Change

Changeling

Lesley Taylor

Changeling

Lesley Taylor

Lesley Taylor

All rights reserved. No part of this book may be reproduced or distributed in any form without the prior written permission from the author

First published in Great Britain 2023

Copyright © 2023 Lesley Taylor

ISBN 978-1-3999-5147-0

Cover design by www.chandlerbookdesign.co.uk

For all my family, friends and fellow writers who have encouraged and supported me.

CHAPTER 1

Chane

I had tried to forget the morning's misfortunes, but hadn't quite succeeded.

'Chane, what did Dillard say that got you so riled? Or could I guess?'

I had slid on damp cobbles, and Dillard had smirked, accentuating his heavy jaw line. Scared?'

It would take more than his size to daunt me, but I lost my temper when he named me 'Changeling'. I might have killed him if the swordmaster had not intervened and sent me to work in the armoury.

Dern's question hung in the wind. 'You could, but nothing Dillard says is worth repeating.' His taunts had mattered once, but I had since learned how to defend myself.

'I swear one of these days I'll–'

Although I appreciated Dern's support, what I wanted right now was to relax over a measure of ale. Shoving the Bridge Inn door open I walked into a wall of men and warmth. The rest of Dern's promise disappeared in the clamour of the crowded bar.

His eyes widened. 'Strewth! Colis will be up till midnight counting his takings.'

'With this many to serve he'll still be pouring ale at midnight.' Most customers recognised us as Duke Reys' guards and cleared our path to the bar. Face to face with a stranger, I touched my sword hilt. 'Stand aside, sir, if you please.' The man stepped back hastily, and I claimed space for two at the bar.

Dern grinned. 'Was that a hint or a threat?'

He knew me better than that. 'I asked him politely to move. If he chose to see it as a threat, that's his problem.'

'Um. What's attracted this crowd, Colis? Are you offering free drinks tonight?'

Colis, stout and ruddy cheeked, raised a hand in greeting, directed a server to a corner table and hurried to draw two tankards of ale. 'Don't be daft, boy. Folk have heard about the singer, Kadron.' He nodded towards a Vethian whose tattooed face and black braids contrasted strikingly with his companion's fair hair. 'His pal's Garanth.'

A Vethian this far from the border? They rarely had business in the empire.

'That's not like you, Colis,' Dern said.

The innkeeper shrugged. 'We made a deal. You two on duty?'

'Not yet.' I took a mouthful of ale – just what I needed. 'Why, what should the Duke know about Kadron?'

'Nothing I know of. Just seems odd for him to be here, with a companion who isn't Vethian.'

Dern leaned on the bar. 'Did he give you a share of his takings last night?'

Colis beamed. 'He certainly did.' He bustled off. 'I'm coming!'

Kadron finished his song, swept up a handful of scattered coins and pushed through the crowd to the bar. His gaze drifted towards us.

I returned the look. At first glance his over large, worn and faded black jacket and breeches suggested a man in want of coin. His deep blue eyes might mean he spent his earnings on okoa, something reputedly common among Vethian tribesmen.

'I fancy the redhead.' Kadron's guttural accent was slight, as if he had spent some time in the empire.

Dern nudged me. 'It's your glorious hair and that new jacket. You should have saved your finery for tonight's reception.'

I shook my head at the singer. He struck up a love song, and nearby drinkers hushed. As the last notes died away, he stepped closer and held out his hand expectantly.

'That's a fine song.' Dern tossed him a coin.

Kadron caught it, inclined his head in thanks and turned to me.

'Don't push your luck.'

He shrugged, moved to the next table and sang the opening lines of Northern Girls.

A mountain lass lit the fires of lust . . .

I emptied my tankard and listened. A roar of acclaim drowned the chorus.

Northern girls are good as gold,
Northern girls are true.

Customers shouted and whistled. Some tried to join in the verses, but the singer had changed the words.

her angry brothers gelded me

Dern's hand slipped, ale splashed from his tankard, and he mopped his chin with the back of his hand.

Kadron sang the chorus in a high-pitched tone, and the nearest drinkers howled with laughter. Silence fell for the last lines.

A northern girl gave me back my life.
She'll do the same for you.

Everyone applauded, including Colis. Kadron raised a hand for silence. 'Don't be misled. She only likes geldings, but I'll solve that problem for anyone who's interested.' He toured the tables, collecting coppers and bowing in appreciation of the few silver pieces.

I was still laughing when he sang O Lonesome One and looked at me expectantly. That almost set me off again. 'Well done.' I dropped one of my remaining silver coins into the singer's open palm.

He smiled. 'My thanks, Most Generous One.' He raised his voice. 'One last drinking song!'

I joined in the chorus and glanced at Dern. 'Time for us to go.'

Kadron passed his instrument to Colis. The innkeeper settled it on a low shelf behind the bar. While his back was turned, a youngster bumped into Kadron and grabbed the singer to steady himself. Kadron thrust him off, and the youth staggered.

'Dern.'

'I saw it.'

I slipped between the tables, and Dern followed.

Kadron's voice drifted through the chatter. 'The redhead paid well. Do you think he likes me?' He swung round, clapped his hand to his belt and cursed as he sprang after the thief.

Garanth seized a balding man by his coat, wrenched him to a halt and held his dagger at the man's throat. 'Stand still.'

Finding his escape blocked by the doorkeeper, the young thief fumbled for his belt knife. Kadron closed his hands around the youth's wrist, planted a leg behind his captive's and twisted sharply. With a yell of surprise, in a waft of unwashed clothes, the thief fell heavily. His face twisted in pain, he drew his knife and scrambled to his feet. 'Son of a Vethian whore!'

I drew my blade and disarmed the thief with a resounding ring, as Kadron darted back, his hand on the hilt of his undrawn sword.

'Aah!' The youth cradled his hand. 'Aah, 'e attacked me.'

I stepped forward, my blade threatening him. '*You* robbed him and drew a knife on him. The magistrate has sworn to rid Bridgetown of pickpockets. As for murderers, by all means try his temper if you feel lucky. He hasn't ordered a hanging recently.'

The youth stood his ground. 'I'm no thief. Search me.'

'He passed Kadron's purse to this fellow,' Garanth said. The balding man gasped, and Garanth withdrew his dagger slightly. 'I warned you not to move.'

A bearded man pushed through the crowd, tankard in hand. 'I saw that.'

'They robbed *me* too.' The speaker, a short, plump man, wore dark-green velvet and a worried expression. 'Search them both.'

The youth flinched, and the tip of my blade touched his nose. 'Don't move again.'

Dern stepped forward, but Colis waved him back. 'My inn, my right to search.' He gestured two of his men forward.

One searcher found a knife and two purses. He shook one. 'Hardly worth the effort.'

'That's mine,' Kadron said. 'Every coin counts.'

'And the other's mine!' the plump man shouted.

The other searcher had found nothing. 'Do we strip them?'

'Check his boots,' the thief's accomplice said. His recommendation produced a filthy knife and a handful of coins, some of them silver.

'Colis, will you see these two delivered to the cells? The magistrate will require statements in the morning.'

He nodded to his men, who escorted the prisoners outside.

I sheathed my sword. 'They call me Chane, and this is Dern. Where do you keep your other purse, Kadron?'

'Where it's safe. I am grateful for your intervention, Chane.' He thrust his lightweight purse into an inner pocket.

A grateful Vethian? The few I had met would rather die that admit they needed help to defend themselves and their belongings. 'I'd hate to see the rewards of your night's singing wasted on that pair.'

Dern looked the singer up and down. 'Talking of singing, would you perform for the duke tonight, if you know some halfway suitable songs?'

'I have songs fit for taverns and mansions, for palaces and brothels. The Duke would have no reason to complain. Does he pay well?'

A glint showed in Dern's eyes. 'He will pay what you deserve, Singer of Many Songs.'

I shook my head. Reys might not welcome the arrival of a travelling singer, especially one as out of place as this Vethian. Nonetheless, it was the duke's responsibility to question such strangers.

'What kind of audience might I expect? Sober guests with silent wives?'

My lips twitched. Kadron would cause a stir among the guests at Reys' dull reception. Maybe not. He had judged tonight's company nicely. 'Exactly that. And an overnight guest.'

'Does the guest have a name?' Garanth asked.

'Sarrech, late of Tahurn.'

All colour left Garanth's face.

Kadron frowned. 'Indeed? I should like to meet him.' There was an edge to his voice. 'Such a rarity, a man from Tahurn.'

I glanced from Kadron to Garanth. There was something between them – these two and Sarrech. It was worth testing. 'Will you come?'

'I will. Garanth comes with me. Unless you object?' He passed some silver coins to the innkeeper and retrieved his instrument case. 'Lead on.'

*   *   *

'Does the Duke often welcome travelling singers?' Garanth asked.

'No,' Dern said. 'But tonight is a formal reception for Bridgetown dignitaries. Most will be glad of something different by now.'

'And that endured sober? Does the Duke bears grudges?'

'He doesn't suffer fools,' I hoped Dern remembered Duke Reys was not fond of volunteering information to strangers.

'Is he wed?'

'Indeed he is,' Dern said. 'To Lady Iylla, daughter of his predecessor, Duke Arnull. She–' I trod on his foot.

'Has he a large family?'

'He has not been wed long,' I said sharply. If Kadron was disinclined to take the hint, I would withdraw the invitation.

Garanth stopped at the brow of the hill. 'That's one hell of a wall for a ducal residence.'

'Once this was merely a fortress on the town wall,' I said. 'Over the years the fortifications have been extended, and living quarters added. Duke Reys has made few further changes.'

'Bridgetown is hardly border territory,' Kadron said. 'Has there been much need to defend the town?'

'The border is close enough for us to take precautions. The walls have served us well over the years.'

'And we've had to reinforce the border garrisons, when the Imps were off hunting demons,' Dern said.

Kadron stared at him. 'Indeed? Then I trust imperial forces will guard your walls in return when demons come here.'

Cap Tharen stood in our path. 'Who's that with you, Chane?'

'Kadron comes to sing for the duke, Cap. Garanth accompanies him.'

'Go through. You two, go with them. Watch your guests well, Chane.'

'I'm watching,' Dern murmured.

I bit back a laugh. The two guards hadn't served the duke long, but I preferred inexperience to someone like Dillard.

Holin stopped me at the door. 'There's no one else on the guest list, Chane.'

'They're here to entertain the Duke's guests. Check with Cap Tharen if you want.'

Holin shook his head. 'If Cap didn't approve, he wouldn't have let them through the gate.' He opened the double doors and stood back. 'What kind of entertainment?'

'Naked wrestling,' Kadron said. 'Do you want to join in?'

Holin snorted. 'Very funny.'

I stepped into the hall. The door opposite leaked light and subdued voices.

'It's quiet,' Dern said.

The lamps on the right-hand staircase burned brightly, but those on the left were dark. I stopped. 'Who's on duty and where is he?'

'Dillard was here earlier, Chane,' the younger guard said. 'He'll likely have gone for a piss.'

'And snuffed the stair lamps before he went?' I turned to the older guard. 'Take his place, until relieved. And you, tell Cap Tharen Dillard's missing from his post.'

The younger guard hesitated, staring at me.

'Now!' He ran off. I glanced at Kadron and Garanth. 'Stay here.' I drew my sword, ran up the stairs and strode along the passage trying doors as Dern lit the dark lamps.

Kadron and Garanth followed. Damn them! Was Dern still watching them?

A glint of light showed under the fourth door on the right, an occasional guest room. I threw it open. Flickering candlelight fell on the polished tabletop, a wine flask, two wine goblets and on the pale face of Iylla, my foster sister, lying on the bed.

CHAPTER 2

Kadron

Sarrech paused in his task of undoing the woman's buttons. He looked up, his eyes narrowed. 'I do not believe I invited you to share my conquest.'

Chane sheathed his sword, gripped Sarrech and flung him away from the bed. 'Iylla!' She did nor stir while he stroked her cheek and brushed her hair back from her closed eyes. He whipped his sword from its sheath. 'What have you done, Sarrech?' Fury coloured his voice. If he had known

Sarrech as I did, he would have run him through before he asked questions.

'*Lord* Sarrech to you.'

Garanth sniffed the empty wine goblet. 'Falseberry juice, a common tool of seducers.'

I glanced at Garanth, who gave an a*ll's well* hand signal: Sarrech did not know him, nor had he recognised me.

Sarrech stood in the passage, cradling his elbow. His eyes flicked from Dern's naked blade to Chane's. 'You have broken my arm.'

'*You* have broken all the laws of hospitality. The Duke will deal with you as you deserve.'

'I am his guest. He invited me to take my ease.'

'Not with his wife!'

'Ah.' Sarrech's eyes gleamed. 'Then I have been mistaken. I thought she was a kitchen trollop.'

Chane stepped forward, his expression a mixture of disgust and anger. 'Tell that to the Duke.'

Sarrech sneered as he took a pace back. 'Indeed I shall. I do not answer to underlings.'

Dern aimed his blade at Sarrech's chest. Chane stepped between them. 'Peace, Dern. He will–'

Sarrech retreated another step and half turned away.

'Beware!' I cried.

Garanth ran back along the passage, ging Dern with him. Chane remained in the doorway, ready to move in any direction, I kKept my eyes on Sarrech.

He drew his sword, raised his free arm and tossed a small, dark object towards us. I pressed myself against the wall, but I was not Sarrech's target. Chane ducked, flinging his arm up to protect his face.

Too late to interfere, I identified a gysun. It struck Chane's plated jacket and clung there.

A rattle. A movement. Chane paled, looking for help. Dern and Garanth were intent on Sarrech, who had retired to the far end of the passage. I alone had some knowledge of gysun. Chane gathered his breath to shout, and the creature on his shoulder stirred. Two steps would take me to Chane's side or encourage the gysun to strike.

I glided forward, dagger in hand. 'Be still.' I spoke softly. 'Gysun respond to movement and sound.'

Swords clashed somewhere along the passage, but Chane kept his attention on me. 'Kill it,' he breathed. The creature clawed at his jacket. He stiffened.

'Close your eyes.'

He obeyed, keeping his breathing shallow.

I covered his eyes with my left hand, set the flat of my blade against his neck and urged the heartbeat in my ears to slow.

Sarrech's taunts carried over the ringing of blades. Someone cursed. I trusted Sarrech carried no more gysun.

Sweat beaded Chane's brow The gysun dug its fore-claws into his skin. A scrape, a clicking sound. I hummed softly, and the gysun stilled.

I eased my blade lower. Its edge grazed Chane's skin. For a moment I expected him to move, which would likely be fatal for both of us. He remained motionless.

The gysun reared. I pressed my blade hard against Chane's skin and flicked it loose along the passage, lending a waft of air to carry it over Dern and Garanth. I dropped my hand from Chane's eyes. 'You may look now. It has gone.'

Chane looked round. 'Where is it?'

'Where it belongs, with its master.' I took a napkin from the table, wiped my blade, sheathed it and turned to Iylla. Her breathing and heartbeat were slow but steady. 'Lady Iylla may be safely left for a short while. Come and see.'

Chane drew a deep breath and followed me.

Garanth and Dern stood further along the passage, their backs to us. Sarrech crouched beyond them. His sword lay on the floor, beyond his reach. The gysun clung to his right arm, glistening dark green, almost black.

Sarrech attempted to shake the gysun off, but failed to dislodge its long claws. Slowly he drew his belt knife and stabbed at the gysun's back. His blade slid off its armour and plunged into his arm. The gysun reared and lunged forward. Sarrech struck once more, sweat glistened on his ashen face, as blood dripped from his arm. Again, his knife failed to penetrate its scales.

The gysun did not recognise Sarrech as its master. Nor had he understood the need to prise it loose, as I had. It clicked its mandibles, sprang over his knife, landed on his cheek and struck at his eye. Sarrech screamed as the gysun shook its head, its serrated tail sweeping from side to side. The forepart of its body advanced into the hole it had made. Its claws tore a greater space for its mid-section. Sarrech's knife dropped from his fingers. He fell, clawing at his face, his howls bestial.

A tremor ran through Chane. 'Dear God!'

Captain Tharen, Holin, the door guard, and a stocky man of medium height, Duke Reys I assumed, thrust past Dern. The Duke stared at Sarrech. 'Put an end to this!'

'No! Let him die the death he sought for another,' I said.

Duke Reys dragged his gaze from Sarrech's death throes and frowned. 'Whose death? Who are you that you dare give orders in my house?'

'Sarrech tried to kill me,' Chane said. 'I would have died that death, if Kadron had not intervened.'

The Duke's jaw dropped. 'In God's name, why?'

'He planned to seduce Iylla. I interfered.'

'What!'

'Garanth, bring lamps and more oil.' I ran forward, slid my booted foot under Sarrech's shoulder, rolled him onto his side and drove my sword through the back of his skull. Dark liquid rolled sluggishly from the wound and hissed on the blade. I leaped back. Garanth, always my shadow, dropped two lamps on Sarrech's corpse and sprang clear. As smoke rose, I passed my blade through the flames and retreated.

Duke Reys stood transfixed, shock etched on his face.

'Sir!' Chane seized his arm and spoke softly. 'Reys, come with me.'

The Duke came to himself and snapped out a stream of orders. 'Holin, make sure that all my guests have departed. Captain Tharen, I want a report on Dillard's condition. Set a watch on these flames.' He coughed. 'See they don't spread. Damp down the floor here and in adjoining rooms if necessary. Bring these two to the main hall. Chane and Derwin, stay with me.'

*   *   *

Our four man escort allowed us to wash, for which I was grateful, although the stink of death and smoke remained in my nostrils. Satisfied with our appearance, they took us to Duke Reys.

Duke Reys sat on his ducal chair, Chane and Dern stood at his side, and a weasel-faced servant, probably his steward, lurked behind. Duke glanced at us and frowned. 'Take their weapons.'

'No.' I spoke quietly, but clearly, and with authority. Our guards hesitated.

'I repeat, who are you to dare give orders in my house?'

'He named himself Kadron,' Dern said.

'So I did. The name suits me even in this guise.' A wave of my hand indicated my blue facial decorations and braided hair. I had dropped the Vethian accent. 'I ask your pardon for abrogating your responsibilities, Duke Reys. In the circumstances, It was necessary. I am supreme commander of the imperial armies and heir to the imperial throne, sworn to act against devilry in all its forms.'

'Be damned to that for a lie!' the steward shouted. 'He's a Vethian – an okoa eater! The imperial heir would not journey alone.'

I scowled at the steward. 'My travels may be your concern, Duke Reys, but I do not propose to share them with your servants. For your information, I am not alone. Garanth is my right hand, sworn to protect me. My men await my summons at Mondun. If my captain does not hear from me within three days, he will require you to explain my silence.'

The Duke stared at me. I could imagine his difficulty. My claim would sound ridiculous, yet I had saved his wife's brother's life at great risk to my own.

'Prove it!'

I met his gaze. The steward sniffed loudly and whispered to Duke Reys. I walked forward, my hands clear of my sword belt. At the foot of the dais immediately in front of the Duke I halted and extended my right hand. On my middle finger I wore a silver ring engraved with a crowned triangle above two wavy lines, the imperial insignia.

CHAPTER 3

Chane

Reys thrust himself upright and stepped down from the dais. 'My Lord!' He bent his knee and bowed his head. Ollery, his face ashen, scrambled to prostrate himself in the full imperial salute.

'You may stand, Duke Reys.'

Reys stood, with a glance at Ollery that boded ill for the steward. 'My Lord, will you be seated and take refreshment?' He beckoned the nearest guard. 'Have wine bought, then leave us, except for two men at the door. Take Ollery with you. The effort of organising this evening's reception has been too much for him. Chane, Dernwin, you will stay.'

Kadron took a seat facing Reys, and Garanth stood behind him.

Reys turned to me. 'Will someone explain to me what the hell happened here tonight?'

I gave a brief account of my encounter with Sarrech. 'I didn't see who disarmed him.'

'Garanth,' Dern said, 'he made it look easy.'

When wine was served, I drank deeply. Kadron swirled and sniffed his before he sipped. 'A fine wine, Duke Reys.'

'My predecessor's choice, my Lord. You knew Sarrech?'

Kadron's fingers tightened on the stem of his goblet. 'He came to Tormene to make demands of the Emperor. When refused, he insulted me. He would have done well to remember that, but he did not recognise me.' He laughed, but his eyes did not share the joke.

'Why on earth would Sarrech turn that thing loose against Chane?'

'I can only guess at his motives, Duke Reys. He would not have been pleased to have his seduction interrupted. Did he know of your connection with Chane?'

'If he enquired, anyone might have told him, my Lord.'

'Then perhaps his attempt on your wife and her brother was designed to hurt *you*. Did you do or say anything to displease him?'

Reys' expression changed to disbelief. 'He asked for employment as a swordmaster and turned down a lesser alternative. Surely no man , however arrogant, would kill someone he didn't know for such a reason!'

His Lordship's eyes were cold. 'It would fit what I knew of him.'

'What was the creature that killed him, Chane?'

I shuddered. 'Ask His Lordship, sir. He has experience with such things.'

'Not so, Chane. I have some knowledge, but had not encountered a gysun before tonight.'

'Why did you not kill it sooner?'

In his dismay, Reys had forgotten to use His Lordship's title.

'As you saw, Duke Reys, the gysun was well armoured. I could not penetrate its underbelly while it clung to Chane. Not without endangering him further.'

'Whatever Sarrech's crimes, there was no need to allow him to suffer for so long my Lord.'

'There was every need. Once released, gysun do not rest until they have fed. Only then are they vulnerable. I had no mind to become its victim, or endanger others.' His gaze rested momentarily on me. 'Duke Reys, I am accustomed to deliver justice. Sarrech deserved his death.'

'He did.' I emptied my goblet.

Reys took a deep breath and let it out slowly. 'Where did Sarrech find such a thing, and why did it turn on him?'

'Gysun are creatures of the cursed wood. Once loose no one, not even its mistress, could have prevented it from hunting its prey.'

'The cursed wood!' Rey's jaw tightened. 'Sarrech ventured there?'

'Apparently so.'

'If the tales are true, a man would take his own life rather than become a plaything of the sorceress.'

'The lady of the wood might have permitted Sarrech to walk free bearing one of her creatures if she had received a mighty gift in return. When I last met him, he owned nothing that might have tempted the lady.'

Reys leaned forward. 'My Lord, we owe you a great deal. Name anything you wish, and you shall have it.'

'I thank you for your generous offer, Duke Reys, but my requirements are few and easily provided. Some provisions for my journey would be much appreciated. My immediate concerns are quite other. Firstly, your wife will require careful tending. The effects of falseberry juice are sometimes unpleasant. Garanth will provide a precautionary draught for her to take. She should not be left alone until she has recovered.' Reys nodded. 'Next, the remains of the late Sarrech must be sealed in a lead lined coffin. No one is to touch him unless wearing leather gloves and using metal implements. Every speck of ash is to be sealed inside the coffin. Do you have accursed ground here?'

'We do.'

'Use it. I wish to see Sarrech's gear, his horse, saddlebags, everything he had with him when he arrived.'

'You will have it, my Lord.'

His Lordship turned to me. 'How are you, Chane?'

'Unharmed, my Lord, thanks to you. I owe you my life and offer you my service.'

Reys sprang to his feet.

His Lordship stared at me as if he doubted my word. 'Gratitude is a friend that does not endure long. I merely repaid my own debt to you.'

Merely? There was no comparison! 'Ingratitude is a poor bedfellow. I did not risk death, and such a death, for you.'

'No? If you serve me, you may come to such an end. Are you so minded?'

'I am, my Lord. I will serve you if it costs me my life.'

He sighed. 'You may accompany me until I dismiss you or you choose to leave my company. I will not accept your sworn service, Chane. One man bound to me by an unbreakable oath is more than enough.'

'As you will, my Lord.'

'My guards can search Sarrech's belongings,' Reys said.

'That would be unwise. The late Sarrech may have carried other gifts. I would not wish any of your men to be taken by surprise.' Garanth whispered something in his ear. 'Perhaps our horses might be brought from the Bridge Inn.'

Reys beckoned one of the door guards. 'See that my guests' horses are brought from Colis' stable.'

His Lordship finished his wine and stood. 'By the time we have done with Sarrech's bags, neither of us will be capable of sensible conversation, Duke Reys. That must wait until tomorrow.'

Reys frowned. 'I beg your pardon, my Lord. What is there to discuss?'

'You were expecting an officer of the imperial army. I am he.'

*   *   *

The passage stank of smoke and death, but only a dark stain on the flagstones marked Sarrech's end. His pack contained a change of clothes, razor, comb and some silver coins. Garanth delved into the bed coverings and under the bed, holding the drapes aside. When he emerged, lamplight glinted on the small round box in his hand.

His lordship took it from him and tilted it to inspect the worn engraved leaf design on the lid and sides. The box held half a dozen red beads. 'Quit seeds. We might have expected that.'

'Well for Lady Iylla he used falseberry juice rather than one of these.' Garanth said.

Sarrech's horse, an ageing gelding with no distinctive markings, showed signs of hard usage, though someone had treated his hurts.

Garanth detached a crossbow and a half empty quiver from the worn saddle. 'I wonder what he hunted.' He found nothing of interest in the saddlebags, and looked up at the beam above the empty stall.

I turned at the clatter of hooves, and directed the stable boy who led a bay gelding and a chestnut stallion to adjoining stalls at the far end of the stable. He soon settled the horses and left.

'Chane, see what you can find up there.'

'No need.' Garanth reached up, felt along the beam and retrieved a sheathed sword, wrapped in dark cloth. He dropped it instantly.

'Garanth!' His lordship leaped across the small heap of Sarrech's possessions, took Garanth's hands in his and examined them closely. 'Your guardian angel is with you today.' He knelt, gripped the cloth and tugged sharply, uncovering a long narrow sword in a plain sheath, with a small pommel, crossguard, and leather-bound hilt. Torchlight drew a dull gleam from four dark stones set in a zigzag line between the hilt bindings. It looked identical to the sword his lordship carried.

'No!' He covered his face and stifled a sob. After a moment he reached for the scabbard, but did not touch the hilt. 'Oh, my brother!'

Garanth gripped his lordship's shoulder. 'How is this possible? Sarrech could not have slain Varryn.'

'Such as Sarrech would have resorted to treachery, or taken this after Varryn's death.'

'Then when did Sarrech enter the cursed wood? Before or after he met Varryn, dead or alive?'

'And what did the lady of the wood accept from Sarrech, when she had no use for this?'

Garanth withdrew his hand. 'We heard—' He broke off, anguish in his face.

His lordship rewrapped the sword with care. Holding it by the wrapped sheath, he stood, his eyes on Garanth. 'I cannot leave these questions unanswered. I must enter the cursed wood and speak with the lady.'

'*We* must,' Garanth said.

'I will come with you, my Lord,' I said. However good a swordsman Garanth might be, another sword would be useful. I met his gaze.

'If you still wish to serve me, Chane, you may come as far as the border of the cursed wood and not a step beyond. The lady of the wood has no power to harm me, but I cannot protect you if you choose to enter her realm. That applies to you also, Garanth.'

I nodded. Garanth didn't, regardless of any sworn oath.

'You may as well burn the rest of Sarrech's rubbish. I must sleep now, if I am to speak sense to Duke Reys tomorrow. Chane, pass on my best wishes for his lady's swift recovery, if you will.'

CHAPTER 4

Kadron

Despite the hour, Reys' housekeeper led me to a guest chamber, ensured I required nothing more, and wished me a good night's sleep. Garanth remained on guard outside my room, as was his custom. He did not take chances with my life. I sat on the bed, which promised a more comfortable night than the Bridge Inn, and cursed my folly. I should have foreseen Chane's misguided offer of service, freely given and impossible to refuse.

Why had he chosen to stay close to me? Was he an honest man, a liar or worse? If only that were all. It could not be, until I knew the truth about Varryn. The shock of finding my brother's sword had been worse than recognising the gysun. My fingers still trembled and my heart likewise. Ironically, Garanth's reaction, and the touch of his hand, had brought me to myself.

My father had not anticipated this outcome, or he would not have insisted that I trace Varryn 'at any cost'. Now irrevocably committed, I knelt, bowed my head and gave thanks for my life, for Garanth's and Chane's. In desperate hope I pleaded for Varryn's life or, if too late for that, for his soul and for his son's safety, while silent tears trickled down my face.

Stripped of my armour and boots I lay on the bed, waiting for sleep to claim me or for dawn to demand that I rise to pursue my search, futile though I feared it.

* * *

When I descended the stairs, Duke Reys stood in the hall, the stern judge of last night now a smiling host. 'Good morning, my Lord. I trust you slept well.'

'Well enough, I thank you, Duke Reys. I trust that Lady Iylla is recovering from last night's ordeal?'

His smile broadened. 'She is, my Lord. I believe she will be quite herself in a day or so. Breakfast is waiting in my office. We will not be disturbed.'

I allowed him to heap my plate, before I spoke. 'I understand that neither you nor your guards have experience of fighting karyth.'

'That is so, my Lord. Some of my men have seen karyth attacks from a distance, but have not participated. My wife's father, the late Duke Arnull, witnessed several such battles. He understood that karyth numbers had been much reduced.'

'They were certainly reduced, but so were our defenders. I am rebuilding imperial army numbers, but I fear karyth will be ready to move against us in force before I have sufficient trained men to repel them.'

The duke pushed his barely touched plate away. 'You need the support of any lord who has a force of fighting men.'

'Exactly, but I do not plan to absorb your men into the imperial army, Duke Reys. My preference is to ensure that every lord has a force able to stand against karyth. Once trained, by those with relevant experience, your men will remain here to defend Bridgetown, or elsewhere only at greater need. Are you willing to assist in this endeavour?'

'I am, my Lord. Only a fool would reject your offer. Against such a foe, we must unite.'

'My thanks, Duke Reys. I must be gone. Will you see this is delivered to the magistrate, and this to my captain at Mondun? He does not need to make an unnecessary visit to Bridgetown.' I handed him two sealed packets.

'Gladly, my Lord.' He accompanied me to the stable yard, where Garanth waited with Chane and Dern. 'Will you take a pair of packhorses?'

'I appreciate your offer, Duke Reys. However, I prefer to travel light.'

Garanth, always reluctant to leave a useable weapon behind, had brought Sarrech's crossbow and quiver. His own recurve bow hung on his back as always; a tug would bring it to his hand. I strapped my brother's sword to the bay's saddle, took the reins from Garanth and mounted. Although I hoped to return Varryn's sword to him or his son, failing either alternative I must present it to my father.

'I am grateful for your hospitality and for your generous provisions, Duke Reys. I see Dern has decided to join us. I shall endeavour to return your brother and his friend to you unharmed.'

'I will pray for your safety, my Lord Not so, Chane. that of your companions. My blessing on your travels.' He turned to Chane and Dern. 'Farewell. God speed you home.' He clasped Chane's hand. I did not listen to their private farewells.

Few walked the narrow streets as we clattered downhill, but heads turned as we entered the market square, where traders were setting out their wares. The stallholders stepped aside, some with a cheery greeting for Chane and Dern. My appearance drew some stares, while Garanth's stallion attracted more attention than his fair hair.

One fellow seized Dern's bridle. 'Who are they?'

'That's the duke's business.' Dern freed himself.

Another call came as we turned the corner. Chane looked up. A pretty girl waved from her window. Chane waved back, and Dern blew a kiss. The girl vanished, and another took her place. Chane waved again and urged his horse through the confusion of partly erected stalls.

Once we had passed through the South Gate, Garanth took the lead. He set a sensible pace, one that would not overstretch the horses. Market traffic reduced as we took the road alongside Hawater, which followed the river downstream past the lush pastures of Hawdale.

Under pale cloudy skies, the chill of the morning soon faded. I urged the bay into position alongside Dern. 'You could have said farewell to your girl.'

Dern shrugged. "I'll make up for it when we get back, my Lord.'

'I knew a man who said something similar on leaving home. He never returned.'

Chane drew level with Dern. 'Don't worry, Dern, I'll watch your back.'

'Huh! Will you comfort Etta if I don't come back?'

'I doubt it, I'll be too busy trying to escape Zina's leash.'

Dern laughed.

I chose to ignore the joke. 'You need not address me as "my Lord", unless you prefer me to call you Dernwin.'

He grinned and shook his head. 'What should I call you then, sir? Kadron is not your name, if I understood you correctly?'

'It is not. Garanth uses Kadron. You may do the same.'

'Is it a title?' Chane asked.

We had caught up with Garanth. 'It means "commander", more or less,' he said

'Its true meaning is closer to big chief, biggest cock or, depending on your intent, blunderer. I know Garanth's preference. What's yours?'

Dern's face flushed.

'As you wish, Kadron.'

'I am used to it, Chane. Are you still determined to accompany me?'

'I am.'

'I'll stay with Chane.' Dern said.'

'Then you should know my rules. You will both obey any order of mine without question or delay. In the event of my absence or incapacity, you will do the same for Garanth's orders.'

Dern opened his mouth and snapped it closed. He nodded.

'Understood and accepted, Kadron,' Chane said.

'I expect you to be alert at all times. We will alternate overnight watches. Any questions?'

'What was your business with Duke Reys, Kadron?'Chane asked.

I raised an eyebrow. 'Does the duke habitually share such matters with you?'

'Mostly. If I were in Bridgetown now, he would have mentioned it. Unless you forbade it .'

'And you would have enlightened Dern.'

'Only if it concerned him,' I said. 'He *can* keep his mouth shut when needed.'

Dern cast Chane an aggrieved look.

'Have either of you fought karyth, the creatures you call demons?'

'No,' Chane said.

Dern frowned. 'Are there such things? My granny told me stories about them. She didn't believe in them.'

'Why should she? She would never have seen any.'

'Duke Arnull knew karyth were real.' Chane's gaze challenged me. 'Did you mean what you said to Dern last night? Will they attack Hawdale?'

'Possibly. I take no chances where karyth are concerned. Five years ago, when you reluctantly took over border watch, Dern, they and their masters wiped out close to half the imperial army.'

The colour drained from Dern's face. 'I beg your pardon, Kadron. I knew nothing of these creatures.'

'It was not common knowledge.' I gave a brief account of my talk with Reys, which silenced Chane.

Dern's face fell. 'We'll miss the training.'

'You will have to rely on my lessons then,' Garanth said, 'and Kadron's.'

*   *   *

Nearing sunset Garanth chose a neglected copse for our campsite, unloaded his stallion and rubbed him down. I took care of the bay's needs.

'Are you trying to catch a fly, Dern?' Chane asked.

I glanced up and met Dern's stare. 'Would you prefer me to order you to do my work for me?'

'Most army officers I've met would, Kadron.'

'I would not. My men know I am willing to dirty my hands when needed.'

'That's Chane's habit too.' Dern bent to check his horse's hooves.

'What manner of name is Chane?'

Chane scowled. 'The kind that sticks.'

'According to one of the duke's guards, he doesn't have a name,' Garanth said. 'The late Duke Arnull tried to give him one, but folk named him Changeling, which soon got shortened to Chane. As he says, the name stuck.'

Dern's checks reddened. Chane clenched his fists, and then unclenched them. He might lose his temper, but I needed answers. 'Why have you no name? Why Changeling?'

Chane shook his head.

'Duke Arnull found him as a youngster. He claimed to remember nothing, neither name nor origin. The duke took him in and brought him up as his son.'

Through gritted teeth, Dern said, 'You have an ear for gossip, Garanth.'

'It has its advantages.'

I raised a warning hand and turned back to Chane. 'When was this?'

'Twelve years ago.'

'Do you remember nothing still?'

'I remember the last twelve years, Kadron.'

Garanth snorted. Chane had conveniently dodged my question. Was that by choice or necessity?

CHAPTER 5

Chane

Late the following day we turned south, away from Hawdale's green fields and orchards, into a sparsely populated region of rough grassland and thickets. That night we made camp at dusk on a grassy slope between two stunted trees. After supper, I watched Kadron and Garanth practise their swordsmanship by the light of the campfire. They were well matched, fast and fearless.

Kadron fell back, and Garanth failed to press him. 'You did well to disarm Sarrech,' I said.

Garanth laughed. 'Did you believe his claim of swordmastery?'

'Why not? A falsehood would be easily disproved.'

'Would *you* risk your life against a self-proclaimed master, Chane?' Kadron asked. 'Even if you doubted his word.'

'No.'

'You said you'd train us to fight karyth,' Dern said.

'I did.' Kadron sheathed his sword.

Garanth sheathed his. 'If you're eager, we could make a start.'

'Listen carefully,' Kadron said, 'and remember. This knowledge may save your lives. Karyth prefer to hunt in darkness, but are sometimes seen around dawn and dusk. They swoop on unsuspecting men as owls snatch up mice.'

Dern leaped to his feet. 'They fly! How big *are* they, if they can take men like that?'

'They are strong enough to carry you off somewhere where they will rip you open, lap up your blood and eat you.'

God forbid! 'How do we defend ourselves, Kadron?' *If I had understood this threat, would I have left Bridgetown?*

'Stay indoors, barricade all doors and windows, however small, and keep fires burning. If caught outside, stay in a group and watch each other's backs. Use fire to keep karyth at a distance, but do not risk losing your night sight. If you are alone, you would be unlucky to have more than one or two karyth interested in taking you.' A rustle in the trees drew Kadron's attention. His hand on his sword hilt, he gave a slight shake of his head. 'Ensure they can't surround you. Set your back against something solid, a rock face or stout tree. If they are flying, *and* you have sufficient light *and* can judge their speed, one or two arrows might bring them down. That's easily said, harder to do. When they're close, use your sword and guard against their teeth and talons. Keep your weapons in good order and always at hand.'

'Even when you take a piss or a nap,' Garanth said. 'Karyth scales are tough. You need a strong blade, a clear target and your weight behind your stroke. Take its head off, if you can. If not, aim for, its wings or limbs to disable it, or trim its talons to give yourself time for other options. It's not very different from fighting a man, although *they* rarely attack from above.'

'Can we try now?' Dern asked.

'Not tonight,' Kadron said. 'I'm ready for sleep. We'll see what you remember tomorrow.'

* * *

After an early evening meal, Kadron stood and stretched. 'I prefer to know how you two handle yourselves before we show you how to deal with karyth.'

Garanth turned to Dern. 'You're with me. Remember your sword isn't blunted.'

Some guardsmen had never trained with sharpened blades, but Rey's swordmaster insisted we practise that now and then. Dern winked. 'I'll try not to kill you.'

I met Kadron's eyes. 'So will I.' Whatever the penalty for wounding the imperial heir, I had no wish to experience it. Dern and Garanth had drawn their swords and were already pretending to chop chunks out of each other.

Kadron smiled. 'Good. Let's find somewhere quieter. Distractions have a habit of being fatal.'

As the clang of swords and Dern's curses faded, Kadron looked up at me. 'Are you ready?'

I whipped out my sword. He did the same. The blades met with a resounding clash. I stepped back.

He stepped into striking range. 'I take that as a *yes.*'

His lunge met mine, and the tip of my blade touched his shoulder. I caught his sword on my dagger, and forced it away from my chest. A warm trickle ran over my hand.

'Are you wounded?'

'Just a scratch.'

Kadron caught my hand before I could wipe it on my jacket. 'Never do that! You might not care whether you stink of blood, but karyth will smell you from a distance and track you down.' He wrapped an embroidered square of linen round my hand and sniffed it. 'That will serve for now. Garanth will anoint it later.'

His warning had chilled me. Then a loud shriek tore the silence apart and curdled my blood.

He raised his sword and swept it down, aiming for my neck. I ducked and thrust at his sword-arm. He sidestepped, parried my blow and would have taken my arm if I hadn't sprung clear.

In the instant I took to recover my balance, Kadron had vanished into the darkness under the trees, and I had worked out that the shriek came from him and not a nearby karyth. A bough overhead creaked, gaining me just enough time to skip back and set my back against the tree trunk. If I hadn't moved fast enough, he would have landed on me and won the fight. As it was he alighted in front of me, and lunged for my heart. I quarter-turned, which spoiled his aim. His blade thudded into the tree. I whipped my dagger from my belt and slashed at his hand. Unaccountably, and fortunately, I missed my aim.

'What do you think you're playing at, Kadron?' Garanth whispered. 'You invite karyth to an unexpected feast!'

'Calm yourself, Garanth. There are no karyth within hearing distance. Neither would one or two rogue karyth trouble us unduly. Chane has proved his ability to defend himself. Has Dern?'

Garanth snorted. 'He has. Don't play the karyth again, Kadron.'

'Don't worry. Once was enough.' He returned to the campfire.

Dern was already there, adding more wood to the dying blaze and stirring the embers. He straightened and rubbed his sword arm. 'Do karyth always take live captives to kill later?' His voice trembled, as my hands still did.

'Sometimes they sweep down, grab your head with their fore claws and crush your skull,' Garanth said.

'I've seen men die like that,' Kadron said. 'You need to keep your wits about you. If you're going to be sick, Dern, kindly face the other way.'

Dern shook his head. 'You said, "they and their masters", Kadron. What masters?'

'Concentrate on karyth. You would be unfortunate indeed to have to face one of their masters.'

Dern swallowed. 'Do *they* eat men too?'

'Not to my knowledge,' Kadron said. 'They deal with their prisoners differently.'

My scratch attended to, I lay awake wondering how he knew there were no karyth within hearing distance, if he did, and what else he hadn't told us.

*   *   *

After riding for hours against an increasing wind, I was relieved when Kadron called an early halt.

Garanth returned from his usual scout ahead. 'There's an old ruin not far off. The walls will provide some shelter.'

He was right. *Some* shelter was all the walls gave us, the roof having collapsed long ago, but we had seen nothing better on Kadron's choice of tracks.

'Dern, -if you can provide some fresh meat for the pot.'

'I don't mind trying, Kadron, but Chane's the best I know at setting snares.'

'I'd like to see that,' Garanth said.

'As you wish. Dern, take care of the horses while I gather wood.'

Garanth, bow in hand, trod as lightly as I did. When we came across a well-used rabbit run, I turned right and Garanth followed. The rustle of wind in the trees deadened other sounds.

A burrow opened at the foot of a slope. I set a snare across the entrance, another on the far side and retraced my steps, ensuring I had left no tracks. At a fork in the run, I set two more snares, while Garanth watched. 'Simple, but likely effective. Who taught you?' His voice was barely a whisper.

A flash of memory happened sometimes, meant nothing, and was soon forgotten. This was different. After setting a few more snares, I walked away from the run and sat cross-legged at the base of a tall tree. 'It works well for small game. I taught myself.'

Garanth sat facing me and leaned against a tree trunk. 'How?'

'I was hungry. Nothing to eat for two or three days or longer. I found a long dead trapped squirrel. Undid the loop and moved the snare somewhere that didn't smell of death. Retied the knot and waited. Caught a young rabbit.

Took a while to prepare it for cooking, but I prefer meat cooked when I have the means.'

'So do I. Kadron's less squeamish.' He grinned. 'From raw ant eggs to rat brains, and fried maggots to bull's penis, he claims to have eaten it.'

A laugh escaped me. 'I can't imagine the heir to the imperial throne accepting such things.'

'Sometimes it's to avoid insulting his hosts. Once he accepted a challenge to swallow the most disgusting food, and won. If you stay with him long enough you may see such an event for yourself, but I don't recommend it.' He frowned. 'Why didn't you answer him when he asked you about your past?'

I met his stare. 'Because snares are one of the few things I can remember. Anything meaningful has gone for good.'

'Now, who taught you how a handle a sword?'

'I pestered a man who had the skill, but no sons. He refused at first, but I persisted. Eventually he gave in. He didn't regret it. Neither did I.'

'I don't intend to stay with Kadron longer that it takes to pay my debt to him.'

He snorted. 'Keep your stay short, or he'll trap you, as I was trapped. Members of the imperial family tend to get what they want.' He stood. 'I'll try hunting fowl that haven't been caught by your snares.'

I watched until the trees hid him from view. My experience of Kadron contradicted Garanth's suggestion that Kadron had trapped him. Either Garanth had lied, or Kadron wasn't the man I thought he was. The scars on his face didn't help me judge his age, though to be given charge of the imperial troops he must be more than twenty, but probably less than thirty. Maybe his title of *Commander* meant nothing in reality.

The first two snares had trapped rabbits, and Garanth had two bulging game bags slung over his shoulder. He handed me one. 'These are yours. I was lucky too.'

* * *

Days and nights passed without incident. While Dern and Garanth took up their bows to aim at a gaping gash in a rotten tree, Kadron slipped off to bathe at a nearby brook.

Garanth's voice, quiet but clear, carried. 'How long have you served Duke Reys?'

'Two years,' Dern said. He retrieved his bolt from the centre of the target. 'Before that I served Duke Arnull. Why did you swear an oath to Kadron?'

'I swore an oath to his brother, Varryn, eleven years ago. When he left home, five years since, Varryn refused my company, and Kadron inherited my service.'

'He wouldn't release you?'

Garanth didn't answer, but if that was his grudge his advice made sense. I would heed it.

At supper Dern nudged me. 'I must mind my manners, I suppose, even if he doesn't,' he muttered

Kadron had been tearing meat from a skewer with his teeth. 'Perhaps no one's allowed to bring knives into the imperial presence,' I said

'There are rules regarding weapons, certainly,' Kadron said. 'However, palace knives are invariably blunter than one would wish.'

Clearly I had spoken louder than intended. 'Thank you for that information, Kadron.'

After a while Dern nudged me again. 'I thought he had a sense of humour. He must have lost it.'

'You'd lose yours if you thought one of your brothers had fallen prey to the sorceress of the cursed wood.'

Dismay paled Dern's face. 'Oh oh.' He glanced round. 'He didn't hear me did he?'

'Doesn't look like it.'

CHAPTER 6

Chane

One evening Kadron insisted on testing the horses with fire.

'The duke's horsemaster has us doing that regularly, Kadron,' Dern said.

'When was the last time?'

Dern shrugged and glanced at me.

'A while ago. Another session won't hurt,' I said.

'Good.' Kadron took the lead and had the horses jumping over the blazing campfire until Dern complained his boots were beginning to singe.

He pulled his boots off and checked for damage, before he tugged them on again, 'Do you expect to find your brother alive in the cursed wood?'

'No, I believe my brother is dead.'

'Then why do you want to go there?'

After a pause, Kadron spread his hands. 'To learn the truth. Varryn disliked the marriage chosen for him and disputed my father's choice each time the subject was raised. Finally my father lost his temper, disinherited him and bade him depart. I have had no direct message from Varryn since. Two months ago, I received word that Varryn's wife had died and her unborn child with her. Varryn took his firstborn son, and left the house of his wife's father. If Varryn is dead, as I fear, there is still his son. Living or dead, I cannot abandon him. My father waits for news, good or bad.'

Dern lowered his head.

'May God grant you what you seek, Kadron,' I said.

'Amen to that,' Garanth said.

Dern asked no more questions that evening.

Garanth tried to persuade me to bet against Dern questioning Kadron again tomorrow. I shook my head. Though I knew Dern well, I was short of coins to risk.

'How much further is it to the cursed wood, Kadron?' Dern asked.

'Not far. In two days we ford the Cold River and pass north of the river they call the Singer. A further day's ride will bring us to our parting. I shall make the second crossing of the Cold alone.'

'I've never heard of a singing river.'

Neither had I, but unlike Dern I would not have questioned Kadron further.

'The Cold River does not sing in the foothills, but its song can be heard further south where it falls from icy heights of Mount Stinnun. It takes on a different chill from passing so close to the accursed realm. There are shorter routes, but the northern and eastern approaches to the lady's realm are well guarded on both sides of the border. We would not have passed the sentries easily. Nor have I a mind to give the lady notice of my approach.'

I caught Dern's eye. Kadron's explanation confirmed my suspicions. I knew little of the emperor, and that by hearsay, but I doubted he would permit his heir to enter the cursed wood, unless with an army to force the sorceress to give up any hostage she might hold. At the first opportunity, I whispered to Dern. 'What will become of us, if Kadron enters the cursed wood and never comes out?'

Dern paled. 'How can we stop him?'

'We can't.'

'Then we do nothing and hope for the best?'

'Or go with him into the lady's realm.' My voice sounded strange in my ears.

'Good God, no! I'd rather face the emperor with the news of his son's death!'

'Truth be told, so would I.' Kadron apparently intended to enter the cursed wood alone and emerge again unscathed. How was that possible? Yet he did not have the air of a man about to kill himself, and Garanth, who surely knew him well, seemed to trust his ability to negotiate with the sorceress.

* * *

The Cold River churned and thundered in a deep rocky gorge. Dern peered over the edge. 'We're crossing this?'

'A man who travels with Kadron must have a head for heights.'

'I've no problem with heights, Garanth. It's the depths and the force of that washtub that bothers me.'

A narrow path twisted its way down the cliff. Kadron led his bay, its hooves dislodging loose stones. Garanth followed. I stroked the grey's neck. 'You've seen how it's done, boy. Let's make it look easy.'

Once down I stared at the Cold. Unlike the shallow fords of Hawater, tall, steeply angled boulders broke the flow of the rushing water and white spray drenched the rocks scattered across the riverbed. After a little searching Kadron pointed out a line of large stepping stones. Wet, uneven and dangerous, they were our only choice. Kadron's bay walked slowly across, and we followed. The path on the far side, as narrow and steep as the descent, my grey took as readily as if it were a paved road.

That evening I was glad to be sheltered from a chill wind in a small dell. For once Kadron permitted the small fire to remain lit all night.

At the change of watch, Garanth said softly. 'Walk warily. The lady's servants are forbidden to cross the border, but there may be other strays from the cursed wood. We patrol the rim of the dell and no further.' I repressed a shudder.

My watch over, shivering, I settled closer to the fire, determined to forget the gysun and like horrors.

A man cannot control his dreams. I woke with a cry that brought Kadron to my side.

'Nightmares?'

I sat up and wiped sweat from my face with a shaking hand. 'Yes.'

He studied me. 'We must be wary tomorrow. Such fears will increase as we approach the lady's realm. Perhaps I should leave you here.'

'You are sure she regards the Cold River as the utmost limit of her realm, Kadron?'

'That is one thing I am certain of. She would not dare cross it.'

'Then I will stay at your side until the river.' He glanced at me.

I hesitated. If the sorceress had willingly given a gysun to such as Sarrech, she might dare anything. Kadron might be wrong. How did he know so much about her? Despite my doubts, self-respect demanded I wait with Garanth – it would seem an endless vigil for a lone man. I straightened my back. 'So will I.'

Dern's face reflected my worries. Even Garanth seemed uneasy, though he would surely insist we wait for his master's return. However long that might be. Kadron directed his gaze northwest.

Riding through long grass towards a distant line of dark forest, I shivered despite the blazing sunshine. Beside me, Dern wiped sweat from his brow, but my hands were icy. 'Why is it so cold?'

Kadron pulled up, his glance travelling past Dern to me and Garanth. The expression on his face changed abruptly. 'Flee,' he cried, 'back to the river!'

Dern hauled on his reins. I caught a movement from the corner of my eye and drew my sword. Garanth, bow in hand, fitted an arrow.

'Hold!'

Garanth stilled his hand. I tightened my grip on the hilt as a smell of damp rot assailed me. Cold air, heavy with moisture. Gleaming grey-green men, on mossy green horses, unarmed unclothed, sexless. Covered in mucus. Not men, though man-sized. Slime men, their features blurred and their green-tinged eyes glazed.

Nausea and giddiness threatened to unhorse me. I wrenched my gaze away from the creatures, spoke soft nonsense to my nervous horse and rubbed his neck. Dern, his face drained of blood, stared at the slime men. The dun tossed his head and sidled. Dern did nothing to control him.

Garanth forced his stallion past Dern's mount and alongside Kadron. 'What now, Kadron?'

Envying Garanth's calm, I strove to steady my breathing. When Dern's horse barged into mine, I held the grey in check and gripped Dern's arm. 'Steady,' I whispered. Against my will, my eyes were drawn towards the nearest creature.

'Welcome t' lady's realm.' The creature's voice echoed strangely. 'We take you t' her.'

Straight-backed on the motionless bay, Kadron displayed the same authority he had shown Duke Reys. 'You are mistaken. The lady's realm ends at the western arm of the Cold River. You have no right to be here and none to hinder our passage.'

The slime man's laughter vibrated through my ears. I swallowed, and tore my gaze away. The sky remained blue, and the grass green beneath the grey's hooves, yet the nightmare continued.

"'Tis you who mistake. Treaty has nearest river as boundary. Southern river an't flowed since spring. Northern river now boundary. You come t' her.'

God in heaven!

Kadron held the green man's gaze, his eyes very cold. 'We *will not* accompany you. You *shall* permit us to leave.' He made it sound like a command. How could even the imperial heir command creatures such as these?

The slime man's glazed eyes wavered and fixed on me as if it read my mind. I wrenched my attention back to the grey, to Dern's struggles with the dun. The green man drew its horse closer to Kadron, who did not flinch, though the bay tried to back away against his hold.

The creature leaned forward. 'You dun't give orders here. Seize them!'

Kadron whipped his sword out, and the slime man recoiled, withdrawing to its former position. 'Do not touch us,' Kadron ordered. He gestured, a downward movement with his hand flat. Garanth slid the arrow clear and shouldered his bow.

I hesitated. Better to die than be taken alive-if death could be certain. I slammed my blade into its sheath.

Kadron raised his naked sword aloft, and the green men kept their distance. Led by the one who had spoken, they swerved to herd us north and west.

Disbelieving, I cast a longing glance southwards and understood Kadron's sudden capitulation. A line of green horses and riders extended as far as I could see from west to east, blocking any escape attempt.

I followed Dern closely, Kadron's earlier words ringing in my ears. "I cannot protect you if you choose to enter her realm." I hadn't chosen this. None of us had. The grey pulled against my guidance. I kept as close as possible to Dern and refused to consider what lay ahead.

CHAPTER 7

Kadron

My choice of route had provided no opportunity to see the Singer's empty bed. I had thought the easy crossing of the Cold a blessing, rather than an indication the water level was suspiciously low for the time of year. Anyone with more wit and less learning might have wondered whether some dislodgment in the mountains had restricted its flow, and likewise that of the Singer.

    Chane's nightmares should have warned me. Even Garanth, who usually trusted my judgement, had been concerned enough to query my knowledge of the lady. May he forgive me. I knew little outside the treaty, although I had learned that word for word, including paragraph references, dates and legal analysis. Those who drafted it believed the lady of the cursed wood feared retribution too much to break its terms. Such was likely true once, but the world the lady had known vanished long ago. I doubted we could now restrict her powers and imprison her within her chosen territory.

I should have seen the effect of her extended boundary on my companions in time to flee while escape was possible. They would pay the forfeit, unless I found a way to prevent it. I had not kept Garanth alive against his will to lose him in such a manner. Nor had I brought Chane with me to hand him as plaything to the lady. As for Dern, whether he came for friendship or duty, it would be poor repayment for his faithfulness to abandon him here.

We had been driven here as cattle were herded for slaughter, yet I would not yield to despair. The lady would not kill us swiftly or painlessly. She would play with us as a cat plays with a mouse. When she chose to strike, that first blow would not fall on me. Rather, she would torture and slay those she assumed to be my underlings. Proud and friendless herself, she would not deem them of any value to me. Indeed, they were not my friends, though Garanth was as close to me as a brother.

Nonetheless, for honour, for duty, and for pride, I would not permit her to act as she desired. Having walked into the trap, as a fly blunders into a cob's web, I must engage the spider's interest until an opportunity arose to extract my companions from her wiles. Failing that, it would be fitting that I paid the price for my mistakes.

The lady had feared to take Varryn's sword from Sarrech. I trusted she was equally reluctant to lift her hand to my blade. Either would be useless to her: She would find it impossible to add the force of Varryn's sword or mine to her present source of power. While I knew her limitations, I trusted she did not know mine. That lack of knowledge gave me an advantage, slight though it was.

* * *

Unlike the first crossing of the Cold River, the western branch flowed broad, shallow and quiet. The water came barely to the bay's knees. Once across I demanded a short halt to water the horses and fill our water bottles. The lady's servants stared at us, and in return I watched them closely.

When at last we came to the dark margin of the forest, I halted in sunlight. 'Tell the lady I will speak to her here.' My voice was quiet and steady.

'You dun't give orders in this land. You wun't be warned agin.'

The lady's servant turned towards Chane. He swayed and lurched forward, clutching at the grey's mane.

'Stop!' I turned the bay to place myself between Chane and the lady's servant. 'These men are bound to me. You *shall* not harm them.' The evil directed at Chane ceased.

Utter silence fell, lasting for heartbeats. Chane straightened in the saddle.

The creature hissed. 'Come, or die.' It turned into the shadow of the wood, and I followed.

The lady's servants surrounded and crowded us. Their nearness and stench did not disturb me, but it was otherwise with my companions. Garanth, who feared nothing natural, shuddered. Both Chane and Dern blinked as the darkness under the trees momentarily blinded them. The horses fidgeted, seeking a way out of the trap, but finding none.

Dern slumped over his horse's neck, and the dun stumbled. Chane caught the dun's reins. 'Don't despair, Dern. Kadron will save us all. Believe it.'

'What can he do? This is worse than the gysun. At least I could see that.' He shook his head. 'Here, I don't understand what threatens us. I only know it does, and it's evil.' His eyes met Chane's. 'A-all right.' He drew himself upright and tried to smile. I was not fooled. It was a brave effort, but terror ruled Dern.

Chane successfully returned Dern's smile. 'We'll come out of this safely.'

He might hope that I, whose misjudgement had trapped them here, had a plan to deliver them. That the man who had known how to deal with the lady's creature, the gysun, would know how to deal with the lady. If only that were so. I could not yet see any possibility of overcoming the odds against us.

Garanth watched my back as I dismounted, and then swung down as if nothing were amiss. Chane followed. Dern took his time, clinging to the saddle, his eyes darting everywhere. 'Do not speak in the presence of the lady of the wood. Leave that to me. Above all, do not meet her eyes.'

CHAPTER 8

Chane

When at last the sorceress came, I would have given a great deal for her absence. She glided through the trees, dripping grey-green mucus that left a slug-like trail, and the slime men cleared a way for her advance. Tall, shaped like a woman, draped in lichen, her emerald-stranded hair piled in mossy cushions about her shoulders, she swept her gaze across her captives. My heart raced as her fern-green and rust snakeskin stare lighted on me. I hastily looked away.

'Put up sword.' Her voice, harsh as a raven's call, drew my gaze despite my revulsion.

Kadron made no move to sheath his weapon. 'Does my sword frighten you, Lady?'

The sorceress laughed, and echoes of her amusement stirred the trees. A cloud of winged creatures rose and wheeled deeper into the wood. 'Fine gifts you have brought me.'

'They are not for you!'

I realised, sickened, what the sorceress wanted - men for her amusement, us.

'Why did you cross the river, Lady? Was the wood no longer large enough for you?'

'I cleave t' letter of treaty.' Her voice had changed. Slow, seductive, it ate at my senses. 'I in't responsible for changes in my borders. You strayed into my realm. My rules apply.' The rhythm of her speech, rising, falling, sliding one word into the next, pausing mid-word, mid-sentence, echoed the green man's speech. No, its speech copied hers. Or she controlled it-them. She meant to force us to meet her eyes. To be enthralled. I shivered.

'You would be wise to release my companions now.'

The lady's eyes drifted towards Dern, pale, hand on sword hilt, to Garanth, calmly waiting Kadron's orders, and rested on me. She smiled, and the glint in her eyes came close to freezing my blood. I forced my gaze down, away from her spells. 'What gift d' you offer me in return?'

'What did Sarrech give you in exchange for the gysun?' Kadron's voice had hardened.

The lady's eyes glittered. 'He swore t' use it well. I admit yielding t' temptation.'

And the bitch cared not who he might loose it on! Hot anger at her casual comment drove the chill from my bones and the tension from my guts.

'He found a use for it, but his enjoyment was short-lived.'

The sorceress smiled at Kadron, her emerald lips parting to reveal gleaming fangs. 'He brought me good news. I wished t' reward him. His fate in't my concern.'

'What good news, Lady?'

'Death of emperor's son. Good news for me, if not for you.' Cold laughter hissed between her lips. 'Emperor, he calls himself. I remember when his family herded swine.'

Kadron's expression did not change. 'I say again, release my companions, or it will go ill with you.'

'Threaten *me*, would you!' The lady's glittering eyes glared. She raised her hand and spat on the grass. Immediately a vivid yellowish-green stalk sprang up.

Dern leaped back, came close to colliding with the creature behind him and clutched my arm to recover his balance.

Kadron pointed his sword at the ill-gotten growth. It fell in smoke-darkened ruin. Dern's sigh of relief found an echo in my chest.

The lady's eyes narrowed. '*If* your gift pleases me, I release your friends. Boy stays here.'

Kadron's hand jerked on his sword hilt, and the sorceress stepped back. 'Dun't touch me!'

'There is nothing I will not dare, do you press me too far, Lady. What boy?'

'Ah, you know him,' her voice gloated. 'T'will be a long wait for his manhood, but I have patience, and have known longer waits.' She beckoned, and a slime man brought forward a boy, perhaps three or four years of age. His hair was as black as Kadron's, but his skin and eyes were glazed like the lady's creatures.

'Name your price.' Kadron's voice had steadied, although the knuckles on his sword hand showed white.

The lady licked her lips. 'A man.' Her finger moved sideways and halted, pointing directly at me.

A wave of giddiness swept over me, so violent that I came close to falling. Only Kadron's calm, as sure as when he faced the gysun, kept me upright. I remembered to breathe.

'He is not for sale.'

The sorceress tapped her long pointed nails together. 'So I keep boy. You must pay for your release.'

'Kadron,' I spoke softly, seeing no alternative, though the air in my lungs had thickened and my heart thumped enough to break through my ribs.

'Peace!' Kadron turned back to the lady. 'I am an uncomfortable guest, as you are aware, my Lady, and your right to keep the child has not been established.'

'Tahurnan brought him t' me, claiming boy t' be child of Varryn, late son of swineherd emperor. Will not emperor pay well for his grandson?'

'He will pay nothing, because you cannot send word to him, and I *will* not. You must deal with me, Lady, and it will not profit you, as it did not profit Sarrech.'

'D'you suppose such as he concern me?' She paused, her eyes glinting, her face eager. 'Did he die?'

'The gysun turned on him. It seems to be the way of such creatures. Consider your options, Lady. They are fewer than you imagine. We shall speak again.' Kadron turned his back on the sorceress, remounted, urged his horse on, and we crowded close behind him.

The lady's laughter rang in my ears, and my back crawled. Facing her had almost undone me. When I looked over my shoulder, trees blocked my view, but my dread of her still lingered.

Kadron halted in a small clearing, dismounted, sheathed his sword and stroked the bay. 'Garanth, Dern, take charge of the horses. Loosen the girths only. Ensure they cannot stray. Do not approach the trees. The grass is safer. Chane.' He beckoned.

I followed him to the centre of the clearing, glad to distance myself from the discoloured tree trunks, spotted with growths and giving off a rank odour.

Kadron dropped onto the damp grass. 'Do not think to offer yourself to the lady.'

'You might find it convenient, Kadron.' Better one man lost than four, and a child.

'You would lose your soul.' He spoke with certainty.

'I lost my soul some years ago.' The priest had told me so.

'Souls are not so easily given up.' Kadron's deep blue gaze forced me to lower my eyes.

I had nothing to do, except watch the horses. Kadron warned us against sleep. Although I would not give voice to my fears, I dared not take my eyes off my companions, drawing strength from their ability to act as usual. Perhaps they saw in me a confidence I did not feel and were also encouraged. I had no appetite, but Kadron insisted we eat and forbade the use of water from the streams and pools of the wood. As if I could have brought myself to drink from the garish, steaming water we had passed.

'We will be thirsty tomorrow,' Garanth said.

'Tomorrow is another day.'

Not for the first time, Kadron had responded to a comment other than the one I heard.

I shared first watch with Kadron and brushed the horses, which calmed them. The grey nuzzled my pockets, seeking treats. I gave him a handful of oats and stayed with them, offering an occasional touch or soft word. All was dark under the trees, but stars shone clear and bright above the glade, enabling me to see enough for reassurance. Kadron stood alert, watching the edge of the clearing and listening to the uneasy sounds of the forest.

My watch finished, I slumped on the grass. The terror of the darkness beyond the clearing, barely noticeable when on my feet and caring for the horses, returned in full force, keeping me from any desire to sleep, even without Kadron's warning. He sat nearby, his hand resting on the hilt of his sword.

The night wore on. After the pre-dawn watch, sick from lack of sleep and constant disquiet, I dropped to the grass. Dern stood guard. Garanth sat beside Kadron, his master's head resting on his shoulder.

'No!'

The cry roused me from drowsiness. I opened my eyes in panic, and scrambled to my feet. Garanth looked up from brushing his stallion's tail. Dern stood nearby, arching his back and stretching.

Kadron knelt on the far side of the clearing, his sword upright before him, both hands on the hilt. The tip of his blade rested on the ground. 'Oh God, what have I done?'

Garanth patted the chestnut, crossed the clearing and gripped Kadron's shoulders. 'All is well here.'

Kadron slowly raised his head to meet Garanth's eyes. The growing light shone on tears tracking unevenly down his tattooed face.

'If there is something to be done, permit me.'

Kadron slowly shook his head. 'It is done. Would I could undo it. God help him.' He stifled a sob with his sleeve.

Darkness receded from the edge of the clearing. I choked down some morsels of food, drank the last mouthfuls from my water bottle and soothed the horses. Hours of daylight dragged by.

* * *

The lady's summons came late afternoon. Kadron glanced round. 'Come. Do nothing except by my command.' He took the bay's reins and followed the messenger, his naked blade held upright before him, as before.

The walk seemed shorter than yesterday's ride, but felt worse. In the stifling, dank, shifting shadows of the cursed wood, nothing grew as it should. Shafts of daylight uncovered its warped and twisted growths. I averted my eyes from the escort of green men, but the trees did not make comfortable viewing either. Strangely coloured branches and leaves swayed and dipped overhead, but no wind rustled leaves within this wood. I focused on the grey's mane. Whatever crawled and swung behind the unnatural foliage, better not to know its nature - God send it stayed there!

The slime men halted and withdrew, leaving Kadron face to face with the lady of the wood.

The lady's eyes flashed. 'D' you suppose my people would steal your horses? They have no need of such.'

'I would not leave even a horse alone and afraid in this your realm, Lady.'

'D'you fear me?'

'All wise men fear you, Lady.'

'Will you bargain?'

'I will not. You *will* release the boy and my companions.'

'And keep you? I have no use for you.'

'Then we have nothing to say to each other.'

The lady's fury seared my flesh, but Kadron did not flinch, and his blade daunted the sorceress still.

'I will bide your change of mind.'

Sweat glistened on Garanth's brow and Dern's, the only trace of fear either showed. While they stood firm, I would not give way to panic.

Kadron asked softly, 'If I choose to give you a man, what then, Lady?'

The lady's eyes glinted. 'Then all manner of possibilities remain open.'

'I need more assurance than that. Wait then.' Kadron led the gelding a little way apart.

My heart beat fast and loud in my ears. I breathed with difficulty in the thick air. Horse's hooves thudded on the ground. Had I imagined it? No, the distant sound had caught Kadron's attention.

CHAPTER 9

Chane

A horse emerged from the trees – his rider a young man, dark haired and ashen faced. He brought his horse to a halt and dismounted, his whole body shaking.

'Kei!' Kadron beckoned.

The rider released his grip on the reins, and his horse fled. Kei stumbled forward, bent his knee and bowed his head. Kadron passed the bay's reins to Garanth, took Kei's hand and half lifted, half dragged him to his feet.

The sorceress stepped closer, and Kei jerked back. 'This I will take. You may have t' boy.' The eagerness in her face turned my stomach.

I clenched my fists until they hurt. Oh God! Kadron will not permit this. When will it end?

'Kei will remain, and we four will leave freely with the boy?'

I stared at Kadron in horror. He couldn't mean it.

'I have said.' The lady stretched a hand towards Kei, but he would not look at her.

Kadron drew Kei to him and kissed his brow. 'Kei, I name thee my athan, the first of my adopted sons.' He kissed him again, full on the lips, a lingering kiss, such as lovers might exchange and released him 'I shall remember thee at nightfall and forever, my athan. Remember me, I pray thee.'

Kei's eyes had widened. He nodded. Then the lady seized him and dragged him away from Kadron. His face reflected despair, but the light in his eyes suggested otherwise.

'You presume on my favour, the sorceress hissed. 'You will not touch my property.'

Kadron dropped his gaze. 'I shall not touch him again.'

'Well.' Rage faded from the lady's face. The open desire that replaced it forced me to look away, trying to focus on something other than the lady's face, or her victim's.

'You acknowledge my right t' take him. My right t' land as far as river.' It was not a question.

'As you say.' Kadron turned to Garanth. 'Take the boy. Let us go.'

Garanth took the child from his slime man captor, set him on the chestnut and mounted behind him. Dern and I hastily followed him into the saddle.

'You will release the boy from your spells, Lady.'

'He will be free once across t' border.'

Kadron frowned, shook his head, mounted and dug his heels in. 'Go!'

Garanth needed no encouragement. Somehow he avoided low branches, distorted tree trunks, dark mires and steaming pools as the stallion crashed through the rank undergrowth. We followed, making the most of daylight while it lasted. Too soon the last rays of sun glinted through the forest roof, and darkness engulfed us.

The thud of hooves and snap of twigs deafened me to all other sounds. Bent low over the grey's neck, I was conscious of little other than the desperate need to escape the sorceress and the wood haunted by her creatures. Trusting the grey to follow Garanth's stallion, I clung on.

Garanth slowed. 'Fire ahead!'

A shriek sounded behind us: a cry of fury and vengeance. Dern cast a distracted look behind. The hairs on my neck stood, and I shuddered.

'Ride!' Kadron shouted. 'Fire is our friend here. Our hope lies northward!'

The stallion sprang forward. Dern chased after, I followed with Kadron only a few strides behind. Garanth, crouched over the boy, might see a clear path, but I did not, willing the grey to sense obstacles before I saw them.

The dun staggered, and Dern leaped clear as his horse fell.

I pulled the grey up as the dun tried to rise, but fell with a squeal as a leg folded under him. Dern turned back. 'Leave him to me!' I sprang down and boosted Dern into the grey's saddle.

'Ride with me, Chane,' Kadron said. 'I am lighter than Dern.'

I slapped the grey's rump to send Dern off, and cut the dun's throat. 'Are you sure, Kadron? The bay will fall behind.'

'I have lost one man tonight. I will not lose another.' He slipped his foot from the stirrup. I mounted behind him. 'Hold fast!'

Kadron regained the stirrup, and the bay lunged forward, striving to overtake the others. I held Kadron's waist lightly, finding my balance as the gelding twisted and jumped to avoid unseen obstacles. Kadron talked to the bay continually, reins in his left hand while his right hand held his sword aloft, the blade gleaming bright in the enclosing darkness.

I should have understood sooner that his sword was no ordinary blade. In Hawdale, Garanth had recoiled from the touch of Varryn's sword. Even Kadron had been reluctant to touch it. Here, in her own realm, with scores of her creatures at hand, the sorceress had not ventured close to Kadron. Throughout he had held his sword in plain sight, in opposition to the sorceress and her creatures. Now he used his blade to keep pursuit at a distance. It gave me fresh hope.

Not for long. The bay slowed and the sound of pursuit grew louder. My skin crept.

Kadron's sword and its power notwithstanding, we would end trapped between the lady's wrath and the fire ahead. Speed might improve Kadron's chances of escape. My blood ran cold, but I loosened my grip, determined to drop off before terror locked my muscles and destroyed my will.

My movements gave me away or Kadron read my mind. 'Stay with me. We are near the edge of the wood and safety.'

A cloud of small dark winged creatures dived out of the darkness. I slashed at them, and they scattered. Kadron struck once, twice. His blade gleamed with blue fire, and the winged creatures vanished in acrid smoke. We rode into firelight, the vivid glare momentarily blinding me. The bay reared, Kadron slipped back, and his sword arm drooped. I threw my weight forward, concentrating on keeping my awkward balance. Until our combined weight forced the terrified horse down, I failed to notice the dart projecting from Kadron's neck.

I dropped my sword, slipped my left arm under him and lifted, bracing his weight against my body. When I closed my right hand over his failing grip on his sword hilt, my arm began to shake, tremors reaching me from Kadron or perhaps from the sword. 'Hold on,' I gasped. 'We'll make it yet.'

Dead ahead fire blocked our path, its bright flames leaping from tree to tree, spitting sparks and spreading fast. Garanth and Dern struggled to control their plunging and wheeling horses.

Garanth forced his wild-eyed mount alongside the bay. 'Kadron, we're trapped! We cannot persuade the horses through that!'

Kadron did not answer. I lifted his hand, and aimed his sword at the flames. The blade remained dark. Pursuit came nearer every moment. 'Kadron! You can do this,' I said. He did not respond.

Rather death by fire, than be retaken by the sorceress. The bay agreed, sidling towards the roaring heat.

I risked a backward glance. A host of green men were emerging from the trees. I dug my heels in and shouted, 'Go!' The blade flashed, quenching the blaze directly in front of me, and the bay bolted forward. Fierce heat touched neither me, nor Kadron, nor the bay, all secure behind the defending sword. Then we had passed the soaring flames, and Garanth and Dern rode alongside.

Kadron moaned, and his hold on his sword loosened. I tightened my grip. The bay burst through the last of the trees to run on long grass. The flames ahead were now merely campfires and handheld torches. Relief flooded my mind and body. Pulling gently on the reins, I spoke to the bay. 'Ease up now, my lad. You've done it. Time to rest.'

The horse slowed and hands took the reins. Other hands lifted Kadron down, helped me dismount, guided me to a campfire, made me sit, gave me clean water to drink and held my hand steady while I did so. When I had drained the cup, I looked around.

A whole troop – no, more than one – guarded the edge of the burning forest. A dozen soldiers stood around the campfire. Dern sat nearby, talking quietly to the boy, who did not look at him. I struggled to my feet, feeling my empty scabbard. Nearer the campfire, Garanth knelt beside his master, supporting him with one arm and speaking urgently. Kadron's hand closed on his sword and, with Garanth's guidance, he sheathed it. Garanth laid him down and called the officer.

'A surgeon is on his way. A tent is ready for the commander.'

'No. We must make all speed to Althein. Nothing else will serve.'

The officer glanced from Garanth to Kadron. 'Very well.' He barked his orders and shortly afterwards a trooper helped me mount a fresh horse.

Garanth lifted the unconscious Kadron up to me. I opened my mouth to protest, but remembered Kadron had given the boy into his care. I settled Kadron in front of me, hoping this would not be a long ride and swiftly discarding that hope. Despite my weariness, I preferred to leave the cursed wood far behind. The officer ordered six of his men to accompany us, two alongside each rider. If I fell, there would be one to catch Kadron and one to catch me. I had not fallen from a horse much in recent years. Just as well, their orders would likely be to save Kadron and leave everyone else.

His weight seemed less than before, as if the sheathed sword were lighter than the naked blade. We rode for hours, stopping only to change horses. When offered water I drank gratefully. Kadron did not move as he was lifted from one horse to another.

Miles passed in a blur of exhaustion and aching limbs. Unburdened, I would have slept in the saddle, as Dern slept despite our speed. If Kadron were to be saved, speed was essential, but I feared he was already beyond help. Since he had sheathed his sword, he had not stirred. Fiery pain shot through my supporting arm, across my shoulder and down my back, but I dared not move lest I lose my balance and drop Kadron, living or dead. If he lived, the fall would kill him, and the emperor would see that I paid accordingly. I gritted my teeth and held on.

At last, our pace slowed. Dern sat upright in the saddle. I could not face another change of horses. Nor could I ride further, even unencumbered, whatever pursued. Hands on my reins brought the horse to a halt and Kadron was taken from me. I was not aware of dismounting.

CHAPTER 10

Kadron

I remembered little of our flight from the cursed wood and the ride to Althein, but that hardly mattered. More importantly, my nephew, Garanth, Chane and Dern left the cursed wood unscathed, if not unchanged. Although my decision to take Chane on my horse came close to costing me my life, I did not altogether regret my choice. He was under my protection; how could I have abandoned him to the fate Kei would have endured had I not intervened? Further, I have been well repaid. He wielded my sword in that wild ride and saved us all.

The border watchers knew me. They would have let me pass, but turned away my followers, even Varryn's son, in ignorance of his identity and dread of his appearance. Garanth took my part, refused such a dismissal, and repeated my orders that we should not be parted. The watchers referred the question to those in authority, and one of the elders permitted entry to Althein. Separation was then inevitable: Chane taken with me to the healers, and Dern removed to separate custody in the guise of lodging. Varryn's son and Garanth, for he would not leave the boy's side, led to an isolated lodging to await the complete withdrawal of the lady's sway.

I slept through the arguments. By the time ilen deemed me fit to leave my sickbed, Althein's elders had determined that Varryn's son was free from malign influence. Garanth remained with him, claiming that his oath bound him to protect the boy. So much my carers told me.

Whatever one's desires and personal priorities, there were always niceties to be observed. I asked to see Master Ydrin, who had all the appearance of authority in Althein, although the reality might have been otherwise.

He entered unsmiling, and I rose to greet him. 'Master Ydrin, I am grateful for Althein's shelter and healing, for myself and for my companions.'

'You are always welcome here, child. As is anyone who travels with you. I am glad to see you recovered.'

The formalities over, I embraced my grandfather. 'May I be permitted to see my nephew?'

He led me to Lady Kirra's house. I had no need of guidance, but was glad of his company.

I did her a courtesy, but my lady mother would have none of it, sweeping me into her arms and kissing me as if I were still the child Ydrin named me.

We spoke of Varryn, the child who had shown such promise, the impetuous youth, the man who determined to follow his own path.

'His son is very like him.' She smiled, and I dried her tears. 'I wish I had known his mother.'

'I shall pursue Varryn's trail as far as Westaven. My father requires it.'

My mother's expression changed. 'He would.'

I had given up hope of my parents' reconciliation. 'Wilem will rejoice to know his grandson lives.'

'As I do. Tell him he and his are welcome here. They should know Ryny and be known by him.'

The name brought a smile to my lips. Ryny had been his father's childhood name, dropped as Varryn yearned towards manhood.

Ydrin returned. My nephew walked slowly beside his great-grandfather, his small hand in Ydrin's. Garanth followed a step behind. My mother spoke truly: Ryny was unmistakably Varryn's son.

I knelt before him. 'Ryny, you are my brother's son and my kin. I hope we shall be friends.'

Ryny stared at me, his eyes large in his thin face, their colour the grey-green of the Outer Sea. He pointed to the decorations on my face. I laughed. 'These marks will not last, I shall wash them off and untie the braids. Then my hair will swing loose like yours, and my face will be like yours too.' His finger traced the lines across my cheek, and I laid my hand on his. I thought he might resist such a touch, but he did not.

'He likes to be held,' my mother said.

I lifted him and held him against my shoulder. As he relaxed into my hold, I felt his breath on my neck, the warmth of his small body, and wept. Garanth took Ryny from me and handed him to Lady Kirra. She smiled at me over his tousled hair. 'You should release Garanth from his oath. He should not be required to serve two masters.'

I shook my head.

Garanth answered for me and for himself. 'Kadron released me from my oath before we made the crossing of the Cold River. I chose to serve Lord Ryny. As I loved his father, so I love him.'

My mother said something I did not hear as I walked away without a backward glance.

Ydrin came with me. 'Do you begrudge Ryny Garanth's love? He will never know that of a father or mother.'

'I begrudge him nothing.' Always ranked below Varryn, despite being my father's favourite, it did not occur to me to hold it against the emperor or his first-born. I understood the hierarchy of rule. In Althein, things were not so straightforward. Master Ydrin had status here, but I did not know the extent of his authority. Until now, it had not mattered. 'May we speak together?'

He nodded. I walked with him to his house, where he bade me sit and sent for refreshment. 'You should not exert yourself unduly.'

My thoughts were elsewhere, or I should have told him how much I appreciated his care for me. 'This is a matter of concern to Althein, Master. You may wish to invite others to listen.'

'I will hear you, and share this matter with those who need to know.' He had always understood me.

I waited until the boy who served us departed before I told him what I feared, in as much detail as I could recall.

Some events in the wood were hazy, while others retained a hideous clarity. He did not need to know everything, but I wished him to understand my grief and guilt for Kei. That was incidental to this matter, deep though it was written in my soul. Ydrin listened in silence, sympathy in his eyes.

'I had overdrawn power, in an attempt to defend my companions from the lady of the wood, and had little strength left. The dart removed my last capacity to wield my sword. I thought it was the end, for us all, but I could do nothing to avert that fate, not even pray. Then Chane's hand steadied mine. As he touched my sword hilt, power flowed into him and a little into me. Together we cut a path through the fire that barred our passage. I soon lost consciousness.'

Ydrin sprang up, knocking his cup over. 'Are you sure that Chane drew on your power?'

'I am sure of nothing. Only that Chane touched the stones, and the flames were quenched.'

'You had unexpected reserves. That is more likely than that Chane should suddenly display an ability to draw on power.'

I shook my head, set his cup upright and refilled it. 'Neither are likely. I fear there may be a third possibility.'

Ydrin's hand trembled as he drank. 'Spit out your fears.'

I took a deep breath and let it out slowly. 'Chane may have known his power and deliberately kept it secret. He might be a halaryth in disguise.'

'God forbid!'

'Amen to that. We are God's hands to act. That we must do, swiftly, to establish whether Chane has power and discover his intentions.'

Ydrin placed his cup carefully on the table and pushed it aside. 'I agree. He must be tested soonest.'

'Tested and guarded. I will take Dern with me. You do not need two potential enemies here. Dern would not knowingly support a halaryth, but would fight to the death to defend the man he regards as his friend. Be wary of Chane, until you learn his abilities, or prove he has none.'

'Will you teach me my work?'

'I would not endanger you. May I request that the elders consider a linkage of power?'

Ydrin shook his head. 'I cannot recommend that. Nor will I permit you to speak to the council.'

I had expected such an answer. 'Then, Master, I urge those entrusted with this task to take the utmost care. I would not lose you, or any other in Althein.'

His smile enveloped me. 'You will never lose me, Varia. I am here.' He touched my brow and my heart.

'I would have you here in the flesh.' I dropped to my knees before his chair and embraced him.

He held me close, as he used to do. 'I shall not live forever, but I shall take care to do nothing to shorten my days. Will that satisfy you?'

'Thank you, Master.'

'God's blessings go with you, to Westaven and wherever your duty takes you.'

My duty as army commander called, but first I must be sure of Varryn's fate. My heart told me to hope, but my head knew otherwise.

'Take care. You may be mistaken in your reading of Dern.'

I might. On taking my leave of my grandfather, I began to remove all traces of the Vethian tribesman from my appearance. The process took several hours.

CHAPTER 11

Chane

The sorceress' gaze lingered on me as if I were the main dish at a feast. Unable to tear my eyes from her face, I cried out in dread and despair. A man laughed, a strange sound here in the lady's realm. I wrenched my head around and saw Kei, astride his horse, galloping after the others. The sorceress' hand closed on my arm. Her touch burned me, and I screamed. She burst into emerald flames, but the blaze did not consume her.

Fire surrounded and invaded me. Its roar deafened me to all else, my skin pulsed with white heat, the stench of burning flesh filled my nostrils, and my nerves screamed in agony.

The flames dwindled. Hot tears burned my eyes and sealed my lids. Thirst tormented me. Meaningless words drifted around me.

'He does not respond, Lady,'

'Leave him to me.'

I feared the sorceress more than death, more than pain. As I fought to move, to escape, hands restrained me. I cried out, but no sound reached my ears.

A voice broke through my terror. 'Be still. Nothing will harm you here.'

A supporting arm lifted me, a cup touched my lips and I drank. Cool liquid soothed my throat. Lowered onto the pillows, I slept and did not dream.

I half woke, swallowed what was placed in my mouth and slept again.

* * *

Slowly awareness came back to me. I lay in comfort, my mind at peace. Birds sang sweetly somewhere close by. A soft breeze cooled my face, bringing the scent of flowers and grass. A linen sheet lay soft against my skin. All trace of pain had fled.

'It is time for you to wake.' The quiet voice caught my attention. I opened my eyes. Sunlight brightened the room, dappled with the shadow of a tree outside the open window. My gear hung from a peg, and my pack lay underneath. A man dressed in grey stood beside the bed, his grey hair streaked with white, but his face that of a younger man. Clear grey eyes met mine. 'How do you feel?'

I considered the question. 'I'm exhausted, but that's ridiculous. I must have slept for hours.'

'Perhaps you will feel better when you have eaten.'

I could not remember my last meal. My stomach rumbled.

The man smiled. 'It is not good to ask the body to fast for long.' He turned to speak to someone outside the room. 'Zako will bring food and drink. The boys address me as Master. You may call me Ydrin.'

Recollection of the previous night came flooding back: the cursed wood, the sorceress, Kei's fate, the dart that felled Kadron, pursuit and overwhelming terror. 'What happened to the creatures that hunted us?'

His eyes darkened. 'The creatures of the wood are not your concern. However, for your comfort, I may tell you this. It is thought that most, if not all, of the lady's creatures perished in the fire. Those who have been appointed to investigate will ascertain how far that may be true.'

'And the sorceress?'

Ydrin's eyebrows lifted. 'You are persistent, are you not? That lady is most definitely not your concern. It is possible that she also fell victim to the fire. That was Lady Varia's intent, after all. Again, those responsible for such matters are working towards verifying the lady's fate. Whether she lives or not, you are safe here.'

The name Varia meant nothing to me. 'What of my companions?'

'Neither Dern nor Garanth were harmed. The child is under our care. Lady Varia could make no sense of that. My lips shaped the words soundlessly. 'Lady Varia?'

'Ah. I see that Dern was not the only one taken in by her disguise.'

I recalled snatches of conversation. Kadron: 'The name comes close to matching my choice of appearance.' Disguised as a Vethian tribesman, she might draw attention, but not the kind a young woman would attract.

The sorceress: 'I have no use for you.' *She* recognised Kadron as a woman!

It all made sense now – Kadron's overlarge padded clothes, his braids and the scars on his face, his frequent wish for privacy. 'You must think me incredibly stupid.'

'No.' The warmth of Ydrin's smile lifted my spirits. 'Varia's disguise might have deceived even the emperor, but I know her better than most.'

Was he suggesting the emperor did not know his daughter, his heir? It happened. And some men hated their children, even those they were sure were theirs and not some other man's. Where had that last thought come from?

'Here is Zako with your breakfast. After you have eaten, your friend Dern will come to say his farewells.'

"Farewells?" What the hell! By the time I had my thoughts in order Ydrin had gone. Zako, having set the breakfast tray within easy reach, shook his head at my questions and left. Hunger deferred curiosity, but I did not have to wait long. Partway through my meal, Dern strode in whistling, and I unleashed a torrent of questions.

'Whoa!' Dern held up a protesting hand and reached for a piece of fruit. 'My leg's fine now. One of the healers said I'd just twisted the knee. He rubbed some balm on it, which hurt like hell at first, but then deadened the pain. My leg aside, I don't know much more than you, they're tight-mouthed here. What I do know, I wheedled out of Garanth. I don't suppose you remember much about our arrival?' He perched on the edge of the bed. 'They name this place Althein. It's a chain of islands in a huge lake with marshland all round. If you don't know where the causeway lies, it would be almost impossible to find. They don't usually allow strangers past their borders. I gather they made an exception for us because of Kadron. They took you and him-I mean her– to the healers straightaway. I thought they'd be more concerned about her, but they were extraordinarily worried about you, I don't know why. You didn't get hit by another dart, did you? Still, you recovered eventually.'

'What do you mean "eventually"? How long have we been here?'

'Five days. Long enough for me to find out why no one mentioned Kadron and why I kept hearing whispers of "Lady Varia". Was that a surprise! I suppose it explains why she wasn't afraid of the sorceress. *She* wasn't wanted as the lady's plaything!'

'No.' I said between clenched teeth.

'She was on her feet within two days. Mind you, I gather she mostly healed herself with her sword. God knows how, more's the pity.'

'What about the boy?'

'Young Varryn? Garanth calls him Ryny. I haven't seen him since we arrived, but Garanth says he's lost that green covering and the fixed stare, so he looks quite normal now.' He shivered. 'Whether he's right in the head after being in that place for months, who knows?' He shrugged. 'Garanth plans to stay with him.'

'Isn't he bound to Kadron – Lady Varia – by an unbreakable oath?'

'I thought so, though he did say he served Varryn first, didn't he? Maybe he reckons his oath is fulfilled by protecting Varryn's son. Anyways, he stays here, and I get to be her bodyguard, while she goes and reports to the emperor. I don't suppose I'll keep the position for long, but it won't be for want of trying.'

I knew Dern's capacity for trying. 'Don't tell me you volunteered for that duty?'

Dern stared at me. 'I didn't, she asked me, and I couldn't think of a reason why not.'

'Good God, Dern! There are a dozen reasons why not. She's the imperial heir and, if anything happens to her, you'll have to explain to the emperor, though that would be difficult because you'll likely be dead. In any case, you're not free to take service with her because you are still in service to Duke Reys. You promised him you'd see me safely back to Hawdale, and I'm not there yet. She said she'd enter the cursed wood alone, but we ended up there anyway, because she couldn't count rivers. Or–'

'Enough!' Grinning, Dern lifted his hands in surrender. 'I bet she pays better than Reys, though.'

'I wouldn't count on it. She has her own plans, and I very much doubt they include making you a rich man. She might provide a horse, bed and board, but you'll be lucky to see any coin out of this.'

Dern's grin was still optimistic. 'Well, it's too late now. I said I'd go with her, so I'm stuck with whatever she provides. I hope you're wrong.' His grin faded. 'Look, Chane, you know I wouldn't have left you–'

'Forget it. There wasn't time to think. If you'd hesitated, we'd both have died.' Best to think of it that way, although death at the lady's hands would have been neither fast nor clean. 'You would have taken me up if my horse had foundered. In fact, you did exactly that two winters past, didn't you?'

Dern's face brightened again. 'Right. I'd better be going. Mustn't keep the lady waiting on my first day of service.'

'No.' I hesitated, and then said quietly, 'Dern, don't trust her.'

'Why not? Damn it, Chane, she saved your life! Twice, if you count the ride in the wood!'

'I know. I haven't forgotten. It's just that – maybe she had her reasons – but she lied to us. If I'd known she was a woman I wouldn't have–'

'Maybe that's why she didn't tell us. I'll be careful.'

Reading his face, I knew that despite Dern's apparently casual attitude, he had taken my warning seriously. 'Fortune ride with you. I suppose they won't let me come too.'

'I haven't asked, but I doubt it. You aren't fit to ride today or for some days yet, and we're leaving now. Good luck to you. I'll send a message to Hawdale when I can. You will go home when you're well enough, won't you?'

'Where else would I go?'

Dern gripped my hand. 'I've been promised a horse. The grey will be here for you. You didn't rescue my bow, did you?'

For a moment I had no idea what Dern meant. Then I remembered. 'No. The dun rolled on it, smashed it to bits.'

'Damn. I hope Lady Varia will provide a replacement.' He raised a hand in salute and strode out.

My appetite had vanished. I pushed the tray away and closed my eyes.

*　　*　　*

When I woke, a fresh meal had replaced the breakfast leavings. After eating I swung my legs over the side of the bed, tried to stand and fell back as my legs gave way. Fool that I was, I had rushed things. When the room settled, I eased forward, levered myself up, took two uncertain steps to the security of a low chair and sat, shaking with effort, trying to control my breathing and waiting for my heartbeat to slow. I told myself my condition resulted from lazing abed for five days, but I did not believe it. If I had slept for that long, I had been seriously ill. After a half-hour or so, I stumbled back to bed and fell asleep again almost immediately, woke in time for an evening meal and slept again.

For days, I did nothing but eat, sleep and try to walk about the room. Every day a little more strength returned to my weak muscles, and I stayed on my feet a little longer.

One morning, an older boy, tall and well-built, brought me fresh clothes: clean linen, a white shirt, plain brown breeches and a matching belted tunic, just like his. He stood outside while I bathed, shaved and dressed. Then he led me along the path to an open clearing where Ydrin waited, his gloved hands resting on the hilt of an unsheathed sword.

The boy bowed his head. 'Master.'

'Thank you, Eward. You may go.'

I watched Eward until the trees blocked my view. When I turned back two others stood beside Ydrin. A man of middle years, dressed in green, a sword on his belt. His cold eyes studied me as if he were consider ways to use it on me. The woman was tiny. Her light brown hair, in a thick braid, showed no hint of grey, and her small heart-shaped face was smooth, except for laughter lines. Why were they here?

At a movement behind me, I swung round, groping uselessly for my lost sword. A hard-faced woman stood there, clothed and armed like the man. Her hand rested on her sword hilt.

CHAPTER 12

Varia

Dern stared at me as if I were a stranger. Perhaps he had expected me to wear female garb. I wore the black as before, my hair tucked under a black cap. At a distance or in poor light, I might pass for a youth. I mounted the dapple, a gift from my mother.

  Dern looked the grey mare over, tested the baggage fastenings, accepted a bow and quiverful of arrows with a quiet word and a smile. He swung into the saddle, and we set off. The paths of Althein are often misleading, but I knew enough to take a narrow track that wound through the woods. Dense foliage closed off every view. Judging by Dern's expression, he was concentrating on his position as my bodyguard, unaware that unseen guards watched over us. I did not intend to enlighten him, the less he knew about the workings of Althein and my intent the better.

The trees ended at a stretch of open water. Bright green reeds bordered the causeway, a continuation of the track, and the only land access to Althein. A mile or so later, where reeds gave way to a grassy plain, nine mounted men waited. The sergeant saluted. 'Name's Raneth, milady.'

His men took their positions: two in front, two at the rear and two on each flank. Raneth rode on my left. Dern, on my right, turned to look back, but the reeds would block his view of the causeway and track.

'Althein is well guarded, by fens and man. No uninvited stranger will find his way to the isles.' I meant it as a warning. If he chose to leave my service, he would be turned away from Althein.

He nodded his acknowledgment.

* * *

A dark haze appeared in the southern distance, the remnants of Captain Heksun's fire. Whatever his choice of action in my absence, I trusted it had sufficed. Slow hours passed before we came close enough to see the extent of the damage. A vast smoke cloud hung in the still air, dimming the sky. Blackened trunks pointed skywards or lay toppled in thick beds of ash. The rank odour of burnt wood mingled with rot poisoned the air. I turned west, and a light wind wafted away the worst of the stench.

Here the fire had burned fiercest. Not a skeletal trunk remained, only a thick carpet of grey ash where pockets of embers glowed red and spirals of smoke rose, drifting in the gentle breeze.

Heksun's men patrolled the margin on foot and on horseback. An officer came to greet me, his gear ash spattered. A man of middle years, his eyes reddened above a cloth covering his nose and mouth, he wore the two bar insignia of a senior captain. I did not recognise him until he lowered the protective cloth and saluted me.

'The border is secure, Commander. Nothing has left the forest.'

'You are sure of that, Captain Heksun?'

'Raithen keep watch with us. They are sure.'

'And further west?'

'I sent Captain Frenn west. It's been a long time since someone checked on the coastal villages.'

My eyes narrowed. 'A full troop?'

'Half a troop, Commander, I could spare no more.'

I nodded. 'I would speak with such raithen as may be available.'

'They're resting or on patrol now, Commander. Unless you wish to join them on patrol, you must wait till dusk.'

'No matter. How fare your men?'

'They are holding up, Commander.'

'You have done well, Captain. The emperor shall hear of it.'

Following Heksun's directions, I turned away from the remains of the wood and, two or three miles later, rode into an army camp. Men came to take charge of the horses, guided me to the centre of the camp and brought water and food. Raneth and his men settled into their bedrolls soon after sunset.

'Sleep while you may, Dern. I must talk with raithen.'

* * *

Those I spoke to had little information. Other raithen had turned south and might have more to report. Unfortunately there were no callers among them. I woke in the grey light of dawn, in time to question the exhausted patrols. They had followed the lady's trail, marked in the bones of horses and green men. Now they planned to move south in force to investigate further. I did not presume to give advice. I gave them my blessing, and spoke briefly to Heksun, before we set off westwards. I did not explain my choice of direction. Raneth would stay with me until I dismissed him and his men. Dern would surely resist such a dismissal. He was quieter than he had been in Chane's company. I could not blame him for that. Much had changed since we left Bridgetown. My thoughts were occupied with fear of the lady's escape, and how I might break news of Varryn's uncertain fate to Wilem. Other considerations aside, I must improve my relationship with Dern before his ignorance of the dangers attached to me resulted in his death.

As the afternoon waned, I drew the dapple alongside the grey mare. 'You are very quiet today, Dern.'

He met my questioning gaze. 'Where are we headed?'

'West.'

'I thought you wanted a bodyguard. My lack of knowledge of what's afoot might kill us both, Lady Varia.'

My lips twitched. I had underestimated him, as I had Chane. 'True. We are following Captain Frenn to Westaven. Wilem is kin to me by marriage. He may be able to tell me my brother's intended destination. If nothing else, he deserves to know that Varryn's son lives.' I paused. 'Why did you address me as "Lady Varia"?'

'Thank you for that information, Kadron.' I raised an eyebrow, and he grinned.

The next day, I felt his eyes watching me. Good for him; the better he knew me the greater our chances of survival. I rode alongside the troopers where possible and spoke to them as equals. They responded with respect, as to any officer. Raneth tried, not altogether successfully, to curb the amount of swearing that came naturally to most of his men. The coarser jokes were either cleaned up for my benefit or whispered out of my hearing, which was a pity. I had laughed at Dern's crude jokes and then capped them. Dern alone named me Kadron.

* * *

We rode single file along the narrow forest track, Dern behind trooper Grice on his unpredictable sorrel. I followed. A scout whistled, the sorrel shied and slammed his rider against a tree trunk. Grice let loose a string of curses while Dern eased his mare wide of the sorrel and looked over his shoulder.

'Make way!' I called. The troopers ahead drew as far off the track as possible, I rode past and Dern followed.

Raneth turned his head. 'Tobe's found something, milady.' He stood in his stirrups. 'Full alert! Grice, control your mount.'

'I wouldn't pin my hopes on Grice's sleeve,' a trooper muttered. 'That horse'll be the death of him one of these days.'

'Trooper!'

'I heard you, Sarge. Full alert.'

The trail twisted, turned downhill and broadened into a small clearing. Tobe, the forward scout, stood beside his ugly piebald, crossbow ready, his eyes scanning the trees. 'Take a look at this, Sarge.'

I caught the rusty scent of blood. Dern's mare backed away, and he sprang down, looped his reins over a handy branch and rested a hand on her neck. 'Easy, girl. It's not going to hurt you.'

'It's a dead bear cub, Tobe. Nothing to concern us.'

'How did it die, Sarge?'

Raneth sighed. 'Male bears kill cubs all the time.'

'No bear did that, Sarge.'

I crouched to examine the remains, and Dern leaned closer. The cub had been ripped apart. Bloodstained body parts and shreds of fur littered the forest floor. A ragged, bloody paw lay almost at Dern's feet. The stink of shit, blood, and something else proved my instinct correct. Dern stepped back.

Raneth frowned. 'What then, milady?'

I stood. 'This is the work of karyth, violence for its own sake.'

Dern shivered.

'I thought they didn't come this far south.' Raneth's weather-beaten face had greyed.

'I have received no reports of karyth movement in the west, but they have ventured great distances on the eastern border. This may be a rogue.' My fingers tightened on my sword hilt. 'It may not. We must reach the Tower of the Winds before dark.'

'We'd best keep watch for the cub's dam,' Tobe said. 'She has reason to be angry.'

We had covered no more than half a mile when Tobe found the bear's dam, close to the trail. Raneth barely gave the scattered remains a glance. 'Troop, close in. Scouts, stay with us. Trot!'

He set a fast pace, and the troop matched it. Dern watched the shadows. We emerged from the trees into the glare of the sinking sun, which half-blinded us to any attack from the west.

Tobe whistled and pointed at a dark speck in the northern sky. Sergeant Raneth shouted, 'Halt! Take defensive stance. Bowmen, hold your shots until you can make them count. And remember that thing can move faster than you.'

'Will it come that close?' Dern asked.

'If we are fortunate,' I said softly. 'Karyth are not wise enough to trail us at a distance. A halaryth would keep out of bowshot and bring a host of karyth down on us when we think ourselves safe. If you are minded to pray, make it brief.'

Dern nodded and reached for the bow he had acquired in Althein, then changed his mind and drew his blade. Mine was already in my hand.

I had lost the creature against the fierceness of the dying sun, though I could sense it above us, not yet close.

A black object dived at us. 'Loose!' Tobe cried.

All around me horses plunged and wheeled, and men shouted conflicting instructions. Dern leaned left to avoid a low bolt, and swung his mare clear. Grice screamed as the karyth hurtled past him. Raneth lunged for its body as it came at us again, but misjudged its speed and had to duck to avoid its talons. Dern struck at its wing, an easier target. The karyth faltered. I stood in the stirrups and swept my sword down, slicing its head from its body. Dark blood spurted towards Grice's horse. The sorrel reared, and flung Grice off.

'Don't touch it! Watch the sky, there may be more.' I leaped down and tossed my reins to Dern. The karyth lay in a puddle of dark blood, its head two paces from its body, a bolt still quivering in its back. 'Leave it to me. We cannot delay here. How is Grice?'

'Dead. Broke his neck. He hated that horse.' Raneth looked round. 'You heard milady. Stay alert. Catch that blasted horse and tie Grice to his saddle. We're not leaving him here. Move it!'

I set fire to the karyth corpse while Dern's gaze followed the troop. The karyth consumed, I cleansed my sword in the dying flames, retrieved my reins and remounted. 'Let us make haste.'

*   *   *

A horn sounded near dusk. 'Halt, in the name of the emperor! Who goes there?'

'Sergeant Raneth with eight men, escort for Milady Varia and her bodyguard. Where's your captain?'

The sentry stepped into view. 'You are welcome, Lady, with your escort and guardsman.' His horn sounded a two-tone signal. 'Go on up, Captain Frenn is at the tower.'

Some few hundred yards and two further challenges later, I rounded a cliff and joined a path winding up a series of steps towards an old watchtower.

Another sentry directed the troop to the tower and led me to the right. 'Watch your step, Lady.'

Dern followed closely, as I picked my way through tumbled stones and tree roots in the fading light. I guessed we had half circled the main tower when our guide halted and called, 'Captain! Lady Varia is here.'

A dark figure appeared out of the gloom, wiping his hands on his breeches, and saluting. 'Lady Varia.'

'Call your men inside the tower, Captain Frenn. We downed a karyth earlier. There may be more hereabouts, or worse. We must stand ready to defend the tower.'

'See to it,' Frenn ordered, and his man ran off. 'This way, Lady.'

'What news, Captain Frenn?'

'Come inside. You will be glad of rest and refreshment.'

'Glad indeed.' I looked up. 'Night is falling. Let it find us within the walls.'

CHAPTER 13

Chane

'I ask your forgiveness, Chane,' Ydrin said. 'We rarely welcome guests here, but that is no excuse for neglecting the duties of a host.' The tiny woman touched his arm. 'Nyth reminds me that I have not introduced my companions.' He gestured. 'Here is Nyth, one of the elders of Althein, and there Burll and Maris, both raithen.'

I nodded to Nyth. She smiled. Neither Burll nor Maris responded, but I had not forgotten my manners. 'There is nothing to forgive, Ydrin. I've been well looked after.'

His tension eased. 'You have not yet regained your full strength. Do not overexert yourself.'

The last thing I wanted was to set back my recovery.

'Varia asked me to give you this, to replace the sword you lost in her service.' He offered the blade, hilt first.

I reached for it instinctively, and stopped, my hand still outstretched. The hilt design was familiar, identical to that of Kadron and his – her –brother Varryn. I could not bring myself to touch it and withdrew my hand. 'No.' The stark refusal sounded ungrateful, but my distrust of the sword was irrational, and I had no wish to appear a fool before witnesses.

'Why do you fear this sword?'

As a guest, indebted for the care provided, silence was unacceptable. 'I don't desire such power.'

'"I will serve you if it costs me my life." Those were your words to Lady Varia. Would you retract them?'

'No.' Any possible explanation eluded me.

'She bade me test you with the sword. Do you wish me to tell her that you will not be so tested?'

Burll, raithan,–whatever that was – stepped closer. Ydrin waved him back and Nyth whispered something.

'Well?'

'No.' Unarmed, weak and outnumbered, my only choice was to play along with Kadron's game, whatever it was.

Ydrin visibly relaxed. 'That is well for you. For your comfort, there is no power in the sword. It is merely a tool to channel power. If you have no power, you will not be able to use it.'

"Merely a tool to channel power." The phrase disturbed me. I hesitated.

'Take it.' The fine lines on Ydrin's brow deepened.

I took the hilt reluctantly, forced myself to handle it as if it were merely another blade. Willed myself not to fear it– the sword would find no power in me.

Light and well balanced, the blade glinted with the clean brightness of burnished steel. The leather hilt binding showed little sign of wear, except for dents in a diamond pattern. It might have been Lord Varryn's sword, once studded with gems, but the one remaining dark stud was no glittering jewel. Its dull sheen, like dirty glass, contrasted oddly with the shining blade. At the first chance I would be rid of that.

'Do you see or feel anything different, perhaps a tingle in your flesh, a slight warmth or a glow?'

I shook my head. Nothing like that. 'I have no power. For me, this is a sword like any other.' To my great relief I had failed the test.

'Show me your hands.' Beads of sweat had formed on Ydrin's face.

I tucked the sword into my belt and turned my hands palms up.

Ydrin held my hands and inspected them closely. 'As you say.'

Nyth took my right hand in her small grasp, then the left and the right again. She looked up at me. 'Interesting.'

'How?'

She raised an eyebrow. 'If you are ready, Chane, we will proceed with the testing.'

I stared at her. Surely I had failed the test. Whatever they expected hadn't happened.

'All power is dangerous,' Ydrin said. 'Here we teach children to control the power within them, so they endanger neither themselves nor others.'

'I have no power,' I said between gritted teeth. 'You've seen that.'

'The stones defend themselves against the unwary. You touched Varia's power wielded at her utmost capacity and were not consumed. Nor are you marked by the stone in the hilt of that sword.. You have power.' He linked his fingers. 'I'm told you have no recollection of any time before Duke Arnull of Hawdale found you twelve years ago.'

A chill touched my heart. I nodded.

'I judge you found power as an untrained boy and came close to destroying yourself. That might account for your missing memories.'

The icy grip on my chest tightened. I shook my head, unable to trust my voice.

'Those who have power can turn anything in their imagination into reality, as a means of defence or to heal. The test for power is simple. First, you must be able to hold a one-stone weapon unmarked. You have done that. Secondly, you must be able to shield yourself, and lastly you must demonstrate that you can make the object of your imagination real. Close your eyes, shield yourself and build a defensive wall, stone upon stone.'

'How?'

'Form a picture in your mind. If you believe it to be real it will be.'

He had said Lady Varia demanded I be tested. I must attempt the test –and fail– to obtain my release.

Not daring to consider the possibilities further, I closed my eyes. Shield myself? Reys' armourer sometimes described shields large enough to protect every part of the body. I thought of such a shield held in front of me, willed it to protect me and filled my mind with a memory of the strongest fortress wall I knew. I shaped the wall slowly, carefully. Time passed, while I felt nothing but shame at being forced this childish game. When I opened my eyes, the wall I had imagined loomed over us. Shock ran through all my nerves, my fingers sprang open, and my sword fell as I stared in horror.

'Stand well back.' Ydrin took a slim crystal rod from his tunic pocket and pointed it at the wall. Nothing happened.

Burll stepped forward, and Maris followed. While they conferred with Ydrin, Nyth gazed at me, her expression unreadable. Then she smiled. 'It seems we must allow Chane to undo his creation. Leave your sword where it is, Chane, and release all control over your wall.'

I did, but the wall stood.

Nyth turned to Ydrin. 'Have you ever seen such control in a new student?'

Ydrin shook his head. 'Never to this extent, though Varryn came close.'

'Did he now?' Nyth smiled. 'Well, Chane, you have surprised us. Think back to your creation of your shield and the wall, what did you ask of them?'

'The shield to protect me, and the wall to stand until no longer needed.' My voice was not my own.

Burll grunted.

Ydrin exchanged looks with Nyth. 'Take your sword, Chane,' she said. 'Keep your shield in place, tell the wall it has served its purpose and dismantle it as you built it one stone at a time.'

'Starting at the top and working down,' Ydrin said.

Of course, but if they were used to training boys, they had learnt to be cautious. I retrieved the sword, tightened my fingers on the hilt, and faced the wall, feeling all kinds of a fool. Nevertheless I followed Nyth's instructions, stone after stone toppled from the wall and dissolved into nothingness. When all had vanished, I released the shield.

Ydrin stared at me a moment longer. 'Did you see Chane's shield, Nyth?'

'I didn't,' Burll said.

Maris shook her head.

'No, Ydrin,' Nyth said, 'but clearly Chane has power and the ability to use it. We should not delay his training over an initial difficulty with shielding. Many students encounter that problem.'

Ydrin sighed. 'Give me the sword.' His tone was gentle, his eyes implacable.

I handed it to him, hilt first, wishing him to keep it.

He withdrew something from a pouch on his belt and fitted it to the hilt. 'Take your sword.'

I willed my hand to remain steady and reached for the sword. My fingers closed on the hilt, the metal guard cool against my knuckles, the leather binding almost smooth. Ydrin had added another stud, twin to the first. I stroked them, removed the second stud from the hilt and rolled it over in my palm before replacing it.

'You live dangerously, Chane. The stones should not be handled lightly.'

'What are they?' My voice was almost under my control, its slight hoarseness barely noticeable.

Ydrin held his rod for my inspection. Three stones were inset near one end, that closest to his hand. He tucked the rod away. 'I will not speak of their origin, or the discovery of their use. Their numbers are limited.

'There are two uses of power: for healing and for, I suppose you might say *war*, although we in Althein prefer to use the term *defence*. Ilen are healers, raithen defenders. Individual ability varies, but no ilan holds more than three stones, no raithan more than five. Sometimes great strength runs in the same family, but not always. My daughter is a three-stone ilan, her husband a five-stone raithan. Their children each earned five stones, but my son...could not use the stones to focus power.

You believe I'm raithan?' The idea was ridiculous. This whole situation would be a joke, if I could return the sword and ride out of Althein.

'You are a man of war, accustomed to a sword. Raithan is more likely, but if you are ilan, it will be seen in the testing.'

I stared at the stones. 'You have three stones, is it safe for you to handle more?'

'It is not. I took care to protect myself. We will deal with that later. Do you see light in the stones, or feel warmth or a tingle in your flesh?'

'No.' Neither, though the sword felt familiar in my hand, as if it had always belonged to me, the more so since the second stone had been added. My mind must be playing tricks.

'Ilan, or raithan, the power we harness is the same,' Ydrin said, as calmly as if he were describing his midday meal.

'How could I have such power without knowing it?' Either the wall had been an illusion, or Ydrin had created it to deceive me. I did *not* have power.

'Without the stones, you would find it difficult to focus the power, difficult but not impossible. Did you never do anything you couldn't explain?'

No. .. Maybe. Once I had – and the darkness retreated. 'No!' I sank to the grass and covered my face with my hands, attempting to block the fragment of a long-forgotten memory.

*   *   *

'Try again,' Ydrin said. 'Give the wall more substance this time.'

I looked up to meet his steady gaze. 'I beg you, let me leave.'

'I cannot. You have power, Chane. Only the extent is uncertain. You must be trained. Will you co-operate in your training?'

'Do I have a choice?'

'There is always a choice. You may remain here at your will or ours.'

Call that a choice? Unless he was playing with me. I took a deep breath and let out slowly. 'I will not resist.'

Ydrin's expression softened. 'Rebuild the wall.'

With my eyes open, I could not. 'Why can't I do it with my eyes open?'

'The will to succeed is vital. Lack of confidence or disinterest both result in failure. Closing your eyes is recommended at first. It helps you to relax, clear your mind and concentrate. In time, you will learn to use power successfully with your eyes open. I hope so.' His smile was wry. 'It would be a short-lived raithan who entered battle with his eyes shut. Try again.'

He had not reminded me to shield myself, and I didn't think of it. I closed my eyes and built the wall anew instantly. Ydrin walked round it, peering as if he saw something I could not – like the invisible light, the missing tingle in my fingers and the lack of warmth that puzzled him.

'With practice you will be able to dismantle the wall as fast as you created it. Until then slow and sure is best.'

I heard his warning, but the idea of the wall's instant disintegration was stronger. When I sought to move the first stone, something cracked. The wall shattered, flinging lumps of stones everywhere. A sharp pain in my temple brought darkness.

CHAPTER 14

Varia

Under the tower's looming walls, darkness had descended. Wind soughed through the trees. A screech that had weapons drawn signalled nothing worse than a hunting owl. Nonetheless, Frenn lengthened his stride. Two of his troopers waited at an arched doorway at the head of the broken steps leading up to the tower doorway. Once inside, they heaved the iron-studded doors shut and dropped the bars into place, reinforcing the barrier with old timber and rubble.

Frenn preceded me up the narrow stairs and through a large chamber crowded with his men and Raneth's. On the floor above, an internal wall had collapsed leaving an open landing. Wind gusted through arrow slits, despite makeshift shutters, and reduced the brazier's glowing heat to barely acceptable. Frenn's men served hot food and warm spiced ale. Dern, his back against the wall to avoid the worst of the draughts, ate and drank his way through all he was offered. I did not have his appetite and soon set my platter aside. Frenn questioned me at length on the possibility of a karyth attack. I reassured him. Whatever damage time and neglect had wreaked on the outbuildings, the thick-walled tower with its single door was our best defence. The window slits would not admit something the size of karyth.

While we might be safe here, the coastal communities had no such defences. Tomorrow I must send warnings to Captain Heksun, to the emperor and to the western coast settlements. 'Tell me your news.'

'We discovered the remains of two men here, Lady. One wore the imperial signet.'

Frenn was right; his news was bitter. I laid aside the cup I had been nursing. 'Was it possible to make out how they died?'

'One shot in the back, the other beheaded, Lady.'

Varryn would not have fallen prey to an easy ambush. 'How do you read it, Frenn?'

He waited until the man who came to collect our platters had returned downstairs. 'I believe they came to the tower to make a defence against a pursuing wolf pack. Animal bones were scattered back along the trail and under the tower walls. I judge they found the tower door barred against them. Those who held the tower shot Lord Varryn, picked off the wolves, and then came out to kill the other man. It was foul murder, Lady.' He paused. 'It looked as if they tried to steal the imperial ring.' He cleared his throat. 'They broke his finger, but could not force it off.'

His guess made sense. Sarrech had lorded it in his high tower and taken his revenge on the imperial family. He had no use for an imperial ring, but would have delighted in mutilating Varryn's body. May he burn in hell for all eternity! 'Only one man held the tower.' My voice was harsh.

Frenn met my eyes across the brazier. 'May justice be done on him!'

'It has been. A creature of the cursed wood ate him slowly.'

Frenn's eyes widened. His hand shook as he made the sign against evil. He took several breaths before he could speak. 'Lord Varryn's death is a great loss to us all, Lady.'

'It is.' I paused. 'His son lives.'

Frenn sprang to his feet. 'How is that possible?'

I shook my head. He did not need to know the details, and I had no wish to relate the horrors of the cursed wood. 'He is safe. That's all that matters.'

Frenn stared at me, torn between disbelief and joy. 'That is indeed good news, Lady. May I tell the men?'

I gave my consent, and he left us, his boots echoing on the stairs. Cheering broke out, but soon died away. Frenn would have reminded the men of my nearness.

On his return he led us up another flight of broken stairs to the top chamber. As on the floor below, only a pile of broken stone remained of the wall between the stairs and the uppermost chamber. 'I'll have the brazier brought up, Lady. It will be cold here, but overcrowded below, both on the first landing and in the lower room.'

I had spent too many nights in crowded sleeping quarters. 'This will serve, Captain Frenn. The men may keep the brazier.' Other officers might have expected me to offer to share my privacy with them, so that they did not need to sleep cheek by jowl with common soldiers. Frenn was neither so proud nor so foolish, but Dern's face reflected his discomfort.

Frenn saluted and ran downstairs. I settled myself in a corner. Dern arranged his bedroll at the top of the stairwell. Comfort was relative, but the chamber was dry and partly sheltered. The alternative, sharing the overcrowded floors below, was not an option. A woman taking a man's role must be seen as a woman and respected accordingly. Lying beside common soldiers is apt to confuse them. When men lose respect for a superior officer, they act according to their nature. As for Dern, he had not yet learned to relax in my presence. For him, it would be a long night.

* * *

I lay in near darkness, except for a slim ray of moonlight. Wind tapped twigs against the stone wall and rattled the shutters. Dern, a dark shadow on the floor, stirred and propped himself on one arm to arrange his bedding more securely about him. At a sound from below, he scrambled to his feet.

I sat up. 'I am sorry to have disturbed you.'

His response was swift. 'You've nothing to apologise for. You're entitled to grieve for your brother.'

Despite my sorrow, I laughed. 'He chose his own path and found happiness for a time with the woman of his choice. May I do as well!'

He hesitated. 'I imagine you have many suitors. How will you chose between them?'

'My father chose a husband for me last year. He did not ask for my consent.' I did not expect Dern to understand the issues surrounding my marriage.

'Will you wed your father's choice, Kadron?'

'I killed my father's choice in the cursed wood.' Dern's silence shamed me. I should not have burdened him with my guilt. While I attempted to think how to retrieve my blunder, if that were possible, I saw the flash of his gaze as he turned to look directly at me.

He took an audible breath. 'Tell me, what happened there? Why did Kei come into the cursed wood? Surely he knew its dangers?'

'I gave him a message to relay to Captain Heksun, who had orders to set fire in the wood under certain conditions, or on receipt of orders from an imperial authority. I had already sent messages to warn him that such an order was likely. At that time Kei was the only raithan near enough to receive my message and pass my instructions on. He did so, but he also decided to seek me out, to do what he could to help. That I neither wished nor foresaw. I would have given much to have deterred him.'

'He chose his path, Kadron. You are not to blame.'

'It was his duty to serve me and mine to protect him. I am responsible for his death.'

'When I was unhorsed Chane intended to take me on his mount. If he had died because of it, I would have grieved, but I don't believe I would have blamed myself. He counts me as his friend. He is free to die for me if he so wishes, as I am to die for him. Was it Kei's duty that made him risk the sorceress for you, or was it something else?'

Moonlight illuminated our sleeping place through another gap in the inadequate shutters. I turned my face away so he should not see my tears. When I had control of myself, I stood. 'Are you cold, Dern?' It was long past time to treat him as the brother Garanth had been.

'Yes, Kadron.' He spoke no blame for my refusal of the brazier's heat.

'So am I. Once this place was known as the Tower of the Winds. The name is apt.' I took one of his blankets, wrapped it around a broken stone and returned it to him. He held it close. His shivers would soon cease and then he would sleep. I warmed another stone for myself and lay down again.

Dern remained standing, his eyes fixed on the blanket-wrapped stone I had given him.

'Thank you for your kind words, Dern. You should sleep now.'

He retreated to his chosen place and lay down, drawing his bedding close. I completed my silent prayers. Afterwards, his even breathing lulled me to sleep.

* * *

I woke early, left Dern to his slumbers and found Captain Frenn finishing his breakfast. He wiped his mouth and stood. 'Good morning, Lady.'

'Show me the graves.' My voice was not my own, but Frenn did not know me well enough to notice.

Daylight revealed two fresh graves in a clearing in the trees, each marked with a rough wooden stake: the left-hand marker carved with the imperial symbol, the right bore the crude outline of a bird's wing.

I made a sign of reverence at the right-hand grave. Its occupant had been with my brother at the end and deserved my respect. He may have been kin to Wilem and therefore to me through Varryn. Now it fell to me to take news of his death to Wilem and mourn with him. I hesitated, unwilling to leave Varryn's friend unnamed as I prayed for his soul, but God knew all names and heard all prayers.

Frenn had left me. Two troopers stood guard at a short distance. I knelt at the left-hand grave and bowed my head.

Formal prayers for the dead are lengthy, but it was not my place to recite the full service. I spoke for God's hearing, and perhaps also for Varryn's.

'In thy mercy, Lord above all lords and God above all gods, grant to Varryn peace in the presence of thy glory. May he therein know an end to his restless striving. May he be reunited with his wife and second son whom thou, in thy wisdom, did take from him in pain and distress. I beseech thee, reward thy son Varryn for his merits and forgive him his faults. As thou hast promised, so let it be.'

I lingered, unwilling to leave my brother and his friend. One of the troopers cleared his throat. I looked up. The sky had brightened. I must give Frenn his orders.

CHAPTER 15

Varia

In the outer courtyard, Raneth shouted orders as his men mingled with Frenn's to saddle horses and pack supplies. Frenn, his cheeks flushed, turned away from me. I watched order emerge from the muddle. Frenn had separated his troopers into two sections. Raneth and his men were already mounted. I fastened the dapple's saddlebags. Dern strode towards me. The grey mare lipped at his hand, and he rummaged in his pockets.

'Try this.' I dropped a small biscuit onto his palm. He fed it to the mare before he looked up. 'Thank you, Kadron.'

My anger with Frenn, probably unjustified, drained away. I attempted to smile. 'One biscuit now and then won't spoil her.'

'Did Frenn have bad news from Westaven?'

'He never reached it. A sea fog blanketed the cliffs. He would have lost men making the attempt. We must try again.'

'God grant all's well there, Kadron.'

'I pray so, Dern.' I glanced at Frenn, talking to two of his men. 'I shall make my peace with Frenn, but not until he has calmed down.'

'He looks safe enough now.'

I gave him a sideways look, tightened the girth and mounted.

Dern swung in between me and Raneth, who had the sorrel's lead rope fastened to his saddle. Frenn followed with the larger of his sections. Raneth muttered to himself, the only clear words being 'ignorant' and 'fool'.

'What's Frenn's problem?' Dern asked.

'He's in a hurry to report back to base and didn't expect milady to overrule him. Now he's concerned for her safety.'

'How would that be his responsibility?'

Raneth snorted. 'Right now, he's the senior officer here after milady.' He glared at one of his men. 'Watch what you're doing! I have no wish to turn back and bury you next to Grice!'

Raneth was partly right about Frenn's misgivings. My news of our karyth encounter had also unsettled Frenn.

* * *

Early next day we crossed the ridge. Leaving two laden packhorses with Raneth, Frenn took his men north. Raneth's troopers drew lots to avoid taking the lead rope for Grice's sorrel.

Tobe lost. 'If he doesn't behave I'll eat him, hooves, saddle and all.' He grinned, and took rearguard while another scout led westwards.

I guided the dapple into thick forest. Almost immediately the ground fell away, and I loosened the reins for the steep descent. Mist thickened as we descended. By the time the trees came to end, I could barely see the horse and rider ahead. I shivered in the chill damp air, finding some sympathy with Frenn's earlier decision to turn back.

As the morning wore on, the wind direction changed, bringing a briny tang and clearing the mist. I called a halt on a stretch of rough grass that ended abruptly a dozen paces ahead. Dern peered over the edge. Dark rolling waves swept in to crash against the stony shore.

Below us the rock face fell away. To our left, the shore curved around a shingle beach backed by dark cliffs. On our right, a headland cut off the view. On the far side of the headland, steps had been carved into the cliff face. The cliff edge had given way in places, its rock shattered on the beach below, but the area around the steps remained largely intact.

Raneth left two men with the horses, everyone else was loaded. I had no fear of heights, but the condition of cliff edge suggested I watch where I stepped. Taken with care, the descent proved uneventful.

In the shelter of the headland, a cluster of grass-roofed stone huts stood above the high tide mark. Only three roofs remained intact, while some huts were no more than piles of stone. I had not expected such dereliction. Where was everyone?

Below the huts, the shingle beach sloped down to the water. A lone man sat on the skeleton of the furthest jetty, facing out to sea. I tugged off my cap and shook my hair loose. My boots crunched on the pebbles, but the man on the jetty did not turn until I spoke. 'Wilem.'

'That's my name.'

'I am Varia, daughter of Virreld. We are kin through my brother.'

'Aye. He spoke of you. Is he dead?'

'He is.'

'And his companion?'

'Also dead. I have avenged them.'

Wilem's eyes were shadowed. 'Vengeance will bring back neither my son nor my son by marriage.' He sighed. 'Varryn wished to take Ryny to meet his family. Bry chose to leave with them, and I had no heart to stop him. Now I have no sons, daughters or grandchildren. Many of my people have perished.' He rose to his feet, 'Leoric, we have guests!'

A boy of about ten years ran out of one of the huts, stopped and stared. A woman and an old man followed him. The boy seized the woman's hand, she took the old man's arm, together they made their slow way towards us.

'We four are all that remain – Alen, his grandson Leoric and my wife's aunt by marriage, Mae.'

Only four! 'I am Varia. Varryn was my brother.'

Mae gasped. 'Was?'

Leoric burst into tears. No longer supported, Alen sagged. Dern stepped forward and braced him with a hand under his arm. I took in the white film covering Alen's damp eyes, and his misdirected searching stare. 'What happened here, Wilem?'

'There were few enough of us, even before Varryn and Bry left. Two winters of sickness followed his departure. This spring we lost two boats and their crews. We have no future here, but we will not leave.'

I understood that feeling. 'Not even for the sake of Varryn's son, your grandson?'

'He lives? Truly?' Wilem's eyes shone, and Alen's hand grasped Dern's arm.

'He lives and thrives.'

'Where? Where is he?'

'There is a land in the east, where the waters are still and sweet, silver fish rise to the bait, birds flock in the trees of evening, and the water reflects the blue of the sky. You would teach him to fish and hunt.'

Wilem turned to Mae, who nodded.

Leoric wiped his eyes. 'Can we go there?'

Alen shook himself free from Dern and clutched at Wilem. 'This is my home. How will I know this new land?'

Before Wilem could answer, I stepped forward and enclosed Alen's shaking hands in mine. 'Uncle, Varryn's son will take your hand and lead you until you know your new home as well as Westaven. That is not all. In Althein, the place of sweet waters, there is one who will remove the film from your eyes. You will look upon Varryn's son and be glad.'

'Wh-who can do this?'

'Varryn's grandfather will restore your sight. His daughter will welcome you for her son's sake and for her grandson's sake. You will know laughter again.'

'Mistress Varia,' Wilem said, 'if you can promise this, we will come.'

'You have my word, Wilem.' I took his hand. 'Will you show me your daughter's resting place? I would say farewell to my sister by marriage and her child.'

Wilem led me to the far side of a rock stack, the stony beach there as uneven as the rest. He stopped in front of a low mound. 'Here lies Eneve, her babe with her.'

Mounds stretched back to the base of the cliffs. On the stone ledges above, dense patches of green and pink provided a startling contrast to the otherwise dark grey rock face. 'Did she die in childbirth?'

Wilem shook his head. For a moment he was silent. Then he lifted his head, and his eyes met mine. 'We were fishing, the men and the older boys. When we returned after three days, we expected the women to run to greet us and help unload the fish. As we secured the boats, Mae came, alone. She clasped my hand and Varryn's and told us what had happened.

'Not long after we left three men had come begging for shelter. Most of the women wanted to provide food and send them on their way, but Eneve disagreed. She said we must not turn away Tahurn survivors, and invited them to stay for one night. Early the next morning, food was taken to the guests, but they had gone. Eneve was not in her hut, nor anywhere they searched. The tide brought her in later. She had been raped, her arms and legs broken so she could not swim. They had thrown her into the sea to drown. Why? Why would they do such a thing?'

I wept. Willem waited for an answer which would bring him no comfort. At length I succeeded in controlling my grief. 'Their leader named himself Sarrech.'

Wilem stared at me. 'He did.'

I swallowed bile. 'He had a grudge against the world. Nothing could have saved Eneve.' Except Varryn's presence.

I knelt beside Wilem and said my silent prayers for my sister and her unborn second son. When I stood, Wilem turned to me. 'You have given us hope.'

I embraced him.

Back at the village, Mae prepared a meal, and one of Raneth's men produced flat bread and cheese. I sat by Wilem. We talked of Bry, Eneve and Varryn.

I accepted a plate of smoked fish, shellfish and cooked seaweed with thanks. Dern stared at the dark green mush and opened his mouth. I kicked his ankle. 'It's a delicacy of coastal communities, Dern. Tell me how you like it.' I held his gaze as he hesitated.

Dern cleared his plate. 'Thank you, Mae. I've never tasted anything like that before. I wish I hadn't eaten so much bread and cheese. I haven't enough room for seconds.' Mae blushed and smiled at him.

'That was delicious, Mae.' I had eaten many worse.

At Leoric's urging, Willem told a tale of the sea. When he had finished, he pointed to Leoric. 'Sing to us, lad.'

The boy sang in a clear high voice and asked everyone to join in the chorus. I already knew the words, and Dern soon picked them up.

The crash of waves on the rocks lulled me to sleep.

*　　*　　*

No one felt inclined to linger in the morning, and only Leoric looked back. Alen displayed agility at odds with his age and frail frame. Nevertheless, for his sake and Mae's, Raneth ordered a rest break at the clifftop.

Wilem's face lit up when he saw the horses, and Leoric ran towards them.

Tobe grabbed him. 'Don't startle them. Let them see you coming.'

One of the packhorses was unloaded, and the packs fastened onto the sorrel. Tobe lifted Leoric onto his piebald and swung up behind him. Mae clung behind one of Raneth's men and Alen behind another.

Wilem mounted the packhorse as if he had known horses all his life. When Dern questioned him, he beamed. 'I haven't ridden for years. They say you never forget.'

By midday on the third day after leaving the tower, with a rising wind behind, we crested the ridge. Mae and Alen looked longingly at the turf, but Wilem stood in the stirrups gazing out to sea. 'A storm is coming, a bad one.'

'Feels unnatural, it does,' mumbled Alen.

I conferred with Raneth, who nodded. 'There's no shelter here. We can make the tower by nightfall. Let's go!'

We reached the tower soon after dark. I shared the middle floor with Dern, while Wilem and his people occupied the ground floor with Raneth and his men. The storm rumbled in the distance, but the wind was favourable. Nothing disturbed my sleep.

* * *

Under Raneth's sharp eye and sharper tongue, equipment and supplies were packed and horses tacked up before dawn, but I delayed our departure. Wilem wished to visit the graves, and his friends went with him. When they returned, Tobe lifted Leoric onto his piebald.

The boy looked down at Dern. 'How long have you been sleeping with the lady? What happened to the other man?'

Dern stared at Leoric, but Raneth snatched the boy down, cuffed his ear and swung back for another blow.

'Hold!' I cried.

Raneth pulled his blow and released Leoric. The boy turned to look at me, a bewildered expression on his face. Wilem dismounted neatly and pushed past Dern, begging an apology for Leoric, but my gesture stopped him.

'What do you mean, Leoric? What other man?'

'I don't know his name. He has bright hair and a bright sword.'

A reader! I had not expected it. 'His name is Garanth. He slept at my door. Now Dern does the same.' I laid my hand on his shoulder. 'When you come to Althein, tell Master Ydrin that Varia sent you to him.'

'Why, Mistress?'

'Do as I ask.' My eyes followed him as he scrambled back on the piebald.

* * *

Four long days of riding bought us down from the hills to the northern plains. A day later I ordered Raneth to escort Wilem and his companions to Althein. 'I shall ride for Tormene with Dern.'

Raneth scowled. 'My task is to protect you, milady.'

'Your task, Sergeant Raneth, is to ensure these four reach Althein safely. It is Dern's responsibility to protect me. I have every confidence in him.'

Raneth muttered something inaudible.

'Well?' I glared at him.

'Very well, milady. You'll want your share of supplies.'

'We will manage with what we have.'

Raneth glanced at Tobe. 'Will you take the sorrel then, milady? He might make good eating.'

I nodded to Dern. He suppressed a sigh and attached the sorrel's lead rope to his saddle.

I took affectionate leave of Wilem and his people. 'My blessing for your journey. May God be with you.'

CHAPTER 16

Chane

When I opened my eyes, blood filled them. I cried out.
'Lie still. Head injuries often seem to bleed heavily. It may not be serious. Let me see.'
When I closed my eyes, my eyelids showed red. I lifted a hand to wipe away tears of blood.
'*Still*, I said.' A gentle touch lifted the pain from my forehead and eyes. 'You may look now.'
Ydrin's face wavered and came into focus. 'I can see,' I whispered.
'Good. Make a fist. Move your feet. Count from ten backwards.'
I obeyed.
'You have been fortunate. Rest.'

I dozed. When I stirred, I lay in a bed. 'Sleep will restore you,' Ydrin said. 'Someone will watch over you. If you have needs, ask. Your sword is safe. I shall return it tomorrow.'
'Why–' But Ydrin had gone.
A woman seated beside the bed said, 'Sleep.' She touched my head, and I slept.

* * *

A frown disturbed Ydrin's face. 'Your carelessness and inattention could kill others, as well as yourself. Is that what you want?'
I shook my head.
'What are the aspects of the test for power?'
I didn't hesitate, the damn things were unforgettable. 'Hold a one-stone weapon, shield yourself, make the object of your imagination real.'
'Don't *ever* forget to shield yourself! Make your shield as strong as you can, even if you only draw on a small amount of power.' He handed me the sword. 'Show me.'
I set a shield in place.
'Stop. Describe your shield.'
'I can't see it.'
Ydrin sighed. 'Open your eyes.'
'Eyes open or closed, I can't see the shield I believe I created, or feel it.'
'*I* can't see his shield,' Burll said.
I whirled round and returned his glare.
'Can *you*, Master Ydrin?' Maris asked.
'No, but as Nyth said, that's common with new students' Ydrin looked as if he might be sick.
'He is a freak. If–'
'Let me finish, Burll! I have discussed this with Nyth. We agree that you and Maris should persevere with Chane's training, until it is clear what Chane can or cannot do. Until then, Nyth or I will be present at every session, in case of unexpected problems or questions.'

Burll inclined his head. 'As you say, Master.' He glanced at Maris then turn to me. 'Are you tired of building walls, Chane?'

'Yes.' Tired of pointless exercises. No wall would stop a karyth.

'Let's move on. Raithen don't use walls in battle, but we do throw fire.'

'Start with a small blaze, away from the trees,' Maris said. 'You need to set boundaries, otherwise the flames will spread. And you must be ready to quench the flames quickly if sparks make the fire grow beyond your limits.'

'A raithan must always control his own creation,' Burll said. 'For his own safety and that of other raithen or any onlookers. Are you ready?'

'I am.' I reinforced my shield, at least I hoped I did. Until I could be sure it existed and knew how strong it was, I had no surety. Maybe that would come in time. I pictured a small campfire, on a rough stone hearth, with enough wood to last for cooking, opened my eyes and watched the flames leap up. For the first time I felt I had achieved something useful. Ydrin nodded.

'That will do,' Burll said. 'Let the fire die.'

It did.

'I've watched many students,' Maris said. 'None have made fire at the first try. This is going to be interesting.'

After several repeats of the fire, larger, smaller, nearer the trees, all successful, Maris produced three practice swords. She gave one to me and another to Burll. 'Shall we have some swordplay?' She lunged at me with the her practice sword before I answered.

I dodged her opening strike, propped up my invisible and unfelt shield, parried her next thrust and aimed for her throat. She dropped her sword and laughed. 'You have no qualms about fighting a woman then, Chane?'

'I've done it before.'

'Who won?' Burll asked.

'No one. We stopped before we did serious damage to each other.'

Burll stared at me. 'You weren't using sharpened swords? That's crazy. Ready?' He barely waited for my nod before he struck hard and fast.

We were evenly matched, my height and reach against Burll's solid strength.

At length, bruised and panting, I fell back. 'Well fought. Was that a draw?'

'This time. In future I won't hold back.' Burll turned his back and walked away, leaving me the practice sword.

At least he was honest about his intentions.

* * *

Ydrin dismissed Burll and Maris for the day and took me across a bridge to a cluster of small cabins.

The healer – ilan – looked up as Ydrin and I approached. 'Master.' She smiled, her eyes bright with curiosity. 'You must be Chane.' She clasped my hands briefly. 'My name's Lenathe, I'm pleased to meet you.'

'And I you, Lenathe.' I returned her frank appraisal. Plump and shapely, she was younger than I had first thought; strands of silver in her long brown hair had misled me. A crystal rod like Ydrin's hung from a loop on her wrist.

'How's your patient?' Ydrin asked.

'She's asleep. Would you watch over her for me, Master?'

'For a little while.'

Ydrin entered the cabin, and I walked with Lenathe into the woods. Sunlight glistened on long willow leaves. A small bird trailing a wing hopped through the long grass.

Lenathe raised her rod. The bird stopped, cocked its head to look at her and stood quivering. She knelt, closed her hands carefully around the bird's body and sat back on her heels. 'Watch closely.'

I dropped to the ground beside her. When she uncurled her fingers, the bird crouched on her palm, watching her. I drew my sword cautiously, not wanting to disturb it. With the naked

blade across my knees and my hand on the hilt, I closed my
eyes and concentrated.
Lenathe stroked her fingers lightly across the damaged wing.
Broken bones realigned and knitted together, feathers
interwove and straightened, pain fled, and the bird chirruped.
Lenathe lifted her hand and smiled. 'You may go now.'
The bird opened its wings, ruffled its feathers, hopped to the
ground, flapped its wings strongly and flew. A series of short
whistles floated down from the treetops.
'Did you see?'
I opened my eyes, swallowed and nodded.
'Excellent. Come and see more.'

* * *

The small figure lying on the bed was not a child, but it was
hard to judge her age. Except for her distended belly, she was
painfully thin, her bare limbs covered in scars and old bruises.
'This is Nona. It's the only name she knows. Her master used
it and laughed, saying it was short for "no name".'
I knew how that felt.
'He beat and starved her when she didn't please his friends,
and punished her again for falling pregnant. See how the babe
is lying. He gives his mother constant pain.'
I closed my eyes and focused. The baby was small and thin
like his mother, his body strangely twisted. Half-starved and
broken before birth. Damn whoever did this!
Lenathe met my gaze, and my anger died. 'If we had found her
sooner, we might have been able to heal her sufficiently for a
normal birth. It's too late for that.'
'Will you cut the baby from her?'
'I have no alternative. A midwife without power would cut
only as a last resort, with small hope of saving either mother or
babe. Nona would not survive the loss of blood, and the child
is already damaged.'
'Why do you–' I had intended my question for Ydrin, but he
had slipped away. I started again, my tone calmer. 'Why do

you force such as Nona to come to you instead of going to the towns and villages where you're needed?'

'I've done so. Those in greatest need came to me for healing, although they feared me and my kind. This is the result.' She pulled her robe aside to reveal a long scar under her arm. 'Well for me that I could heal myself.'

'You might have healed the wound to leave no scar.' I was sure of it.

'I was tempted to do that, but wiser friends bade me leave it as a reminder of the peril ilen face beyond Althein's borders. Whenever I feel I should go to those who need healing, this reminds me how much folk fear those who wield power, even when it's for their benefit. So I stay here and hope that those truly in need will come to me. Do you imagine it is an easy choice?'

'Forgive me, I spoke without thinking.'

'You are raithan, able to defend yourself. See that you do so, always.'

Her unexpected advice unsettled me more than my ability to see her healing. 'Why are you studying my hands, Lenathe?'

She laughed. 'I wondered whether you had always favoured your right hand. It was just a thought.'

A thought that lingered. Between Lenathe's teaching and exhaustion, I had no spare time try using my left hand instead. Over the next few days I followed Lenathe's clear instructions and learned: when and how to reduce my power to a feather touch, as thin as spider's silk and as strong; when and how to increase its strength to force broken bones together and weld them into an unbroken whole. If I was a healer that explained why I couldn't do Ydrin's tricks to his satisfaction.

Sometimes Lenathe used potion or poultice without power. At others she used power and herbal remedies. She rarely relied on power alone. I began to make my own decisions regarding effective treatment.

When I despaired of memorising the numerous ingredients, she laughed, 'Use your power to understand their effect.'

In time, I learned to do so, studying them with my eyes closed and feeling – that was the sensation – the uses of leaf, root, flower and distilled essence.

*   *   *

'What are you puzzling over, Chane?'
'Everything.'
Lenathe laughed. 'Oh dear. If you like explanations, Faril's the man you need. I'll ask him to come over when he's free.'
'Thank you.'
'Meanwhile, I'll answer your questions if I can.'
'Am I unusual in seeing with my eyes closed?'
She hesitated. 'Perhaps. Do you object to being thought unusual?'
'Doesn't everyone?' I tried to keep my tone light.
'Some new students find it easier to concentrate with their eyes closed, but I discourage it, for two reasons. One, it's a hard habit to break. Two, it's dangerous. Life is risky enough for ilen and raithen without making it harder. My advice, Chane, for what it's worth, is try to see with your eyes open. It does become easier with practice.' She smiled. 'You've been one of my most rewarding students, I'm sorry to have to send you back to Master Ydrin.'
I stared at Lenathe in dismay. 'Why?' Although she insisted I was raithan, healing came easier to me and felt more natural than the exercises Ydrin insisted on.
'Because healing alone will never suffice for you, and you cannot make it do so.'
Before I could deny it she had turned away to attend to a young girl who stumbled in, her cheeks tear-stained. Whatever ailed the girl, Lenathe did not intend me to be concerned with it. I returned to my raithan lessons like a condemned prisoner seeing the gallows.

CHAPTER 17

Varia

Nyth's call woke me. I lay still, my eyes closed. *I hear you, Nyth.*

Chane has passed the test for power, has two stones and had his first accident. He is likely heading for five stones, or more. Ydrin has transferred his raithan training to Burll and Maris, Ydrin and I take turns to watch their efforts. Lenathe has been teaching Chane healing. My blessings.

Raithan and ilan! I opened my eyes .The glimmer of starlight showed only Dern, on watch. A sound from the horses drew his attention. He passed the cold campfire, stopped near the horses, turned back and circled our camp.

I felt the presence of aryth, rose and drew my sword.

Dern stretched, set off on another circuit and stopped when he noticed me. 'What–'

I spoke softly. 'Watch the skies.'

He drew his sword and looked up. A horse snorted. Something glided in the darkness above us. Dern turned to follow its path, but the karyth – I recognised its flight pattern – closed its wings and dropped like a falcon on a pigeon. Dern stood firm, his sword pointed at the karyth. At the last moment he stepped aside and struck empty air as the karyth spread its wings, slowed, missed him by a yard and veered away.

Dern searched the sky. The karyth gained height and swooped back.

'Duck!'

Dern flung himself sideways and sprawled on the hard ground.

The karyth swept past and barely missed him.

Dern leaped up. 'Look out!'

I judged the distance and angle and released a blast of power.

The dead karyth fell out of the sky, bounced and landed almost at Dern's feet. He leaped back, his eyes wide. 'How did you–'

'Do not ask.'

Dern tried to still his trembling sword hand.

'Stand clear. I'm going to burn the carcase.'

He retreated, his gaze fixed on the corpse. When it burst into flame he jumped. I have long been inured to the stench, but he covered his mouth and nose with his sleeve and retreated.

'You did well, Dern. Get some sleep. I shall keep watch, but I don't expect further visitors.'

* * *

Dern rationed our provisions. I foraged around each camp to supplement our meagre meals. He kept me in view. 'How are supplies?'

He did not need to check the saddlebags. 'A small morsel of dried meat and some horse biscuits. I don't recommend the horse biscuits, Kadron.'

I raised an eyebrow. 'They are not ours to eat.' Dern had probably meant it as a joke, but I was in no mood to laugh. Although I did not regret the time this journey had already taken, I must not lengthen it further. The emperor awaited my report. Then I must make the long overdue ride to assess the situation at the border.

However, our track soon joined a rutted road, and my spirits lifted. Worn milestones indicated eight miles to Creikham. Even allowing for local optimism, that likely meant less than ten. 'We can purchase adequate supplies at Creikham.'

Dern's expression did not change. Although he would hardly faint from hunger before we reached Creikham, he might be trying to calculate whether I had already squandered the means to pay for our needs. I resisted the temptation to check.

Just short of the fifth milestone my horse stumbled. I swung down, tossed the dapple's reins to Dern and examined the hoof. 'The shoe is loose.'

'I could probably fix it here, but it will take a while.'

'If we follow that farm track, you can do the task properly while I attend to the matter of our supplies. We'll ride double. I trust the sorrel no more than you do.' I tied the dapple's reins to the sorrel's saddle and swung up behind Dern. He tried to avoid touching me, an impossibility.

'Keep your wits about you, Dern. I have little acquaintance with this area.' Not every countryman welcomed strangers, but I would soften my demands with coin as necessary.

'Understood, Kadron.' I had given him something to think about other than the nearness of my body.

We passed a sign branded with the outline of a tree, rounded a bend and climbed a small hill. From the top, farm roofs were visible, surrounded by fields and woods. Dern urged the mare on.

A shriek brought us to a halt.

Dern drew his sword. 'That sounded human. Should we flee?'

'No. Stay mounted.' I dropped to the ground, cut the sorrel loose and whacked his rump with the flat of my blade. As he raced towards the farm, I tethered the dapple to the nearest tree.

Shouts and squeals confirmed the sorrel's progress. 'They don't like him either. Sounds like we're outnumbered.' Dern had barely spoken when a horse dashed towards us, dragging his rider, his foot caught in the stirrup.

I seized the loose reins and freed the rider. 'Whoa, boy.' Thudding hooves warned me of pursuit. I patted the new horse to send him towards the dapple, who nickered. then other riders were upon us. The mare reared, Dern kept his seat and the mare's hooves came down on the leading rider. His horse shied, and I leapt from its path.

A burly man shouted, 'Kill them!' He rode at me.

I shifted to behind him. My strike cut cleanly through his thick neck.

Dern had dismounted. 'They're all dead.' He bent over the fallen rider. 'They trampled him, not caring whether he was still alive. And meant to kill us, though they knew nothing of us.'

'Welcome to my world, Dern. Let us see what damage they left at the farm.'

We gathered the horses and led them through the open gate into the farm yard. One of the farmhands sprawled against the wall, a pool of vomit at his feet. Another lay in his own blood. The farmer, sickle in hand, stared at us. A third farmhand shouted, 'They've come back!'

'We are strangers, caught in some argument that should not concern us. But we are not used to being attacked without reason. We defended ourselves. Who were they?'

Dern tied the horses to the fence.

'Lord Merken's tax collectors. He will hang us all.' The farmer approached me, his skin grey under the weathering.

I gestured at the sick farmhand. 'Is he hurt?'

The farmer shook his head. 'Nay. He has a weak-stomach. Can't say I blame him today.' He dashed away a tear. 'They killed the lad because I couldn't pay the full money they demanded. Said they'd be back in a couple of hours and would kill another if I didn't pay the rest.' His eyes met mine. 'How is that just?'

'It is not. We will help you avoid Lord Merken's retribution.'

In the leader's money belt Dern found seventy crowns, mostly in loose coins, a stained leather-bound notebook and a pencil stub. The other men's pockets contained only coppers.

I opened the notebook and read the last entry. 'You are Larent of Ash Farm?'

'Aye.' He set his jaw, his eyes darting from me to the blood drenched body of "the lad".

'How much did they demand from you, Larent? Ten crowns?' There were five entries for the day, each showing that amount, which did not tally with the crowns in the money belt.

Larent grimaced. 'Fifteen.'

I wrote ten in the notebook and replaced notebook and pencil in the leader's pocket. 'Get these fellows on their mounts. Dern, take Larent's men and deal with it. Quietly. Leave the horses near Creikham where the road runs close to the cliff edge. Throw the men into the river. It's far enough from here.'

Larent stared at me. 'You know these parts?'

I shook my head. 'I read maps and listen to travellers.'

Dern wiped his sword on a saddle cloth and washed his hands and face at the pump. By the time he had remounted, the dead men were tied face down on their saddles. Larent's men, mounted on ponies, held the leading ropes. Dern nodded to them and urged his mare through the gateway.

The sooner we left Ash Farm the safer Larent, his family and farmhands would be. 'I will help you bury the lad.'

It did not take long. Larent wiped his face with the back of his hand, and glanced round. Someone, likely his wife, had swilled and brushed the yard and the farm track. The money belt hung over the fence. I handed it to Larent. 'The dapple has a loose shoe. If we may borrow your tools, Dern will fix it when he returns.'

Larent stared at the belt. Then he grinned. 'I'll do the shoe. You can be off as soon as your friend returns. Take your horse to yon barn. I won't be long.'

While he worked, I persuaded him to talk about Merken and the difficulties high tax rates caused the locals. Then I offered him the sorrel. 'He's only good for the stewpot, I'm afraid.'

Larent looked up. 'That'll suit us fine. The stewpot's been empty for too long.' He patted the dapple. 'This'un will do for a bit.'

'You need to hide that belt somewhere Merken's men won't find it. If you are willing to trust your neighbours with your life, you can use the smaller coins to help them. Don't let your men speak of it.'

Larent stared at me. 'Who *are* you?'

'A friend. I will do what I can to have Merken replaced. Until then tread warily.

* * *

Dern entered the farmyard as I mounted. 'Where's the sorrel?'

'He's for the pot. I thought him a fair price for a new horseshoe.' Larent sent his men indoors and waved farewell.

I turned away from Creikham, keeping the dapple to a walk. After two miles, I urged him into a trot. A full half-hour passed before I handed Dern a honey cake. 'We'll save the rest for later.'

Hours passed before I drew rein at a small stream. 'We should rest for a bit.'

Dern watered the horses and refilled the water bottles while the horses grazed. 'What else did you buy, Kadron?'

'A small length of blood sausage. They had little to spare.'

'I'd rather go hungry than eat blood sausage right now.' In the failing light, I could not see his face.

'So would I. Like you, I've seen enough blood today. Tomorrow the sausage may be more acceptable.' I passed him several honey cakes and he gave me a small piece of dried meat.

'That's almost the last of the meat. Are we finishing the cakes now?'

'Why not? We've ridden on a tight belt for three days. I must forage for a day or two. If all goes well, we shall eat heartily in a few days.'

'And if it doesn't?'

'We may never need to eat again. If we do, there's the blood sausage.'

When Dern had finished coughing, he tried to copy my light tone. 'I'll look forward to it.'

I gathered the reins, remounted and he followed. An hour later, I turned off the road to follow a broken dyke and slowed the pace.

'Kadron, were the tax collectors working for Lord Merken or only for themselves?'

'Both. Merken set the tax at ten crowns each quarter. The standard rate is ten crowns a year. It's no wonder that Larent couldn't pay.'

Dern whistled. 'Damn them!'

'Exactly. Merken's men demanded a further five crowns a quarter for themselves. Their own record contradicted their lies.' I sighed. 'I suspect those men knew that this Lord Merken has no more entitlement to his claim of lordship than you have.'

'What!'

'Larent told me Merken came to power three years ago. I know the name of every man appointed to rule in the empire. Merken is not among them. While this so-called lord chose to beggar his victims, his underlings left them with nothing. Larent was forced to sell seed corn to pay only part of the sum demanded. He will have a reduced harvest this year and doubts his ability to feed his family and workers for the coming winter.'

'You will not leave Larent and his neighbours to starve, will you, Kadron?'

'Ah, you know me! I will not. Larent has hidden the money belt well. I have warned him to be cautious in using its contents. As soon as I can, I shall have this usurper lord replaced and brought to justice, and the excess taxes repaid with compensation. Until the local farmers can recover the lost harvests, I shall ensure that grain is sent to them. However, none of that will happen until I have the ear of the emperor, and that is yet some days away. Let us ride!'

CHAPTER 18

Varia

I did not call a halt again until the moon had set. Dern dismounted, loosened the girth and let the mare graze. He stretched and said, 'Kadron, will you not rest?'

'For a little while.' I spread my bedroll and slept until Dern woke me.

Breakfast was a drink of water. We rode in silence for hours.

'Are there no troops nearby that you could use to remove Merken, Kadron?'

I shook my head; a lock of hair fell from my cap and I tucked it back. 'There are no imperial troops closer than the

Ridges. The nearest troops are Lord Ossner's. I do not intend to ask for his support in this.'

'Why not?'

I smiled ruefully. 'Ossner considers his own interests first and last. His oath to the emperor will hold only while it does not conflict with his profit and pleasure. Did I bid him oust Merken, I might well find myself with Ossner in his place and Merken's men added to his own. I can spare only a small force for this task. My captain does not need me to increase his challenge!'

* * *

By mid-afternoon, I would have given a great deal for a respite from the sun's heat and a flagon of cool spring water. Dern sagged in the saddle. 'Cheer up. Our destination is in sight.'

Dern straightened up and squinted along the dusty road towards the walled town. 'Is this where Lord Ossner rules?'

'Marrton, where Lord Ossner has ruled for more than two decades. I hope he will give us an acceptable welcome.'

Dern blinked at me. 'You don't trust him, do you!'

My confidence in his lordship varied with circumstances, but now was not the time to attempt an explanation. We were nearing the town gate and a farm cart was about to force us off the road. Dern guided the mare left, and I urged the dapple right, passing within spitting distance of one of the gate guards. He neither wished me good day nor brought me to a halt for questioning.

Once through the gate Dern glanced at me. 'Sloppy,' he muttered. 'Duke Reys would've had them on West Tower night watch for a month.'

I laughed. Even discounting the threat from aryth, which few considered real, threats tend to come from the north and east. In Duke Reys' place, I would also require counts of owls and bats.

As we rode along the main street, Dern commented on the number of closed shops. 'And those with open doors have few items for sale. It looks as though–' He broke off to stare at two men wearing smocks and woven-grass hats. His gaze followed them as they trudged past, head down, each carrying a laden basket on his back.

I reined in outside a large house that dominated the town square. Like most others we had passed, the door was closed and windows shuttered. When Dern's knock brought no response, I turned the dapple down a side street and along an alley, and gestured at the postern door. Before I asked, Dern jumped down to open the main gate.

No one came to challenge us. Dern left the gate open, took the reins and looped them loosely over a rail, in the shade within reach of a water trough.

'Wait here.' I left him fretting and opened the kitchen door.

'Who do you think you are, sneaking into my kitchen?'

'An old friend, Colia. Do you still bake the best cakes south of Tormene?'

Her mouth fell open. 'Lady Varia? Well, I never!' She bobbed a curtsey 'Milord's out hunting. I'll tell master Berist you're here.'

'There's no need, Colina. I'll wait for Lord Ossner outside. You're busy, but could you provide food and drink for two, to keep us going until tonight's feast?'

She beamed. 'That'd be my pleasure, milady. 'We'll do better for you later.' She called to the spit boy and soon had a tray loaded.

Dern took it from me and set it on the mounting block. There was plenty to share: a large jug of cool ale, broth, cheese and bread fresh from the oven.

He wiped his lips with the back of his hand. 'This will do for an hour or so.'

'It will have to. The kitchens are busy preparing dinner for when Lord Ossner returns from his hunt.'

'Will he welcome you as his guest?'

'He dare not offend me. In that he is wiser than Sarrech was.'

* * *

The drum of horses hooves brought me to my feet. 'Come.' I untied the dapple and mounted, sweeping off my cap and shaking my hair loose. Dern swung into the saddle and followed. Turning into the square, we met a group of horsemen. In their midst sat my target, a bulky man dressed in fur-trimmed brown velvet despite the heat. His face glowed red between his grey beard and his velvet cap.

I rode forward. 'Lord Ossner! Greetings.'

A flicker of disquiet crossed his face. He forced a smile and bowed from the saddle. 'My Lady, you are most welcome. May I offer you my poor hospitality?'

'I should be delighted to accept, my Lord.'

As Ossner's gaze reached Dern, his smile faded. He ushered me into a long, dim and stuffy reception room and sat opposite me. Dern stood behind my chair. Ossner offered wine and biscuits. I accepted, responded to his attempts at conversation, and deferred the subject of aryth until I had emptied my goblet.

That matter discussed, Ossner rose and led me to a suite of rooms on an upper floor. He glanced at Dern. 'Your man can be accommodated in the servant's wing.'

'Dern stays with me.'

Ossner gave a short bow. 'As you wish, my Lady. Ask what you will. If it is in my power, I will meet your requirements.' He waved a hand at the manservant standing in the doorway. 'Berist will serve you.'

I inspected the spacious rooms. 'Open the windows, Berist. Bring hot water for bathing, more towels, drinking water, wine and fruit.'

Berist bowed and closed the door behind him. I sank into one of the ancient leather chairs and leaned back. 'You have stood for long enough, Dern, sit down.'

'Are we to trust Lord Ossner then, Kadron?'

'Did you notice his reluctance? It serves his interests to welcome me, and the emperor through me, but I trust him no further than that. I shall need you to taste my food and drink while we are here.'

Dern frowned. 'Would he harm a guest in his own house?'

'I believe him fully capable of that, did it suit his purpose. At present I doubt it does, partly because he will expect me to be wary. Do not fear, I have survived greater threats than any Ossner may pose.'

'That's great consolation, Kadron.' His face contradicted his words. I laughed.

Berist headed a parade of servants loaded with my requirements. Their purpose achieved, I dismissed them. 'Bolt the door, Dern.' I drew a bag of herbs from my pocket, measured doses into two cups, added water and stirred, handing one to him and taking the other for myself. 'Drink.'

He pulled a face. 'What is it?'

'A mixture that will provide protection against most common poisons.'

Dern finished the bitter drink and set the cup down with a steady hand. 'I trust Lord Ossner is not familiar with uncommon poisons.'

'I doubt he would take such trouble when the most commonly available are invariably effective. However, it would be wise to avoid heavily spiced or sauce-smothered dishes.' I emptied my cup, broke the seal on the wine flask and poured wine for both of us before selecting and peeling a piece of fruit.

'Shouldn't I taste that, Kadron?'

'Ossner has scarcely had time to meddle. We are most at risk at dinner. I trust the cook, but she cannot watch all the kitchen staff and servers.' I wiped my hands on a yellowed linen napkin and took my pack into the bedchamber, leaving the door ajar.

Although I travelled light, I had packed a shift and a dark green silk dress. Bathed and dressed, I donned my mail coat, buckled my sword belt at my waist, turned my ring to conceal the imperial insignia, tugged my boots on, brushed my hair to fall in a loose twist on my shoulder and opened the door fully. 'You may take your turn now.'

Dern's jaw dropped, and his eyes widened.

I raised an eyebrow. 'Ossner will expect me to dress as a woman. I prefer to remind him that I am not an easy target.'

Dern took a deep breath. 'You will frighten him half to death.' He closed the bedroom door behind him.

I reopened it before he had unfastened his shirt.

'Kadron!'

'Ossner is the kind of man to have secret doors in the walls. I will not provide him with an easy target. Nor will I permit you to do so.'

Dern gauged the distance from the panelled walls to the bathtub and nodded. He drew his sword and placed it on a stool within easy reach of the tub.

When he returned to the sitting room I looked him up and down. His efforts to improve his appearance were adequate. 'Leave your laundry by the door; a maid will see to it.'

In the crowded and noisy dining hall, Lord Ossner, wearing blue velvet, bustled forward. A hint of sweat and camphor accompanied him. He greeted me by name and lead me to the high table, where he introduced me to a handful of guests, who stared, but clearly had no idea who I was. Dern kept as close to me as possible, while attempting to remain unnoticed. Lord Ossner honoured me by offering the seat at his right hand. I pointed Dern to the empty seat on my right.

Dern accepted every dish and cup I gave him to taste, swilled each mouthful of wine round his mouth before swallowing, and chewed every morsel of food slowly and carefully before nodding to me. I followed my own advice, choosing from plain roast joints and fowl, cheese and bread, rather than dishes of unidentifiable meat floating in strange-coloured sauces. When one of the serving men offered Dern a platter directly, he shook his head. The server turned to me, I considered the platter and declined with a smile.

Dinner ended at last, the boards were cleared and musicians and dancers replaced the serving men. I glanced at Dern and rose to retire.

Lord Ossner stood to bow to me. I returned a small curtsey. 'Goodnight to you, my Lord.'

Dern followed me upstairs. He checked both room and inspecting the bed. 'A lumpy horse hair mattress. It will be full of fleas and bugs.'

'Undoubtedly.'

'You would sleep better in a chair, Kadron.'

'Or the floor.' I took the heavy quilt and pillows from the bed and arranged them on the rug in the centre of the room.

'Kadron?'

'We take turns to keep watch as usual.' I overrode his protest. 'I need you alert tomorrow. Wake me at once if you feel unwell.'

CHAPTER 19

Chane

Nyth greeted me with a smile. 'Lenathe tells me you have taken to healing.'

'I should like to learn more.'

'Good. I'm sure that can be arranged. Ydrin tells me you still cannot cast a shield.'

'I don't know whether I can or not. I can't see or feel any shield I try to cast.'

'Hum. Which hand do you use?'

'My right hand.'

'Ilen use either. Most raithen favour one hand for the sword, so that's the one they use for power. Try casting your shield with your left hand.'

I awkwardly drew my sword left-handed, cast a strong shield and stared. I could see and feel it, though my eyes were open! That wasn't all. I could feel a tingling in my fingers, and see a glow in both the stones. I laughed.

So did Nyth. 'You found it difficult to see power at work when you held your sword with your right hand.'

'Unless I closed my eyes.'

'Ydrin believes you found power as a boy. Being untrained, you came close to destroying yourself. But all you lost was your memory. He may be right. I assume your early ability was instinctive, and the tendency to use your left hand deep-rooted. Your swordmaster told you to fight right-handed, and trained the left-handedness out of you. Using your right hand for swordplay became a habit, difficult to break. When you were reintroduced to power, your deeper instinct, buried and long-forgotten, awoke and replaced the learned right-handedness.'

'What now, Nyth?'

'Instinct is harder to fight than habit. You must learn to wield your sword left-handed. Burll might help you with that.'

'I grew out of fighting with a blunted sword some time ago, Nyth.'

'Ah! Burll was always inclined towards caution. I will speak to Garanth.'

'He is watching over Ryny. I don't expect him to desert his charge.'

Nyth smiled. 'He is not an oathbreaker. I will ask him to leave Ryny for a short time, now and again. It will do you both good. Ryny will be safe with his father's mother. She is always well guarded.'

'His father's mother? I didn't know she was here.'

'Not many do.'

'I'm grateful for your help, Nyth.'

'Chane, I will do everything possible to assist you in learning to control your power. As will others. Don't refuse our help.'

I met her steady gaze. 'I won't.'

* * *

I rehung my sword on my right side. At first, I fumbled the draw, but as when I learned to use a sword right-handed, a smooth draw came with practice. If Maris and Burll noticed the change, neither remarked on it at first.

'Chane!' Maris said. 'I can see your shield. It's strong!'

Burll turned to stare at me. 'That's better. Let's see whether it says that way.'

'It's time we taught Chane the fire game,' Maris said.

'Long past,' Nyth said. 'Chane, instead of throwing or kicking a ball, we use power to send fire to each other. You will need to keep the fire intact when passing it on. If you can't, quench the flames. I will start. Ready?'

A flaming ball soared though the air. Before it reached Burll, it swerved, heading for me. I stopped it and aimed it at Maris. She sent it spinning. 'Chase it, Chane.'

I summoned the ball, entwined the burning twigs and tossed it to Burll. He returned it to Nyth.

'Faster,' she said. She was now some distance from the three of us, though I hadn't seen her move.

The ball sped towards Maris, who slung it at me.

It was in no state to pass on. I extinguished the flames, quenched the smouldering grass, created a new fireball and flung it at Burll. He threw it towards Maris.

Its speed increased as it neared her. She stepped aside and sent it spiralling back to Burll. He dodged. The fire vanished, then took fresh hold in a tree.

'Fire in the tree,' Maris cried. Even as she spoke, the flames died.

'That was too close, Maris and Burll,' Nyth said. 'You should know better. Chane, can you heal the damage?'

Short of climbing the tree, I couldn't see the fire damage. I walked closer. If I imagined the branches and leaves whole and healthy, would they recover in a snap of my fingers? I willed it.

Nyth looked up at me. 'You did well in the game. We will have to wait and see how the tree fares.' She smiled. 'I am confident.'

'Bah!' Burll turned and left us.

'My mistake,' Maris said. 'I misjudged the distance.'

'And I the players,' Nyth said. 'Let us be more cautious next time.'

CHAPTER 20

Varia

Ossner offered us a change of horses: a glossy black and a sturdy piebald.

'I am grateful for your hospitality and supplies, Lord Ossner, but I am reluctant to part with the dapple, and I'm sure Dern feels the same about the grey.' I handed him coins to cover his hospitality.

He pocketed them with a smile. 'I wish you a safe journey, my Lady.'

Once outside the walls, Dern turned to me. 'Was that a test, Kadron?'

'Did I not say that Ossner serves his own interests? He would wish to profit from our stay and has, but not so much as he might have done had he declined my coin. If I had not paid him I should have incurred his anger, which I can do without.'

'You said you don't trust him, but he made no move against us. Unless his supplies include a parting gift.'

I shook my head. 'I doubt that. He decided the risks outweighed any reward. What did you think of him?'

Dern paused for thought. 'He wore fancy clothes and drank from silver cups, but the servants we saw were slovenly and the guest rooms shabby and ill cleaned. He did you a favour in not giving you your full title, Kadron. If he had, there would have been a line of hopeful beggars on the road.'

'There would, but he did not omit my title to spare me. He prefers beggars to make their supplication to him, it being his responsibility to care for his people.'

'He doesn't care for them, does he? The townsfolk we saw didn't look very prosperous. Neither did most of Lord's Ossner's guests.' He patted the grey's neck. 'So why would he offer us quality steeds?' He struck his forehead with the heel of his hand. 'Because they're easy to spot.'

'Exactly. Our road passes through the Ridges, which is bandit country. Ossner would have done us an ill turn with his showy horses, whether deliberate or no.'

'He still might. The dapple's colouring is striking.'

The dapple's dark head and forequarters contrasted with his pale grey back and hindquarters and his almost white tail. The mare though, dust already clouding her coat, would not stand out like Ossner's rejected piebald. 'That can be mended.'

* * *

Around noon, I called a halt among tall trees, where the road bridged a shallow stream. I rummaged in my pack and handed a small pot to Dern. 'Try lightening the dapple until he matches the grey.' I walked downstream until I found what I sought. Having ensured that Dern was out of sight, I sat on the grass, removed my boots, rolled up my breeches and stepped into the water. My dagger had not been made to cut reeds and flowers, but it served for that purpose. Once gathered, I sorted them, unrolled my breeches, tugged my boots on and began weaving.

I had eaten a bite of lunch, pulled my shift over my other gear, hung a garland round my neck, donned a hat and was finishing the last hat when Dern appeared. He stopped and stared at me.

I tucked away a trailing end and tossed him the hat. 'You have good timing. This was the last.'

Dern turned it over. 'Neat work, Kadron.'

'It's one of the few uses I've found for my stitching and weaving lessons. Do you remember seeing a couple of farm hands wearing smocks in Marrton?'

He grinned. 'I'll find my spare shirt and wear it loose.'

I draped a garland round his neck, wreathed the horses and plaited the dangling stems into their manes. Finally, having cut slits for the horses' ears, I placed the two remaining hats on their heads and knotted the loose reeds to the bridle. The dapple shifted uneasily, and I soothed him.

'The horses look ridiculous, and so do I.' Dern's hat shaded one eye and his unconfined shirt had caught on his sword belt.

'These hats are common wear locally.'

Dern adjusted his hat. 'Why the flowers, Kadron?'

'It's a wedding custom.'

Dern snapped his mouth shut and helped me stuff grass and leaves into the saddlebags and packs until they bulged.

I straightened my hat and mounted. 'Keep to a walk and slump in the saddle. Act as if you're a country bumpkin on a borrowed horse.'

*   *   *

Dern held his grey alongside the dapple as the road climbed into the foothills and passed into the shade of the pines.

'The road soon narrows to a track and winds steeply. We must go single file, but follow me closely. After we cross the stream, the track hugs the cliffs to avoid a sheer drop. Take care. The track is often treacherous.'

'For a stretch, we'll be out of sight of anyone above us. Lose your hat when I drop mine and tuck your shirt out of the way. When the track turns back on itself, we'll be in the open. Ride fast, stay low. If needed, use your sword freely. Stop for nothing. Where the track divides we keep right and take the wide track downhill.'

'Understood, Kadron.'

I urged the dapple on, and Dern followed. The rush of the stream in its stony bed covered the clatter of hooves.

As we climbed, the drop on the right increased. The main stream thundered from the cliff above, missed us and crashed onto the rocks below. However, the overflow splashed down the cliff face, pooled in hollows and dripped onto the slippery track.

I dropped my hat and stuffed my shift into my belt. As we neared the corner, I drew my sword, dug my heels into the dapple's flanks and flattened myself against his neck.

The dapple charged into a band of men on hill ponies, halloing and whistling, intent on blocking my path. I shielded myself and Dern. He had ignored my orders and now rode at my left-hand. When a man tried to snatch my reins, I severed his hand. Ignoring his shriek, I swung my blade sideways, and the next rider folded in the saddle with a groan.

'Watch out! They're armed!' shouted one of the band.

Another aimed a coward's blow at the dapple's foreleg. I blocked it. The pony reared, its rider yelled and both were down, trampled by plunging hooves.

I could not see Dern, but heard his curses.

A horn sounded, bringing with it a detachment of Imperial soldiers. Shouts and clashes of weapons increased. Pressed by sheer numbers and fighting to create enough space to escape, the remaining bandits lost all interest in me. The dapple shouldered a riderless pony aside, leaving me facing an Imperial Sergeant. He curbed his lunge. 'Commander!'

'Well met, Sergeant. Don't let your men kill my bodyguard. Dern rides a grey mare.'

He stood in his stirrups.'Dern! Identify yourself to the nearest trooper.' He eased into the saddle. 'I'd prefer you away from this skirmish, Commander.' He pointed downhill and cleared a gap for me.

I urged the dapple forward. As the trail twisted right, I rode into the shade of a group of large boulders, reined in and turned. Two men cantered towards us, one on a grey horse. I dropped the shields.

'You have earned my thanks, Sergeant . I shall remember this.'

'From what I saw, Commander, you and your bodyguard were successfully defending yourselves before we arrived. If you'll excuse me, this won't take long.'

'I trust that's not your blood, Dern.'

'Not mine, Kadron. And I hope that blood's not yours. Looks like the Sergeant was right, we must have accounted for at least half of them.' He frowned. 'They're bringing three ponies.'

An hour or so later, the Sergeant called a halt at a grassy knoll where a spring formed a small pool. He directed sentries to their posts, ordered one trooper to ride on to the camp, two more to check on the wounded and the rest to water the horses.

I washed the blood from my blade and hands. 'It doesn't look as if anyone is seriously injured.'

Dern had changed into his spare shirt and attempted to wash the blood from the other. I handed him my soap. 'Rub this over the blood and scrub the shirt under water. Wash your hands well, when you're done.'

He had barely finished when the Sergeant gave the order to ride. The downward trail zigzagged through gullies, across streams and in and out of trees. It was late afternoon when the lead soldier turned off, answered challenges from hidden sentries and led the way into a well-organised camp. A one-bar Captain was waiting.

I dismounted. 'I expected you to have returned to Tormene some time ago, Captain Barys.'

He accorded me the Imperial salute. 'Lord Ludran forgot to send us a relief troop six weeks ago, Commander.'

Damn Ludran! Did he imagine I had appointed him Commander in my absence? 'I shall cure his memory. How did you fare with the bandits, Captain?'

'Not as I expected, Commander. We set out to clear their camp. Another gang got there before us. They tortured and mutilated their rivals before leaving them to die.'

'Bloody hell!' Dern muttered

'Dern, meet Captain Barys.' They exchanged nods. 'How many dead?'

'We found eight mutilated bodies, and three headless bodies with fatal wounds, but otherwise intact.'

'They took the heads of their own men?' Dern said.

'It sounds like it,' I said. 'Unless they took captives. Are you short of men, Captain?'

'Some are hunting and fishing nearby. They'll join us before sunset.'

I invited Barys to share our supplies. He readily accepted that and my offer to help with the wounded. I stitched a trooper's wound, and splinted a broken wrist. My first patient bore my administrations in silence. The second objected to the sling.

'The sling is to prevent further damage. Do you want to risk losing that hand, trooper?'

He gulped. No, Ma'am. Beg your pardon, Ma'am'

In my absence Dern had watered and brushed the horses and himself and cleared the padding from the saddlebags. I unpacked Ossner's provisions. 'Have we any blood sausage left, Dern?'

His face was in shadow. 'I believe so, Kadron.' He opened a saddlebag, pulled out the package and added it to the rest.

Barys called a trooper. 'I appreciate this, Commander.'

'It's my pleasure, Captain.'

Dern succeeding in containing his laughter until they were out of earshot.

'He looked as you did when offered honey cakes. Come. I'm hungry, if you're not.'

The cooks dished out the food, ensuring that each man had a fair share of meat. I took a portion of trout, avoided Dern's eyes, and kept my face straight as I declined a portion of blood sausage.

'I hope some of the loot is edible,' Dern muttered.

'What, tired of roast goose, already? Shall I find you some rat brains?'

'Did you really eat that, Kadron?'

'Hunger has a way of lowering a man's standards.'

'And a woman's?'

I raised an eyebrow. 'Women are sometimes finicky about such things.'

Barys joined us. 'The gang's camp was reasonably well supplied. We now have adequate provision for three weeks, and a little wealth. I regret to report that this was among the coin and jewels.' An imperial token lay on the palm of his outstretched hand.

'Damn them!' The life of an imperial messenger should be sacred. 'Coin and jewels only? No trade goods?'

'None. I suspect the murderers took those. I should have suspected two gangs. We've been following pony tracks, but we've also seen lone men at a distance and found evidence of rope bridges, partly dismantled and tracks covered.'

I sighed. 'They must wait. You've done your duty here. I trust the road is clear for now. Ready your men for departure at dawn, Captain. We ride for Tormene and ride fast. If any of your men can't keep up, you must make other provision for them.'

'Understood, Commander. I'll see to it.'

When the camp settled down for the night, Dern chose his sleeping position, nearer to me than to anyone else but not markedly so. Any soldier attempting to approach me would have to pass him first. Nonetheless I slept lightly.

CHAPTER 21

Varia

Riding with a troop did not encourage private talk. Nor did I respond to Dern's half-hearted attempts to question me about Tormene. My thoughts kept returning to the fate of the imperial messenger, but I could have done nothing to prevent it. Ludran would answer for his actions, but not yet. Not while we rode mountain trails under a blazing sun, descending only to climb again, looping, zigzagging, occasionally backtracking to find a passable route. Dern mopped his brow, his glance on me. I might have cooled myself, but preferred to rely on the old saying that ladies do not sweat.

Barys rode up and down the column. Snatches of talk and laughter reached me. I was not minded to interfere. The troop was its captain's responsibility, and I trusted him to remember it.

He called a halt to water the horses barely a half-day's ride from our destination. I left the dapple to Dern and climbed the riverbank.

After seeing to the horses, Dern joined me 'What manner of man is the emperor, Kadron?'

'What manner of man do you suppose him to be, Dern?' My gaze was fixed on the road ahead, a dusty track that led straight through the forest.

'A jumped-up version of Duke Reys, except he won't know all his subjects as well as Reys does.' I swung round, and he paled. 'I mean–'

'Well put, Dern. That's precisely what the emperor is, although he would challenge your claim that he does not know his subjects well. He is well acquainted with the heart of his realm, the north and some border districts. Only the west coast and deep south are outside his personal experience.'

'I wouldn't call Hawdale border country.'

'No? It's less than fifty miles, as vultures fly, from Bridgetown to Mondun. Hawdale's prosperity depends on a safe border. Without the troops at Mondun, Hawdale would fare very differently.'

'Kadron, what manner of man is the emperor, leaving aside any likeness to Duke Reys?'

'There was a time when he would have been eager to meet you as one who had a hand in seeing his grandson brought to safety, but he has changed. Now he will not concern himself with you, and he will be the loser thereby.'

Barys called, and I raised a hand in acknowledgement. Back in the saddle, I watched the countryside I knew well; at times it seemed I spent half my life on the road.

In the middle of nowhere, the road changed: its dusty surface widened and paved with flat stones, with wide channels each side for spring and autumn rains. 'Cheer up, Dern.'

He grunted. If he had hoped for an early camp, he would be disappointed. In another ten miles we would reach Tormene.

* * *

Forest gave way to farmland, at first the road climbed gently, then steeply, one ridge at a time. As we crested the last height, Torr Menne, the heart of the empire and the mountain of the imperial symbol, welcomed me home. Across the fields, the city clung to the mountain face, its buildings barely visible in the shadow of the peak cast by the sinking sun.

Lost in thought, I paid little attention to the road until the troopers in front of me slowed. The city wall loomed ahead, the gateway wide enough for four horse carts to pass through when both gates were open. One was shut, and the troopers closed ranks to pass through. I noticed Dern's upward glance at the drop gate. 'The chains are secure.'

'I should hope so.'

The guards, three on each side of the gateway, saluted. Barys returned the salute. I glanced over my shoulder at the archers on the wall, then concentrated on the road ahead. The clatter of the troop's approach had shoppers hastening aside into doorways, side streets and alleys.

Dern chuckled. 'Just like Bridgetown, only bigger.'

After the Low Gate, the width of two carts, with four guards, we rode single file up the steep cobbled roadway that twisted across the Torr's slopes.

'Where is everyone, Kadron?'

'The Low Gate is always guarded, by custom it is open to anyone with business at the palace by day, and closed to those without imperial authority overnight. Look down to your right. You'll see the southern harbour.' The harbour below glittered with toy-sized fishing boats and several larger ships, some at anchor, others entering or leaving port. Those in the fiord were dwarfed by the towering cliffs on each side.

Dern gave a low whistle.'How do the boats avoid crashing into each other?'

'Only experienced captains may enter the harbour. They must follow channel markers and harbour rules. Accidents are few and penalties severe. The distance between boats is greater than it seems.'

The road passed through the High Gate, four guards, and into the tunnel. Dern looked up, but the murder-holes and arrow slits were hidden in darkness. We rode through the inner gateway, a twin of the outer gate, with its reinforced doors and hanging drop-gate, and entered the vast walled courtyard. Dern stared.

'Is it large enough for you, Dern?' I slid to the ground and handed my reins to one of Barys' troopers.

'Too big.' He followed me through a postern gate and short tunnel, across the inner courtyard and up a short flight of wide steps to a carved stone doorway and the open gilded door. The entrance guards saluted me. Porel, short and wide-shouldered in his rich robes came forward, smiled and bowed.

'You are welcome indeed, Lady Varia. The Lord Emperor awaits you in the lesser audience chamber.'

I took his hands. 'Thank you for your welcome, Porel. Will you take care of Dern?'

'Certainly. This way, Master Dern.'

I walked unescorted along the galleried hall and followed a side passage to the lesser audience chamber. A private meeting with my father would have taken place in his office, or mine, depending on his mood. His choice of meeting-place meant he wished one of his advisors to be present or he distrusted his temper. I must keep a hold on mine; we have quarrelled too frequently since Varryn's departure.

One of the sentries saluted, rapped on the door, threw it open and called, 'Lady Varia!'

Two men sat at the oval table before the blazing heath. Tertel stood and bowed, but I had eyes only for my father. He remained seated, a frown darkening his face. 'You come late, Varia.'

'My Lord.' I bowed. 'Tertel.'

The emperor tapped the documents before him. 'Reports have reached me of your actions. You have a great deal to explain.'

'Yes, my Lord.' I met his fierce gaze. He valued courage above submission.

'I will not have it said that the empire breaks its treaties at a whim. Why did you order fire to be set in the accursed wood?'

'The lady of the wood broke the treaty, my Lord. I merely did what I could to limit her evil.'

His eyes blazed. 'Do not seek to rely on an argument regarding the borders of her territory! Tertel informs me that, although the Cold River was intended to mark the southern boundary of the sorceress' realm, that did not form part of the treaty.'

'So I understand, my Lord. However, the treaty is clear on two points. Firstly, no one having entered the cursed wood willingly may be permitted to leave. Secondly, nothing from within the lady's realm may be released outside her borders. Is that not so, Tertel?' I glanced at him. 'The relevant references are Clause six, subparagraph three and Clause eight, subparagraph two.'

Tertel turned pages until his hovering finger lighted on one paragraph and a second. He looked up. 'That is correct, my Lady.'

'My Lord, Sarrech, late of Tahurn, entered the lady's realm of his own choice. Whatever his dealings with the lady, he bore away a gysun, which he carried to Bridgetown in Hawdale. There he used it to attempt murder.'

The emperor sprang to his feet. 'What became of the gysun?'

'I returned it to Sarrech, my Lord, along with my wishes for his future. After the gysun brought about his death, I destroyed it by blade and fire. Its remains, together with those of its late master, were sealed in a lead lined coffin and buried in accursed ground.' Since he had not asked, I added, 'Sarrech's intended victim survived.'

'So.' The emperor sank back in his chair. 'Why did Captain Heksun choose to obey your orders rather than mine?'

'He set the fires according to my longstanding orders, after the sorceress' underlings had been sighted outside the wood.'

'How foolish of her!'

'She was angry, my Lord.'

'Enraged at the death of her chosen prey. How did Kei die?'

I kept my voice steady with an effort. 'I poisoned him, my Lord.'

The emperor's expression changed. 'What had he done to deserve such a fate?'

'He came to my aid, willingly. As Tertel has confirmed, the treaty would have bound him there. I would not leave my athan in such hands.'

'Athan?' His voice was soft, but no less dangerous.

'I made him so, before I left him.'

'You take much upon yourself, Varia.'

'I have your example, my Lord.'

His mouth relaxed into a smile, and his eyes told the same story. 'Tertel, might it be argued that Lady Varia and her companions entered the lady's realm willingly?'

'My Lord, the paragraphs in Clause six refer specifically to the cursed wood, rather than the realm. As I understand her report, Lady Varia did not enter the wood willingly, but was forced therein by the sorceress' attendants.'

'That is so.'

'What would you have done, Varia, if the said attendants had not forced you into the wood?' His voice was stern, but the remnant of his smile remained.

'The situation did not arise.'

'Very well.' He nodded to Tertel. 'You may leave us.' He beckoned the footman standing at the door. 'Bring wine.'

When we were alone, he stood and drew a chair forward for me. 'They tell me you were wounded. Be seated.'

I took the chair he offered. 'Thank you, my Lord. I am fully recovered.'

'No doubt.' The emperor waved the hovering footman away and poured the wine himself. 'Thank you for your reports. Why did you use such unorthodox means?'

I resisted a temptation to smile. 'You trust your messengers, my Lord. I trust mine.'

He nodded, and opened the subject closest to his heart. 'What of Varryn, did he die in the accursed wood at the sorceress' hands?'

'No, my Lord. From Captain Frenn's report and that of Wilem, I believe Varryn, and his friend Bry, Willem's son, fell into a trap set by Sarrech at the Tower of the Winds and died there. Then Sarrech took Varryn's son and entered the wood.'

'And the rest we know.' He sat back in his chair and drank his wine.

'What news from the wood, my Lord?'

'Raithen report the sorceress dead, or escaped southward.'

I set my cup down. 'There is a world of difference between those two possibilities. I should like to see for myself.'

'I forbid it. You have other duties, and there is yet much evil there. Raithen are investigating.'

'As you will, my Lord.'

'You are weary. We shall continue this discussion tomorrow.'

'There is something else you must know, my Lord.'

The emperor raised an eyebrow. 'Continue.'

'Duke Reys lent me two of his guardsmen for my journey. When I was injured, one of them wielded my sword through me. I have never felt such power.'

His brows knitted. 'Is this possible, an untrained raithan to surprise you with his power?'

'Or an aryth in the guise of a man, my Lord.'

His hand, which rested idly on the stem of his wine cup, jerked and wine splashed onto the table. 'Do you fear that?'

'I hardly know what I fear. The late Duke Arnull of Hawdale found him twelve years ago. He claims to have no knowledge of his origins.'

'You do not believe his claims.' He put his hands together and rested his chin on his knuckles.

'I do not. He goes by an ill-omened nickname, yet the nature of that name does not concern him. I left him in Althein, having asked Ydrin to ensure his testing, to have him closely watched and to call me at need.'

'Then you have done all you could. Will you return to Althein to learn the result?'

I suppressed a sigh. 'I will, but first I must go to Hawdale to question Duke Reys about this man. Then I must proceed to Getheer. I have a long delayed duty there.' I stood. 'I shall keep you informed, my Lord.'

'Do that, and do not fear this ill-omened stranger. I think it unlikely that any untrained raithan could surpass you or an aryth disguise itself to fool you. Possibly, in your extremity, you yourself called up the necessary power. Go. Rest.'

My father did not appreciate being contradicted, and I would not do so. Time would tell which of us was right. 'Good night, my Lord.' I bowed.

'Good night, Varia.'

* * *

It would be strange indeed if I had misjudged Chane, but no one is infallible. My mother would say that to the emperor's face, but I am more cautious. I climbed the narrow staircase to the small chapel in the north tower, now rarely used. The emperor preferred the newer, brighter, larger sanctuary in the west wing. The chapel was dim, lit by a single oil lamp over the altar and several smaller lamps placed in prayer bowls. The scent of hot oil reminded me of family prayers.

I knelt at the rail and prayed for Varryn's soul, for Kei's, as I had every evening since his death, and for Varryn's son. The healers of Althein had told me that the horrors of his time in the sorceress realm would leave no mark on him. I hoped they were right, that the lady's spells had shielded Ryny from the worst of that experience. My prayer for Invar was, as ever, unspoken. I prayed for Lady Kirra as I often did. Last but not least I prayed that my fears regarding Chane's powers might prove groundless, that as my father had said, I had attributed to Chane my own acts.

If I lingered I would fall asleep where I knelt, I rose, lit lamps for Varryn and for Kei and, with a trembling hand, one for Invar. As the flame steadied, I reached for him across the distance that separated us, hoping against hope that, dead or alive, my brother might know he was not forgotten.

CHAPTER 22

Chane

A violent sword fight with Burll made a change from playing with power, though I would have preferred a bout with Garanth, if he was still here. Afterwards I practised pain relief and making bruises fade. Intent on that, I didn't notice Lenathe's approach.

'Am I disturbing you?'

'If you are, the interruption's welcome.' I pushed my right sleeve up, revealing a string of large blue and purple bruises. 'Can you help?'

'That's why I came. I thought you might be as battered as Burll, and I didn't expect you to come asking for help.'

'You're right.' Given Ydrin's restrictions on my movements, I couldn't if I had wanted to. Burll's plea for healing gave me some small satisfaction. 'Since you're here, can you tell me what I'm doing wrong?'

Lenathe gently lifted my bruised arm. 'If you want to learn, you must watch.'

I drew my sword.

'You've changed hands. Has it made a difference?'

'Nyth suggested the change. Once I used my left hand, I could see the effect of power with my eyes open.'

Lenathe laughed. 'Thank goodness for that. But if you're struggling to heal yourself left handed, try with your right again. It will serve you well to be able to use either hand. Otherwise, what would you do if your sword arm was badly damaged?'

Ydrin never thought to tell me that. I stared at my right arm and could see the damage in detail – a chipped bone and broken blood vessels surrounded by blood.

'Some injuries heal themselves, but there's no need to suffer when we can speed the healing. Are any bones broken?'

'That one's chipped.' I pointed.

'Heal it with your right hand on the sword.'

The chip vanished.

'Excellent. Now a careful touch of cold on the bruised area should shrink the blood vessels.'

My arm chilled. 'A slight shrinkage, I think.'

'Good. Any healer would apply heat after two days, to help the skin absorb the blood, but there's no reason to wait. Don't be too eager, better less heat than deep burns.'

Warmth spread through my arm. The loose blood spread, and I dropped the sword.

'Don't panic. Take another look.'

There was less blood than before.

'Leave it for today. If you need it, a little tomorrow won't do any harm. Just be cautious.'

I flexed my elbow. 'That's better. Thank you.'

She smiled. 'I appreciate a grateful patient. When healing is freely available, some take it for granted.'

I wouldn't.

* * *

Ydrin stopped at the edge of a wide channel. 'Turn around.'

I clasped my hands behind my back so I would not be tempted to draw my sword. Since I had started using my left hand, I could see and feel the effects of power with my eyes open, even when my sword was only part-drawn from its scabbard. Assuming Ydrin did not want me to see his power at work, I waited.

'You may turn now.'

Ydrin stood on the far bank. There had been no sound of splashing, and Ydrin's shoes were dry. 'It's your turn to cross.'

I leaned forward. Clear, fast-flowing water rippled over a stony bed. Was it shallow, or deeper than it looked? I drew my sword. A power-wrought rope bridge would serve, but something made me pause. I focused on the channel and sensed some distortion in the flow of water. I stared at the current. Something else was there, neither stone nor water.

I stepped forward. My foot landed on a solid, dry surface. Catching my balance, I walked forward, my eyes fixed on the barely visible substance supporting my weight. When I stepped onto the far bank, Ydrin's smile greeted me.

'Well done! Few students have passed that test. They seem to prefer making the crossing the hard way.'

When I looked back, all trace of the crossing had disappeared.

'You're beginning to see the workings of power. Excellent. Why don't you find your own way back?' He walked towards a wooden bridge partly hidden by foliage.

Yet another bridge I couldn't use, but cursing Ydrin would achieve nothing. I drew my sword and focussed and imagined an almost invisible walkway like Ydrin's. It appeared. Willing it to last until I told it to vanish, I took a tentative first step, and walked on. When I stepped onto the far bank, Nyth stood there, a smile on her face.

'Good morning, Chane. That was well done.'

'Thanks to your suggestion to change hands. That's made a hell of a difference, Nyth. I'm sorry I didn't mean–'

She laughed. 'Don't mind me. I've heard and said worse in my time. Best to watch your tongue in front of the boys, though. They're used to copying their teachers, and learning bad language isn't what they are here for.'

'I'll consider myself reprimanded, but I do appreciate the change it's made.'

'Come with me, Chane. I have something to show you.'

I recognised the clearing where we'd tossed a flaming ball at each other, and a tree had caught fire. Until Nyth pointed it out, I couldn't pick out the burnt tree.

I stood under the branches and stared. 'It looks as if nothing happened.'

'Nothing did, thanks to you.'

* * *

Morning brought rain and a fresh determination. Reluctant to endure a soaking for the sake of more space, I considered the room. Even if I pushed the bed to one side and moved the table and chair closer to the window, there would not be sufficient room.

Every power-wrought creation had a life of its own, its form whatever I chose to give it. The choice was mine, to build anything, give it the substance of rope, stone, metal, wood or anything else I thought of. The only limit was the number of stones. No – the limit was my ability to use power. Ydrin had said the stones were just a tool to help focus. I opened the door. Under the shelter of the overhanging roof, I had space to work, but not enough to create anything noteworthy.

A boy wearing a hooded rain cape brought breakfast. 'Good day, sir.'

'Does rain interfere with lessons?' I doubted it.

'No, sir. Most huts have a roofed over outside space.'

'That's unlucky.'

'You mean lucky, sir.'

I stifled my laughter. Like master, like student. No sense of humour. I ate outside, thinking things through. Leaving the tray by the door, I swung my cape over my shoulders and set off. This island had no stream. No matter. I just needed space.

*   *   *

The bridge shone like light, rain running off its smooth surface. I did not pretend to be a builder, but I had melded and strengthened its substance until I judged it would bear my weight. More, it would take the grey's weight with me on his back. I roughened the surface. That done, I had no more excuses. Sword in left hand, eyes open, I held my creation in my mind and ran across the bridge. It held. I turned and walked back, stopping in the centre to jump. As solid as the Low Bridge across the Haw. I set my sword on top of the arch and walked away. Retrieving my sword, I left it twenty paces from the bridge and crossed. The bridge stood.

Setting a careful boundary to my undoing, I unmade the bridge in order to make it anew. After several repetitions, I had managed all possible variations, including raising the bridge so it hovered above the grass. Eyes open or closed, left hand, right hand, the result was the same, but the seeing, creation and endurance had become quicker and simpler using my left hand and with my eyes open.

My next step was to improve my shield-casting. Maris had said my shield was strong, Burll hadn't agreed. More practice would be useful. I looked up. Why not a rain shield? Anything to keep the constant rain from trickling down my face, soaking my hood and cuffs, and seeping into my jacket. I flung a lightweight, transparent cover over myself and watched droplets slide down the sides. I hadn't thought of making the shield breathable. That must have been instinctive. How could raithen wield power through a shield? Did the shield allow power to pass outwards but not inwards, because it was part of me? I would have liked to ask someone. Not Ydrin or Burll. Perhaps the teacher Lenathe suggested, Faril, or in his continued absence, Nyth.'

I walked back to my room, the rain shield serving its purpose admirably. A true shield needed to be strong enough to deflect an arrow, a sword thrust, fire, a bolt of power, but that was for tomorrow. Today I wanted to dry off and relax. After I had stripped off my wet cloak and boots, and towelled my face and hands, I considered drying my clothes with power, but I'd likely burn the place to ashes, and myself too. I shivered, remembering Lenathe's warning.

* * *

Ydrin fitted a third stone to my sword hilt. 'The third stone is an important mark of progress. No ilen and very few raithen are able to progress beyond three stones. Today I saw a student earn the third stone and lose it again by misplaced pride in that achievement. I hope he learns his lesson.'

'Do you ever take all a student's stones?'

Ydrin shook his head. 'That would be a last resort. The body accustoms itself to the stones, and the removal of all stones is invariably fatal.'

He might have curtailed my power by merely withholding the stones and could yet take them all. I dragged my gaze from his. Why was he pushing me so hard? Why had he given me a third stone?

CHAPTER 23

Varia

My father invited me to take breakfast with him. He listened to the remainder of my report without comment until my final point. 'Heksun's troops to provide additional patrols along the full length of the northern and western borders. He did well at the cursed wood, with raithen assistance. I propose the same arrangement.'

'Has Heksun any experience with karyth?'

'He had a tour of duty at Getheer at a time when karyth were active. That gives him more experience than any other available captain.'

He sipped his tea. 'I cannot argue with that. Leave the negotiations with Althein to me.'

'As you will, my Lord.' Today he was his former self. Long might that last!

An hour spent with my captains encouraged me further. I deliberately delayed my confrontation with Ludran, knowing he would rile me and aware my orders would enrage him. Nonetheless, I must make an example of him. He had sent Barys to the Ridges, disregarded standing orders by providing neither regular supplies nor a relief troop, and risked the success of the endeavour and the lives of imperial soldiers. Barys had done well despite his extended duty and shortage of supplies. However, I could not permit any captain, let alone one as senior as Ludran, to display such flagrant unconcern for orders and the safety of the troops under his command.

In the privacy of my office, Ludran did not seek to justify his actions, but his eyes reflected his fury. A traditionalist, he was unable to accept the concept of a woman in command, or the possibility that a young captain's capabilities might exceed those of an older man. I gave him an opportunity to demonstrate that age and experience might count for more than bright ideas and enthusiasm and trusted he would do so.

*   *   *

Responding to the emperor's summons, I found his mood had changed since this morning. At first I thought that Ludran had hastened to him to complain of me, but the problem was quite otherwise. The emperor wished to return to the subject of my marriage.

'I gain the impression that you prefer to remain unwed. Do correct me if I am wrong.'

I chose my words carefully. 'Allow me time to mourn Kei before I consider his replacement.'

The tic in his cheek throbbed, something rarely seen since Varryn's departure. 'There are few potential suitors, Varia. I should prefer to settle this matter before you leave for Getheer.'

'Father, I beg you.' I did not often I ask him for anything, and his expression softened.

'Very well. I shall give you until your return from Getheer. Perhaps you might use your spare time to consider the matter on your travels.'

'I am grateful, Father. I will add this to my already lengthy list of concerns.' His eyes twinkled, and I relaxed a little.

'I trust the future of the empire is high on your list.'

'As of this moment, my Lord, the safety of the empire, the security of its borders and our continuing alliances are indeed my priority. The rule of the empire after your death and mine comes a poor second.'

'I would see you wed to a strong man before I die.'

'Long may that be delayed.' I took formal leave of him and ordered a meal to be served in my office.

Porel carried the tray himself. 'I trust you slept well, Lady Varia, and remembered to eat at midday.'

'Yes, to both of those.' He had brought me a platter of fowl and vegetables, sufficient to feed two hungry men, but I had regained my appetite and thanked him.

'Lord Ludran is a fine man.'

'He is much admired.' I had forgotten Porel's admiration of Ludran.

'He would make a fine consort for a ruler.'

A cold finger caressed my heart. Porel had always taken good care of me. If he pursued this line our friendship would end. 'My father will decide that, Porel. I'm afraid my choices must concur with his.'

'I will bear that in mind, Lady Varia.'

I had cleared my plate when one of my guards knocked and opened the door. 'Training Master Dom is here, Commander.'

'I'll see him now.'

Dom saluted and ignored the chair. 'You asked for a report on today's maze run, Commander. It went well. The runners got through with only bruises to show for it, and the attackers likewise. Everyone needs more practise, but that's easily achieved here, and similar runs could be set up in other garrisons.'

'That's good to hear. How did Dern fare?'

'Your new bodyguard? It'll take him some time to rival Garanth with a sword, but he has a good reach and quick reactions. He did well in the maze. Especially for a first attempt. Whether he'd keep his nerve facing karyth . . .' He shrugged.'

'He has so far. Twice.'

Dom bit back what was undoubtedly one of his stronger curses. 'Good for him. But two attacks on you, that's ill news, Commander.'

'As long as karyth strike we must train men to fight them. Good work, Dom.'

*   *   *

I met Dern and Jonnan in the main courtyard and nodded to Dern. 'Are your men ready, Captain?'

'Yes, Commander. Ready and eager.'

The squadron, six score mounted men came to attention. I acknowledged their salute. 'There is no need for such formality until we reach Getheer, Captain.'

Jonnan grinned. 'The men will appreciate that. Troop, mount!'

Dern stared at the black mare in foal. 'I trust you to take care of her, Dern. She is a gift for Lady Iylla.

He whistled. 'If the black is half as good as the grey, she'll do for Lady Iylla. But I'll miss the grey.' If I read him correctly, he had something to tell me.

We were some miles south of the city walls, and riding out of earshot of the main troop and the rearguard, before he spoke quietly. 'Why should Lord Ludran wish me ill, Kadron? He knows nothing of me.'

My hold on the reins tightened involuntary and my stallion turned his head, reproach in his eyes. I loosened my grip and patted him. 'Sorry, boy. Tell me about Lord Ludran, Dern.'

'I had to skip out of his way sharpish as I left the mess hall. He didn't look best pleased to have to stop, so I begged his pardon. He asked if he should know me. I told him I had arrived the day before yesterday and was leaving today. Captain Jonnan ordered me to hurry and I did.' He frowned. 'The captain said I wouldn't want Lord Ludran asking too many questions and described him as a bad enemy.'

'Dammit! If it's any consolation, Ludran's anger was directed at me, not you. Unfortunately, you happened to be in his path at the time. You did well not to boast of your association with me, but our arrival and departure together will have signalled it, even without gossip from Barys' troop.'

'Why is he angry, Kadron? What have you done?'

'Given him command of the troop to replace Barys in the Central Ridges. Let's see how well he can scavenge while patrolling the mountain trails.' Dern raised an eyebrow, and I laughed. 'I have countermanded his orders, restricted his supplies and chosen half his men for him. He's not pleased.'

'And Barys?'

'Has been given the command that would have gone to Ludran, if he had behaved differently. Barys will arrest Merken, the usurper at Creikham, and rectify his misdeeds.'

'I thought you would do that yourself, Kadron.'

'If I could split myself in two, I might. As it is, I am overdue at Getheer.'

'Why are we going to Getheer, Kadron?'

'*We* are going to Getheer to replace part of the garrison. *You* will leave us at Bridgetown. I have kept you from your duty to Duke Reys for long enough. You will be glad to be home.'

Dern opened his mouth, and closed it again. 'Yes, Kadron.'

'What, no argument?'

He met my eyes. 'Would it succeed?'

'It would not, but I doubt that weighs much with you.'

He grinned. 'You might be right, Kadron.'

I inclined my head and moved off to speak with a burly young man on a tall tan gelding. Called Blackie by his fellows, he cooked the first night's meal. The result was as black as his hair and his fast growing stubble. In the merciless ribbing around the campfires, one of his fellows shouted, 'You're not supposed to be working at your father's forge now, Blackie!'

'Give me better quality meat to work with then.'

Dern chuckled. 'You could do better than this, Kadron.'

I spat a lump of gristle into the heart of the fire. 'Even you could improve on this.'

Dern was voted camp cook the following evening. Contrary to his personal preferences, he served the meat still oozing pink juices. To my surprise, it was both tender and tasty. Blackie and several others asked for second helpings.

I raised my cup. 'To the best meal in two days. I challenge tomorrow's cook to do better!'

* * *

'Dern.'

He raised his eyes from the knife he was sharpening. 'Yes, Kadron?'

'I've a request to make.' I paused, and he regarded me expectantly. 'You have kept the events of the past weeks to yourself. Continue to do so.'

Dern nodded.

'I'll have no gossip regarding our time together, from leaving Bridgetown until your return.'

He did not argue. I had made my point, and he clearly had no wish to rile me. 'I require you to act the part of a true friend to Chane, to stand between him and his other friends.'

He scowled. 'What are you asking, Kadron? My friendship with Chane is not your concern!'

'My reasons are my own, Dern. I will have your promise on this matter: you *will* stand beside Chane, defending all others from him, and you *will* keep silent on the events of our journey. Give me your word.'

His fingers tightened on his knife until his knuckles whitened. I had asked him to betray his friend.

'I am waiting.'

He let me wait. I had lost his allegiance, but I had no choice. He swallowed. 'Very well, *Lady Varia*, you have my word.'

'Thank you, Dern.' I took his free hand and held it between mine. 'I accept your word and bear witness that you will fulfil your oath.' Having no comfort to give him, I released his hand and walked away.

* * *

We clattered into Bridgetown under the imperial banner. I wore the garb of the imperial heir, which concealed my mail. Townsfolk stopped to stare, leaned from windows or rushed outside. Young boys ran alongside the horses, and girls threw flowers. The news of our arrival soon outpaced us. Beyond the open fortress gates, the duke's guardsmen stood to attention and saluted me. I raised my hand, and my standard-bearer dipped the flag in acknowledgement.

'Troop, dismount!'

I alighted in front of Duke Reys.

He bowed. 'Welcome to Hawdale, my Lady.'

'Thank you, Duke Reys. It is good to be here under happier circumstances.'

Seeing Reys at a loss, Dern intervened. 'Sir, this is Lady Varia, Commander of the Imperial Armies and the imperial heir, once known to you as Kadron.'

Reys' eyes widened, but he barely paused. 'Then you are doubly welcome here, Lady Varia. Will you come inside, with your captain, and take some refreshment? Your men will be looked after.'

'By your leave, Kadron, I'll stay with my men,' Jonnan said.

I nodded. 'Gladly, Duke Reys.'

The duke beckoned Dern, led me to his private hall and gave orders for refreshments. Once seated, he gazed at me, his face stern. 'Lady, I lent you two men, but you have brought back only one. You give short change.'

'Chane should have been back by now.'

I frowned at Dern. 'Chane does my bidding, Duke Reys. I am not ready to release him.'

'Lady,' Reys' tone and expression were both accusing, 'you said you would not accept Chane's sworn service.'

'I also said that he might stay until I chose to dismiss him. That he does.'

'Of his own free will?'

Under my cold stare Dern studied his dusty boots.

I met Reys' gaze. 'His choice.'

The duke sighed. 'Well, Lady, how may I serve you?'

'Two nights' accommodation is all I ask, for myself and my men.'

'That is easily granted. It will be my pleasure.'

Dern's eyes were still lowered. Nonetheless I felt his gaze on me.

A servant brought in a laden tray. Reys served me and took a cup for himself. I sat back in my chair. 'How is your wife, Duke Reys? I trust she is fully recovered from her ordeal.'

'Thank you, my Lady. She is well. It will be my pleasure to introduce her to you later.'

'I shall be happy to meet her.' I sipped my wine. 'There is a further favour I must ask from you.'

Reys leaned forward. 'Name it, my Lady.'

'I understand that the late Duke Arnull accepted Chane as his foster son, but never formally adopted him. He had enquiries made, but never found anyone who claimed to know Chane.'

'That is so, my Lady.'

'How is that possible, Duke Reys? Hawdale is small community. Strangers will surely stand out.'

'It is, my Lady, but the place where Duke Arnull found Chane was remote. No one lives there in winter, and in summer you would find only hunters and miners.'

'Lord Arnull was hunting when he found Chane?'

Reys brow creased. 'Yes, my Lady.'

'Will you show me the place?'

'I will, my Lady, but it's a long ride and late to start today, if you do not wish to spend the night in the mountains.'

'Did Duke Arnull not camp on his hunting trips?' I took a mouthful of wine.

'He kept a hunting lodge, my lady, but that has long fallen into disrepair. If we start at dawn tomorrow, we will be back before dusk.'

'So be it. Deduct the cost of two nights' accommodation from your next tax payment. I shall authorise it.'

Reys blinked. 'My Lady, Hawdale can afford to keep your men for two nights.'

I shook my head. 'The emperor does not ask his people to incur costs covered by taxes.' I drained my cup.

CHAPTER 24

Chane

Raised voices caught my attention. When I looked up, two boys were arguing on the far side of the water. The taller, well-built one looked like Eward, the boy who had taken me to meet Ydrin on the first day of my training. If I had known what it would lead to, would I have risked trying to escape then?

The younger boy, slim and curly haired, snatched something and ran off. Eward shouted, 'Murry!' He gave chase, his longer legs soon reducing Murry's lead.

Murry neared the water's edge, too busy looking over his shoulder and laughing to see his danger.

'Look out!' I shouted.

Murry turned his head, slipped, wavered, lost his balance and fell into the water. Eward ran up to the bank, red-faced and panting. 'He can swim. He'll come up in a moment.'

'Unless he hit his head or got tangled in the reeds.'

Eward's face paled. 'I never thought of that. I'll get help.'

I stripped off my armour and boots and dived into the cold water. It was deeper than I expected. When I half drew my sword I found the boy, caught in the tangle of reeds at the bottom of the channel. A hand reached up, but the other remained tightly clenched. His mouth had fallen open.

My first instinct had been to cut him free, but that would mean entering the matted reeds, and risk trapping myself. Drowning beside Murry might prove my lack of power, but I preferred to live. I flung a shield over the boy, shaped power into a blade and slashed at the reeds. Murry floated free. I dropped the shield, seized him, slammed my sword fully in its sheath and kicked for the surface.

Eward helped me drag Murry onto the grass. 'She's coming.' He stared at Murry's still face. 'Is he dead?'

Not if I could help it. I turned Murry's head to one side. Water trickled from his mouth. Drawing my sword, I forced air through the water in his airway and lungs, watching for signs that he was breathing.

'She's here.'

Lenathe knelt at my side, rod in hand. 'Don't stop. I think–'

Murry coughed, part choke, part splutter. He spat out water while I supported him. When he could speak, he croaked, 'Take it. It burns. Judin–' He screamed.

I uncurled Murry's fingers, but could not free the stone without tearing his flesh. I blocked Murry's pain and cooled his hand.

'Nicely done, Chane. Hold it like that while I cut the stone loose. I can't avoid taking some skin with it, but we can deal with that later.'

Lenathe cut swiftly and cleanly, but the cut sealed itself behind her power, leaving the stone stuck fast. 'I've never seen anything like this. Eward, fetch Master Ydrin. Quickly!'

'I could try shielding him as you cut.'

Lenathe glanced at me. 'Do it.'

Intent on protecting the boy, I did not attempt to follow Lenathe's progress.

'It's done. Release the shield and leave him to us.'

I let the shield slip and gradually reduced the pain relief and chill. Sitting back on my heels, I attempted to ease my headache.

'Chane?' Lenathe touched my forehead.

My headache vanished.

'What happened?' Ydrin asked.

'Murry took one of the boxes,' Eward said. 'He whispered Judin had dared him to do it, and he'd put it back once he'd shown Judin. Then he ran off and fell in the water.'

'He was caught in the reeds.' I said. 'I cut him free.'

'Why would he take the stone from the box?' Ydrin asked. 'He knew the danger.'

Lenathe said, 'If the box came open when he fell, he would reach for the stone without thinking.'

'I would have too.' Eward's eyes avoided Ydrin's.

'Thank you for helping, Eward,' Lenathe said. 'Don't worry. His hand will heal. I hope he's learned his lesson.'

'Don't talk to anyone about this, Eward.'

'I won't, Master.'

'Off with you then.' Ydrin's eyes followed Eward, then snapped back to me. 'Did you use power to cut Murry free? You might have seriously injured him.'

'I shielded him first, that's what gave me the idea for shielding him while Lenathe cut the stone free.'

'Indeed? Go and rest. Lenathe, we must talk.'

* * *

Lenathe tapped lightly on my door. 'Nona's labour is near. Will you come to watch and learn?'

Childbirth was not the most tempting of lessons, but I could not resist the invitation. I snatched up my sword belt, buckling it as I strode beside Lenathe's hasty step. 'You said you would cut her to take the child.'

'I must, whatever the outcome. Here, in Althein, we do not blame failure, unless it is failure to make the attempt. I may need your help. Childbirth can be unpredictable.'

I glanced at her. Surely there was someone more experienced. 'You asked me to learn. I will do what I can.'

Nona lay still, her eyes closed, her lids fluttering and dribble seeping from the corner of her mouth. A grey-haired woman leaned forward and wiped the girl's lips. 'This is Sylve,' Lenathe said. 'She will help me. I've given Nona a sleeping potion, which I'll explain later.' She sat on the bench opposite Sylve. 'Sit here. Childbirth is one of the most challenging aspects of healing. Labour can be exhausting for even a healthy mother. Our problems here are greater due to the abuse Nona has suffered, which has damaged both her and her babe. Watch carefully, but do nothing unless I ask it. Save your questions until afterwards. You mustn't distract us.' Her eyes met mine.

I nodded, hardly needing Lenathe's warnings. When attempting to wield power, even a small thing such as a gust of wind or a rustle of leaves could disturb my concentration. In a sense, I found it encouraging that an experienced ilan such as Lenathe had the same problems. As for trying to help, I hope I was not such a fool as to do anything without Lenathe's guidance.

'Let us begin.'

Sylve folded back the covers to expose Nona's distended belly. The girl's breathing was soft and regular.

'Ready?' Lenathe moved her hand across the under curve of Nona's belly, the power-made cut as neat and clear as if she had used a sharp knife.

My hand on my part-drawn sword, I watched the tissues part. A fine red beading edged the opening, less that I had expected. The clotted blood held traces of one of Lenathe's herbal extracts — I couldn't remember which one.

'I have cut through the outer flesh to expose the womb. Sylve will hold it back and stop any blood leakage. Now I shall cut the womb open.'

A strange mix of colours made it difficult to see what was happening. I eased my sword further from the sheath, focusing harder. Sylve and Lenathe had each cast a healing glow across Nona's belly, covering her womb. The pale leaf-green of Lenathe's power overlaid Sylve's delicate primrose yellow. Both made me think of spring, of new growth and vigorous life.

Their combined power held back the flaps of taut skin and weak muscle, blocked blood flow, resealed blood vessels, prevented pain from reaching Nona's mind and strengthened her heart and lungs. The spring green and yellow also brought new life. It wouldn't be enough.

Lenathe slipped her hand into the gap and lifted the babe. 'How is she, Sylve?'

'Holding on. Let's make this fast.'

'Chane, take the boy. Wrap him warmly. Mind the cord. I'll cut it later.'

I eased closer to the bed, took Nona's bloodstained son and wrapped him, aware of the babe's warmth, the softness of his wax-patched skin and his quiet heartbeat. I held him close as Lenathe detached the afterbirth, cleaned away oozing blood, closed and sealed the womb opening and the belly cut. Unlike Lenathe's scar, Nona's was already merely a thin pink line. Lenathe nodded. 'It will be barely noticeable soon.'

'All's well,' Sylve said.

The babe gave a weak cry, and I turned from Nona to her son.

Lenathe tied and cut the cord, took the babe from me, partly unwrapped him and laid him on his mother's bare skin. 'Closeness is best for mother and babe. Will you watch them, Sylve?'

'I will.' Sylve bent over her charges, one hand resting lightly on Nona's thin shoulder, and the other cradling the babe's head. Only one finger touched her rod. A pale yellow cloud of healing covered her patients.

'Nona will live to take her son in her arms and name him. After that her life is in God's hands.'

Outside the air was fresh and the wash water clean. I made an effort to order my thoughts. 'How did Nona come here?' I contained my anger. Lenathe was not to blame for Nona's treatment.

'A friend brought her. Her master would never have called in a midwife or even allowed one of his girls to care for her. You're right to be angry, but let's make better use of our time than cursing him. Describe the drug I used to bring sleep and reduce blood loss.'

I explained what I had seen, and Lenathe showed me the plants, detailing their preparation, storage and other uses. She answered my questions, explained actions that I had missed and asked my to repeat everything she had said.

She smiled. 'You'll make a fine midwife when your wife's time comes.'

Laughter banished the last of my anger. 'Can you see my colour?'

Silence issued from Lenathe's mouth. Her face stiffened, and her eyes widened.

I had asked the wrong question.

'What colours did you see?' Her voice sounded like a muffled echo, far away and too quiet.

She's afraid of me, as Ydrin is. Why? 'Leaf green and primrose yellow.' The silence took on a different tone, lighter and brighter – the quiet of Althein's peace.

Lenathe blinked. 'It's been known for ilen to see the colours. I know of none here who can.'

'What about raithen?'

'I doubt it. Do you want to ask Master Ydrin?'

'Why shouldn't I?'

She pursed her lips. 'To be honest, I don't believe he'd tell you. If you really want to find an answer, you might try

Faril. He has a bewildering knowledge of obscure and dusty facts.'

'The colours weren't dusty. I'd be happy to talk to Faril, but he hasn't managed to find me yet.'

Lenathe laughed. 'I'm sorry. I'm so used to him I forgot you don't know him. He does things in his own time.'

'Fine. I hope I'll meet him before I die of old age!' I swallowed my renewed anger. 'I'm sorry too. I shouldn't take my frustrations out on you.'

'Why are you frustrated? Is Master Ydrin pushing you too hard or not hard enough?'

'Yes. No. Both of those.'

'I remember the feeling. The answer is always practice. Study your body and everyone else's. Understand health. That will help you to undo injury and sickness. The more you do, the more you can do. Carefully. Especially when Master Ydrin or Nyth aren't with you.' She smiled and shook her head. 'Every student has practised in secret.' Her smile faded. 'Some paid for it with their lives. Make haste slowly, Chane.'

It had become strangely cold in the sunshine. 'I will.'

* * *

The episode had raised my hopes that I might after all be ilan rather than raithan. When I said as much to Ydrin, the master studied me, his brow knitted. 'In the world of power, almost anything is possible. However, I've seen few ilen achieve what you have and none in so short a time. Show me what you've taught yourself.'

I created a series of bridges, each longer and stronger than the one before. In quick succession I cast a rain shield, a defensive wall that withstood everything Ydrin threw at it and a shield that protected me from his blows. I drew light from an unfilled lamp, lit fire in an empty brazier, created a breeze to cool Ydrin, let it die and warmed the air. I threw a shield around him, not expecting it to last. It did not.

Ydrin met my gaze. 'You frighten me. You should not have been able to do that.' He brought a hand to his face and wiped his mouth. 'Many three-stone raithen could not have shielded me.'

'It wasn't strong enough.'

'It was enough to distract me. You might have used that instant's inattention to kill me.'

I might have been tempted once. No longer.

'You're right. You do need to make the shield stronger, as strong as the wall you created earlier and the shield you wove for yourself, but that will come with practice. Your main failing is speed. When you fight with a sword, do you consider your enemy's strategy before you strike?'

'If I did, I'd be dead.'

'Then you know you need to resolve that problem soon.'

'Yes, Ydrin.'

To my dismay, Nona died fifteen days after her son's birth, having named him Joy, because he brought her such happiness. Lenathe hoped she and Sylve together might achieve some straightening of Joy's twisted spine. 'Healing must continue as he grows, otherwise his growth spurts will undo our work. Common sense would tell us to wait until he is full-grown, but why should he be crippled for all those years?'

Why indeed? Lenathe's hope was almost enough to bring a smile to my face. Almost.

CHAPTER 25

Varia

Reys stared at me. 'My Lady, I believe Dernwin is in *my* service. Or are you proposing to take him with you when you leave us?'

'I beg your pardon, Duke Reys. I have become too used to making decisions regarding Dern's actions. I have no objection to him joining us.'

Traddin, who claimed to have accompanied the late Duke Arnull on all his hunts, led our small party, which included six of Jonnan's troopers. I rode alongside Reys, and Dern took up a position close behind. Since I had forced him to swear an unwelcome oath I had maintained a shield between us, in case he attacked me. I thought such an act unlikely, but my death would free him from all my requirements. He would not long survive me: the emperor would make a public example of him and might regard Reys as equally responsible. Hence the shield.

Shortly after noon we came to the lesser pass. Traddin muttered something about his aching back and bollocks, stood in his stirrups and pointed. 'There!'

Forested slopes hid the track ahead and greened the approach to the White Mountains. On the right a great scar of bare rock cut through the trees, from the jagged peaks across the valley almost to the foot of the lesser pass.

'What happened here?'

'Mountain tossed out its fiery innards, milady, and lit up the sky. Rock melted and ran down the far side of the range. Only a little stream of fire came this way, but t'was enough to do this.'

'Where was Chane found?'

'The changeling?' Reys glared at Traddin, who took no notice. 'Yonder, under that ledge.'

I urged my horse forward, dismounted short of the ledge and handed my reins to one of the imperial troopers.

'Nuffin to see. We searched, all them years ago. Found nuffin, did we? Only the lad, and him naked and burnt. No trace of anyone else or any belongings.'

'He was burned?'

'Aye. Blistered and raw. Screaming in pain, but healed quick and no scars. So couldn't ha' been too bad, could it?'

'Did he say anything about himself? His name, his family, his home?'

'Maybe. Cried out a lot he did, at first. No one understood him. Might have been one of them foreign tongues, or an outlandish name. Not a name of anyone round Hawdale, that's for sure.'

'Do you remember what he called out, what it sounded like?'

Traddin shook his grizzled head. 'Nothing that sounded like a human tongue. They might ha' been right, them that called him devil's spawn.'

Reys turned on him. 'That's enough of that kind of talk, Traddin!' His face flushed, he wheeled his horse round to face me. 'Lady, there's nothing more to be seen here. We should be heading back.'

'In a little while, Duke Reys.' I walked towards the edge, glanced at the broken rock face across the divide and studied the line of destruction below. The dead area might mean something important, but I could not read it. Traddin fidgeted and muttered about time passing, and a trooper reminded me of the dangers of riding mountain tracks after sunset. I nodded, remounted, and we returned to Bridgetown.

* * *

Lady Iylla did not appear at breakfast. I found her in the paddock, talking to a brown mare. She turned as I approached, her expression wary. 'Good morning, Lady Iylla. May I introduce you to a friend of mine?'

'If you wish, Lady Varia.'

The black mare lifted her head, and Iylla's face lightened. 'She is handsome.'

'She is yours, Lady Iylla.'

She gasped. 'I cannot accept such a gift.'

I took her small hand and laid it on the mare's neck. 'Her name is Dark Lady, But she prefers Lady. Don't you?' I patted Lady's shoulder. 'This is your new mistress, Lady. She will treat you well, as she has her friend over there. See you look after her.'

Lady Iylla stroked Lady's shoulder, her face averted from me. 'Whatever your reason, Lady Varia, I am glad to have her. You have my thanks. Why hasn't my brother come home?'

I had expected that. 'Are you asking me to shame him by dismissing him?'

Iylla turned, tears in her eyes. 'If you asked him to come home, Lady Varia, he would do so.'

'Perhaps, but I prefer to allow him to make his own decisions. When I next see him, I shall tell him you miss him.'

'Dern will miss him too.'

'I don't doubt it. Perhaps you would be good enough to write to me. I should like reassurance that Dern is settling back into life in Bridgetown, and to know when your brother returns. If you wish to enclose a letter to your brother I shall see that it reaches him.'

'I will do so, Lady Varia.'

'I look forward to receiving your news. Now I must take my leave.'

Reys watched the troopers mount. 'My wife tells me you have given her a generous gift, Lady Varia.'

I swung into the saddle. 'You have a fine stallion. The mare is appropriate for Lady Iylla and will serve her well.'

'She is indeed a fine gift, Lady Varia. Shall I send you the foal when he is old enough?'

'No indeed. The foal is for Dern. You might call it payment for services rendered.' I laughed, and turned my stallion to follow the troop.

* * *

I had not inspected the garrison at Getheer recently, but was aware of its reputation as the worst garrison for a two-year tour of duty. Garrison Commander Turrard's reports failed to include vital facts, which an unnamed trooper had brought to my attention in an unsigned, misspelled and unpunctuated note delivered to me by the captain in charge of a supply train. While most troopers have grievances, this one had courage.

yuw need to no comander turards lost hiz grip
trupers quarrel drink an smoke dreem smok an okwa
wun por bastad fela as bin ear over 5 yers
need releaf trup beefor wurs trubul

Turrard's reports had dated the last skirmish with bandits nigh on a year and a half ago. No wonder the troopers were bored. Turrard's service record showed he had commanded the garrison at Getheer for more than thirty years, at least twenty years too long.

The garrison's horn rang out in welcome, and Jonnan's trumpeter responded. Troopers lined the battlements and leaned from windows. Turrard had not seen fit to assemble his troops for my inspection.

I accepted his salute and ignored the onlookers.

'Welcome to Getheer, Commander. Come this way.'

He turned towards the East Tower. I beckoned Jonnan, who fell into step behind me as the garrison horn gave warning of an approaching rider. In Turrard's place I would have waited for the rider's report, but he preferred to lead me to the musty gloom of his shuttered office and gestured to a chair.

Five years ago I had spent nigh on two months here. I had soon decided to leave the window ajar by day and endure the resulting dust. Turrard had chosen otherwise. I remained standing. Hurried footsteps sounded in the passage, a trooper rushed in and saluted.

'Sergeant Norys sent me back, sir,' he panted. 'A rockfall has blocked the track on the far side of the Outcrop. The sergeant would have had everyone dismount and lead the horses and mules through. But the merchants refused to try it. They want the track cleared. He told them that meant spending the night there, and he couldn't guarantee their safety, but they won't budge, sir.'

Turrard sighed heavily. 'Go, get yourself a drink and something to eat, trooper. And tell Sergeant Bohan to report to me soonest.'

'Wait!' I stepped forward. 'Are rockfalls a common problem along the track?'

'Not big ones, ma'am. There's always grit and small stones, but I've seen nothing like this before.' He glanced at Turrard.

'Be off with you, trooper.'

'Yes, sir!' He saluted and ran off.

* * *

Turrard gave his orders, and Sergeant Bohan nodded. 'Sir.'

Johan stepped forward. 'There's time to reach the Outcrop before sunset.' He had been studying his maps.

'Yes, sir, but not to return here.'

'So?'

Turrard blinked at Jonnan. 'If you are to remain here, Captain, you must familiarise yourself with standing orders. If a patrol cannot make the distance to the next fort before dusk, departure is delayed until dawn. Without exception.'

'Commander Turrard, Captain Jonnan knows the standing orders as well as I do. Have you forgotten that I wrote them? I will not leave the merchants and their escort overnight with inadequate protection.' Bohan stared at me. 'Captain Jonnan will take twenty men in addition to Sergeant Bohan's thirty. We leave now. At the double, Sergeant!'

Bohan saluted. 'I'll have the men ready soonest, Ma'am.'

Jonnan followed him out while Turrard protested. My patience snapped. 'Master Turrard, the length of your service does not permit you to contradict me. When we return I shall appoint Captain Jonnan as Garrison Commander. I trust you will enjoy your retirement.' I left him agape.

The muster bell rang. Jonnan selected his twenty men and ensured that they had fresh mounts and adequate supplies. I stood in the shade watching Bohan's men check armour and weapons, and fasten packs.

'Why are we going out today, Serge?'

'Orders, trooper.' Bohan surveyed his men and nodded approval. 'We're going out now, to save sorry Norys. He's got himself trapped between a rockfall that's blocked the track the far side of the Outcrop and a pack of lazy merchants who refuse to move.' He raised a hand for silence. 'We're taking twenty of the new troops along with Captain Jonnan and the army commander.'

'Bugger that!' The comment echoed, and Bohan pointed a finger at the culprit. 'Enough! We're going to work alongside the puling babes and show them how to behave themselves. Whether we face a rockfall, bandits or something worse, I expect you to act like men, not fools. Anyone carrying okoa, dreamsmoke or liquor can dump it now. I want everyone alert. The army commander,' he paused, 'is a woman.' Ignoring laughter and jeers, he said, 'She's neither a whore, nor a skivvy. You will treat her with respect at all times, and you *will* obey her orders, keeping your thoughts on such orders to yourselves. Do I make myself clear?'

'Yes, Sarge!'

'Move out!'

* * *

Jonnan spread his men among Bohan's. The old hands knew the trail and would tell the newcomers that bottomless pits cast by the fierce evening light were merely shadows. Bohan's men knew that leaving Getheer mid-afternoon was a bad idea. Even the 'wet-behind-the-ears new boys' might guess it, but no one said it or much else as I rode alongside.

Blackie rode with two of Bohan's men. 'I suppose you get used to this track.'

A trooper snorted. 'No. Ask Regert.'

'Best not to look,' said Regert. 'The drop to the desert below draws you if you stare too long. Tempts you to fly. I've seen one or two try it. Nearly made me give up dreamsmoke. It'll be dark soon, then you won't have to see it. Where were you based before this?'

'We had a month's training in Tormene,' Blackie said.

'What's the army commander like?' Tedur asked.

'I reckon she'll do. Captain Jonnan's her man, and so am I.'

'Couldn't be worse than–'

Regert had noticed me. 'Trooper! Never criticise the command. I hope you're right, Blackie. We need the best captains out here when the shadows lengthen and anything can lurk in the darkness above or under the cliff.'

I moved up to the head of the column.

'Looks like Norys has shown some sense after all,' Bohan said. 'He's kept the merchants and mules by the track and spread his men out on the lower slopes of the Outcrop. It's the only defensible site before the Peak. It'll be a while before they see us.'

Their campfires signalled their position to us and anything else. I searched the skies and found them almost immediately: a pack of karyth, aiming for the Outcrop. 'Sergeant Bohan, can we increase our speed?'

'No, ma'am. What is it?'

'Karyth. They will reach the Outpost long before you do. Warn Captain Jonnan and your men, and make haste safely.' I sprang from my horse, drew my sword and shifted.

CHAPTER 26

Varia

I landed on a narrow ledge above the highest campfire. Karyth wheeled above the Outcrop, black shapes barely visible against the dark sky. Hatred poured from them. Harsh screeches pierced the air. Dark winged shadows, scaled and clawed, swooped down to rend and eat. Archers loosed arrows.

   I drew my sword, and my stones flared. Karyth hesitated, as though they had sensed my presence, then they soared up and formed a swarm to aim for me. An unexpected trick! Nikaryth and halaryth could recognise raithen, but karyth had never shown such ability, until now.

I extended the range of my shield and strengthened it, summoned flame from the campfires, shaped it and flung the ball of fire into the air. Spinning the whirling sphere around the swarm until its fiery tail joined its head. Stretching it over and under the swarm to form a blazing barrier. It closed on karyth, spitting flames and blinding karyth, creatures of darkness. I shielded my eyes from its brilliance and my ears from karyth's piercing shrieks.

Silence fell. I held my breath for a moment, then undid my creation. Campfire embers burst into life once more, ash fell on living and dead, and a cloud of smoke drifted upwards. I scanned the ground and sky. Some karyth had avoided the swarm and resumed their attack. I could not extend my shield to cover everyone. Nor could I fling power about without endangering troopers. However, I could pick out individual karyth, my actions unnoticeable except by other raithan.

Something moved in the shelter of an overhang, troopers, and karyth targeted them. I blasted a karyth and shifted. 'Stay under cover.'

Regert ducked back. Blackie swung his sword at a diving karyth. A third trooper leaned forward and loosed an arrow. His scream cut off as a karyth dropped on him. Its foretalons pinned his arms to his side, and its tusks crunched through his skull. Regert whipped his blade across and swept the karyth's head from its body. I impaled the last karyth.

'Tedur!' The trooper had fallen at Regert's feet, dead before he hit the rock ledge.

'Don't touch him, Regert!' Blackie shouted. 'Karyth blood will kill you.'

I acknowledged Blackie and shifted to the huddle of merchants, who were too shocked to answer my questions.

Their guards had slain four karyth. I commended them. The sky was clean again.

Moonrise lit the last stretch of the way for Bohan's men. Jonnan took command, and I supervised treatment of the wounded. I am no ilen, but I could at least ensure that would-be helpers knew enough to cauterise severe wounds, or amputate limbs. And understood the amount of pain relief required. For those exposed to karyth blood, thorough cleansing was necessary.

The stench of burning karyth smothered the smell of sweat, piss, the sweet charcoal odour of cauterised flesh, and competed with the throat-catching aroma of the herbal liquor cleanser. Jonnan and Bohan reported thirteen dead and seven injured, Sergeant Norys among the dead.

I ordered Bohan back to Getheer with two-thirds of his force, the caravan and the dead and injured. The merchants were now frantic to return to the protection of the garrison. Jonnan and his men would accompany me to the Peak, with the rest of Bohan's force.

Bohan called, 'Regert!'

'Sarge.'

'Take command of our men.'

'Yes, Sarge.' He turned to me. 'You probably saved my life, Commander. Pity you didn't get here sooner.'

Jonnan sucked in his breath.

'You might have saved Tedur. I don't suppose you got his note.'

'I did, I am grateful for it, and sorry for his fate, Regert. It is hard to lose a friend.' I nodded to Jonnan. He gave the order to move.

The scramble across the rockfall would be a challenge in this light. Beyond the gorge, the track narrowed and climbed steeply, twisting to catch out the unwary. However, Regert and his men knew the track and its dangers. Jonnan's men, now blooded, must follow his lead.

The karyth strike was the first massed attack on the eastern border for four years. One thing was clear from the shape of their attack and their mistakes: this was an opportunist attack, not driven by their halaryth masters. When acting on their own urges, karyth are swift to rend men, while halaryth seize any chance to torment their captives. Tales abound of their cruelty and boundless capacity for amusement at their victims' suffering.

Whether this attack was the first of many or not, I could only guess. My presence might have drawn them as a lamp attracts moths. Whatever the cause, Bohan would brief Turrard, who must continue acting as commander until Jonnan's return. I would warn the small detachment keeping watch from the Peak. Depending on the tribe currently on duty, the watch would be alert, celebrating our downfall, or sleeping their duty away except for a handful who had lost the draw. Hence the need for speed and for hope that the tribe now holding the Peak was friendly towards the empire and prepared to listen to a woman. Otherwise, Jonnan would need to take over, with his lack of tribal languages and his merely theoretical knowledge of tribal intrigues.

Acting Sergeant Regert led the single column, I followed close behind and Jonnan took the rear. The men mingled so that those who knew the dangers of the track watched and guided those who did not. The merchants might well have decided against risking their mules and valuable goods, but like Norys, I judged the scattered and broken boulders passable, on foot, leading the horses. Jonnan and Regert concurred. I ordered silence, and my troopers obeyed. Nonetheless boots and hooves crunched on shattered stone, men grunted involuntarily as feet slipped, leather creaked and loose stones rolled to whispered curses. The listeners on the Peak would hear our approach.

Remounted, we rode slowly towards the Peak, its watchtower in darkness, and the path leading to it treacherous.

* * *

At the foot of the watchtower, dark robed and hooded shadows stepped forward to greet us. Jonnan rode forward. One sentry, his eyes glinting above his veil, pointed to the tower door. Another held the curtain aside and lamplight lit the broken stairs. I stepped ahead of Jonnan, trusting he had kept his night sight. Tribesmen despise clumsiness as they scorn those who take orders from a woman. The door guard spat at me. Fortunately for him, his spittle missed me. I answered him with the back of my hand. To have ignored the insult would have confirmed his assessment of me as a whore in man's clothing.

Jonnan, hand on sword hilt, entered behind me and immediately stepped to the side, setting his back against the wall.

The leader at the tower, identifiable by his embroidered veil, remained seated, but his eyes flashed to me. He muttered, 'Whelp of a pig,' in his own tongue, that of the mazrak tribe.

I responded in the same tongue and a scathing tone. 'He who does not welcome an ally is a coward and weakling, deserving of death.' That brought him to his feet, sword in hand.

The slight figure now standing with his back to the doorway, his veil hanging at his neck, laughed and said, 'Do not throw away your life so lightly, my brother. Here is my cousin, hear her.' The word he used might mean relative, but was often a courtesy title, as now. However, its use gave the mazraki reason to hesitate. My cousin, Vithz, crossed the uneven floor and embraced me in tribal fashion, kissing me on both cheeks and brow.

I returned the greeting.

'We saw your fire, cousin,' Vithz said. 'What did you cook for us?'

'A wing of karyth.'

Vithz's hands tightened on my shoulders. He said in the common tongue of the empire, 'Come sit with us, you and your officer. My brother, meet Varia, heir to the empire. Cousin, this is my brother Dru.' The term 'brother' likely signified blood-brother, but it might also be that Dru was brother to one of Vithz's wives. Thus are tribal alliances made and often forfeited.

Dru sheathed his sword and sat cross-legged, his eyes fixed on me as I sank into the same position between him and Vithz. Jonnan's attempt to sit opposite me was less practised.

'Jonnan,' I said. Vethians have little use for titles of rank.

'Your cousin's dog,' Dru said.

'This dog bites,' Jonnan retorted in the same tongue, which I had not known he possessed.

Dru laughed, and his amusement brought peace between us. Wine, meat and fruit was brought. Tribesmen of the Vethian Desert do not discuss business or war during meals, but Vithz broke the custom. 'It is long since karyth troubled us. One may fly over the northern heights once or twice a moon, but that is far from our camps.'

'Do they land to eat your horses, brother?' Dru asked.

'The boys bring them down with practice bows. We will send word to the tribes, Varia. When they come again, we shall be ready for them.'

'Beware of halaryth, Vithz. Tonight I saw none.'

'I hear you. Men are needed to deal with halaryth.'

We discussed arrangements to protect caravans. The tribes rely on traders for certain goods, much as they volubly despise them. If karyth, with or without greater demons, chose to target the eastern border, the garrisons and tribesmen would be hard pressed to keep trade routes open. No one said it openly, but the thought hung in the air. The tracks were vulnerable to ambushes, and merchants valued their lives as much as their profits.

I did not tell my cousin and his brother the night's death toll. A score of casualties against mere karyth did not bode well for the future of cross-border trade. Might tonight's attack be linked to the reappearance of karyth in the far west? I could not rule out the possibility. While I must not linger here, I needed to learn the extent of the karyth incursions into tribal territory.

One of Dru's men interrupted. 'Will you show it to the soft ones?' Among the desert tribes, 'soft' is a term reserved for young children and eunuchs.

'No.'

Careless of Dru's reaction, I said, 'I will see this thing.'

Dru met my gaze. 'This is not your concern, cousin of my brother.'

'All aryth are my concern. What have you brought down that you are ashamed to boast of?'

His breath hissed between his teeth. Nonetheless I had won the argument.

Dru refused to have the discovery brought inside, and Vithz backed him. Dru's man led us to a sheltered corner of the outermost court where torchlight revealed the karyth. It had not died easily. Pierced by two arrows, it had clawed one of them from a hind limb. The oversized carcase sprawled in a puddle of its own blood. Karyth were unmistakable: scaly body, four limbs ending in long curved talons, wide mouth overfull of sharp teeth, large sunken eyes and vast black leathery wings. They stank of filth, rotten meat and a pungent chemical odour. Some named them 'dogbreath', but that was an insult to dogs.

Dru bent over it, and used the arrow imbedded in its belly to turn it fully onto its back. He was careful not to touch the body, which was foul with blood and the leaked contents of the creature's guts.

Vithz took a bone-handled dagger from his belt and pointed with the tip of the blade. The scales he indicated were smooth and pale grey, rather than the usual wrinkled, pitted, age-old, dark grey-black.

I borrowed his dagger and scraped clean a larger patch. All the karyth's frontal parts were the same, while the head, back, wings and rear limbs were dark and rough.

Dru sat back on his heels. 'What does the claw-beast say to you, cousin of my brother?'

I changed my grip on Vithz's dagger and carved a deep incision into the pale belly, made a second cut across the first, drew my dagger and prised the flaps of tough skin apart. My fingers sprang apart, I dropped the daggers and stood, my breath short.

What the claw-beast said was best not shared with common soldiers, but Vethian view of status does not always accord with those of the empire. I retrieved my dagger and handed it to Dru's man. 'Clean it.' I returned to the tower, where Dru repeated his question.

'It says to me, brother of my cousin, that this is something we have not seen before, a breeding female.' The tribes understood how to breed horses, cattle and messenger birds to obtain certain qualities. They knew that aryth, when breeding karyth, their hellhounds, destroyed those that did not meet their standards and that karyth had never self-bred. I had forgotten to breathe, and my heart skipped a beat.

Vithz laid his hand on my shoulder, his gaze intent. 'Courage, my cousin.'

Dru placed his hand on top of Vithz's. 'We will warn the tribes to seek out and destroy these most unnatural beasts. Trust us, cousin. We take no chances with devils' spawn.'

CHAPTER 27

Chane

I sighed. Lenathe's advice might be useful, but the boys who brought my meals and fresh linen rarely lingered long enough for me to see much. It became a challenge – to make a rapid assessment of a boy's health and check it again the next time he came. I tried it with my teachers too. That produced interesting results. Both Nyth and Maris looked forward to to pressing me to achieve something new. Burll was irritated before and after each session. Ydrin was relaxed before and anxious after, his head aching.

'When you're healing someone, can you see their emotions?' I asked.

'Of course not, Ydrin said. "I see signs of injury or sickness. As for emotions, body language often suggests pain, but sometimes embarrassment or anger.'

Was I reading their emotions or body language? At least Ydrin had given an answer of sorts, rather than his usual 'You aren't ready for that.'

Sword practice proved a diversion from my thoughts, and my left-handed swordplay was improving, but that didn't make my bouts with Burll easier. I had to rein in my temper. As I had in my first miserable months in Bridgetown, where Duke Arnull's favour had earned me no friends, and the label "Changeling" had stalked me by day and haunted my nightmares.

Although now well aware of the potential uses of raithen tricks, I sought ways to convince Ydrin of my ability to heal. To that end my solitary walks took on a different purpose. I watched the creatures of woods: birds, small mammals, even insects. One morning I came upon an alder that had been struck by lightning – another opportunity to learn. I dried the dew-dampened grass – gently without scorching it – and sat down. New grass had grown in patches in the bare soil around the damaged tree. Its branches were blackened and shrivelled, and the trunk bark charred, but the heartwood and some sapwood had resisted the heat, and the roots had been resilient. Flames had spread across the leaf canopy first. Could the alder produce a new trunk from the roots or merely new growth to replace the damaged bark and sapwood? If studying healthy people helped me to heal sick ones, maybe studying healthy trees would give me the answer. I laughed and decided to keep my plan to myself.

* * *

My shield casting was not yet swift enough to satisfy Ydrin, but more successful than my attempts to fly.

'Tush!'

'I'd have wings if I were meant to fly.'

'Give yourself some if you can.' Ydrin said with hard-held patience. 'Birds and bees need wings to move through the air. You do not. I did not ask you to fly. You need to master the instant transfer of your body between one place and another.'

'Why?'

Ydrin's eyes flashed. 'Because I require you to learn that skill!' His tone softened. 'You are a soldier, would it not be useful to vanish from your opponent's sight and re-emerge behind him? To travel an hour's ride in a blink to warn your duke of an attack? To escape a prison cell or torture chamber? Enough, this lesson is ended.'

Next morning a swift scan revealed Ydrin's agitation and his headache. I apologised for my continued failure. 'I'll try again.'

'Wait here. A different teacher might help.'

When the boy came, I stared at him, having expecting Burll. 'Your name's Eward, isn't it?'

'Yes, sir. Master Ydrin said I might be able to help you with shifting.' His cheeks reddened.

'I hope you can. Before we start, for the love of God don't "Sir" me. Call me Chane, nearly everyone else does. I'm just a student with a problem.'

Eward lifted his hands. 'That sounds good to me, Chane.'

'Is that what you call it, *shift*?'

He nodded. 'The masters have different names for it, but we, the boys I mean, just say shifting. It's easier and seems to fit.'

I smiled. 'It does. So what am I doing wrong, Eward?'

'Maybe nothing. You need to decide exactly where you want to shift to and make sure there's nothing in the way.'

'Does that mean I can't shift through a wall?'

'It can be done. But best not try that just yet. For shifting through empty space you just have to think yourself *away* from where you are, before you think yourself *to* the place you want to be.'

'That sounds simple enough. Master Ydrin's instructions had me confused.'

'I was lucky, sir. Master Faril was my teacher. He manages to simplify the hardest things, even calling another raithan or ilen at a distance.'

'Is that what you did when Murry nearly drowned, called Lenathe?'

Eward flushed. 'You have to concentrate on the person you're trying to reach and hope they're listening. I chose Mistress Lenathe because she always listens out for us.' He hesitated. 'Shall we try it? We need an open space with no trees. Then there's less chance of an accident.'

We didn't need to go far.

'Here will do. I'll shift away from you. Then you try shifting halfway between us. Understood?'

'That's clear enough.'

'Always shield yourself before you shift and remember it's two moves, *away* and then *to*. Once you've mastered that, it gets faster and feels like one move, but it isn't. If you forget, that's when accidents happen.'

'I won't forget.'

Eward drew his sword and vanished, appearing again roughly twenty yards away. 'Your turn!'

I wiped my sweaty hands on my breeches, drew my sword, cast a shield and steadied my breathing. Focused on shifting *away* and then *to,* and found myself closer to Eward than before.

'Well done!' Eward walked towards me. 'That was slow, which means you were concentrating on the two moves. You need to do that every time. Now shift back to your original position.'

After several more successful shifts, Eward lengthened the distance. In a series of short shifts, he led me to the bridge. 'I'm going to shift across the water. Wait till I raise my arm before you follow.'

'Won't the sentries intervene?'

Eward shook his head. 'They're used to it. Anyways Master Ydrin has given permission for this. No one argues with *him*!'

Except me. Perhaps that's another lesson to learn from Eward.

'Shifting across water is the same as shifting on land. There are usually no obstacles though.' He shifted.

From. To. I had barely landed when Eward shifted back. I followed.

'That's pretty much it.' Eward grinned.

'Can you shift somewhere you've never been?'

Eward's grin disappeared. 'Don't! Unless another raithan calls you. If he does, you must focus on his call. He'll draw you to him as you shift, and help you avoid anything solid in the way.'

'Such as?'

'Mountains.' Eward shook his head. 'You don't want to smack into solid rock, or trees. We'll try calling, but not today. Let's finish on something a bit more interesting than the shifts so far.' Eward shifted, and stopped a yard above his former position.

'How on earth!'

'With power, you can stand on anything – ground, air or water. Water's trickier, specially if there's a current or waves. And avoid air if it's very windy. Try it now, but don't go too high.'

Face to face with Eward, I laughed and promptly hit the ground with a thud.

Eward shifted down. 'Are you hurt?'

'No. I was so pleased with myself, I forgot to concentrate.'

'I did that the first time.' He wagged a finger. 'Don't do it again.'

'I won't. Thank you. You make a fine teacher.'

Eward's cheeks coloured. 'Please don't practise on your own. Master Ydrin would be cross with me.'

'As you say, *sir*. Can we continue tomorrow?'

'After lunch. I have a class in the morning.'

I watched Eward walk away with mixed feelings. Shifting might be useful, but it was another step in a direction I still wasn't sure I wanted to go.

Ydrin gave his approval to further shifting lessons with Eward. 'If he can teach you to shift, I might ask him to take over your shielding lessons too.'

I wished he would, but did not say so. Nor did I dwell on Ydrin's problems. New alder shoots were growing. And, for the first time, I had disarmed Burll left-handed.

* * *

Eward waited with Nyth and Maris. 'Burll has other duties,' Maris said. 'Go on with your lessons, Eward.'

'Let's go over the basics of shifting again. What do you remember, Chane?'

'Check there are no obstacles, shield, then shift *from* and *to*. And if I'm standing on air rather than something solid, I mustn't stop concentrating.'

Maris laughed 'I've done that too. Eward, you're in charge. Let's shift.'

Eward glanced at Nyth. ' One at a time to start with. Follow me, Chane.' He shifted to the far end of the clearing.

I did as instructed. It felt quicker, though I made sure of the two moves.

'Maris and Nyth, will you join us please?'

They were with us instantly.

'This is where it can be dangerous,' Eward said, 'when raithan are shifting at the same time.'

'Which is what we do in battle, 'Maris said.

'And it's why students are taught to play shifting games together,' Nyth said.

'Let's move two at a time. Nyth and Maris, back to where you were before. Then stay there until Chane and I have landed.' They shifted. 'Chane, I'll shift to between Nyth and Maris. Before I do, you should decide where you're going to land. While shifting, you should try to keep aware of where I am. We mostly shift in straight lines and don't want our lines to cross. Are you ready?'

'Yes. I'll land the other side of Maris.'

We shifted, and landed as planned.

'Well done, Chane!' Maris said. 'The next step is the fire game, if Nyth approves.'

'I do. Today we add shifting to the game you tried last month, Chane. Shall you and I thrash the men, Maris?'

'I think we might.'

'Good. I appoint Eward and Maris team captains. Bearing in mind that games sometimes go horribly wrong, I require full battle shielding for everyone. If necessary, any player can stop the game and all players must stop immediately.'

Maris nodded.

'Understood and agreed,' I said.

'Me too. Is this going to be a free-for-all?'

'Indeed it is, Eward. Why don't you start the game?'

'Shields!' Eward shouted as he slammed a flaming ball at Maris.

She hurled it straight at me. I shifted, and the ball missed. I snatched it up, reshaped it and sent it spinning to Nyth. She aimed it back at me. Eward shifted, took control of the ball and tossed it to Maris. I shifted to the air above her, felt Eward shift towards me and shifted down quenching the flames as I dropped.

'Stop!' Eward shouted.

I bounced off Maris' shield and caught my balance in time to avoid crashing into Eward.

Nyth shifted to join us. 'Maris, Chane, are you injured?'

Maria shook her head. 'My shield held.'

'So did mine,' I said.

'That's just as well. What went wrong?'

'I underestimated Chane progress with shifting,' Maris said.

'And I shifted at the same time at Chane, to the same place. It could have been serious if Chane hadn't put out the flames.'

Nyth pursed her lips. 'Let's do something different. We're supposed to be testing Chane. The three of us will chase him as our enemy and corner him. We will not use weapons, or power against him.'

Maris punched the air. 'Yes!'

'That's hardly fair,' Eward said.

'Nothing's fair in war,' Maris said. 'Don't moan about it.'

'Nyth, Ydrin forbade me to leave this island without escort. That limits my options.'

'And limits your chances of harming yourself or anyone else by shifting to somewhere unknown.'

'Eward's already warned me about that,' I said. 'What about somewhere I know, outside Althein?'

'Ydrin's rule applies,' Nyth said. 'I will count to ten before we try to follow you. One–'

I cast my shield, imagined myself to be invisible and shifted to the lightning-struck alder tree.

No one found me. Nyth came close, but didn't see me. When I was hungry I walked back to my lodging. Maris' curses would have embarrassed any company.

CHAPTER 28

Chane

Zako was bursting with excitement when he brought my evening meal. 'What's happened?'

'Lady Varia has returned, sir.'

'Isn't it time you stopped calling me "sir"? I'm a student just like you.'

Zako's eyes widened. 'No, sir! Not like me! You have the greatest power, everyone knows it!'

When I repeated this stupidity to Ydrin, he was not amused. 'It is so.'

I stared at him in dismay. The greatest power – God help me!

The lines on his forehead deepened. 'You will achieve nothing until you accept that you have power. Do you imagine control comes easily? Our students train for seven years, and at the end of that time some have produced less result than you have in only four months.'

'Four months?' I had failed to keep track of the days, never mind weeks. Four months!

'Did you think it less? It is easy to lose track of time when working with power, easy and perilous. Now, show me the defence you practised yesterday.'

I raised my blade and, abandoning caution, flung a solid flaming shield between myself and Ydrin. The sword vibrated in my hand, a red glow burst from the stones, white light blinded me, and a high-pitched whine pierced my ears, leaving a sharp pain in my skull. I managed to retain my grip on the hilt, but it took all my willpower to release the power slowly and let it fade. My vision cleared.

Ydrin had fallen. I ran forward, flung myself down at Ydrin's side and dropped my sword in revulsion. A faint cry pierced the ringing in my ears.

'Ydrin!' A slim, dark-haired girl ran to Ydrin and dropped to her knees beside him. 'Take up your sword and heal him.' Her voice sounded distant and muffled.

'I can't.' I've killed him.

She seized my arm and thrust my hand on my sword hilt. 'I cannot. You must. Look at him. You must undo the harm you have done him. There's no time to bring another ilan.'

A voice in my head continued to protest, but I instinctively looked into Ydrin. He lay still, as pale as death. Blood trickled from his mouth and nose, but he was alive. I hastily assessed the toll of his injuries: broken bones, crushed organs, and blood everywhere, filling his lungs and clogging his airways. Oh God! The girl was right. Ydrin would die before either of us could find an ilan. If the master could be saved, I must act now. I drew power and fought to focus. Remembering Lenathe's teaching, I touched Ydrin's hurts lightly. Working speedily but carefully I realigned broken bones, holding them in place while I closed tissue ruptures. I breathed air into Ydrin's lungs, fused bones, stopped internal bleeding, repaired torn muscles and bruised organs. Finally, I dispersed blood, located the nerves still sending messages of pain to Ydrin's body and brought relief.

Someone guided me to a place of rest. I lay down, closed my eyes against the stabbing pain in my forehead and forbade my mind to dwell on what I had done.

* * *

When I woke the pain in my head had subsided, leaving only a hint of tenderness. The usual birds' greeting to the dawn and leaves rustling in the wind sounded slightly muffled. I eased myself into a sitting position, swung my legs over the edge of the bed and stared in dismay at my bloodstained hands, blood splatters on my rumpled clothes and bloody smears on the sheets. Was there that much blood? I stripped, bathed and dressed in fresh clothes, then examined my sword and scabbard in disbelief. Neither bore any trace of blood, as if nothing had happened yesterday. At the very least, there should have been bloody finger marks on the hilt and scabbard. Unless someone had cleaned both for me. My stomach knotted at the thought that anyone might handle three stones casually. A faint rusty tang wafted from my discarded clothes and from the bed. It was stronger in my memory, causing my empty stomach to lurch.

I stripped the bed, dropped the stained sheets and clothes outside, and washed my hands again. Breakfast had been set on the table, but I couldn't eat. I sat outside, my back against a birch tree, my gaze unfocused, as I attempted to wipe out the memory of yesterday.

When I looked up, a tall, pale young man stood a few paces away. 'May I?'

I made a gesture of agreement, and he sat on the grass. There, his height was less noticeable. His clothes draped loosely, disguising his thin build, which was evident in the pronounced bones of his face and his wrists.

'I am Faril. I understand you have no name.'

True, as far as it went. 'They call me Chane.'

Faril's solemn face softened. 'It is hard to be known by a name that fits, but does not belong, even in jest.' He smiled. 'When I was training, they called me "One Stone". His smile faded. 'Kei also.'

Kei! 'You knew him?'

'We studied together. I accepted my limitations, but Kei saw himself as a failure. He asked permission to leave Althein, which was granted. Even so he remained sensitive to the power wielded by the woman he loved. When she most needed it, he answered her call. You were there, were you not?'

I nodded, remembering the expression on Kei's face as he faced the sorceress. Faril made it sound as if . . . 'Are you saying Lady Varia deliberately drew him to his death?' I had every reason to resent her interference in my life, but I did not believe her tears for Kei to be fake.

Faril's pale blue eyes widened. 'Did you not understand her difficulties? She could not wrest Lord Varryn's son from the sorceress of the wood without sacrificing one of her companions. That she would not do. She could not attack the sorceress directly without breaking the treaty. Nor would she permit the sorceress to keep the child. A sacrifice was necessary, and Kei chose to make it. Lady Varia allowed him to do so, but she would not leave him to face the torment he would have endured at the hands of the sorceress. Were you not present when she give him the poison that spared him? Then the sorceress, in her wrath at his untimely death, sent her creatures after you. The army had orders to set flame to the trees if any of her creatures passed out of the cursed wood. They did so.'

I shook my head. 'No. The trees were alight long before we neared the edge of the wood. The pursuit was behind us.'

'And before you. The sorceress never intended any of you to escape her clutches. Flame was set only after the border was passed and the treaty broken.'

My blood ran chill. It had been so close, that race to safety, a finger's breadth from failure.

'You kept Lady Varia safe and, in doing so, saved yourself, your friend, Garanth and Lord Varryn's son. I envy you. I shall never know the joy of using my power to save others.'

'It's not a joy, I assure you.' My mouth was dry, and my voice sounded strange in my ears.

As if he had not heard, Faril said, 'I teach those who may, one day, do what I cannot. That suffices, it must.' He placed his hands carefully on his knees. 'Master Ydrin was my teacher too. He taught me to fear power. Do you fear it enough?'

'I know the risks, to myself and others.' How I would face using power again?

Faril shook his head. 'That is not what I meant. Have you heard of those who, long ago, stole many stones to channel their power, to use it for themselves and not to help others? They wanted to hold mastery over others, to enslave them. The stones were not made for such purposes. Those who misused them became other than human.'

'How?' Why didn't Ydrin tell me this?

Faril continued as if I had not spoken. 'Some call them demons. They have troubled us time after time. Those thieves created lesser demons, karyth, which haunt the northern and eastern borders, forcing the emperor to keep half his army on roving patrol. Against karyth, skill and speed often suffices, but when the greater demons, nikaryth and halaryth attack, great power is needed. Power such as the emperor and his children hold.'

'Lord Varryn is dead.' Lady Varia had feared it, and the sorceress had confirmed it. Unless she had lied.

'Leaving only the emperor and Lady Varia capable of wielding five stones. Only they have the power to face nikaryth. Alas for Lord Invar!'

'Who is Lord Invar?'

'He *was* the youngest and finest of the emperor's children.' Faril raised his head, his eyes full of grief. 'Lord Invar was strong and bold, and he loved to laugh. He lightened the hearts of all who knew him.'

'What happened to him?'

'Has Master Ydrin said nothing of his grandson?'

'Nothing.' I had not understood the connection until now. Lord Invar had been Lady Varia's brother. Ydrin was her grandfather. Surely he could not be the emperor's father. His daughter must have been the emperor's wife. Perhaps still was, for all I knew.

Faril sighed. 'With the loss of Invar, the emperor changed. He laid his sword aside and became solitary. The lady empress left him. Lord Varryn took to consorting with peasant girls, and his father banished him. Now Lady Varia bears her griefs alone and not least among them is the grief of losing Kei.'

I stared at him. I could not take it all in, but I had at least a glimmer of understanding of what I had done. Yesterday my recklessness had come close to killing Ydrin, and adding to Lady Varia's griefs. She would hate me, with some reason. Did Faril know of my folly? I would not ask.

'I am told you have questions regarding raithan training.'

My list of questions had been growing ever longer, until yesterday. Now all I cared about was Ydrin's wellbeing.

'I believe you should ask Master Ydrin. As your instructor, he knows what is appropriate for you to know at this point.' Faril seemed to have done talking. He sat in silence, and I bowed my head, my mind full of memories that had nothing to do with Faril's words. When I looked up, he had gone, as silently as he had come.

I had no idea how many hours I sat there, thinking or trying not to think, before I forced myself to move.

* * *

'Chane.'

I whirled, drawing my sword, and Garanth leaped back. 'I didn't mean to startle you. How are you?'

'Fair.' I wasn't about to discuss my health and prospects with Garanth, who already knew too much about me. 'And you?'

'Pretty good. I'm looking forward to leaving Althein.'

'Are you? I thought you were staying with Varryn's son. Where are you going?'

'Wherever Kadron goes. Ryny doesn't need me. That's been made perfectly clear.'

'So you're bound by your oath still.'

Garanth's eyes widened. 'God love you, no! Kadron freed me from that oath before we crossed the Cold River.' He laughed at the expression on my face. 'Did you imagine she kept me bound by that oath for her benefit? It was for mine.'

'I don't understand.'

'Do you remember Sarrech?'

'How could I forget?'

'He was of the ruling caste of Tahurn. I was not.'

I stared at him. I had heard of the disaster that had wiped out Tahurn and its inhabitants, but not in detail.

'My father was a fisherman. I learned swordsmanship at the whim of a foreign trader, but had no prospect of advancement in Tahurn. A fisherman's son could not be permitted to enter a gentleman's profession, nor could his skill with a sword be recognised. So I left, but always returned. Eventually I found work teaching the emperor's children. I swore an oath to Varryn later.

'When he left Tormene, his father would have dismissed me, but Varia begged him to allow the transfer of my oath to her. The emperor had already disinherited Varryn and appointed Varia to her brother's former titles and honours. He granted her wish.'

Now it made sense.

Garanth nodded as if he had heard my thoughts. 'Autumn rains brought the mountain down on Tahurn. That day I lost everyone dear to me – wife, sons, daughter, brothers, father, uncles, cousins. Varia held me to my oath. She forced me to live. Day after day, I begged her to free me, but she would not. She knew that, once free, I would join those I loved. I was a trial to her.

'Grief remains, but despair does not last forever. When at last she set me free, I no longer wished to throw my life away. I owed her too much to leave her to face the sorceress alone. And afterwards I had Ryny to consider. He is very like his father.' He was silent for a moment. 'We'll be off as soon as Kadron's finished here.' He winked. 'This place gets you down after a bit, doesn't it?'

'It does.' I didn't want to talk about it.

'I understand you've changed to left-handed sword use. Do you want to try your luck with me?'

'There nothing I'd like better. It will be a challenge.'

'Why did you swap hands?'

'I think I'm naturally left-handed. The duke's swordmaster always insisted I fight right-handed. Ready?'

Garanth grinned. 'Need you ask? Unless you prefer to use practice swords?'

I glanced at the blade in my hand. 'I never thought. Burll always reminds me.'

'He's the careful type. Shall we live dangerously, Chane?' The gleam in his eyes revealed his own preference.

'Let's do that!'

The strokes came naturally. I noticed neither the passing of time, nor the scratches I received.

Garanth called a halt, wiped the sweat from his brow and rested his sword on the ground. 'I'd say you fight better left-handed. Your swordmaster was a fool.'

'It came easier with you than with Burll.'

'That's the problem with blunted swords. You make more of an effort if there's a risk of being killed.' Garanth grinned. 'I could use a drink. Will you share a jug or two?'

I shook my head, the satisfaction of a good performance fading. 'I can't.'

He frowned. 'You're not permitted a draught of ale?'

'It's not been offered, and I haven't asked. No. I'm not allowed to cross any of the bridges without escort.' I did not mind telling Garanth what I would have died rather than admit to Burll. But Burll probably knew all along.

'What! You must have cell fever. I'll have a word with Kadron.'

'Don't. Hopefully it won't be for much longer. Thanks for the fight, Garanth. Enjoy your ale.'

'I intend to. Good luck. I hope you'll be free to drink with me when we meet again.'

'I'll look forward to it.'

CHAPTER 29

Varia

I might have acted to help my grandfather. Although I lacked skill in healing, I knew enough to stem bleeding, to force air into lungs, to suppress pain. That may have been sufficient to have kept him alive a little longer. However, without the care an ilan could provide, the shock of his injuries would undoubtedly have killed him. Any delay, even a short one, might have led to his death. Guilt would have lain heavy on my heart.

Would I have blamed Chane if he had failed to save Ydrin? I did not know. Had it been possible, I would have preferred any other ilan. As it was, I added a touch of my power to Chane's, and prayed while he worked. It was said that God has broad shoulders to bear our griefs and recriminations? I longed to believe it. Answered prayer demands gratitude. I gave thanks for my grandfather's life, and for Chane's actions.

The ilen who cared for Ydrin told me he would recover his full strength faster without visitors bringing their worries to him. I accepted that, and asked to speak with the elders. A messenger brought their response, 'The rule of Althein is not your concern.'

Have they forgotten that Althein was part of the empire, and that whatever went amiss in Althein had wider repercussions?

Lenathe described Chane as an apt pupil and praised his healing skills. I would have trusted her instincts even without seeing his ability for myself. Yet his unmeasured potential troubled me. Lady Kirra told me I worried too much. I did. Among my cares, I wondered why Faril took it upon himself to speak with Chane on matters Ydrin had kept from him. While I might need to enlighten Chane someday, that time has not yet come. If he were to turn against us, could I control him?

Nyth summoned me. No one else in the empire would do such a thing, save my father, and he would couch the invitation in courteous phrases, to be delivered by respectful servants. Here things were otherwise: I was an uninvited and not very welcome guest, with no recognised status or authority. However, Nyth disregarded many rules. She was, I believe, the oldest teacher in Althein. No one knew her age, and she never referred to it. She had taught both my mother and grandfather, who recalled her with affection and her instruction with awe. I remembered only one talk she gave, which perplexed my fellows, but revealed to me a shining path of understanding and purpose.

She stood erect, skin taut over fine bones, hair veiled. I knelt before her slight figure, and she took my hand. 'Stand, daughter of Virreld and Kirra.' She sat on the bench outside her door and invited me to sit beside her. 'You concern yourself with the wrong man. Ydrin misjudged the healer-defender's abilities.'

The term "healer-defender" shook me. The discovery of a healer-defender was not an everyday occurrence.

'Ydrin will recover, but he should not attempt to teach the healer-defender again.'

'I shall do that. I should not have asked Master Ydrin to do my work for me.'

Her eyes were deep pools of wisdom and sympathy, but her words quite otherwise. 'You will teach him? To what purpose? Is he a mystery to be solved or an asset to be used?'

'Or an enemy to be destroyed?'

She raised her delicate eyebrows. 'Do you imagine you can destroy him, child of Virreld? You cannot. He is beyond you, beyond all of us, acting singly or together.'

I had feared it, but Nyth's certainty enclosed my heart in ice. Invar's loss, Varryn's death, the rise of karyth on the eastern border, a fertile karyth and the healer-defender Chane together formed a pattern I did not like. Events were beyond me, and Nyth's advice would be welcome. So I thought, but when it came I did not receive it gladly.

'You might trust him.'

Trust the man who had lied from the outset! The man who might have the power to wield more than five focus stones. The man who was a freak, both defender and healer. However, Nyth's judgement had never been wrong, and she knew the dangers better than I. Whatever the risks, I could see no alternative.

CHAPTER 30

Chane

I walked slowly towards the place where I was used to meeting Ydrin. If only I had taken more care! My time with Garanth had lifted my spirits, but a restless night had left me weary and reluctant to accept a substitute teacher. Further lessons with Eward would not be permitted. Besides, I wanted to show Ydrin what I had learned. Though I hoped that might be possible, I feared bad news.

    To my surprise, the girl stood waiting for me, her face giving nothing away. Now I could see what I had missed before. I accorded her the full imperial salute. Rising, I asked, 'Lady Varia, how is Master Ydrin?'

'He will recover.' Her voice was hard and angry. 'I shall take his place.'

Relief weakened my muscles, but I would not give her the satisfaction of collapsing in front of her. 'Why could I heal him, when you could not?'

'I am raithan. We have learned to heal ourselves readily, assuming consciousness, but healing others is a different matter.'

'Am I not raithan?' I waited. She didn't want to answer. No one here knew what I was.

'It seems you are not. You are something else, both healer and sword wielder. Such a mix is rare, almost unique. In all the years of power, there have only been two we know of: Selthel and Falcsen.'

My throat was dry, but I needed answers. Faril had refused me, and Ydrin . . . At last, I found my voice. 'When?'

'Before Althein was founded. That was close to three hundred years ago.'

Three hundred years! Too vast a time for me to grasp. 'A legend then.'

She shook her head. 'Raithen and ilen history has passed down the generations by word of mouth. The existence of two healer-defenders would surely be unforgettable. It is said that Selthel exhausted himself caring for others. After his death, Falcsen disappeared. A tale based on truth.'

I relaxed my over tight grip on my sword hilt and massaged my fingers. 'It seems that healer-defender is not a happy thing to be.' My throat was dry, and my eyes stung. A fool and a coward. What would *I* become?

'Before Althein, no system existed for training ilen or raithen. Now we watch each other to ensure that no one expends himself unduly. We will watch you.'

'That does not comfort me.' I sat on the grass without asking permission. 'Why did Master Ydrin not tell me this? He led me to believe I'm raithan.'

'We were unsure until two days ago.'

The day I almost killed him. 'And now?'

'You have demonstrated that you can heal with power and heal well. Eward tells me you have learned to shift. I gather that Master Ydrin's lessons have focused on defence rather than attack, yet you still find shield creation difficult. Let us see whether you can achieve an adequate defence against me. I shall not hold back.'

I leapt to my feet. In almost killing Ydrin I had learned a bitter lesson. My shield creation had improved, but Lady Varia's five stones against my three? I didn't stand a chance. Taking care, I cast a shield, seized my sword, slid it clear of the sheath and raised it in one swift movement, sidestepping Lady Varia's downswing. She thrust for my chest. I sprang back and parried. She slid her blade away from mine and swung low. I blocked her blade. She swept her sword at my neck. I ducked, aiming for mid body, and my blade rebounded from a shimmering barrier. She changed hands and lunged for my left shoulder . Her blade bounced back, but a blast of power brought my shield crashing down, showering me with shards.

'Enough.' She watched my cuts heal, as I recovered my breath. 'Better than I expected, but not good enough. There are two-stone raithen who could do better.'

'I have not spent years learning.'

'That time is for children to practise self-control until it becomes as natural as breathing. You're not a child. Don't think. Act.'

I stared at her, the heat of my anger cooling. 'Did it come easy to you?'

'How will my answer help you? If I say *yes*, you will be discouraged. If *no*, will you use that as an excuse?' She did not give me time to answer. 'Some tricks are easier to achieve than others. Do you fail to form a strong shield because you don't regard me as a serious threat? You know better than to wait for the enemy's arrival before raising defences against him. If you cannot fend off my attacks, how will you shield yourself against those who wish you ill? An enemy may strike when fear, hunger or fatigue make defence more difficult. You must be able to produce a strong shield at will and at speed, whatever the circumstances, even half asleep. Set your mind on what is needed and do it.'

I did my best, though I doubted whether I would ever need such ability. Although I had not forgotten Faril's warning, I pushed the thought of "greater demons" to the back of my mind. If I were fated to meet them, I would not attempt to escape that fate. In any case, if Lady Varia expected me to defend the empire against such things, I thought Ydrin or Nyth would have warned me. Faril might have lied to me. His knowledge of events suggested he was closely involved with Ydrin and Lady Varia, although his description of himself had painted a somewhat different picture. I had begun to trust Ydrin. Whatever my feelings about Lady Varia's deception I did not want to doubt her motives. Maybe Faril had deliberately misled me, but worrying about it wouldn't help me cast an impenetrable shield.

* * *

Having to defend myself against Lady Varia's attacks, with sword and power, strengthened my defences, and taught me uses of power I had not considered. I told her so.

'I would have undertaken your training myself, if that had been possible. However, I cannot be in two places at once. Eward will make a fine raithan, but I will not risk him in combat with you.'

'He made shifting easy.'

She laughed. 'Varryn would have valued such a teacher. He struggled with the concept for months, until he formed an attachment for a girl who lived more than half a day's ride distant. Then it came easily.'

A long-distance romance held no appeal for me.

'Has Eward mentioned that you can call another raithan from a distance and draw him to you, or the other way round?'

'He did, but–'

'–he couldn't show you that? I'm going to shift and call you to me. Focus on my call and trust me. Above all, remember Eward's teaching.' She vanished.

I shielded myself, which was as well – her call struck me like one of Dillard's hammer blows. I staggered, recovered, reinforced my shield and focused. Disbelieving, I recognised her direction, northwest, perhaps three miles away. She stood on a stone causeway. Water lapped its base. I concentrated, remembered to think *from* and *to*, and shifted, feeling her call draw me.

I also remembered to bend my knees as I landed, and took no more than a short step to steady myself.

Lady Varia lowered her sword. 'I'm amazed. Let's see if you can impress me. Return to your starting point and call me to you.'

I did not know how to call her, but reached out towards her position and recognised her power. I had felt it when we fought and when she called me to her. For the first time I understood that I had sensed her power in the cursed wood without realising it at the time. I called on that power, and remembered to bring her clear of the intervening trees. She might have known to avoid them, but I could not be sure.

She appeared, walking on air before landing. A stone wall appeared behind her. 'Shield yourself, draw power through the stones and destroy the wall.'

I did. A tingling warmth raced through my sinews, and the wall exploded.

Lady Varia nodded 'Practice that. You will find it useful.' She held my gaze. 'Have you released all power?'

I dropped my shield, released my grip on power and nodded.

She took my sword, added a fourth stone and returned my blade. 'Well?'

I had not expected such a thing from her hands. 'Thank you, Lady Varia.'

'Don't get cocky.' With a casual flick of her sword, she built a wall of power around me. It was twice my height and allowed me to move only two paces in any direction. 'Escape from that if you can.' She walked away, leaving me trapped and cursing imperial heirs and five-stone raithen.

I tested the barrier. It withstood my assault as if I had struck it with a feather. When I attempted to shift myself outside it, nothing happened. Yet I had done everything right:

shield, from, to. Why didn't it work? What had she done? None of my efforts to break the barrier worked either. By nightfall, I was hungry, thirsty and too weary to be proud. She could free me when she felt like it, unless she intended to starve me to death. I curled up on the grass and slept.

In the greyness before dawn, I woke stiff, cold and furious with myself and with Lady Varia. I summoned all my resources and hurled power at the wall. My power rebounded, flinging me back against the opposite side. Pain slammed into me. Dazed and winded, I slid down the wall and hit the ground. At first, I thought I had broken every bone in my body. I lay still, fighting for breath and attempting to separate the widespread clamour of my nerve endings in order to discover the extent of the damage. By the time I could breathe normally again, I had established the only bone broken was in my sword arm. That apart, I was merely badly bruised.

I had dropped my sword. Levering myself up with my good hand, I closed the fingers of my left hand around the hilt and cried out as the bone ends ground together. Fool! Why didn't I shield myself before I blasted the wall? Pain, hurt pride and irritation hampered my first attempt to self-heal. In desperation, I drew more power than ever before and shifted, *to* high above the barrier, and then *down* on the outside. Stumbled and sprawled on the grass beyond the wall. The agony of my broken arm overwhelmed my elation. I took a deep breath, and set about putting that to rights.

Lightheaded with relief, I walked slowly and shakily back to my lodging, eased myself onto the chair, ate last night's meal and drank deeply. Afterwards, I washed, changed my clothes and returned to the scene of my – I did not know whether to call it success or failure. I studied the barrier from outside. A faint image of power topped the wall. She had set a trap for me, and I had tried to shift into it! No wonder I failed.

Lady Varia had likely expected me to break her wall rather than bypass it. I had repeatedly failed to do so yesterday. She had told me not to think about what I was doing. If I acted as though undoing her creation was possible, perhaps it would be. Reluctant to stare at the wall, I turned my back on it, drew my sword and concentrated on dismantling her barrier. In my mind, it dissolved and faded away. I turned. The wall had vanished. I rebuilt it slowly, carefully, willing it to be as strong as her creation. Then I demolished it again.

I muttered, 'Well done, Chane. Now all you have to do is erect it with one wave of your sword, as she did.' I could not. At dusk, I gave up.

* * *

I did not seek Lady Varia out, and she did not appear. I continued to practise my defence skills, improving my shield-casting daily.

Ydrin came as I was finishing a noon meal. I stood to greet him. 'I'm glad to see you well again, Master.'

'Varia tells me I am old fool for attempting to teach a healer-defender, and a complete idiot for not shielding myself.' Ydrin smiled. 'I believe I've learned my lesson. Have you? Show me what you've learned.'

Ydrin watched, instructed, encouraged and chided me. By evening I completed every task he set. 'That will do.'

I stared at him.

He smiled. 'Between us we have taught you what you need to know.'

A shiver passed through my body.

'You may leave us if you wish. You will know when to return.'

This was what I had been working for. 'Thank you, Ydrin.'

He left. I returned to my lodging, ate half the waiting meal, abandoned the rest and stepped outside. Gazing at the stars, I wondered why I felt nothing, not even relief.

After a dreamless sleep, I ate a light breakfast, dressed in my own clothes, buckled the sword belt, shouldered my pack and walked to the bridge.

Zako ran to meet me. 'Lady Kirra awaits you, sir. Come with me.'

I followed him across the bridge and along a path. We crossed three more bridges before the path ended at a small pavilion, set in a wide grassy clearing. A dark-haired woman sat on the veranda, and a small boy played at her side. Zako beckoned me forward.

'Lady Kirra?' My gaze was drawn to the boy, a dark-haired child with pale skin, his eyes the same deep blue as Lady Varia's.

The woman smiled. 'Ryny, here is Chane. He is our friend.'

Ryny stood and offered his hand. I shook it solemnly. He looked up at Lady Kirra. She nodded, and he ran off with Zako.

I wrenched my gaze from him. Lady Kirra's eyes were grey, but otherwise . . . I realised who she must be.

Her words confirmed it. 'I have to thank you for preserving the lives of my daughter and my grandson. We owe much to your courage.'

'Lady, I could not have done otherwise.'

'Then I will not embarrass you with unwanted praise. Will you accept this with my good wishes?'

A piece of crystal dangled from a silver chain, a stone set within the crystal. Once I had not wanted any stones. How Althein had changed me! 'Gladly, Lady Kirra.' I slipped the chain over my head and tucked the crystal under my shirt.

She nodded. 'It is best kept hidden. Do not remove it, for any reason. If you lose your sword that stone will keep you alive.'

Ydrin had said something similar. 'I'll remember.'

'We hope to welcome you back soon.'

Unable to reply truthfully to that, I said nothing. Nevertheless, a touch of sadness crossed Lady Kirra's face, as if she knew my mind. I bowed low and turned away.

My horse, the grey gelding once lent to Dern, was waiting, full saddlebags and a bedroll already tied in place. Attached to the saddle I found a full purse and a plain, but well-made scabbard. When I exchanged it for my worn one, the sword fitted as if the sheath had been made for it. I took the reins in hand, mounted and nodded to the boy who had held the bridle. 'My thanks.'

'Farewell, sir.'

I dug my heels into the gelding's flanks and did not look back.

CHAPTER 31

Chane

My destination was Bridgetown, but I was unsure what welcome I would receive there. At the very least, Reys would have something to say about the length of my absence. While relieved to have left Althein, I was reluctant to think further ahead than Iylla's face when she saw me. For a moment I wished Duke Arnull could be there waiting for me too. Tears pricked my eyes, and I blinked them away.

I had no reason to hurry, so let the grey choose his own pace. Althein's supplies were generous, but I bought more when chance came for fresh bread, cheese, fruit or ale. Arriving mid-afternoon at a farm, I stayed for two days and helped with the harvest in exchange for shelter and meals. The farm folk were friendly, and I did my best to make conversation, but missed the tranquillity of Althein. I would have to get used to this kind of bustle again.

Towards the end of my journey, the wind veered and brought with it sporadic raindrops. I stopped to don my waterproof cape. As daylight waned, the few drops of rain became a downpour. I urged the grey on, heaving a sigh of relief when the lights of Bridgetown came into view.

I did not recognise the guard at the South Gate. 'I have a message for Duke Reys.'

The fellow waved me through, and I urged the grey on up the empty streets. He trotted up the final slope without need of encouragement and clattered into the courtyard. Two guardsmen ran out from the shelter of the overhanging roof.

The foremost peered at me. 'Chane? You'd best go right in. There's trouble. We'll see this fellow's taken care of.'

I sprang down and hastened inside, throwing off my cape as I passed through the door. A young man I did not know ran out from the old steward's room. 'You took your time. Oh, I beg your pardon. I thought you were the physician.'

'Who's ill?'

The young man's eyes widened. 'Lady Iylla, she–'

I pushed past him and ran upstairs. The door to Iylla's chamber was open. At first glance the room was full of women. One moved to bar my approach, and I brushed her aside.

'Out. All of you.' My gaze swept the room. 'Marytha may stay.'

Reys' voice sounded clear above the protests. 'Go.'

The room emptied, and Marytha closed the door. Reys knelt by the bed, his face pale and strained. Iylla lay still, her breathing shallow, her eyes closed, her face deathly white. I threw back the covers, and Reys cried out.

Marytha seized Reys' arm, holding him back. 'Do you imagine he would harm her?'

Iylla lay in a pool of blood. I drew my blade. A drug had eased her pain and slowed the blood flow, but her strength had failed. A low moan escaped her lips. I focused on her womb. The baby lived yet, but time was running out, for both Iylla and her son. Remembering Lenathe's lesson, I cut swiftly and cleanly, staunched the bleeding, drew out the baby, sealed the cord and handed him to Marytha. Stripping away the remains of the afterbirth, I cleansed Iylla's womb, repaired the torn flesh and damaged nerves, and closed my cuts. Setting a pool of healing around her, I sped the renewal of her blood and removed all memory of pain. Reassured, I turned my attention to the boy. Marytha had cleared his airways, wrapped him warmly and was massaging his chest. 'Give him to me.'

The boy breathed. His heartbeat was fast, like Nona's son, but unsteady. I settled him on Iylla's chest and enlarged the healing area. Instinctively, I drew more power through my sword and increased the rate of healing until Iylla's body responded. Her son's heart settled into the rhythm needed to pump his blood. I maintained the flow of healing and energy until I was sure both mother and child were strong enough to survive unaided and eased them both into sleep.

Reys caught me as I collapsed, guided my shaking hand to sheathe my sword and helped me to a chair. He bent over Iylla, touched her cheek lightly and rested his hand on his son's back. Marytha drew the covers up, tucked them carefully around Iylla and the child, and stepped back. Reys kissed his wife, fondled his son's head, rested his head onto his arms and wept.

* * *

I woke in a strange bed. After a moment's panic, I found the sheathed sword lying on the bedcovers beside me.

'You have a strange bedfellow,' Reys said. The strain of yesterday had lifted, taking years from his face.

I met his questioning gaze. 'It wasn't my choice.'

'I don't suppose it was.' He paused. 'My wife and son live, thanks to you. Your arrival was timely. Welcome home.'

Home. I closed my eyes and slept.

When I woke again, hot water stood on the washstand, along with a razor and a change of clothes – my own. I took my time. My hand, at first prone to tremble, steadied when I lifted the razor, and my legs bore my weight. I buckled my sword belt, opened the door and only then realised I had slept in Reys' chamber.

Iylla's room was clean and fresh, and Iylla herself, still pale, turned her head and smiled as I entered. She took my offered hand and, as I bent to kiss her cheek, pulled me into a close embrace. When I straightened up, she retained her hold on my hand. Her gaze drifted to the cradle beside the bed. 'He is well.'

'Has he fed?'

'Thrice.' She smiled again. 'He is gaining strength. As I am.'

'Rest while you may, my dear sister. Your body will need time to recover.'

She squeezed my hand gently. 'I'm so glad you came home.'

'Where else would I go?'

Reys rested a hand on mine. 'We wish to name him for you.'

I sprang up, breaking free from his grip. 'No! No,' I repeated more quietly. 'Chane is no name for a man. Call him Arnull.'

Reys exchanged a glance with Iylla and nodded. 'As you will, Arnull he shall be.'

* * *

Some of the servants gave me strange looks and went out of their way to avoid me, but most guardsmen greeted me with enthusiasm, and Dern embraced me. 'Well!' He held me at arm's length. 'It isn't true, after all.'

'What isn't?'

Dern winked. 'That you can't teach new tricks to an old dog. What else have you been doing?'

He wouldn't believe it. I longed to tell him everything, but had no idea where to start. In any case, I must be careful what I said in front of an ass like Dillard. 'Nothing worth mentioning. You didn't get to keep your new job, then?'

'Nah. I told Lady Varia I didn't want to work for her after she came here asking all those questions about you.'

'She did what! What did you tell her?'

'*I* didn't tell her anything. S*ome* people told her what she wanted to know.'

'Which was?'

'Where you were found, when, what you weren't wearing, what state you were in, what language you didn't speak, whether you could read or write, or use weapons, what steps Arnull had taken to try to trace–'

'Duke Arnull to the likes of you, Dern,' Tharen said.

'–to trace your kin, why he kept you as one of the family, why he didn't adopt you, why they called you Changeling.' Dern scowled at Dillard. 'Any question you could think of and some you couldn't, she asked it.'

'And was answered?' I could imagine a few folk keen to tell Lady Varia what they thought they knew of me.

'Aye,' growled Holin. 'Apart from Duke Arnull's reasons, which no one knew.'

'There's no harm done, though. After all, it's common knowledge, isn't it?'

'What's common knowledge, Dillard?' Cap asked.

I outstared Dillard, and he backed away. One by one, the other guards followed him.

Dern grimaced. 'I swear to God, one of these days I'll . . .' He aimed a punch at Dillard's former position. 'Forget her questions, Chane. We're well rid of her.'

It was good advice. I did not expect to see her again. Nor did I wish to.

* * *

I took up my duties as if I had not been absent for months. For several weeks, life at Hawdale was the same routine I had known, before Sarrech's malice changed everything. More than one of my fellow guards had told me about the child I had supposedly gotten on Zina and her belated marriage. Dern, as knowledgeable as anyone else on the subject, thanks to his new girl, Darie, told me no one with any sense believed I was the father. He named the man Darie believed to be responsible, and the man Zina had wed. I listened, but was more interested in how Dern felt about Etta's marriage and the fact that she too was expecting.

Dern shrugged. 'Wasn't meant to be, was it?'

His attitude baffled me. He had been serious about Etta for nearly a year before we had left Hawdale.

Marriages and births aside, only one thing had changed. Reys had dismissed Ollery. Iylla had to say it twice before I believed it. Even then I had to see for myself. The steward's desk had been moved from Reys' office to the old steward's room. Anas jumped up as I entered.

'Master Chane, I owe you an apology for the other night. I did not know you.'

'Why should you? Hardly anyone knew me until I had shaved. Please don't call me Master Chane, that's reserved for reprimands.'

Anas' eyes twinkled. 'That goes for me too.'

'Tell me, if you can, why Ollery was dismissed.'

'I don't know the details, but I gather he offended the duke once too often. I take it you're another glad to see the back of him.'

'I couldn't be more pleased.' Unless Dillard managed to get himself kicked out. I looked around. 'I don't think I've ever seen this room in use. You look busier than Ollery ever did.'

'I prefer to be busy rather than idle. Though I fear the duke would rather I wasn't quite so thorough at times.'

'Better thorough than slack. Good to meet you, Anas.'

'And you, Chane.'

* * *

Iylla sat in her sewing room, Arni on her lap, her embroidery case missing from its usual place. 'Sit here, and take Arni.'

'Goodness, he's growing heavy!'

'Babies do that, you know.' She unlocked a drawer in her cabinet, drew out a small purse and laid it on the table.

'What's this?'

'Payment for the jade necklace you bought, acting for Reys so he didn't miss the opportunity. Thank you, it's perfect.'

For a moment, I had no idea what she was talking about. Then it came to me – the necklace I had bought for Zina with the last of my savings. How it had gone from Zina to Reys? 'I'd forgotten.'

'With everything that's happened I'm not surprised.' Iylla sat on my chair arm and leaned against me. 'I'm so glad you're home.'

'It's good to be with you again.' What else could I say?

Two days later Dern and I were off duty together. 'What happened to Zina's necklace? I asked.

Dern grinned. 'Come with me and meet Darie. She knows more than I do. I need to pick up my new boots on the way.'

Wearing his new boots, Dern greeted the shopwife. 'You'll remember Chane, Mistress.'

'How could I forget? Darie,' she called.'

A small girl ran down the stairs. Her soft brown curls bounced around her pretty face, and her eyes lit up at the sight of Dern. 'You must be Chane,' she said. You've been away a long time.'

'Needs must sometimes. I'm pleased to meet you, Darie.'

'Chane wants to know about the necklace,' Dern said.

'Of course he does. I moved in after Etta and Zina left. The room was a mess, thanks to Zina. It took me three days to clear her rubbish out. Then I found the necklace under her bed. She *might* have lost it while packing, but, more likely, she wanted to hide it from her husband.'

'She would,' said the shopkeeper.

'I asked Dern to return the necklace to you, but he had a better idea.'

'I had no idea when you might come home, and I knew you were broke. I asked the duke if he wanted to buy it from you for his lady. When I explained and told him what you'd paid, he said – Never mind that. He thought she'd love it.'

'She does,' I said. 'Thank you, Dern. And thank you for finding it, Darie.'

I could see why Dern was fascinated. She was pretty, clever and kind. If Dern had not made it perfectly clear that Darie was his girl, I might have been tempted.

CHAPTER 32

Chane

A sense of unease drove me to one of the best vantage points, the ruined east tower. The sentry on the west tower gaped at me. I ignored him, walked the length of the connecting wall, watching out for missing stones, and climbed the worn spiral stair. A bitter wind struck me at the top.. My viewpoint did nothing to explain the trouble – only its direction, currently somewhat north of east, but heading south. I nestled against the outer wall, below the parapet and waited.

Footsteps drew my attention. Dern, inevitably, had come in search of me.

'What's wrong?'

'Can you feel it, Dern?'

He frowned. 'Feel what?'

'They're coming south.'

Dern hunkered down beside me. 'Then you must tell the duke.'

I met his worried gaze. 'They won't come here. They'll follow the border to Mondun.'

'I hear the garrison there was reinforced last month.'

'That won't be enough.' Not against aryth.

'Well, if the Imps need help they'll send for it. They always do.'

'It's too late. They'll reach Mondun tonight. Dammit.' I resisted the temptation to cover my face with both hands.

'Who will?'

'You don't want to know.' My words sounded muffled.

'Tush! I'll find out sooner or later. What are you going to do about it?'

'I don't know.' Dern stared at me. I knew what had to be done, but I could not do it, unless someone called me to Mondun.

'Seems to me it's been a long time since breakfast. You should keep your strength up. Just in case.'

'I've never felt less like eating.'

'What a fib! Less than when Kadron was boasting about eating ant eggs and drinking snake's blood! Never mind the–' Dern broke off as if afraid of losing his own appetite.

The corners of my mouth twitched in a smile. 'Maybe not. What have you brought?'

'Nothing much, only a pack-up each.'

When Dern flipped the lid off, the waft of rich stew almost had me dribbling. He handed over the second can. 'It'll be cold by now. Don't ask me to go down and get it heated up for you.'

'I won't. My thanks.' The stew was still warm, thick with meat, onions, vegetables and soft dumplings. Dern scooped out the solids with his knife and lifted the can to drink the gravy.

'What?'

'Just checking it was cool enough. You'd have yelled if you'd burned yourself.' I ate.

Dern wiped his mouth. 'What now? Are you going to Mondun?'

'If I am, is that anything to do with you? You're not my keeper. Or are you? Did Reys ask you to keep an eye on me?'

'Not exactly. That was Lady Varia.'

'Blast her! She– Don't do it, Dern. You're safer keeping your distance from me, and from her.'

'I'm sure I would be, but I promised her.' He forced a grin. 'So, if you go, I have to follow.'

I took a deep breathe and let it out slowly. 'No. If I go, I'll take you with me. Be ready.'

* * *

When I jumped the last stair, sword in hand, Dern was waiting. He wore a reinforced cap, and tossed me another. 'I should have thought of that.' I settled it on my head. 'Ready?'

'Of course.'

'Put your arms round me, hold tight and pray.'

Dern flung his arms around my neck and clasped his hands together. 'I hope no one sees us. What–'

I concentrated on Lady Varia's call, remembered Eward's instructions, cast a shield to cover us both and shifted.

Dern screamed. Wind whipped the sound away, but he clung and did not lose his grip.

The call cut off, and the wind stopped abruptly as I landed. My stumble broke Dern's hold. He fell with a crash of splintering wood, rolled over and scrambled to his feet, gasping for breath as he drew his sword. 'What the hell happened? Where on God's earth are we?'

'Mondun.' I reinforced my shield and drove my blade into a dark shadow. Although I could not make out its shape, instinct said aryth.

'Karyth!'

Something swooped down. Dern ducked and struck. Long claws snatched at his arm. He jerked back and slashed. I let loose a blast of power, and the karyth shattered.

We stood in the ruins of a marketplace, amidst broken stalls. Flames leaped from a wagon on my left, and cast wavering shadows across a crumpled figure under one of the arches. Ahead a handful of pikemen fought back-to-back against dark winged creatures. The flap of their wings, harsh screeches and shouts filled the air. Dern needed someone to guard his back, but Lady Varia had called me to fight something worse than karyth. She might be anywhere in the deep darkness of the walls around the square. So might karyth. They avoided firelight and torchlight, but we stood in shadow. How well could they see? I had not heard the creature that dived at Dern, but I had felt it.

Muffled screaming came from somewhere behind me, but it was eerily quiet where I stood. A movement from a window high on the opposite wall drew my attention. A bowman. One of the creatures attacking the pikemen shrieked, swerved and plunged to the ground, an arrow through its guts.

Dern seized a torch from a wall bracket and set fire to the remains of the wrecked stall at his feet. The canvas caught quickly, and within moments wooden frames and partitions were ablaze. Trusting Dern could hold his own in the flaring light, I shifted to the opposite end of the square, close to another group of soldiers. Dern ran towards me, setting light to more debris on the way. He sprang away from a sudden movement, tripped over something and fell. A blade glinted, firelight gleamed on fair hair and a familiar voice said, 'On your feet, Dern.'

I felt Lady Varia's call again and answered it. The quality of the darkness above me changed. Karyth scattered. A rush of wings and shrieks pained my ears.

CHAPTER 33

Chane

Soldiers retreated in formation, leaving me isolated, but not alone. Lady Varia stood in the shadows next to me, visible only by the light of her sword and her shield. 'Choose your target,' she said quietly. 'Halaryth distrust each other, but if we join together so will they. I'd prefer they don't. No single halaryth can overcome us. Hold your shield, and do not fear. We *will* prevail.'

  They came, larger than karyth and man-shaped, casting vast shadows around a central darkness. I shuddered. They were nothing like men. The sense of evil threatened to choke me. We *will* prevail! I checked my shield – the strongest yet.

The leading halaryth swooped towards me, its wings a mere suggestion, its claws and teeth shorter than karyth. Yet it presented a far great menace. In the depths of its darkness, hunger glinted from its eyes and teeth, and its claws reached for me. My skin prickled, but my shield was impenetrable, and Lady Varia guarded my back. I cast aside all my doubts of her and trusted her with my life. As halaryth closed in on me, I did as Ydrin had once suggested. I shifted from Lady Varia's side to a point behind the descending halaryth, sliced through its neck, shifted upwards and scythed into its followers. Shifted a short distance to avoid Lady Varia's burst of flame, returned and fought alongside her.

She had said halaryth would attack singly. They did, and died, by sword, flame or power strikes. I had not known battle rage until now. Lunging, stabbing, cleaving, I slew all that threatened me.

Strangely, a lone karyth came slowly towards me, weaving its way through the handful of halaryth that remained. It hovered just beyond the reach of Lady Varia's blade.

'Yours.'

'Mine.' I blasted it, and it winked out of existence.

I cast a power-wrought rope around a halaryth's throat and jerked it tight. Lady Varia struggled against two halaryth, her fire rebounded, and her sword strokes missed her target. They were working together. She needed help.

Remembering her warning about joining together, I hesitated. In that instant, the karyth reappeared. Impossible! I had killed it. Lesser demon or not, I dared not leave it free to wreak its mischief. Lady Varia must save herself.

The karyth folded its wings and gazed at me. Its eyes glowed sun-bright. Suspended in air, it dropped its wings as if they were not part of it. Its contours rippled and buckled, stretching, transforming into true human shape: a woman, even to its garb – robe, cloak and sandals.

I stared, disbelieving. All other karyth had fled. My blood chilled. The she-demon glanced at Lady Varia, her golden eyes glittered and she laughed, revealing sharp, gleaming teeth.

Lady Varia's attackers drove a cloud of karyth at her. She flung fire. Karyth fell in blazing ruin, but another wave followed. The two halaryth still floated just out of reach of Lady Varia's sword thrusts and blasts of power, and struck at her with every opportunity.

The she-demon drew closer. Her long fingers stretched towards me, pointed nails poised to grip – and rend. Then she turned towards Lady Varia.

Hot anger surged through me. I shifted upwards. Extending my shield to cover Lady Varia, I cast a wall of fire between her and the she-demon. Lady Varia staggered back, and I blasted the karyth-woman.

The she-demon laughed as she turned to face me. Her mirth rebounded from the walls below and deafened me.

I had heard that laugh before, seen her luscious body and the gleam in her eyes. 'No!'

Echoes multiplied, rang in my ears, throbbed through my body, shook my resolve. In panic and rage, I fought the dark flames that burned behind her long-lashed eyes.

She closed on me.

Summoning all my strength, all my hatred, I drew power through my sword. It raced through me, my sword hilt warmed, the stones flashed red, and I hurled power outwards as I thrust my blade through her, through the thing that looked like a woman but was not.

Pain surged through my sword arm – the she-demon's last desperate struggles to drain my power. Agony pierced me, but I would not submit. As I fought, the dark flames in her eyes lightened, until white light filled my vision.

The she-demon plummeted to the ground. I fell beside her.

CHAPTER 34

Chane

I lay on coarse linen. Wood smoke and lamp oil competed with something worse – the scent of a startled ferret. I opened my eyes and tried to stand.

Ydrin pushed me back on the bed, his expression unreadable. Lady Kirra sat beside him, her face tranquil, although something in her eyes suggested disquiet. Beyond her stood a stern-faced older woman, and Burll, his years weighing on him. Both Burll and the woman held naked swords. She must be raithan. Something was wrong. 'Lady Varia?'

'She is safe,' Lady Kirra said.

Ydrin glanced at her and turned back to me. 'You felt the presence of aryth at a distance.'

'Yes.' What I had sensed was evil, desiring to rend and consume. Aryth or halaryth – whatever Ydrin chose to name it made no difference to its hunger.

'And you transported yourself and Dern to Mondun in a matter of moments.'

'Lady Varia called me and I came.' It had been night when we left Bridgetown and night when we landed in the beleaguered town. When I felt Lady Varia's call, I had not considered the risk, for myself or for Dern. If I had, the compulsion that had drawn me would still have been irresistible. I had concentrated on the call and ignored Dern's terrified grasp. A true friend would have given him a chance to refuse. He would not have done so. Knowing what he was about to face would not have helped either.

'Did you recognise the nikaryth?'

I shook my head. Faril had talked about different forms of aryth, but I could not remember the details. Lady Varia had named the things halaryth, and I had recognised them as evil, if that was what Ydrin meant. The creature that changed into female form . . . Female or not, it was not human.

'I shall ask you again. Did you know Divasa?'

The name meant nothing to me, if indeed it was a name and not another term for a form of aryth. I did not understand Ydrin's question. The creature that had taken the shape of a woman was familiar only in . . . I vomited.

* * *

I lay on fresh sheets, a clean taste in my mouth. Someone lifted my head. 'Drink.'

Obediently, I opened my mouth and swallowed sweet water. The cup was removed and my head lowered gently to the pillow.

* * *

'Did you know Divasa?'

I opened my eyes to a different room, perhaps a different day. I was as weak as before. Ydrin had once said, 'Constant use of power is weakening. You must conserve your strength.' I had failed to do so in the battle against the she-demon that Ydrin named Divasa. How could a demon have a name and Ydrin know it? Yet the master's question remained in the air, hanging over me. He wouldn't stop asking until he was satisfied with the answer.

I closed my eyes. Recalling the thing named Divasa brought sickness to my mouth again, and I fought to master it. Ydrin had not asked about karyth. I could deny any prior knowledge of those lesser demons, as Faril had named them. I had not seen karyth or halaryth before the battle at Mondun, but something about the demon Divasa had been familiar, chillingly and terrifyingly familiar. I had encountered her before somewhere, somewhen in my forgotten past, though I couldn't remember the details. Or would not. The sorceress was the same kind of demon – more powerful, more evil than the halaryth Lady Varia and I had destroyed. Was she one of the greatest demons – the word came to me – nikaryth?

Duke Arnull had once said, 'Always tell the truth.' When truth had been impossible, silence had become my answer, but that would not serve now. How long was it since Ydrin asked the question? 'Yes.'

A hiss of intaken breath. I opened my eyes. Ydrin stared at me. Lady Kirra had turned her face away. The two raithen were closer than before, the tips of their blades almost touching me. Would they kill me if I spoke again?

Ydrin ignored them. 'Did you have congress with her?'

'No!' Ydrin's question triggered a revulsion that threatened to destroy my already less than perfect control over my stomach and bowels. My eyelids snapped shut. The argument centred on me meant little as I strove with my body.

A woman exclaimed, 'He lies! When has he ever told the truth? He has concealed his name, his power, his knowledge of aryth. Let us put him to death!'

'He has twice saved Lady Varia's life,' Burll said

'She has twice saved his.'

'Peace, Maris.' Ydrin said. 'Is there anything you wish to tell us, Chane?'

I had strength for one word, but more was required. 'I do not lie.' Even to my own ears the words were close to inaudible.

'Then rest. No one here will harm you.'

I sensed movement and heard footsteps leaving the room. Burll arguing with the woman, she saying something about the emperor, and then they were out of earshot. Although at least one raithan might want my death, I thought Ydrin and Lady Kirra would ensure that I lived. Ydrin's reassurance had sounded like a promise. Death might be kinder than this. I should have sought it long ago. Remembering a promise I had once made, I turned my head away from the glow of the lamp beside me and wept.

*   *   *

When I woke, it was daylight and a different room. Soft linen rested lightly on my skin. Wind rattled through the trees, fast-flowing water chuckled and a log fire crackled. The scent of pine and apple wood drifted and warmed the air. Lady Kirra sat beside my bed. 'You do well to fear us. Are we right to fear you?'

'I don't know.' My voice was hoarse. 'I would not willingly harm you and yours.'

She smiled. 'Then it is as Varia has said. You do not know the extent of your powers. You have not deliberately deceived us.'

Her gaze was clear, and I met her eyes for as long as I could. 'Was Lady Varia harmed?'

'Like you, she suffered from the death throes of the nikaryth, but your shield protected her from the worst. She is able to heal herself. Why do you find self-healing so difficult?'

I could heal myself and had done so, but not now.

She sighed. 'You do not love yourself enough. How do you expect others to love you when you do not believe yourself worthy of love?

'I do not ask anyone to love me.' The lump in my throat made speech almost impossible.

'While you live, you cannot cut yourself off from love.' She studied my face. 'Ah, I understand. You wish to die, but you will not take your own life.'

I could make no answer to that, but silence was unacceptable. At last I whispered, 'You are wise, Lady Kirra.'

'Not wise enough, I fear, to help you find a solution.' She rose gracefully to her feet and then, to my surprise, bent and kissed my brow. 'I wish you well. Perhaps the peace of Althein will help you.'

* * *

Zako brought meals and clean linen. When I felt strong enough, I wandered woodland paths. At Ydrin's suggestion, I watched hours of lessons in halls lit by blazing fires or outside in the warmth of braziers. Although I had no need to stay, I was in no hurry to leave. If I stayed long enough, Lady Kirra might be proved right. I did not believe it.

After several days of rain, the skies cleared. Despite a chill wind youngsters spilled out from their classes, laughing and shouting. I retreated to my lodging.

Waking late, I found my breakfast tray waiting and Zako hovering impatiently.

'You'll hear the rumours soon enough, sir. The word is that the emperor sent a messenger to Lady Kirra, but she would not receive him.'

'And?'

'She said, "If the emperor wishes to speak with me, he must come himself." They're taking bets on whether he'll come and, if he does, whether the lady will refuse him to his face.'

'I believe what occurs between the emperor and Lady Kirra is not something that should concern anyone else.'

'Oh, but–'

'Did you hear me, Zako?'

'Yes, sir.' Zako backed away, and whispered to someone outside the door.

Zako's unseen companion said, 'Does that mean he won't place a bet?' Zako hushed him, and they both ran off.

I laughed.

While I had not marked the passing days, it was time for me to leave. I would tell Ydrin my intention after the evening meal and leave the next morning. For Iylla's sake at least, I must return to Hawdale, though it no longer felt like home.

'You are right to leave us, although you will always be welcome here whenever you wish to visit us.'

'Thank you, Ydrin.'

'A horse and supplies will be ready for you tomorrow morning.'

'I'm grateful.'

I was about to bid him goodnight, when Zako appeared. He stood waiting for Ydrin to acknowledge him.

'Yes, Zako?'

'The emperor is here, Master. He asks to speak with you and Lady Kirra.'

'I will come. You too, Chane. The emperor will wish to meet you.'

I had no good excuse, only reluctance to be presented to the emperor as – what did the boys murmur behind my back? – the raithan who saved Lady Varia. 'Very well.'

* * *

Imperial guardsmen stood outside Lady Kirra's dwelling, but when I entered only two men were there, neither of whom wore a crown. Ydrin dropped to one knee before the taller of the two, a man of middle years, his dark hair flecked with grey, his face shadowed and strained. He helped Ydrin to his feet. 'I need your assistance, Ydrin, and yours, Kirra. I beg you both to come with me to Tormene.'

'Why do you need us, my Lord? What has happened?'

The emperor ignored Ydrin, as though Lady Kirra and he were alone.

'His Imperial Highness has not yet enlightened me as to his motive for gracing us with his presence.'

Lady Kirra's voice was soft, but her words were so outside my experience of her I struggled to keep my astonishment to myself.

The emperor's eyes flashed, but his tone was bland. 'You would not answer my summons, my Lady, making it necessary for me to come to you.'

'I am not your servant.' The emperor's gaze was fixed on her, as if he wished to see into her soul, but he said nothing.

Ydrin asked again, 'My Lord?'

'Varia has enclosed herself behind a wall of power. I cannot break it down. She is beyond my reach.'

'Why would she do such a thing?'

Lady Kirra cried, 'What have you done, Virreld?'

The emperor shook his head.

'What do you believe we can achieve, that you cannot?'

The emperor hesitated before he spoke. 'If she fears me, Ydrin, she may respond to you and Kirra.'

'What cause have you given her to fear you?'

Lady Kirra shook her head. 'I will not come. If she indeed fears you, she is now safe from you.'

'She will die!' Virreld's cry held anguish.

'Only if she wishes to.' Ydrin's expression gave nothing away. 'Kirra and I working together could not penetrate any barrier Varia has erected, but I believe Chane could.' He nodded towards me, and the emperor swung round. 'I suppose Varia has told you of him.'

'She has.' Virreld's dark eyes assessed me. 'Are you as strong as she tells me you are?'

'He has been well taught,' Ydrin said, before I could work out what answer to give.

'Will you do this, Chane?'

'I will do what I can for Lady Varia, sir.'

'Very well. We ride tomorrow.' He turned his back on me.

'I will come with you. You may have need of me.'

'I will not be a party to this.' Lady Kirra's voice still had an edge to it.

Virreld bowed his head slightly. 'As you wish. Once you would not have refused me.'

'Once you were a different man.'

The emperor turned on his heel. His companion bowed to Lady Kirra and followed him outside.

Ydrin took Kirra's hand. 'All will be well.'

'I pray so.' A tear rolled slowly down her cheek. Ydrin brushed it away and kissed her.

Finding no words of comfort for Lady Kirra, and having no right to kiss her cheek, I clasped her hand. 'Farewell, Lady.'

CHAPTER 35

Varia

My father and I had often disagreed, but my quarrels with him had never reached the pitch of Varryn's. Twice, to my knowledge, Varryn had drawn his sword against the emperor. The first time, his reward was confinement in the cells for two days. On the second occasion, his imprisonment lasted a week, for he would not beg my father's pardon. It fell to me to make peace between them.

This evening I was tired, irritable and reluctant to discuss business over a glass of wine. Had the emperor delayed his question until morning, I might have answered calmly, but my father's timing and mine did not always coincide. When he raised the question of my marriage, I unwisely lost my temper.

'Who is to be my husband?' I snapped.

He frowned. 'No one as yet. I am waiting to hear your preference.'

If only that were possible. 'You said, "a strong man". I would add a man with sense and limited ambition.'

'To rule the empire? I think not.'

I knew what would follow, but did not have the wit to restrain myself. 'No, my Lord, to support *my* rule. I do not propose to take up my embroidery and leave the empire and imperial forces in other hands.' I noted the tic in the emperor's cheek and waited for his fury to burst over me.

He stepped forward. I might have moved aside or merely lifted a hand. If I had, he would have regained control of himself immediately. Instead I drew my sword, intending to shield myself from his approach.

What I did was somewhat different. Too late, I recognised my error. I had not set bounds to my shield. It held me apart from my father's designs certainly, but also trapped me within walls of fire.

I tried to free myself, but could not. Nor could I release my power. My thoughtless shielding held me motionless, unable to speak or move. My heartbeat so slow and weak it might not existed, and my breathing likewise. Nonetheless I lived, if my stillness could be described as living. It has been said, 'I think; I am alive.' I had not thought to prove the truth of that saying in such a fashion.

My eyes remained fixed on my father. I could not turn away.

'No!' The pain in his voice should have brought tears to my eyes, but I could not weep for him. He drew his sword for the first time since Varryn left us.

I watched unblinking as he attacked my shield, disregarding his own safety. He used power repeatedly and unsuccessfully, until exhaustion claimed him. Then he sank to his knees and wept.

CHAPTER 36

Chane

Since the emperor demanded speed, we rode too fast for comfort, stopping only to change horses, eat and sleep. I was not invited to ride alongside the emperor and Ydrin, but still felt the strain. The escorting troop did not talk much to each other and not at all to me. Tharen would have told them to cheer up, emperor or no emperor. Lacking Cap Tharen, I accepted the prevailing mood and resigned myself to long, dreary days battling a fierce headwind, short comfortless stops and rushed meals. I had done it before. You did what you had to. Ydrin, likely unused to days in the saddle, would be more uncomfortable. As would Emperor Virreld himself, who had already ridden from Tormene to Althein with only one night's rest before the return journey. Except they undoubtedly had the wit to cushion their saddles and shield their buttocks. Belatedly, I did just that.

During an early change of horses, I asked one of the imperial troopers how long the journey would take.

'Twelve days, if we're lucky.'

'Hope we're lucky then.'

The soldier grunted. 'Usually are, when the emperor rides.'

'I imagine so.' I felt someone's eyes on me, checked the girth, walked the horse a few paces and tightened it a further notch.

Ydrin, accustomed or not, rode easily, as silent as the emperor, who had barely spoken since Althein. If Lady Kirra had agreed to come, he would never have considered me. Why had she refused? Whatever her feelings towards the emperor, surely the safety of her only surviving child must come first?

*   *   *

It was late when we finally reached Tormene. Cold and tired, I would have accepted a bed anywhere. Meanwhile, I stretched my aching back and awaited the emperor's orders.

'One night's delay will not change Varia's situation,' Ydrin said. 'We will all benefit from food, hot water and rest. Even you, my Lord.'

If the emperor responded, I missed it. He strode into the palace, leaving Ydrin and me to fend for ourselves.

'This way.'

A middle-aged man, wearing a heavily embroidered robe, waited at a set of high doors. He introduced himself as Sirus, and led us along a series of unheated passages. Dern's description of the palace was not an exaggeration. Though he had failed to convey the vastness of the palace, and that attendants or soldiers stood at every junction, landing and doorway. I lost count after the second score.

In other circumstances, I might have laughed at the size and splendour of the suite of rooms allotted to us. The bright wall hangings, thick rugs and gilded furniture made me feel acutely out of place. However, after the chilly passages and stairs, I was grateful for the warmth of the blazing fire in the hearth and the sight of a table laid for supper.

'Your chambers open directly from this hall,' Sirus said. 'Baths are ready and hot dishes are being brought. If you require anything else, let me know.'

'Thank you, Sirus.'

What more could we possibly want?

I was glad of the bath, but did not linger in it. After a hot and satisfying meal, I lay in a warmed bed and fell asleep immediately.

* * *

I woke early, dressed in the fresh clothes provided and was pulling on my boots when Ydrin came in.

'Breakfast is served. I'd advise you to eat, if you can. Lord Virreld will send for us soon. He is not a patient man.'

Any appetite I might have had dwindled at Ydrin's words. Nevertheless, I served myself from a couple of the covered dishes while I listened to him.

'I don't know what has driven Varia to this. Nor am I familiar with such a shield. If she has not cut herself off from all awareness of her surroundings, she may see you as a threat when you seek to break through her shield. Her five stones against yours?' He shook his head. 'The backlash would consume you both and anyone near you.'

I pushed my plate away. 'If power does not suffice, what will?'

'Power will suffice. You must find a different way to use it.'

A different way to use power? 'How?' Lady Kirra should have come. Varia would not harm her mother or grandfather. I had no idea how she would react to my interference.

'I wish I knew.'

I followed Ydrin, wondering which I should fear more, the emperor's wrath if I succeeded where he had failed, or the failure that would leave Lady Varia trapped in her own fire forever.

Sentries guarded the doors of the emperor's audience hall, but none followed us inside. A circle of lamps illuminated the imperial throne. Emperor Virreld sat there, a servant at his side, the same man who had accompanied him to Althein. His bodyguard? The chamber was vast and cold, its columns and hangings glittered disconcertingly in the lamplight. I turned my gaze to the emperor's left.

Every lamp dimmed in the dazzle of Lady Varia's fire. Its brilliance hurt my eyes, yet I could not look away. She stood erect within her blazing prison, her eyes wide open and her sword raised. To attack or defend?

I walked forward, made a full imperial obeisance before the throne and stood. The emperor did not acknowledge me, but when Ydrin made to follow suit, he lifted a hand to stop him. 'Not now.'

Ydrin bowed his head. 'As you will, my Lord.'

The emperor stared at me. 'Proceed.' His voice was as cold as his eyes.

I studied Lady Varia's fiery wall as I slowly circled her bright prison. Nothing I had been taught at Althein or learned by myself would help me here. After I had freed myself from the trap Lady Varia had set for me in Althein, I had taken her wall apart. This barrier was different, designed not to keep me in, but to keep me out. Or, more likely, to keep the emperor out. My mind refused to focus.

I remembered my own flaming prison – an instinctive reaction to protect me from the nikaryth Ydrin named Divasa.

My mind resisted, but only for a moment. Facing Lady Varia through the wall of flickering white flame, I drew my sword slowly, deliberately and held it crosswise in front of me. Swiftly, before my courage failed, before Ydrin could determine my intent and try to stop me, I held the possibility of success in my mind and stepped into Lady Varia's fire, dropped my blade and released my power. In the instant before my flesh crisped and blackened, eyes melted, bones splintered and blood boiled, I said, 'I am here.' Light, heat and pain enveloped me. I had not surrendered all power, one stone remained – Lady Kirra's gift kept me alive.

'You are not my father.'

In other circumstances I might have laughed. The flames were wearing away my resistance, destroying me. I seized Lady Varia's sword.

Someone screamed in agony. Knowledge, awareness, memory overwhelmed me. Darkness enveloped me.

Sparks flashed before my eyes, shooting stars. Anguish. Colours I did not recognise advanced and retreated. Voices spoke in languages I did not understand; voices I knew but could not name. I fought for air. Another voice spoke. For a moment as long as eternity, I did not recognise the words, then the slow drawl sharpened into comprehension. 'You have sought peace long enough. Now you will have it, if you so choose.'

Ahead, where the voice was, where I longed to go, was only shadow. Light shone behind me, and other voices called. I might ignore them, if I could make sufficient effort. They did not know my true name. I must listen to the one who did.

The effort exhausted me. Tears of grief and weakness soaked my face, scalded my skin. Torn between memories of my painful past and an unachievable future, I tried to call the name of the one I needed to pursue, but no sound came. A soft voice in my head impossibly used my true name, drawing me away from the path I desired. Unbearable agony ruptured my soul. I screamed, 'Don't leave me again!'

Silence.

The effort to speak, to move, brought a wave of agony that rendered me unconsciousness. Forced into part awareness I felt a touch of moisture on my face, coolness on my hands, numbness spreading over my limbs and sank into welcome oblivion.

* * *

I opened my eyes to darkness. Grief smothered me. I cried out.

A voice said, 'Rest. All is well.'

I attempted to speak intelligibly but the words formed by my mind were not those that escaped my lips. I made a supreme effort. 'Lady Kirra?'

A gentle touch held my hand; the blackness dissolved, and the world swam into focus. 'It is I. Do not concern yourself about anything. You have done enough.'

My unspoken questions tumbled over each other silently, my vision blurred again, and I closed my eyes in despair.

'Varia is safe, and you will live. All else can wait. Drink and sleep.'

Having no strength to resist, I swallowed obediently and drifted into sleep.

When I awoke the numbness had eased. Ydrin sat beside my bed. 'This is becoming a habit,' my voice barely a whisper.

Ydrin's lips twitched. 'Are you in pain?'

'No.'

'Good. You will be weak for several days, and it will take longer than that for full feeling to return to your hands. You must reconcile yourself to a stay in Tormene.'

'How long have I slept?'

'You remained caught between death and life for nigh on three weeks, while we struggled to heal you. Afterwards you slept for six days.'

'Why?' It was all I could manage.

'Varia insisted we persevere when common sense told us to give up. You did not want to live.'

I tried to ask, but Ydrin did not need prompting. 'We came close to losing her, until Kirra came. Then Varia recognised us. She is fully recovered. I shall bring her to see you soon.'

'No!' Whatever had happened to me in Lady Varia's fire, I could not bear to have it pored over. Betraying tears slid down my cheeks. I turned my face away from Ydrin's anxious gaze. 'Let me rest.'

'As you wish.'

* * *

I slept, woke, ate and slept again. At times Ydrin came and spoke to me. A day came when I was lifted from the bed to lie on a couch. Thereafter, each day, someone helped me to stand and walk. At first, as Ydrin had warned, my hands would not respond when I attempted even the simplest tasks. I could not name the day when I moved my left hand freely for the first time, but that was the beginning of a swifter recovery. My first shaky effort to feed myself was slow and exhausting, spilling more than reached my mouth. I washed, after a fashion. Within another week, I was able to take care of myself. I walked the length of the room and back, having no desire to explore further. Having no desires. What I wanted was out of my reach.

CHAPTER 37

Varia

I stood tireless, knowing neither hunger nor thirst. For all I knew, I might stand thus forever, while the world outside my self-imposed prison continued without me. I had lost count of the days. The empty chamber provided no distraction; when servants came in to clean or trim the lamps they walked behind me, as if they feared my staring eyes.

Footsteps indicated more than one visitor. Maybe my father had persuaded someone to assist him. If anyone from Althein knew how to free me, it would be Nyth, but I could not see her enduring such a journey at my father's bidding. She would have said, 'You caused this problem, Virreld, you must resolve it.' My laughter was silent.

I heard the murmur of voices, but the throne and those who stood before it were behind me.

Chane stepped into view. I had not expected it. My father knew my former doubts of him, and I had not shared Nyth's advice. Why would he bring Chane into this?

The answer was clear. If my mother had refused him, he was left with little alternative. Working with Ydrin and Kirra, my father *might* have been able to free me. With Chane, he *would* have succeeded, but he had chosen to force Chane to act alone. When Chane failed, he would be a convenient scapegoat, freeing the emperor of any blame for my fate. I controlled my fury. Blaming others was a coward's excuse.

'God in heaven, no!' No sound emerged from my mouth. I was too late; Chane had dropped his sword and was trapped in my fire. His lips moved, but I heard nothing. I spoke, but knew not what I said. He reached out, snatched my sword and collapsed.

So this is transference! He and I were linked: his memories mine. At last I knew the truth about him, the man I had known as Chane, and my lingering doubts vanished. He lay at my feet, unwilling to live, but not yet dead. I could not force him back to life, and I alone knew why. Blinking away a tear, I bent, retrieved my sword, had control of my power again and smothered the flames.

'*Gereyn.*'

He heard me, screamed, the link broke, and I collapsed.

CHAPTER 38

Chane

Ydrin paid me a brief farewell visit. He did not invite me to return to Althein with him and Lady Kirra, and I did not ask to join them. Three days later, two guardsmen entered my room without knocking and beckoned me. I walked slowly and unsteadily along endless passages and down two flights of stairs clutching the cold balustrade for support. Outside, I shivered in a keen wind.

'Here.' Dern raised a hand.

I closed my eyes in relief. The guardsmen re-entered the palace, slamming the door behind them. I stared after them.

'Don't just stand there. Do you want to freeze?' Dern helped me into a windproof coat.

Unused to speaking and unable to find words to express my gratitude, I gripped his hands.

'Can you stay in the saddle?'

I nodded. Dern boosted me up, took my reins and mounted. I did not protest. Clinging to the pommel, I gained my balance after a fashion, did not look back, nor consider where Dern might be taking me. One place was as good as another.

When we stopped, I lifted my leg over and slid into Dern's waiting arms. He half carried me into a barn, eased me onto a pile of straw and brought the horses inside. The horses' needs satisfied, he offered me a drink of water. I drank without spilling more than a few drops and lay back exhausted.

Dern hunkered down beside me. 'You wouldn't consider using this to heal yourself?' His gesture took in the scabbard on my belt.

I shook my head. 'I'm well enough.' The thought of using my sword again, for any purpose, revolted me.

'Well? You can barely stand up, you can't sit on a horse for more than an hour, and you look as if you're ninety years old!'

'Do I?' I felt it.

'Well, forty at least.' He brushed my hair away from my eyes 'I don't suppose you want to talk about it?'

'Talking doesn't change anything.'

'How would you know? You never talk about anything that's important to you! I've known you for six years, nearly seven, and I still don't know how you feel about–'

'About what, Dern? Being named Changeling, seeing people make the sign of evil against me or turn away rather than cross my path? Being thought of as a parasite on Duke Reys? Being forced into carrying and using this damned sword?'

'Are you planning to use it?'

'Not unless aryth attack.' I had no idea whether that was likely. After the initial questioning no one had talked about the Mondun battle. I understood Dern's frustration, but was far from comprehending what had happened to me and could explain nothing

He looked at me helplessly. 'But . . . It's Varia, isn't it? You're in love with her.'

'Don't be stupid, Dern. She's the emperor's heir.' Even if she were some farmer's daughter, she wouldn't want to marry someone like me.

'Are you sure that's a problem?'

I started to say something cutting, but stopped at the bewildered expression on his face. 'What did I say?'

He shrugged. 'I haven't the slightest idea. Does that happen often?'

'Only since I–'

'Have you asked Ydrin about it?'

'I wasn't in any state to question him at first. He left before I could.'

'Or the emperor ordered him to stay away from you.'

I hadn't thought of that, but it made sense. I attempted a smile. 'You didn't take to the emperor either?'

'I haven't met him. Perhaps that's just as well. He strikes me as a bully and a yellow-streaked coward, skulking in Tormene instead of leading the fight against karyth or aryth. Whatever you call them. He's probably afraid of you.'

'Afraid?' It seemed unlikely.

'Well, you can do better than him with that sword, can't you? If you tried, you could probably get Varia as well, and then you'd have the empire. That's probably why he ordered you out, before you could recover enough to threaten him.'

I stared at him. 'No.' I closed my eyes and did my best to sleep.

He let me rest.

By slow and exhausting stages, Dern led me towards Hawdale. As I began to take my own weight and sit upright in the saddle, he increased the length of the day's ride. When my horse threw a shoe, Dern walked until we found a village blacksmith. It cost us two days, but Dern did not seem to mind.

By the time we came to Bridgetown, I was strong enough to withstand Iylla's rush at me and her flood of tears. I kissed her and accepted Reys' embrace. Reys seemed relieved to have me home, but Iylla watched me as if I might melt on the spot under the warmth of her welcome. I came close to it. Later she gave me Arni to hold for a while. He enjoyed being tickled.

* * *

Nothing had changed, but nothing felt the same. It had to be me who'd changed. The first time someone called me Chane, I failed to recognise the name. When Dillard sneered at my swordplay, I disarmed him in one move and might have killed him, if Tharen had not dragged me away. Thereafter, the swordmaster banned me from general weapons training. Only Dern and Tharen were willing to practise with me. Tharen kept asking stupid questions such as, 'Where did you learn that?' or

'What the hell do you think you're doing?' It might have been a relief if he had given up on me too, but Cap was too stubborn. Impossible to answer questions aside, sword practice, with a blunted sword, relieved me of the unbearable weight of the other sword, the sword I hated, but could not now live without. Fighting with Tharen, no quarter given, or Dern, who knew my moves almost as well as I did, forced me to concentrate, instead of dwelling on the unattainable.

Allowing for my irregular sword practice, I had too much time on my hands. Reys had deemed me unfit for routine duties, or merely unreliable. I took to wandering Hawdale, with Dern's silent and unwanted company. Or, more rarely, alone, when I succeeded in evading his watchfulness, but always aware Reys' watchdog was on my trail. God alone knew how this affected Dern's courting. I could not bring myself to care. There was an empty space where my heart used to be, and I had too many problems of my own to sympathise with Dern's. As for Reys' concerns, they were so far outside my understanding I didn't consider them at all.

My greatest worry was confusion. Though I recognised faces, I could not put names to them, or the name I thought of conjured up a different face. Reys' steward was not who he should be. The cheerful young man, who constantly reminded me his name was Anas, occupied a separate office, not the steward's table in Reys' room. The housekeeper's face wore a smile, when she should have been careworn. And Marytha avoided me for no obvious reason.

Not long ago I had trouble recollecting anything. Now I remembered too much. Little of it related to Bridgetown, or anywhere in Hawdale, and even less made sense. Powerless to shut out the flood of recall, drowning in my past life and in images and words that meant nothing to me, I drifted uncaring. Sleepless by preference, because my dreams were overfull of faces I did not know, or knew only too well and had believed gone forever. If only that were so!

Iylla begged me to talk to Father Natram.

If I had trusted in priests, I might have done so, but I did not, and Swineford was a long way to drag Dern. Better to invent an errand in town, so Dern might meet Darie. Of necessity, their time together must be short. Dern had to escort me back before Reys became concerned enough to order a search party. Knowing how much Iylla worried about me, I smiled at her. 'I'll soon find time to ride to Swineford. In the meantime, I'm glad I'm home.' It felt like a lie.

In high summer the deepest shade in Iylla's garden was under the fig tree. Arni sat at Iylla's feet, scarcely visible under a wide-brimmed hat. As I watched, he shuffled backwards and held out his chubby arms. Iylla took his hands and drew him upright. 'You should marry and have children of your own.'

I blinked. While Reys insists on having me guarded night and day? Who do you want to inflict that duty on, my dear sister? Arni wobbled, and I caught him before he tumbled. 'He's going to keep you busy.'

'I should take on a younger nursemaid. Marytha is getting too old to run after him.'

It took me a moment to work out who Marytha was. 'She won't thank you for suggesting that.'

'I won't tell her why, but I must do something. She's determined to carry on as she always has.' She turned her son to face the pool. 'Let's go for a walk, Arni.

* * *

I was working in the armoury when Anas came. 'Duke Reys asks you to report to him immediately, Chane.'

The armourer asked, 'What's up, lad?'

Anas shook his head. 'That's the duke's business.'

I wiped my hands on a rag and set off for Reys' office. He drew me inside and closed the door. A one bar imperial army officer saluted.

'This is Captain Jud. He has a letter for you.'

Jud offered a scroll bearing a scarlet seal. I took it, frowning, but made no move to break the seal.

'Sir, I am bid to wait for an answer.'

No one sirred me. I glanced at Reys, but the captain had addressed me, not the duke. I turned the scroll, recognised the imperial seal and looked up to meet the messenger's eyes. Hot anger gripped me. I'd done the emperor's bidding once. Whatever he wants this time, I won't do it. 'No.'

'Sir?'

I ripped the thick paper in two and tossed it on the floor. Reys cried out in protest. The captain's grab missed. 'I have nothing to say to the emperor. I'm not his lackey.'

'Chane!' Reys stared at me as if I were a stranger. *Perhaps I am.*

The blood had drained from Captain Jud's face. 'Did I deliver such a message, sir, I should lose my head. I beg you to read it, before you consider refusal.' He retrieved the pieces and held them out, his hand shaking.

I stared at him in disbelief. *Even the emperor can't go around chopping off his captains' heads off at a whim.* 'Tell his imperial lordship I refuse to do whatever he asks of me.'

'Chane!' Reys' exclamation clashed with Captain Jud's, 'Sir!'

'Tell him.'

After a moment Jud's jaw tightened. 'I will deliver your message, sir, though I die for it.' He saluted, turned on his heel and marched out.

Reys seized my arm. 'What's wrong with you? You've condemned that man to death!'

'Have I? Consider, Reys, how would the emperor deal with me if I obeyed his summons?'

Reys shook his head. 'How should I know that? You tell us nothing. You're not the man I knew. You were always solitary, but you were never cruel.'

'I have learned a hard lesson, Reys. I treat the emperor as he treats me, with contempt.'

'And the innocent suffer?'

My gaze met his. 'Always.'

Reys turned from me and ran after the captain.

CHAPTER 39

Varia

It still felt strange to sit on the imperial throne, although I was all too aware that no one would tell me that I had no right to be there. For too long I had foolishly expected Varryn to return to take his rightful place. I sighed. He rested in peace while I carried the burden of the empire. Not alone naturally. On my father's departure to Althein his advisors became mine, and they have served me well, unlike some army officers. While my father ruled, my position as army commander gained general acceptance, being backed by his authority. Now his authority was mine, if only temporarily, and I needed to appoint a trustworthy commander, which was no easy choice.

Most junior captains were excellent. My senior officers, with the exception of Heksun, were another matter: overdue for retirement such as Turrard, or self-serving like Ludran.

No word of Ludran's fate had reached me since he left for the Ridges, several weeks later than I had intended. The supply train had neither returned nor reported. Ludran's death would have been no great loss, but silence from both his troop and the supply train augured ill. My men had been overstretched before I doubled border patrols and sent further troops to garrison critical points. As a result, I had to suspend patrols in the Ridges and investigation into Ludran's silence.

'My Lady, Captain Jud has returned.'

'I will see him in my office.' Heksun's experience was needed on the northern and eastern borders. For the time being I must remain commander, and trust my advisors and secretaries to run the empire, as much as possible.

Jud saluted. 'Lady Varia.'

I waved him to a seat. He ignored it, and my heart missed a beat. 'Master Chane refused me then.' I had expected it, but that did not make it any more acceptable.

'He did not open your letter.'

'Indeed?'

Jud, still rigidly at attention, met my eyes. 'He said, "No," tore the unopened letter in two and flung it aside.'

An answer of sorts. My father would have been furious. 'How did Duke Reys react to that?'

'The duke was horrified. He asked me to convey his apologies and explain that his wife's brother had not been the same since his return from Tormene. He gave me this letter.' He placed it on my desk.

I should have expected this, but Chane had not featured among my multiple concerns. 'Is he ill?'

'So Duke Reys said, but he did not look ill to me, Lady Varia.' Jud hesitated. 'He looked out of place, uncomfortable in his skin,'

'Ah. I understand.' Only too well. 'Captain Jud, you have performed the task entrusted to you, and I am grateful. You are not responsible for Master Chane's refusal.'

A little colour returned to his checks. 'Thank you, Lady Varia. May I ask–'

'You may not. You are dismissed.'

Jud saluted and withdrew. Duke Rey's letter confirmed Jud's message.

I must write to my grandfather, trusting that, while supervising the dispersal of raithen and ilen students from Althein, he might find time to advise Chane. However, despite my wishes, imperial matters intruded. I had an appointment with one of my advisors regarding the impact of aryth raids on cross-border trade and the consequent fall in imperial taxes.

CHAPTER 40

Chane

A shout half woke me. A solid body swept my legs from under me. Something clattered to the floor. A baby cried. A patter of bare feet. I stared up at Dern.

'Take him to his mother,' Dern said, 'and tell the duke he's needed here.'

The girl hesitated, and Dern snapped, 'Now!'

She ran to the cradle, lifted Arni and carried him away.

Dern used his blade to knock my sword further from my reach. 'Get up and keep your distance from that sword.'

'I meant him no harm.'

'Then why did you bring your sword?'

'I daren't leave it.'

Dern stared at me. 'Who do you imagine would touch it?'

I would not expose anyone to the dangers of the stones. Not even Dillard. Dern and Reys knew some of the risks of touching my blade, but others might not be as wise – as Faril's tale had made clear.

'Dern,' Reys said, 'take him to his room and lock him in.'

'Reys.' My voice was hoarse. 'Give me my sword.'

He shook his head. 'You must be parted from that blade, Chane. With it you endanger everyone in this house.'

I shivered. 'Reys, I beg you!'

'Take him!'

Dern gestured with his sword. I lurched to my feet and stumbled to the door. 'Sir,' Dern said, 'don't touch that sword. It would destroy you.'

'It has destroyed me.' Supporting myself with a hand on the wall, I struggled upstairs and collapsed on my bed, fingering the stone hanging from its chain. 'Don't tell Reys about this. I–'

'I won't. As long as you accept whatever restrictions the duke places on your freedom and make no move to regain your sword.' Dern retrieved the scabbard from the floor. 'I'm waiting for your answer, Chane. Don't make it worse for yourself.'

I frowned. 'You have my word. I won't oppose the duke's orders, or seek to take back my sword.' I paused. 'It could hardly be worse.'

Dern swallowed. 'I'll do what I can to make it easier for you.'

I shook my head. 'You don't want Reys to turn against you too.'

Dern closed the door and shot the outer bolt.

* * *

When the bolt was opened I stood, determined to accept my lot. I had expected Dern, but Reys came to deliver judgement in person. He closed the door behind him and met my gaze. 'I accept that you did not deliberately plan any harm to my son, but as long as you cannot control your actions I will not allow you wander freely. You may have the use of a practice sword during the day, provided you are guarded. At night, you will be locked in this chamber. You will not pass the gates. Is that clear?'

I clenched my fists behind my back. 'I understand, Duke Reys.' After he left me locked in my room, I considered my options. None! Without the sword, I had no hope of escape. If I had, what would I do, where could I go? Besides, I must consider Iylla's feelings. She was the closest I had to family. I did not want her to suffer as a result of my folly. If I had not offered my service to Lady Varia none of this would have happened.

It was two days before Dern came. 'Where have you been?'

He grinned, as if he had won the pot in the barracks card game. 'Cap Tharen gave me a couple of days off. Said you didn't need me to wet-nurse you. I've been talking to Darie.'

'Did she say yes?' Dern had been plucking up his courage for weeks.

'She did. We're to be married on Fourthday, and we've rented a cottage on Castle Hill.'

I clapped his back. 'My congratulations.'

'I'd like you be my groomsman.'

'Why?'

'God in Heaven, Chane! Don't act stupid. Because I want you to be. You're my friend, even if you have problems at present.'

Problems? That was one way of describing my difficulties. 'I'll gladly be your groomsman. If you're sure you want me.'

'Who else would I ask? How would I manage without you beside me?'

Better than with me. I couldn't manage anything anymore. The loss of my sword might have exacerbated my problems. Maybe not – I couldn't decide. At times I could think clearly and understand what was going on, but those lucid moments were few and, I feared, becoming rarer. Dreams haunted both my sleep and waking, familiar faces appeared in unfamiliar settings, speech became impossible, and my hearing turned words into nonsense. As Dern's groomsman I would not be required to speak. I just needed to stand at Dern's side, as his friend. 'I can do that.'

Dern blinked. 'Good. I have to get myself something halfway decent to wear. It won't do to be the scruffiest man at my own wedding.'

I laughed. 'No fear of that. Dillard will take that prize.'

'Did I invite him? Cuff me for a fool! I did. I told the duke "everyone".'

'Cap will sort Dillard out.'

'Of course he will. You'll keep me from drinking too much, won't you?'

'If I can.' I must check my wardrobe too. I could not remember the last time I had needed to wear my best clothes.

*   *   *

I could not remember. Something was happening today, but the idea fled when I tried to concentrate. Dozens of thoughts occupied my mind, toing and froing, and making no sense whatsoever. I was halfway down the back stairs when Holin came up. 'Aren't you dressed yet? Get a move on, Chane. It's the bride that's supposed to be late, not the groomsman!'

I did not recall accepting a guest invitation to a wedding, nor could I think who might have asked Holin to be his groomsman. I changed into the clothes Holin took from my wardrobe, and he looked me over.

'Comb your hair. You could do with a shave, but there's no time for that. We have to rush. Come on!' He grabbed my arm and dragged me downstairs, through the crowds in the courtyard, to Dern's side. 'Not one of his better days,' he whispered.

Dern drew me closer. 'Just stand there.'

A rosy-cheeked woman waved, and Dern waved back. Who was she? It was probably better not to ask. In any event, I was probably dreaming. Unable to understand why everyone was looking at me and Dern, and uncomfortable with the stares, I stepped back, slipped away through the crowd, found a quiet space and sat on a wooden bench. I had no idea where I was or what was happening, knowing only I could not bear to be surrounded by people. Being alone didn't help, though it was cool in the shade.

'It's cooler in the shade,' someone said.

Did I imagine that too?

'Best you stay seated. You don't want to overdo it in this heat. Hope a breeze gets up later.'

A hand on my arm. I looked up. 'Who are you?'

'Don't worry about it, lad. We'll just sit here until the ceremony's over and the crowds have gone. I don't like all them folk hemming me in either.'

It was easiest to do as the voice advised.

* * *

I stared at Dern. 'Did I miss the wedding? I'm sorry.' I wouldn't have done that for the world. But I did. The sympathy in Dern's eyes was hard to face.

'I know. You couldn't help it. It's all right. Cap kept you company, didn't he?'

Did he? 'I'm sorry he missed the wedding because of me.'

Dern laughed. 'He didn't miss anything that mattered, since he brought you back in time for the feast. I hope your hangover was less than his.'

I didn't remember any of that. What was happening to me? Although the thought sickened me, perhaps I should persuade Reys to return my sword.

I left his office and took the shortest route to the stables. Clipped the reins to the bridle, decided not to bother with a saddle and led the roan outside. Vaulted on and pressed my heels to his flanks. I ignored shouts to stop, but when I came to the gates, they were closed against me. The guards neither acknowledged me nor moved to open the gates. I turned the roan, and hands seized the bridle. The horse pecked, recovered, reared and I fell off. I rolled over, scrambled to my feet and drew my blunted practice sword. Dern and Tharen stood between me and the roan, their unblunted swords raised.

Dern's face was pale. 'The duke's orders haven't changed.'

'He would rather I left.'

Dern's blade still pointed at me. 'That's not what he told me.'

'Ah.' I lowered the practice sword and slid it into my scabbard. 'Will you let me go to Swineford? I'll be back before dusk.'

'Provided you leave that sword behind. I can't let you take a horse, so I won't hold you to a return by sunset.'

I unbuckled my sword belt and held it out, feeling naked without it.

'Go.' Dern took the belt and turned away, leaving Tharen to collect the roan, now thoroughly spooked.

The track leading to Swineford was well maintained. On foot, it would take me nearly two hours. The uphill return might take me more than half as long again. I sighed. Even if I did not linger in Swineford, it would be dark before I had covered half the return journey. I took no notice of clopping hooves behind me. It was probably my mind playing tricks again.

* * *

The sky was cloudy, but the graveyard was light enough for me to make out the lettering on the headstone. *Sulyth and Arnull. Reunited.*

I knelt at the grave, remembering Arnull's kindness to a frightened and bewildered boy.

When I came to myself again, darkness had fallen. Stiff and hungry, I stood and walked towards the church, thinking to pray for Arnull's soul. A voice spoke from the shadows. 'Come inside, son, and rest.'

I hesitated. 'Good evening, Father. I'm sorry, I don't know your name.'

'It's Natram. You must be Chane.'

Heat flooded my body. No! But denial came too late; I had accepted the name long ago, in default of better. Or worse. 'I suppose I must.' The priest would think me a fool. He would be right. 'I have prayers to say yet.'

'Do you believe God hears only those who are weary and hungry? I've enough supper to share. You may say your prayers later. God will surely listen.'

I followed him to the tiny cottage, its door open to welcome me. Father Natram, a much younger man than the strict traditionalist who had made the few years of my regular church attendance a misery and afterwards condemned my absence. 'Your predecessor would not have welcomed me.'

He smiled. 'Sit and eat. Don't trouble yourself with such things. We're all God's servants, but service may take many forms. I welcome everyone to God's house and to mine.'

I took a stool at the small table. Father Natram served me a generous share of stew. I ate hungrily, and wiped my dish clean with the last crust of fresh bread. Only then noticing the poverty of the one-roomed dwelling.

The priest followed my gaze. 'It suffices me.'

'You will be cold in winter.'

'I have an arrangement with Stonn. He lets me sleep in the attic above the bakehouse in the coldest months, and I don't insist he comes to church every week.'

'Thank you for sharing your supper with me, Father. I'll pray now.'

I closed the church door behind me and knelt. For the first time, I did not feel an intruder here. Afterwards, my return walk passed swiftly, though the slopes took their toll on my underused muscles and rendered me short of breath.

Dern waited at the gate. 'You took your time.'

'You should have granted me the horse if you wanted me to move faster.'

'You've missed supper.'

'I ate with the new priest.'

'New? He replaced the old man three summers ago and comes regularly to Bridgetown. Surely you have seen him before today?'

'I don't think so.'

Tharen drew his horse to a halt alongside and slipped from his saddle. 'If you've nothing better to do, Dern, you can take this fellow to the stable. Had a good walk, lad?'

I nodded. That night, for the first time in weeks, my sleep was unbroken and I woke refreshed.

* * *

It was a waking dream, something now common, but despite their frequency I could not become used to them. Iylla spoke to me in a language I did not know and could make no sense of. When I answered, I spoke my own tongue, but she shook her head in bewilderment. 'What's wrong, Chane? Why are you doing this?'

'Do you imagine I have a choice?' My voice rang out in the silent passage. I was alone. Again.

My sword drew me, despite my determination to avoid it, and I followed its tug like a hound on a scent, stopping outside Reys' chamber. I felt its presence in the locked chest. The lock could be easily broken. I shook my head, disgusted with myself. Reys had asked for my oath, and I had given it. I think I remember giving it though I could not trust my memories.

I crossed the passage and entered Arni's nursery. The child lay in his crib, kicking his legs. I leaned over and picked him up. He was heavy, cold, not breathing. I stared at him in shock and horror. He gurgled.

'Master Chane, he is well. Give him to me.' Marytha took the squirming infant from my unresisting hands.

I retreated to the passage. Marytha closed the door against me and shot the inner bolt home. Leaning against the wall, I closed my eyes and counted to ten while I strove to steady my breathing. Achieving a measure of calm, I opened my eyes, straightened up and walked carefully along the passage and down the stairs.

Partway down, I heard music. The tune I knew, well enough to pluck the notes myself, but the singer was not the voice I remembered. This wasn't real. It couldn't be. I sank to the step and covered my ears, but the tune played on in my mind. Each note sounded like a death knell. Unable to bear it any longer, I ran down the remaining steps, and into Reys' smaller reception room.

CHAPTER 41

Chane

A woman was playing the lute. Reys, seated next to Iylla, tapped his foot to the beat, and Iylla smiled. The lute player seemed familiar, but I could not name her.

She's not real. I–

The woman looked up, stilled the strings, laid the lute down and walked towards me. Her eyes burned into mine. Before I realised what she intended, she struck me backhanded across the face. I staggered back, barely saving myself from falling.

'That for Captain Jud. What have you to say for yourself?'

I found it difficult to think. A woman playing an instrument – Lady Kirra. No. A Vethian travelling singer – absolutely not. She had said, 'Captain Jud.' An imperial letter. My mind cleared. 'I have no excuses, Lady – I sought her name – Varia.'

'None? Who are you?'

I felt the pulse beating in my throat. I am . . . Dern was suddenly close to me, his expression anxious.

'I'm waiting,' Varia said sharply, 'for your answer.'

In the shelter of Reys' arm, Iylla buried her face in his shoulder. Reys, like Dern, was watching me.

My legs could not bear my weight any longer. I sank to the floor, and bowed my head. After taking several shallow breaths, I raised my head and met Varia's eyes again. Whatever she wanted of me, I would have no part in it. The thought sounded familiar.

'Stand up.'

My efforts achieved nothing, and Dern bent to help me.

'Leave him, Dern.' Her voice was cold.

'I can't.' I lowered my head again.

'You cannot lift yourself from the filth of the pigsty, Gereyn, Falk's son? You did so, at one time. What are you now, Gereyn, Falk's son?'

Iylla gasped, a small sound submerged in the echoes of Varia's question.

I lifted the terrible weight of my head. Every word was effort. 'You know so much, Lady. Do not ask me to speak.'

'Why? Are you ashamed?' She flung her questions at me like throwing stars.

I flinched. In the long pause that followed I fought to find words that had any meaning. 'Yes, I'm ashamed.'

Ashamed of not knowing my name, my past. Ashamed of living a lie. Ashamed of living.

She waited for me to continue, but I could not. I allowed my head to sink once more.

Varia stepped closer and used the tip of her sheathed sword to force my head back. 'Look at me!'

Dern seized her arm. 'Enough, Kadron!'

She shook him off. 'Don't you want to know the truth, the truth your friend has kept from you all these years?' She turned towards Reys and Iylla. 'Don't you?'

Reys answered her. 'I do.'

Iylla's tearful gaze rested on me. 'She gave you a name, brother. Is it yours?'

I shook my head, unable to come up with a sensible answer. If I had once possessed a name, it belonged to a former life, a life I could not, would not, remember. Disregarded tears flowed down my cheeks.

Iylla sobbed, and I looked up. She didn't deserve to pay the price for what I had done, or left undone.

'My dear brother.'

'Look at me.' Varia's voice had softened.

Reluctantly, I drew strength from the stone touching my skin and met her gaze.

She was smiling. 'Since we first met, you have sought to deny that you have power. When you had a choice, you avoided its use.' She shook her head. 'Such denial is not possible. Healer-defender is what you are and always will be.' She frowned. 'What you did to Captain Jud was unforgivable. Tell me why I should pardon you.'

Why was it her place to absolve me of guilt? As for Jud . . . I remembered the captain's protest. 'What happened to him?' He did not deserve to die because of me.

Her face was stern, as if she had never smiled. 'He lives.'

Who lives? My thoughts whirled. Exhaustion hovered, waiting to claim me. I struggled to recover a thread of understanding. The woman – Lady Varia – played music that had been created for me. She knew what I thought I had buried irretrievably deep.

'How–' I did not recognise the word. My effort to speak clearly took almost all my feeble strength. 'How could you know?'

'Transference.'

I shook my head. 'That's impossible.' I was careful.

'At Mondun, you took every precaution. However, at Tormene you did not shield yourself because you had to choose between protecting yourself and releasing me. You chose to save me because you planned to die. I was not able to shield myself at time.' Her smile was wry. 'I might have come here sooner, but I had my own troubles.'

I would not argue with her. It would be like arguing with the wind, or with – the name would not come to me – and as pointless. She had all the answers. 'You were affected by transference, Lady?' I had remembered her status, imperial heir.

'I was. Duke Reys, you must return his sword. Without it he will die.'

No! 'I don't want–'

'Your wishes are not paramount now, Gereyn.' Ydrin spoke from behind me. 'Dern, bring Chane's sword. Do not touch any part directly.'

As Dern's footsteps retreated along the passage, Varia drew her sword and approached me. I touched my one remaining stone, and attempted to shield myself. Her power swept over me, invaded me, supported my weakened body, cleared my vision and soothed my bewildered mind. I stood.

Dern returned, holding my sword gingerly by its cloth-wrapped scabbard. His eyes flicked to Varia, and she nodded.

I thought that Varia might have arranged a substitute, but I recognised my sword and closed my fingers around the hilt. The scabbard fell away and strength flooded my body as power raced through my nerves. Varia's presence receded.

Ydrin walked forward to face me. 'I have to ask your forgiveness. I misled you, allowing you to believe you could learn to control your power within a few weeks. Rarely does a student achieve full control in less than seven years. Never, in our experience, has anyone who comes to power in mature years survived the learning. Varia warned me. I should have heeded her.'

'Don't blame yourself, Ydrin. I was equally at fault. If I had taken personal charge of his training, I might have understood sooner. None of us suspected he had already been taught, not as you or I were taught, but taught well.

'Gereyn, if I could choose for you, I would have you stay here to regain your strength and be reminded of your life here. Then, in Althein, you would learn which of your memories are not yours, but acquired by transference. I urge you to take that course, but I will not attempt to force you.

When your mind is clear you will be able to decide what you wish to do.'

'Lady Varia,' Reys broke in, the strain showing in his face and his voice. 'It seems that both you and Master Ydrin know all there is to know about Chane. Can he be healed? Must he then remain in Althein to study for seven years?'

'If he wishes,' Ydrin said.

'Lady?'

Iylla, a tremulous smile on her tear-stained face, closed the gap between us, while Varia hesitated. 'My brother, I have asked many things of you. You refused all, and you were right to do so, to choose your own path. You have given me my life and that of my son, and I'm grateful. I will not ask you to take Lady Varia's advice for my sake, but I would have you do so for your own. I want you to be whole and content. I beg you, think carefully before you choose otherwise.'

I looked round at the expectant faces. Dern and Iylla, at least, wished me well. So did Reys, but he would always place his wife and son's safety first. Ydrin would side with Varia, and she . . . Could I trust her? I did not know her – Kadron, imperial heir, commander of the imperial army – she had too many names, too many faces.

I did not wish to return to Althein, but my present life was unsupportable. "Whole and content" sounded good. 'I will take your advice, Lady Varia.'

If she had been able to overcome the effects of transference, perhaps I might do the same, and then I could leave Althein. It did not matter where I went, as long as my destination was outside the empire, beyond the emperor's reach.

CHAPTER 42

Chane/Gereyn

I lay on my bed, fingers resting lightly on my sword hilt, trying to make sense of Varia's revelations. It did not feel right to use her title. I had no need to draw power, but the closeness of my sword was strangely comforting. Several nights of undisturbed and dreamless sleep had restored me somewhat. My body was returning to normal, but my mind was still confused. Varia was right about that at least.

Iylla tapped on the door and came in without waiting for a response. She took my free hand in hers and sat on the bed.

'It's been a long time since you sat there,' I said.

She giggled. 'Father didn't approve. He said it was "unladylike behaviour".'

'It probably was, but I liked it.'

'So did I.'

As Iylla chatted about Duke Arnull, I relaxed and fell asleep.

Every day either Reys or Dern would appear, eager to remind me of past events. Dern repeated "she said" so often I stopped listening.

By the time I was able to stand, talk and understand the replies, Varia had left Hawdale.

I sat in the garden, listening to Iylla and trying to concentrate. I was still uncertain of my identity and the reality of my recollections. Perhaps renewed familiarity with my past would help, as Varia had claimed. At the moment, I was more concerned about Marytha, who sat facing me, her capable hands clutched a large rolling pin, and her expression challenged me to make a move towards Iylla. It would have frightened off anyone who was so tempted.

Iylla talked about life before her mother's death and her father's grief and loneliness afterwards. When she came to the story of the injured boy her father had brought home, I did not recognise myself.

Marytha laid the rolling pin on her ample lap and leaned forward. 'You were burned so badly, we thought you'd never heal, but you did, with nary a scar to be seen.' She turned to Iylla. 'Do you remember the first time you met him? You said you'd always wanted a sister, and your father had brought you a brother. Duke Arnull wasn't going to turn him out after that.'

'I remember.' Iylla's gaze softened.

The rolling pin rolled to the ground where it lay between Marytha's feet, waiting for me to stir.

I ignored it, caught up in the tale. 'I couldn't understand either of you at first, but he was very patient with me. I think he enjoyed helping me learn.'

'Father said you must have come from a long way away, where they speak a different language. Your accent was strange, but I scarcely notice it now.'

A long way away. There was a ship.

* * *

Someone always wanted to talk to me. The more they reminded me of the past, the more some of my thoughts – or memories – made sense. I spent hours in the armoury, working on repairing an old plated jacket.

'You started that a long time ago,' the armourer said. 'Best you finish it. It'll do for practice sessions if nothing else.'

I nodded, rather than shout a reply above constant discordant hammering.

I sparred with Cap Tharen who reminisced about old practice sessions and drunken evenings. 'You always limited your drinking. Scared of Dillard in his cups?'

'Scared of what I might do to him if he pushed me too far.'

'Ah. Thought that might be it. He never did know when to keep his mouth shut, drunk or sober. You were the opposite, and still are.'

Maybe, but at least I know who my friends are. 'You've been a good friend to me, Cap.'

Tharen clapped my shoulder. 'You've given me less trouble than many, lad.'

Dern invited me to the cottage on Castle Hill, where Darie fed me as if I were starving. She told me Zina had just given birth to twins. 'There's no doubt of their father this time.' She laughed and left me alone with Dern who talked about old battles and more recent ones.

Reys quietly described his courtship of Iylla and the early days of their marriage when they were still confident of having children. Hesitating, he spoke of the miscarriages, his fears for Iylla's life, and the bitter decision to set aside any thought of trying to conceive an heir. Partway through relating his meeting with Sarrech and my warning, Reys stopped to ask Dern to join us. Dern told the events of that night, from Kadron's songs to my reaction to Sarrech's attempted seduction, and Kadron's intervention.

Dern dismissed, Reys said, 'We came so close to losing you that night.'

I had forgotten how much he cared. When Iylla had told me Reys wanted to marry her, she had said, 'He wants you to be his brother.'

Reys reached out, and I clasped his hand.

* * *

Dern said, 'Kadron released me from that damned oath. She told me I might as well talk, since you know everything she would prefer to remain unspoken.' He laughed. 'She should have forced an oath from you too.'

I would have said nothing, with or without an oath. Dern talked about our journey to the cursed wood, Kei and the breakneck escape. And his travels with Kadron. 'I hope Wilem and the others reached Althein safely. Perhaps you could ask, when you're there.' His return to Bridgetown. 'I had a hard time answering the duke's questions with that damned oath ready to bite me at every slip.' His discovery that Zina had married. 'I don't know what she thought to gain by naming you the father of her child.'

I shook my head. 'I might have been fool enough to marry her, if she'd behaved differently.' I smiled ruefully, 'She had a lucky escape. By the time I came back, it was too late.'

Dern play-punched my shoulder. 'It isn't too late to find someone else.' He described the breeches-wetting, heart-stopping, soaring hop to Mondun, what had happened there and started on his ride back to Bridgetown accompanied by two of Jonnan's men and a boy called Whistler.

'Whistler? Is he still here?'

'He is, but he has a new name. Horsemaster Riko's taken him on and insisted he change his name.'

'To what?'

Dern grinned. 'He chose "Horsey", but Riko wouldn't hear of it. They eventually agreed on Tad.'

If only it were that easy. 'What happened?'

'Huh?'

'You said it was a nightmare ride.'

'Oh, not much. We were only attacked by two karyth. I finished one off, Madh got the other and Whistler's pony kicked Blackie.'

* * *

There were still lapses, times when I could make no sense of what was happening, could not recognise faces or names, or understand speech, but they were less frequent than before. I had not dreamed, awake or asleep, for weeks.

'Lady Varia asked me to assist you in your journey to Althein, Gereyn,' Reys said. 'She left two men here in case

Dern doesn't want to leave his wife for so long. Dern has vouched for them.'

I felt a throbbing behind my left eye. 'Is Dern wed?'

'He is, and I prefer to keep him here. The last time I sent him off with you, he was missing for more than 12 weeks. That's no way to start a marriage.'

I could not summon a protest. 'I will go to Althein, if these two know the way.'

'Blackie tells me Madh can find Althein.'

'Mad?' A madman to nurse a madman. That fits.

'He's a tribesman who tells me his name means "swift". When do you want to leave?'

'Now' was probably not the best reply, even if Reys was keen to see the back of me. 'Tomorrow?'

'Tomorrow it is.'

*   *   *

Without Dern's help, I would never have been ready. He packed my gear for me, with no fuss and little chatter. Introduced to Blackie and Madh as Gereyn, I looked round to see who Gereyn was. Even when I remembered, the name did not belong to me, though it seemed to have stuck. As Changeling had – even Arnull's wrath had only reduced that to Chane. Yet another reason to resent Varia's interference. But I could not summon up the energy to resent anything.

At some point I apologised to Dern for missing his wedding. 'I've made a mess of so many things. You were probably better off without me there. I'd only have made a fool of myself.'

Dern grinned. 'Don't worry about it. Duke Reys stood in for you.'

'What do you mean?'

'Never mind. I'm shackled to Darie now. It's too late to have second thoughts.' He hesitated. 'Have you seen how the colt is growing?'

'What colt?'

Dern looked at me as if I'd said something that didn't make sense. Did I? Again?

'Come and see him.'

The colt was tall and leggy. He came over to Dern, but shied away from me. 'He has more sense than you.'

'I hope not! Don't say that to Darie. She'd be mortified. He's easily spooked, but I'm hoping he'll learn sense from his dam. His sire's as solid as a rock, and this fellow seems to take after him in height.'

I called the foal softly. He came and allowed me to stroke him, flung himself away again and raced to his dam and back, stopping just out of reach. 'He's a tease. He just wants a treat.'

'He'll get one. He knows I'm a soft touch.' The colt took a piece of apple and moved aside as his dam pushed forward. 'She's learnt to beg. Lady Iylla spoils her.'

'Iylla?' I could not see a connection between Iylla and the black mare. My sister did not ride very often and when she did, her mount was a placid elderly gelding.

'She's been riding her almost every day.' Dern avoided my eyes, his cheeks flushed. 'Lady Varia gave the mare to Lady Iylla and the foal to me.' He shrugged. 'I suppose she thought the dun was mine.'

'Or the foal's your wages.' I laughed.

'If he is, you were wrong about her.'

What did I say? 'Maybe she pays her debts.' I looked round. 'My escort will be waiting. I'd better go.'

Dern took my hand. 'Good luck to you, Gereyn. Stay safe.'

I returned Dern's clasp. Perhaps that would be possible at Althein.

* * *

Madh and Blackie made the long journey bearable and treated me as a long-standing friend, or brother. I was sorry to say farewell to them.

In Althein, as before, I soon lost track of time. With no worries, days and nights passed unmarked. Leaves changed colour in the trees around my solitude. Birds gathered on high branches. I watched until the leaves began to fall and the birds departed. It was time for me to move too. I wandered, finding my way across unguarded bridges, past empty lodgings. Had everyone left, like the birds? It was the first question I had asked since Lenathe's warning, and no one came to answer it.

I followed the sound of laughter and came to a small lodging in a wide grassy clearing. In the tiny garden, three people sat playing at four-stones: a dark-haired boy, a woman who might be the boy's grandmother and a grey-haired man. I did not know them, although I recognised something familiar about the woman.

She came to me, took my hands in hers and kissed me. 'You are welcome here, Gereyn. Now and always. Nyth awaits you. I must not keep you from her.' She turned back to the boy.

The man clasped my hands. 'Forgive me, Gereyn.'

'I don't know you, sir. If there was ever reason for you to need my forgiveness, I have forgotten it.'

'Perhaps you have. It may come back to you. I would not have ill feeling between us. I beg you, forgive me.'

I glanced at the boy, tugging at the lady's sleeve and whispering. 'I'm sorry. I'm keeping you from your game.' I looked into the man's face. 'Whatever you did, I forgive you.'

The man's fingers tightened on mine. 'Thank you. Follow that path.' He pointed. 'You will find Nyth.'

'Or she will find you.' The lady laughed. Her mirth was infectious, and I laughed with her.

'Farewell.' When I looked back, the three had resumed their game.

CHAPTER 43

Gereyn

The path wound through woods, grassland and reed-choked fen. By the time I came to the shore, I had almost given up hope of finding Nyth. Ahead, breeze rippled a wide expanse of water. I scanned the shoreline, saw a boy and hailed him. The boy pulled his coracle into the reeds and waved. Then he shouldered a bag and disappeared. In a former life I might have lost my temper, muttered curses or given up my search for Nyth. Instead I sat on a fallen tree trunk and waited.

A rustling in the reeds announced the boy's return. A faint fishy odour clung to him. 'Sorry. I couldn't keep Nyth waiting.'

'Nyth lives nearby, does she?'

'Over there.' The boy waved a hand to his left, and the fish smell wafted closer. 'She lets me use her coracle, and I give her half my catch.' He grinned. 'If you talk to her nicely, she might share a fish or two with you.'

'Thanks for the tip. I'll try it.'

With fishy wave, the boy vanished into the reeds before I could ask his name.

Without his help, I would have giving up searching long before I found Nyth's hut. Hidden in the reeds, a short distance from the coracle, invisible from the path and from most of the shore.

A tiny woman sat cross-legged in front of her hut, sewing. As I approached, she looked up and stood to greet me. 'You're welcome here, Gereyn.'

It seemed appropriate that she knew my name. 'Thank you for your welcome, Mistress Nyth.'

Her laugh seemed surprisingly deep for her slight frame. 'No one calls me "Mistress". Some of my former students like to use "Aunt" or "Grandmother". You may call me Nyth.'

'Thank you, Nyth.' Questions hovered in my mind, just of reach, but I had learned not to seek them out. I studied her. Her light brown hair, in a thick braid, showed no hint of grey, and her small heart-shaped face was almost wrinkle free, except for laughter lines. Yet I knew – from Varia's memories – that guesses of her age ranged from ninety-eight to a hundred and twenty-seven.

'You took your time coming. I've been expecting you all my life. Sit.'

Her statement sounded an exaggeration, a falsehood, an impossibility, but her face and her voice held truth. I inclined my head and sat.

Nyth took up her sewing again. For a moment, instead of an old lady, I saw Iylla in her sewing room. It had been my sister's favourite occupation, but now ... I could not follow the thought and abandoned it.

'No matter. You are here now.'

Since her comment did not require an answer, I did not struggle to find one.

'Life is a struggle. If you've learned that at your age, you have the beginnings of wisdom.'

'What is my age?'

'Tush, child. What does that matter? Watch the sky, feel the wind, breathe in the smell of these fine fish and look forward to the taste of them.'

'I do.'

She tucked her needle into the fabric and took my hand in both of hers. 'The touch of another human. We miss it when we don't have it. You need us. Don't turn us away.'

Tears formed in my eyes. I swallowed, but could not find an answer. Nyth talked on, explaining some of her daily occupations: collecting reeds and rushes, gathering eggs, grain and seeds and tickling fish.

'The young ones help when they're free. They imagine I'm too old to fend for myself. I never turn them away, even the clumsy ones.'

'I met a boy.'

'Leoric.' She smiled. 'He's a good boy, who sees further than many do. Would you like to hear about him?'

The name sounded familiar. 'From Westaven. Dern told me a little.' I closed my hand gently over Nyth's delicate bones. 'Tell me more.'

I listened while she spoke of Westaven, a prosperous fishing village on the western coast of the Outer Sea. 'Every sea has its hazards, and all seamen know the local currents and the winds, but the Outer Sea keeps its secrets well and even experienced sailors make mistakes. Wilem came from Northaven, further along the coast. There was some trade between the coastal villages, but little reason to linger in a strange port until young Wilem was washed overboard. The current cast him on the shore at Westaven where the villagers cared for him. He worked to pay off his debt and eventually decided to stay.'

Nyth told Wilem's story. His marriage, the birth of a son and daughter. The dwindling numbers at Westaven, messages sent to other ports, hope slowly fading.

I might have listened all day, but she stood. 'How good are you at scaling and gutting fish?'

'I've no idea.' My stomach rumbled. 'I'll try.'

I watched her expert handling of the knife and did my best, but my first attempt was messy.

Nyth chuckled. 'You have a steady hand, but you need practice. Take care of the rest while I set the fire.'

A flap of wings drew my eyes in time to see her light the fire by looking at it. The diver landed beside the fish. Nyth shooed it way empty-beaked.

'You could have let him have the guts.'

'If I start feeding birds, they'll plague the life out of me.' She winked. 'Never seen a fire lit like that before?'

'I don't know.'

'Let it go, boy. It will come when it's ready. Right now the fish is more important.'

Visiting Nyth, listening to her stories and eating with her became a habit. An undemanding way to pass the day. A reason not to think too much.

When I offered to help with her chores, she thumped her hands against her hips and glared at me. 'What have you been doing?'

'Nothing much, except learning how to scale, gut and fillet fish. I could–'

'Nothing much, is it? After all my efforts, you think preparing fish for cooking is more important than learning?'

'Learning?'

'Yes, young man, learning. That's why you are here, for me to tell you all you need to know. So let's have no more talk of chores!'

Iylla's housekeeper, used to dish out that kind of scolding, and there was only one safe response. 'As you will, Nyth.'

'As I will. Humph! As I will, indeed.'

* * *

Nyth prattled on about the imperial family: Virreld's marriage to Kirra and the three children born to them. 'Varryn bold, but easily riled, Invar impetuous, Varia thoughtful.' Their training at Tormene, Althein and, in Varia's case, with the army.

'Why the army?'

'Why not? Varryn was his father's heir, destined to be emperor. Invar, bless him, tried hard, but would never have made a soldier, still less led men into battle. Do you believe a woman cannot take a man's role?'

My memories, Varia's memories, told me how she had done it, but I was still amazed that the soldiers under her command had accepted it.

'Better a capable woman than a fool of a man.' Nyth mentioned Garanth's allegiance to Varryn, which led her on to Varryn's disputes with his father and his departure from Tormene.

Varia told us, when she was Kadron. She wept, her face averted, but Garanth noticed.

Nyth introduced me to Leoric and to Wilem, who talked about Varryn's life in Westaven, Varryn's wife's death and his departure from Westaven with his son and brother-in-law.

Dern had told me. He would be glad to know they were safe here.

The grey-haired man came. Nyth did not name him. He did not volunteer his name, and I did not ask. He spoke of Invar's loss, and Varia's long and hopeless search for Varryn.

He loved them. A close friend, I suppose.

Every tale cleared more confusion, separated my memories from Varia's and convinced me that coming to Althein was the right decision.

'You've done the impossible, Nyth. Now I can leave.'

Her face creased in faint lines of age. 'I've done nothing, except work on your later memories. What of your early ones, those you are determined to forget? In your now perfectly assembled thoughts, where is Gereyn, the child and the youth?'

Nowhere. He does not exist.

'No one comes to this world almost a man, Gereyn. Until you know the truth, you will not be whole. Come back to me when you are ready to be healed.'

I am healed. The thought was instinctive, but deep within, where I rarely looked, I knew otherwise.

* * *

Nyth was not at home. Her coracle lay in the reeds as usual, and her sewing, fishing lines and knives lay in their places, waiting for her return. I waited too, but she didn't come. Perhaps she was sick. A chill passed through me, as if someone I loved had died. Where are you Nyth?

Silence.

I wandered along the empty shore beyond her hut, my boots leaving shallow tracks in the mud Why had I never come this way before? Because Nyth had always been there to talk to. I needed her to complete my healing, to tell me who I was. Someone – Lady Kirra – had asked me why I found self-healing so difficult. She had claimed I did not love myself enough. How could I love myself when I didn't know who I was?

I followed the faint track blindly, oblivious of the encroaching trees until I stumbled over a root. Recovering my balance, I looked round. I had turned away from open water and reeds. A narrow stream flowed past me. Behind me and on each side the trees had closed in. Ahead, sunlight sparkled. I walked on.

The trees parted, and I stood in sunshine. At first, overcome by its brightness, I could see nothing else, but I felt it and shivered. Something to do with power, but there was nothing to fear. Nyth wanted me to come here.

'As you have proved, Gereyn.'

For the first time, I had an inkling that the name Varia had given me had meaning. I did not yet know what it meant.

Nyth stood beside a fallen column. Upright it would have been more than twice my height. The stone had been uprooted, flung aside and scorched with fire. Angular writing covered its sloping sides. This was what had drawn me.

My heart missed a beat. 'This was done recently.'

Nyth nodded. 'The dark moon before you came to us.'

'Halaryth.'

'Or nikaryth,' she said calmly, as if neither were of great importance.

I stepped closer to the stone. Here and there, in the formation of the characters, small dents pocked the column's face. Stones of power. 'How many did they take?'

'None.'

I swung round. 'None?'

'Althein has ever been vulnerable. Secrecy was our best defence. Once that was lost, it was only a matter of time before aryth found us. We prefer to take precautions before disaster. It is less messy than clearing up afterwards.'

How long had that secrecy been maintained? Who betrayed it? Or was it by chance? 'Has everyone fled?'

'Not quite everyone, although goodly numbers have chosen to do so. The younger students are safer elsewhere. As this desecration proves.' She gestured at the scorched column. 'Where we stand was once a place of remembrance and warning, and storage for spare stones, but it has been generations since we had a significant number of surplus stones.'

Halaryth or nikaryth would have taken stones and used them for our destruction. Rage built inside me. I touched my sword hilt, knowing what I wanted to do and believing it possible. I created strong foundations to hold the stone, lifted it into its former position and settled it in place. After walking round to check the stone's security, I erased the flame scars, restored the damaged characters, levelled the surrounding grass and released my power. It had been effortless.

CHAPTER 44

Varia

The glint in Dru's eyes suggested he knew he was not my first choice. However, Vithz was unavailable, pre-occupied with his fourth wife. He would not leave her until her pregnancy was certain. All other considerations apart, Vithz would not interfere in matters outside his tribal territory unless requested to do so. No such invitation had come from Dru or his brothers.

Burll entered the conference chamber with Eward close behind. The boy's face was flushed. His eyes darted from Captain Jonnan to Dru and me. Jonnan glanced up and turned his attention back to the map. Burll pointed Eward to the seat next to Jonnan and took the remaining chair.

I raised an eyebrow, and Burll shook his head. He leaned towards Eward, whispered in his ear, and the boy's eyes widened.

'Dru, this is Eward, one of our more advanced students. I trust him as I trust Burll.'

Dru's eyes narrowed, but he did not object to the boy's presence.

Eward's fingers gripped his sword, and Burll's hand closed on his arm. Burll was not yet at ease with his exclusion from this expedition, although he understood my reasons and had suggested Eward as his replacement. Jonnan had settled into his position as Commander of the Getheer Garrison, which effectively made him guardian of the eastern border.

'Captain Jonnan, what do your scouts report?'

'No movement along the border for the last two nights, Commander. The last reported karyth sighting from the northern tribes was five nights ago, approximately seventy miles southeast of Getheer.'

'Dru?'

He leaned over the map, pointing to the eastern spur of the southern mountains. 'A single demon entered the Jaws of Hell last night. The tribesman who made the report could not be certain of its nature at such distance. He said, "If it was a karyth, it was a large one." Does a single karyth disquiet us, cousin? Or must we investigate to ensure that no greater demon escapes our vigilance?'

'Yes and yes, cousin. Single karyth have rarely travelled any distance on the eastern border, though it has been otherwise in the west of late. Any change in that pattern disturbs me. Raithen destroyed a nest of karyth at the western end of the haunted mountains last winter, but as yet we have found no nests in the east. If there is one near the border or out in the desert, we must all be vigilant.'

'The tribes have reported their kills,' Jonnan said. 'Karyth only.'

'It is so. No tribesman has seen a greater demon.' Dru paused. 'Unless last night's sighting proves to be worse than we suppose.'

Jonnan frowned. 'Why would a halaryth or nikaryth come this far south and east? The frontier has always been well guarded, and the tribes are watchful.'

'In order to kill as the opportunity arises, Jonnan. I trust the worst we might face is a clever halaryth which might choose to stir karyth into action, and then linger behind until our patrols are relaxed.' I glanced round the table. 'I know of nothing in the deep desert that might interest a halaryth.'

Dru's gaze sharpened. 'Is it your guess that a single demon has business there, cousin? The Jaws of Hell ever had an ill name.'

'Why?' I had not heard the name before, understandably: my dealings have been largely with the northern tribes.

'Old men will make the sign against evil when the Jaws are named, but none can explain why. None of my people will approach within ten miles of the peaks.'

'I trust you and your men plan to be an exception to that policy.'

Dru rose to his feet. 'We will come with you. If Burll is willing to carry me.'

'Burll has other duties. We have a dozen raithen who can take your men. Eward will carry you in Burll's place.'

'This boy!' Dru glared at Eward.

The boy's flush died away. He swallowed and nodded.

'Eward is strong in the power, cousin. Prepare yourselves, we leave immediately.'

Dru shot another glance at Eward and stepped outside. Jonnan followed.

'Eward.'

He took a deep breath. 'Yes, Lady?'

'I'm sorry I wasn't able to forewarn you of this plan. We go to hunt aryth. No one is sure what we shall find. I need you to bring Dru. If all goes well, that is all I shall ask of you. Be wary. You have been taught that, against aryth, all manner of things may go wrong. Remember that and shield yourself well.' I stood and offered him my hand. 'Are you with us?'

He stared at me. Eward was young to be thrust onto such a position, but Ydrin had trained him well. I trusted him to obey my orders. Would I could say the same for certain other raithen!

'You will make us proud, Eward,' Burll said. He clapped him on the shoulder.

Eward took my hand. His was damp, but he did not duck my gaze. 'I am with you, Lady Varia.'

I pressed his hand, released it and pointed to the map. 'This is our first destination. We will maintain close linkage. Come. If we are to catch this aryth, we must not delay.'

Burll instructed Dru to grip Eward as if he were riding a horse bareback. Eward flushed. I did not offer to translate Dru's quiet comment in his own tongue.

Our first shift took us to a tribal outpost, a mere huddle of tents, the air thick with smoke and pungent with a mix of animal dung and okoa. A scout greeted Dru, letting loose a torrent of words.

'He says we are too late. The big one fled at our approach.'

'Which way?'

'South.'

'There is nothing there to sustain it.' Dru said. His face darkened. 'It will haunt the tribes unless we can trap it.'

'I fear so, cousin. Are your men ready, Dru? Raithen, with me. Now!'

* * *

I landed on the sloping saddle between the highest peaks of the Jaws. Raithen joined me and formed a loose circle around the tribesmen. Eward, his face pale, stood next to Dru, sword in hand, as safe there as anywhere. Noon light blazed from naked blades and bounced off rock faces, sunlight ever our ally against aryth. An early lesson: aryth prefer darkness; it echoes their black thoughts. Perhaps it was true. No one knew what lurked in aryth's minds. Their deeds were dark enough, but the same might be said of many a man.

A scout climbed the uppermost peak, scanned the horizon and signalled a negative. I had expected it, although I did not share Dru's confidence that the lone aryth would turn back. What sustained aryth? Death and destruction. No living raithan had seen halaryth or nikaryth consume anything resembling food. Karyth ate living and dead flesh, but they were mere tools, pack hounds. Did a huntsman eat the flesh he threw to his dogs?

We searched for the duration of the day. Dusk was approaching when Eward called me mind to mind. When did he learn that trick? I called raithen together and drew them with me.

Eward stood under an overhanging shelf, his shield extended to cover Dru, whose sword pointed to a crack in the rock. 'I defy even your boy to slip through that crack,' Dru said, his eyes glinting.

'Stand back. Shields firm.' I assessed the rock. The crack, at its widest, would admit a small bird, or bat. No karyth could squeeze through. Nonetheless I felt them, as Eward had. 'Shield yourselves!'

I signalled Eward away from the rock face, and Dru retreated with him, step for step.

In a flare of power, I sliced the rock open and lit the scene. Shadows skittered out, sprang in all direction or clung to shattered rock above the enlarged opening.

A tribesman made the sign against evil, and a raithan swore, 'What the hell–'

'Destroy them!' I blasted the nearest.

Raithen and tribesman responded. Fire ignited scales, wings and talons. Blades impaled dark bodies, slit limbs and smashed skulls. I flamed the huddled remnants in the exposed cleft. Whirling, I shouted, 'Watch your backs!'

Dru bent over a creature he had slain, intent on its lifeless form. 'My scout exaggerated. This is the smallest karyth I have seen.'

I met his gaze, and he straightened. 'He who slays a family of lion cubs must guard against the arrival of the cubs' dam.'

Raithen understood me and checked shields. Eward flinched at a movement near his feet.

Dru's sword skewered the karyth. He laughed. 'Have we accounted for them all, cousin?'

'I doubt it. We must continue to search. You and your men should leave this place, Dru.' They would be safer away from the Jaws, as would Eward.

Dru shook his head. 'We will stay. The boy needs more practice in killing.'

He did. Eward's stance would have earned him short shrift from his swordmaster, but with Dru at his side, he was relatively safe. He had recovered from his fright, and his shield was firm.

I left them and joined the hunt. Karyth would hide in darkness or deepest shadow, teeth and claws ready to rend the unwary. God send all raithen had their wits about them. Anyone who thought small karyth an easy target would likely not live to regret it.

I paused, my senses ranging out. If the little ones had been able to fly, surely they would have–

I looked up. 'Skyward!'

Someone screamed. A bow twanged, and another. A shadow fell past the saddle and vanished into the darkness below.

Eward! I swung round, ready to extend my shield. Dru stood facing Eward, laughing, his sword raised. Eward was rising from one knee, his sword bloody, and his face showing astonishment at his first kill, a small karyth missed in the first sweep.

A blur of movement, and Dru was gone.

Eward sprang up.

I cried, 'Hold fast! Shields firm!'
Thud.

Raithen shifted into the air. All but Eward, alone and exposed, staring at the mutilated body parts that had been Dru.

A dark shape dived at him. I lunged from the shadows and impaled it. Still, it fought me: its hind talons locked around my blade. It's weight forced my sword down as its fore talons reached for me. Its fangs snapped shut, clashed against the crossguard. I channelled a shaft of power through my blade. Dark blood spurted, sizzled against my shield. The karyth growled and died. Its body slid from my sword and slumped on the rock at my feet. I stepped back.

'Raithen, keep watch! Mazraki, to me!'

A head count confirmed it. Dru dead and one tribesman missing.

'I should have saved him,' Eward whispered.

I gripped his shoulder. 'He would not have thanked you for it. To be indebted to you would have shamed him in the eyes of his men. He died bravely. You are not to blame.' The responsibility is mine. 'You did well tonight, Eward.'

* * *

No one wished to spend the night at the Jaws, but I refused to depart until daylight. Two karyth had attacked. One lay dead, but only daylight would reveal the truth of the missing tribesman and his attacker. There might be more, lurking on the cliffs, waiting for us to move.

A watch was set, fires lit, scratches tended, water and food shared, and a sip of brandy apiece. Raithen remained silent while tribesmen spoke quietly in their own tongue. I toured those raithen on sentry duty, Eward with me. The tribesmen sentries I avoided. They would not welcome my sympathy for their losses.

Eward offered to take his turn on watch, but I forbade it. He had done enough today, I would not stretch him further.

In dawn's light, I studied the bodies.

'Half-spider, half-bat,' one of the tribesmen muttered.

'Younglings,' spat another.

'Is that what they are?' Eward asked. 'I thought aryth didn't breed.'

'So did we all until last summer when a tribesman shot down a fertile female at the Peak. We've seen others since.' I looked up. 'Four raithen to find the missing tribesman and his attacker. Everyone else gather dead karyth. You know better than to touch them. Over there.'

Crouched beside the oversized corpse, I drew my dagger and opened its belly. Feeling myself overlooked, I glanced up. A tribesman, Zem, cousin to Dru.

'Is it the dam?'

'I think it likely. Perhaps the other was also.'

He squatted on his heels beside me. 'You suspected more than one, but you were unprepared for the younglings.'

'Karyth have ever proved sterile.' I paused. 'I think it unlikely they learned to breed by themselves.'

Zem's eyes flashed. He spat. 'How else?'

I held his gaze. 'Greater and lesser demons worked together to make the first karyth. They have had time to improve on their design.'

'There may be more?'

'We will search, but there are not enough of us to patrol everywhere.'

He grimaced. 'I hear you. It is why Dru asked us to come.' He veiled his face.

'I share your grief.' I stood. 'We will burn these carrion and take our dead home.'

* * *

A stench of death hung over the outpost, obliterating all other smells. Nothing lived, neither tribesman, nor livestock. After the first cries of rage and mourning, the only sound was the wind buffeting collapsed tent covers.

I held raithen apart while tribesmen searched, their faces veiled.

Zem returned, his pace slow, his shoulders slumped. 'No karyth did this. It is the work of a greater demon.'

'May I see?' For a moment I thought he would refuse. Then he nodded, a quick jerk of the head, and led me through the tangle of debris.

When he pointed, I stared at the shreds of discarded clothing, not understanding.

'This was my father.' He held a dagger, its blade discoloured.

I knelt and focused. The powder among the shrivelled strands was not the dust of the desert, but the desiccated remains of a man. Choking back a cry, I gathered my strength, stood and wrenched my gaze from the dust of Zem's father. 'I have seen the work of lesser and greater demons. This is new to me. It cannot be coincidence. The demon that bred fertile karyth has learned a new evil.'

'You believe this to be work of a single demon?'

I forced my over fast heartbeat to slow. 'I pray there is no more than one that can do such as this. I think it unlikely.'

This was not the place to discuss the subject further. 'I must speak with your chiefs.'

Zem's gaze drifted across the remains of the outpost. 'There is no one here to bury. Their souls have departed without guidance. We will come with you.'

CHAPTER 45

Gereyn

Nyth walked around the standing column. 'It is once more the heart of Althein. Few know of it, and fewer still are permitted to come. Now Althein will function again.'

'For how long? Until aryth come again to destroy raithen and ilen? Then the names on the stone will mean nothing.'

Nyth tilted her head back to look me in the eye. 'Perhaps. I prefer to believe that whatever did this came in search of stones of awakening. It has been many generations since necessity drove aryth to take such risks, but now they are few and desperate.'

'Stones of awakening?'

Nyth smiled. 'That was their original name. It was thought touching a stone awakened the power within. Or, in the case of a person without power, burnt flesh was a punishment for their presumption in grasping the stone. A nonsensical idea, but they knew no better then.' She sighed. 'We have learned a little since. The truth is that a holder of power recognises something akin to power in the stones. As for those without power, few survive the encounter to explain it. One woman I questioned said she felt the stone searching her mind. She dropped the stone and ran, but could not live with the thought of a stone entering her mind for any reason. Poor thing. The name, stones of awaking, has lost its appeal. Perhaps understandably. Where were we?'

'How can you be so sure about the number of aryth?'

'Sit down, Gereyn. My neck aches looking up at you.'

I sat on the grass, leaning back on my hands, and Nyth sat cross-legged facing me. 'That's better. We have ever watched aryth, studied their habits, their attacks, their breeding of karyth. When Varia told us of the sorceress' deeds, we sent raithen, and ilen with them, to search the ashes of the burned forest and all the lands around, even to the heights of the southern mountains.'

'What did they find?'

'Why do you suppose the stones were set here?'

'Because too many stones can kill you as easily as too few.' It tripped off my tongue without a thought.

'Precisely. We have discovered that to our sorrow. More to the point, with usage a raithan's power becomes imbued within their stones. Setting a stone aside does not immediately break its linkage with its former user. I trust Ydrin taught you that anyone who dares to touch a newly discarded stone risks grave injury or death. Once a stone is separated from its master, its power will eventually dwindle. Until then its master, or mistress, can use its power without touching it.'

I frowned. 'Is that what the sorceress did – set a stone aside?'

'She was a nikaryth who possessed four stones. When she was confined to the wood, an idiotic notion, but we had tried and failed to destroy her, she, like a spider, created a web to trap her prey. She distorted the natural creatures of that place and made them her tools. To strengthen her hold, to ensure they were forever her creatures, she set two focus stones in the depths of her realm to hold her web in place. She would have planned to replace the set-aside stone with another before its power was dangerously drained. While the set aside stones remained apart, she carried only two, but those two sufficed.'

'Until the fire.'

'Intense heat can do no harm to a focus stone, so long as its wearer holds it and shields himself. We can only guess, but I think it likely that one of the wood's foundation stones had left her hold some time before, perhaps more than a year. That stone being weakened, the fire destroyed it, and the remaining stone could not hold the sorceress' spells. When it began to give way, her creatures sensed her lessening hold and fought her control. Fixed on revenge for the loss of Kei, intended as her plaything, she was slow to realise her danger. One of her not-quite-men took the remaining stone, perhaps thinking to take her place. It had reckoned without the stone's capacity to remember its mistress, but it lived long enough to achieve its aim. The sorceress, unsuspecting, died at the hands of a not-quite-man, and its fellows, seeing what the focus stone had done to their lady's killer, fled south. Raithen hunted and destroyed them.'

I closed my eyes in relief. When no one had hinted at the lady's fate, I assumed she had escaped. I opened my eyes to meet Nyth's.

'So far, so good. However, the elders of Althein had lessened their vigilance. Believing that the nikaryth threat was weakening, they contented themselves with watching the approaches to Althein, leaving imperial troops to patrol the eastern border. That served until last summer, when Varia reported karyth loose in the west. Raithen tracked them to the western extreme of the haunted mountains, and destroyed a nest. The elders were still considering whether nikaryth remained a threat, when karyth attacked traders on the eastern border near Getheer. If Varia had not been present, imperial losses would have been worse. She reinforced the border garrisons and asked the elders to reinstate raithen watch on the haunted mountains and eastern border.'

'I thought nikaryth were the most powerful. How could they not be a threat?'

Nyth pointed to the names on the stone. 'Nikaryth hold more stones than halaryth. We always assumed them to be the most powerful and the most dangerous, but our experience in recent years has been quite otherwise. In every recent battle, nikaryth hung back, leaving the battle to halaryth, or did not appear. Halaryth drove karyth to attack us, while halaryth attempted to kill or abduct four and five stone raithen.'

'If nikaryth joined with halaryth, could they wipe us out?' My skin prickled at the thought.

'It has always been our greatest fear. However, many nikaryth have died in battle over past generations. Maybe the remnants have reconciled themselves to watching halaryth, rather than risking their lives.' She shrugged. 'If you are right, they are conserving their strength, planning a final strike.'

I made the sign against evil. 'God forbid.'

'I trust so. After the latest battle at Mondun, most nikaryth and halaryth retreated to the haunted mountains. The karyth of the eastern border scattered, and tribesmen shot them down with raithen assistance. Recently watchers have reported a lone aryth, initially on the eastern border, then further south, flying through the southern mountains into the desert.'

'Just one?'

'Perhaps. A hunt is underway.'

'Could a single halaryth threaten us, as the lady of the wood did?' I shivered.

'As she did or as Divasa toyed with you. It would depend on their strength and whether they control karyth. If they do, it will not bode well for us. Pah! That is enough chat about such sad vermin.'

'Sad!'

'They made the wrong choice once and condemned themselves utterly. You and I might have done the same if tempted.' She brushed a tear from her cheek. 'Let us concentrate on more important matters.'

She drew a string from underneath her tunic. 'This I never remove.'

I stared at Nyth's stone. If she carried more, I couldn't see them. I touched the crystal through my shirt. 'I wear one here too.'

She nodded. 'That is wise. Now we may begin. I suggest you set aside your stones, with the necessary exception of that you wear at your neck.'

'Why?'

'Why not? You don't take that sword to bed with you, do you? Or wear it when you bathe? Gereyn, I don't want to take your stones from you. All I want is for you to remember what it feels like to experience power without them. That's how you learnt before the elders of Althein interfered with Varia's advice to Ydrin and cocked up your training.'

She laughed at my expression. 'Do you expect me to be a prim-mouthed old lady? I don't feel old, and I don't hesitate to speak plainly. Try it.'

Still chuckling, I unbuckled my swordbelt and cast it aside. She was right. I'd come to rely too much on the stones.

Nyth slid a knife from the folds of her skirt and slammed it into the back of her hand. 'Ah, that was careless.' It was a fish-cleaning knife, its blade still clogged with blood, fish guts and scales. Her eyes twinkled. 'Will healing this stretch your abilities? You haven't practised for a while.'

The hand was that of a boy, sun-browned and calloused from the ship's ropes. The knife's saw edge had cut through bone, flesh and blood vessels. The boy was screaming as the sawbones set to work. The flash of memory faded. 'I could have saved his hand.'

Nyth tugged the knife free and laid it beside her. 'Why didn't you?'

'I was afraid. They cast stowaways overboard.'

'Did you fear death so much?'

'Death, no. But the deep water, and the great fish with teeth . . .' I shuddered. 'Give me your hand.'

Her hand was not a boy's hand, and the cut was straight, not jagged. If the blade had been clean, it would have been a simple matter. As it was – I had done something like this before – I numbed Nyth's pain, repaired the blood vessels, cleared the leaked blood, removed all traces of fish guts and scales and checked the cleanliness of the wound before joining the split muscle and sealing the wound. 'How does that feel?'

Nyth made a fist and reopened her hand. 'It's good. How did it feel for you?'

'Like something I learned a long time ago.'

'Before you crossed the Inner Sea?'

'Yes.'

'Who taught you, your father or your mother?'

My father? An angry man with a stick, who dragged me outside. 'My father beat me.'

'Why did he do that? Was your mother there when it happened?'

My mother always veiled her face. The other veils, that had shut off my childhood for so long, were now torn, drifting away. 'I think . . .' I covered my mouth with my fingers, and swallowed the rage I had endured for too many years. When I dropped my hand, that small movement loosened my tongue. 'His name was Falk. He kept pigs, but never made much money. We were always hungry. My mother . . . my mother was a whore. When she died, my father sold my sister and me, but he kept my brother. I ran away, but couldn't find my sister. For two summers I worked when I could. In winter, when work was scarce, I begged or stole.'

'How old were you?'

I tried to work it out. 'Five or six.'

'That was very young to fend for yourself. You were fortunate that Selthel found you when he did.'

The name silenced me. I had heard it not long ago, but then my memory had been unreliable. This time the name brought to mind a face and a smile. A man who had been kind, and more than that. 'I was always cold and hungry that winter. When Selthel came, I was feverish. "Bag of bones," he said. When I recovered . . .' I thought I was dead and had gone to heaven. I expected to find my mother and sister there. 'Selthel told me he was a healer, and that I was one too. He gave me a place at his hearth and his table, and taught me healing and defence. I worked with him to treat those who came to him for help, until he sickened.' I closed my eyes, struggling to continue. 'I begged him to let me heal him, but he would not allow it.' Tears flowed down my cheeks.

'When he died, I left. There was nowhere to go, but I couldn't stay. I don't know how long I wandered or where I went.'

'Until you crossed the Inner Sea. That was a long voyage to remain hidden.'

'The crew were cruel, and careless. I stole a knife, food and clothes, and left the ship at the first port. I walked for days, taking food where I could. And then–'

'Divasa found you.'

Her understanding gaze made it possible for me to speak again. 'I fled, but she trapped me. When I tried to protect myself . . .' I shook my head. 'I didn't know what I'd done. Only that she couldn't reach me, but I didn't feel safe.'

Nyth nodded. 'You did deliberately what Varia did accidentally, barricaded yourself behind a shield of power. I wish I could have seen Divasa's face when she realised your shield was impenetrable. You waited there until the mountain erupted and woke you.'

'Duke Arnull came. I didn't want to live, but he wouldn't let me die.'

Nyth's eyes were sad. 'You learned to know love again, but you fought it, because it hurts to lose someone we love. You had not discovered that it is more painful to deny love, to cut oneself off from it.'

'I have now,' I whispered.

'Who do you love, Gereyn?'

'Iylla, my sister. Reys and Arni. Dern.'

'No one else? There's a wide world of people out there.'

'Garanth. A man like me, who lost everything.'

Nyth beamed. 'I'm glad. There's a man who needs all the love he can find. As you do.'

I did not argue. She might be right. An earlier thought came back to me. 'Nyth, how do you know so much about the lady of the wood and Divasa?'

She rubbed the faint silver line that was the only remaining sign of the cut on her hand. 'Can you read the words on the standing stone?'

I shook my head.

'Few can. Here is written the name of everyone who has ever held a stone of power, from the very beginning, every aryth, ilen and raithen.'

I leaped to my feet. 'Aryth!'

Nyth rose. 'Here, this side carries the oldest names, they follow round.'

She pointed to the top of the fourth side. 'These are the latest students to be accepted as raithan or ilan.' She had stopped at the first side again and pointed. 'Here is Divasa and here the sorceress.'

Divasa's name was one of the oldest. The lady of the wood's partway down the second face. 'How is that possible?'

Nyth studied my face, and shook her head. 'I will tell you one day, Gereyn.'

CHAPTER 46

Varia

My relief in seeing Vithz was short-lived. He had veiled his face, something only required before strangers or when in deep mourning. Although we were friends and allies, he would not meet my eyes. I lowered mine so as not to intrude on his grief.

Against all tradition, the chiefs permitted me to join their discussions. Zem tersely described events at the Jaws of Hell and the outpost. I added the little he had omitted, reserving only my thoughts on what manner of aryth might have wreaked such vengeance on the tribes.

The spokesman for the southern chiefs broke the ensuing silence. 'Vithz and his brothers have agreed to join the northern tribes to ours in an attempt to counter this menace.' He gestured towards me. 'You will leave our lands, all but one.'

One to remain? For what purpose? I had already ordered raithen to leave. The tribes had always believed in blood for blood. Did that belief still hold?

A tribesman burst into the conference tent. 'The wizards have gone!'

The nearest tribesmen drew their swords. They could not hope to penetrate my shield, but neither could I leave while their demands were unfulfilled. Negotiation might mitigate their desire for compensation, but no chief would permit a woman to bargain for such stakes.

When Vithz stood, all eyes turned to him. 'We will make no progress here. Will you trust me to go to the border fort to discuss terms?'

After a brief consultation, the spokesman said, 'You and Zem. If you return without a wizard, we shall feel free to make war upon the northern tribes and upon the empire.'

'I understand you,' Vithz said. 'We shall not fail.'

* * *

Captain Jonnan had cleared the battlements save for archers. Raithen were close enough to call at need. At present their concerns and mine coincided. I did not doubt they would act on my command.

Sergeant Regert conducted Vithz and Zem to the garrison commander's office and turned me away at the door, stern-faced. 'My orders, Commander'.

I walked to the corner of the parapet and stared unseeing across the empty reaches of the desert. At last I understood my father. Faced with such choices, what could he do but lay aside his sword? I had my father's blood in me, but I would not emulate him. I would neither select an unwilling raithan as a possible sacrifice, nor make war against the tribes. I would not abandon Vithz, nor force him to tell me his grief.

If there were alternatives, I could not see them. I sank to my knees and prayed.

The meeting lasted longer than I might have expected. Good for Jonnan. He led Vithz past me, but Zem stopped. 'We need to talk, you and I, cousin.' His eyes strayed towards Regert, guarding an empty room.

'Sergeant Regert.'

'Yes, Commander?'

'Stand guard on the head of the stairs.'

'Yes, Commander.' He strode past us.

I gestured Zem to precede me and closed the door behind me.

'The soldier does not think of you as a woman.'

'He did once. Since he has seen me fight it is not something that concerns him.'

'I too have seen you fight.' He lowered his veil. 'I will treat you as a man. If I incur Vithz's anger thereby, so be it.'

'I am grateful, Zem.'

'You may think otherwise when you hear what I have to say. You know our customs. Vithz's bride brought him wealth and her brothers. His first duty was to get her with child. She told him that she believed she had conceived.' He shrugged. 'Women may know these things, but men require proof. So Vithz was happy, but not yet convinced. Wedding celebrations continued. Her women helped her prepare for Vithz's coming and then left her. Vithz and his brothers sang, danced and drank.

'Late that nightVithz went to her, expecting her to be wakeful and to welcome him, but his tent was unlit. When he brought a lamp and entered, the stench that covered his wife's perfumes told him she was dead before the light revealed her, but he was unprepared for what he saw. She lay on the bed, her robes ripped away. Blood covered her lower body and the bed. If she had conceived Vithz's son, she carried him no longer. Her belly had been emptied.

'Her face was not the face Vithz knew and loved. It had been melted. Stains of liquid flesh covered the pillows as blood the mattress. Her mother would not have known her.'

I swallowed bile. Dear God! 'This was done deliberately, the attacks on Vithz's wife and on your father, to break our alliance.'

'Could you have stopped it, you and your raithen?' Zem's eyes were wary.

'I do not know. We have few who can stand against the greatest demons. A lesser demon might have acted in the service of its masters or to amuse itself. Perhaps it intends its deeds to convey a message.'

'You believe this creature to be a lesser demon? What message does it wish to give us?'

'I do. The message? Perhaps that raithan can not or will not protect the tribes.'

'Then there is some hope. This is a demon of lesser power.'

'There is indeed hope, if we work together. You must tell your brothers what we face and persuade them to hold the alliance.'

'You must give us a raithan.'

'I will speak with them. If I give you a raithan, will he live?'

Zem shrugged. 'Tempers are high, but we do not squander resources.'

I watched him walk away. If he was right, improved trade deals and a raithan's power might satisfy the tribes. I trusted so.

'Commander.'

'Sergeant Regert.'

'I overheard your talk.'

'You have keen ears.'

'The walls make it easy to hear what is said here. Commander Turrard always posted his sentry at the foot of the steps.'

'I shall enlighten Captain Jonnan.'

Regert nodded. 'I'd like to volunteer to be one of those to accompany the tribesmen when they leave.' He hesitated. 'If you don't mind my saying so, Commander, you should get some sleep.'

When I could bring myself to speak, I said, 'Thank you, Sergeant. I shall consider your offer and your advice.'

* * *

My quarters, a vast, echoing tiled emptiness, had formerly been those of Commander Turrard. Open shutters ensured that fine sand filmed every surface and crunched under my boots. The bed at least was relatively dust-free behind its protective drapes. I had grown soft. Once a little sand would not have offended me. However, my problems were greater than a little dust. Sleep, though necessary, was unlikely to change matters.

A tap at the door. What now? 'Enter.'

Eward pushed the door open and stood in the doorway. 'I'm sorry to disturb you, Lady.'

'You have not disturbed me, Eward. Have you slept?'

'All afternoon.' He twisted his hands together. 'You said it wasn't my fault that Dru died. I . . . He saved my life.'

'I know how that feels, Eward. I am also in debt to a man who died for me.'

Eward flushed. 'They say the tribes want a raithan to help them fight aryth. I know I'm not yet qualified, but . . . Will you consider me?' He held my gaze.

'You are full of surprises, Eward. Why? To repay Dru's family for his loss?'

'No! I know that's impossible. Whatever I do, I can't take his place.' He licked his lips. 'His people have no defence against nikaryth and halaryth. Even karyth – those new things – at close range they're deadly.'

'Eward, whatever I decide, I am grateful for your proposal. I shall bear it in mind. Go, eat your supper and rest again.'

'You too, Lady.' He flushed. 'I mean–'

I smiled. 'You are wise. I need sleep as much as you do. You are not the first to have told me so today. Good night, Eward.'

'Good night, Lady.'

*   *   *

Exhaustion, of body and mind, claimed me until Burll shook me awake.

'While you sleep the world goes to hell.' He had found time to wash, shave and don freshly laundered clothes.

'So I see.'

Burll did not understand irony. 'We must talk.'

'I must eat. Join me in Jonnan's tower.'

Burll dismissed, I washed in tepid, rust-coloured water and dressed in the clothes I had thrown off the previous night. Downstairs, I wheedled breakfast from an undercook, who did not recognise me. He served me an unfortunate mix of army and tribal cooking.

When I entered the tower room, Burll was pacing the floor. Jonnan sat at the head of the table. Raithan had ranged themselves around the table or against the walls. Eward sat on a stool near the empty fireplace, his eyes downcast. Regert closed the door and set his shoulders against it.

I stood at the foot of the table. 'Captain Jonnan, have you been able to improve our negotiating position?'

'No, Commander. I believe Zem is inclined to appreciate our difficulties, but his chiefs are immoveable, and it seems Vithz is no longer our ally.'

'He has reason.'

A two-stone raithan on Burll's left, whose name escaped me for a moment, slammed his fist on the table. 'You should have kept us with you, Lady Varia. We could have shown those Vethians who–'

Burll glared at him, and Jas – the name came to me at last – fell silent.

I took a deep breath and let it out slowly. 'The tribes of the Vethian desert are and always will be our allies. The battlefield has changed. The tribes you despise now form the front line. In this war we must and will support them. They have asked for one raithan. Do you wish to be that raithan, Jas?'

He shook his head, his jaw tight.

'What use is one raithan?' Burll asked.

'Very little, but it's a start.' If he was not to be a blood sacrifice. 'I am minded to send more, as students finish their training.'

Several raithen murmured protests. Jas did not bother to lower his voice. 'You have no authority to do that!' I stared at him, and he glared back.

'It is an extension of what has already been decided. Two have offered themselves for this duty. Does anyone else wish to join them?'

Eward looked up, his eyes questioning.

Silence.

'No one?'

Burll stood. 'I will, Lady Varia. I see the need, and God knows we would have been worse off without the watchfulness of the tribes over the years.'

'Indeed we would.' I turned my gaze to the hearth. 'Eward.'

He walked slowly towards me, his eyes intent on the stone floor.

'Are you still of the same mind?'

His head jerked up, his eyes sparkling and his face flushed. 'I am, Lady.'

'You're going to send this untrained boy to do a raithan's work?' Jas's face was flushed.

'I am going to send a raithan to do the service he requested, the task you did not wish to undertake.' I held his gaze until he looked away. 'Regert.'

'I'm ready, Commander.'

Burll came forward to join Regert and Eward.

I said, 'Burll, you have fought long and bravely against aryth. I charge you to continue that fight while you have strength to do so.'

'I will, Lady.'

'My blessing.' I clasped his hand and kissed his brow.

'Regert, you have served faithfully in the imperial army and have fought aryth. You go to take the place of a tribesman. It may well be that you are required to keep goats rather than fight. Are you ready for that?'

'I hear tribesmen skin a goat with one hand and shoot karyth with the other.' He winked. 'That'll be a fine trick to learn.'

I laughed. 'My blessing.' I gripped his hand and kissed his brow.

'Eward, you have been an excellent student. I name you raithan, qualified to wield the sword you carry in the service of the tribes, protecting them to the best of your ability against all aryth. I name thee my athan, the second of my adopted sons.' I embraced him, kissed his brow and lips. 'My blessing. I shall remember thee, my athan.'

I turned from Eward's glowing face. 'Captain Jonnan, please tell our guests that we offer them two raithen and one soldier in return for our continuing alliance.'

Jonnan leaped to his feet. 'Consider it done, Commander.'

'Jas, give me your sword.'

He remained seated, his brow furrowed as his knuckles whitened on his sword hilt. Then he cried out as his sword flew to my hand.

I prised a stone from the hilt. 'If you wish this returned, you will beg Master Ydrin to enrol you as a student.'

'I will not!'
'Your choice.'
'Never!'

I prised the remaining stone free and tossed it to him. 'You may make your own way in this world. From this moment, you are no longer raithan.' Jas fumbled the catch, his expression disbelieving. All eyes stared at me. Then one by one, raithen nodded.

CHAPTER 47

Gereyn

Nyth's teaching was a reworking of my first lessons, a fresh look at aspects of power I thought I understood.

When I said so, Nyth chuckled. 'Ydrin and I have different methods. She looked at me thoughtfully. 'Drop your sword and light my cooking fire.'

My flames caught and burned steadily.

'Scale and clean the fish. Then cook them.'

I remembered the alder fire, and my carelessly cast shield that came so close to killing Ydrin, reduced the flow of my power, set boundaries and treated the fish as an infected wound to be cleaned. It worked well, but the image and the accompanying stench – surely imagined – destroyed my appetite.

Nyth never repeated a lesson, but she sometimes had me using power to perform the most menial of tasks, for teaching purposes only. 'Cleaning fish is a job for a knife, not power.'

Each time I set my sword aside, Nyth increased the time of my deprivation. That's what it felt like. As if someone had taken my toy away. I laughed, and Nyth asked me to share the joke.

'That's a good example. A child who clings to his toys will never become a man.'

'What will I become if I succeed in throwing away the stones?'

She frowned. 'You will *not* throw them away. This is merely the beginning, Gereyn. While you no longer need to touch the stones to focus through them, I suspect you will still draw on them. If you wish it otherwise, you must increase both the time and distance of separation, a little at a time, which may take months or years. It is not something to be undertaken at the present time. Talk to me about it when our position is less perilous. When you eventually decide you have no need of these four, I will give them to the elders for safekeeping. As for what you will become, tell me when it happens. I should like to see it.'

'I hope you will, Nyth.'

Her smile returned. 'It is certain, Gereyn.'

I walked to my lodging, my feet light on the path, as if I were a fledgling that had dropped from the nest and discovered the purpose of its wings.

* * *

Dern had described Leoric as undersized. Now the boy was head and shoulders taller than Nyth and sturdy, with fresh colour in his cheeks. 'Come fishing with me, Gereyn.'

Looking at his eager face, I could not bring myself to refuse. After I had spent an afternoon sitting on the bank doing little but watch the lines, I understood the appeal.

'You should use a coracle.' He borrowed one for me and sat in Nyth's boat demonstrating and explaining. It looked easy enough.

It was not. The first problem was stepping in. Leoric told me to use the paddle as a prop and hold the coracle steady with my free hand. The lightweight boat was as frisky as Dern's colt and as easy to tip as a mug of ale in the hand of drunkard. Twice it escaped me. On my third try I came close to capsizing and needed Leoric's help to right the coracle. I stepped in on my fourth attempt, sat gingerly on the plank seat and tried to copy Leoric's smooth figure-of-eight paddle strokes.

The boy kept a straight face until I had gained some measure of control. 'Good luck!' He waved and was gone.

When clear of the shore I wended my way through the channels. The conflicting currents and gusting wind spun the boat and tipped it dangerously close to the water. I might have used power to steady it, but it did not feel right. More and more, I preferred not to access power when alternatives were available.

I gave a sigh of relief as I finally beached the coracle near Nyth's hut.

When I told Nyth, she set me a steer-your-coracle-from-a-distance challenge, which ended with both of us rolling on the shore, helpless with laughter. I helped her up.

'You don't laugh nearly enough. When was the last time?'

'I don't keep records.' I thought about it. 'When Lady Varia sang *Northern Girls*. Lady Kirra's version didn't make me laugh.'

That set her off again, which infected me. Eventually she said, 'I taught her both.' Her amusement faded. 'Tell me what you know about transference.'

'Ydrin warned me to guard myself always. I heeded him until . . .' I shrugged. 'You know why I dropped my defences.'

'Do I? Can anyone know another person so well? I want to hear you say it, Gereyn.'

I had learned to trust Nyth as I had trusted Selthel. 'Part of me wanted to die, to be done with pain and regret, but I wanted to free Lady Varia.'

'Why did you want to free her?'

I hesitated – I had not questioned my motives. 'She intervened when the gysun would have killed me, and again in the cursed wood. I owed her my life.'

'And?'

Nyth knew everything else. She might as well know this too. 'I didn't want her to go through what I had, when I came to myself and realised that everything I knew was gone. Not just Selthel, but the world I had lived in.'

Nyth nodded. 'I can understand that. Both of you experienced the confusion of transference: someone else's memories displacing yours.'

'Not displacing. Merging. I begged for food, but slept in a feather bed. And not just memories. Emotions – fear, love, hate, rage.'

Nyth raised an eyebrow.

'I know which memories are mine now, but I still have hers.'

'And the emotions?'

'Only when I'm close to her.'

'That might be embarrassing.'

I shrugged. 'She has good reason to avoid me, yet she came to Hawdale and forced Reys to restore my sword. I'm grateful for that.'

'I don't believe she is avoiding you. Between commanding the army and ruling the empire, she has no time to consider you.'

I should have realised that. 'Is the emperor still dodging his responsibilities?'

'That's not for me to say. If you search your memories and hers, you may find the answer.'

'I'd rather not.' I already remembered too much about her and her family.

'That is your answer. You prefer to be ignorant.'

'Perhaps.'

Nyth nodded. 'What do you know about convergence?'

'How is that different from transference?'

'Fortunately it's not something we have much experience of. I have only known one case. An extraordinarily bright student asked for extra lessons, which were granted. I don't know whether master or student failed to shield adequately or the master's strength overwhelmed the student. Possibly the other way round. I only saw the result: two bodies, one mind. Their personal memories utterly lost. A new being formed from the essence of two separate identities.'

I stared at her, my mouth dry, my heartbeat rapid, my palms clammy. 'I was lucky.'

'You both were.'

'What happened to them?'

'The body of the former student begged us to end her life, but we could not. Her other self wanted to live. It would have been murder.'

'It would have been kindness.' No one could live like that.

'We did not consider ourselves qualified to judge such things. With hindsight, you may be right. For their safety, we watched them both, which was intrusive and unwelcome. So they endured, and day after day the former student's torment increased until she used her new knowledge to destroy herself. She lit a blaze in the centre of her being, and it consumed her from the inside out. We were slow to see what was happening.'

'The former master's body was untouched, but his mind was another matter. He experienced everything she felt in her last agony. By the time her body's life had ended, he was left with only half a mind. He begged for death, and we granted it. I pray never to see the like again.'

'I wish Ydrin had told me this tale.'

'The elders forbade it.' She wiped away a tear. 'It would provide an adequate warning for most students and masters, but there will always be someone determined to try something forbidden or new. It is not worth the risk.'

'Is that what happened to aryth?'

'The desire to accept the challenge of the unknown? We believe so. Greedy, careless of risk for themselves or others, tempted to experiment with power and with life itself. Their victims have paid dearly over the years since aryth took the first stones.' She shook her head. 'Remember that tale, and do not be tempted. Show me your defence against transference and convergence.'

I did so instinctively.

'It is the same as any defence, but with an added element. We teach students to link early, while they have only one stone. It's impossible to transfer or converge at such low levels of power. Linkage increases the possibilities of power, but brings its own risks.'

'Backlash.'

'The protection against backlash will also protect against transference and convergence.' She raised a hand. 'See?'

As I saw the colours of Sylve and Lenathe's healing, so I watched as Nyth's transparent lavender-hued cloud flowed out, touched me lightly and surrounded me. Wispy tendrils pierced my shield – the linkage – but my defence held the greater part of the cloud at bay. I grinned. 'I see it. Do you see my colour?'

'It is brightest gold.'

'How bright?'

'Like sunshine reflected on the waters of Althein. If it bothers you, leave it, boy. Colours are the least of your worries.'

'I have none.'

'No? Have you decided what you are going to do when you leave here?'

I had not given the matter a moment's consideration. Here was where I wanted to be.

Nyth smiled, 'Do you want to live for ever?'

Her question caught me by surprise. 'Of course not.'

'Speech without thought is like meat without salt. Do you wish to die now?'

I stared at her. Nyth looked as defenceless as Iylla, but appearances were deceptive. She was older than anyone else in Althein, except me. If I opened my mouth would I laugh at the thought or scream?

Nyth stood beside me, a steaming cup in her hand. 'Drink this.'

The drink settled my guts, but not my hammering heart. She had asked me a question. 'No.'

'No one does. Faced with that reality, few would choose immediate death, unless life had become unbearable. Age brings weariness of spirit, and for most, the body fails or the mind. It is not so for ilen and raithen, but for us there is always the temptation of immortality.' She sat with her back to the stone so that, facing her, the names hung before my eyes. 'Aryth succumbed to that temptation. 'You were once faced with that choice and resisted because you feared and distrusted the temptress.' She smiled. 'Rightly.' Her smile faded. 'How would you feel if you loved someone enough to share your life with her? Would you wish to live forever with her, young, strong and free from pain?'

I did not hesitate. 'It would not be my choice.' To live on, while my family and friends died would be unbearable, even with one I loved at my side. When I had suffered the loss of Selthel, grief had swept away my desire to live, but I had not been able to die. 'Would the stones keep me alive unwilling?'

Nyth took my cold hands in her warm ones. 'For those used to three stones or more, death can be encouraged. You know from bitter experience that the sudden withdrawal of two or more stones brings confusion, weakness and a form of madness. If the withdrawal is gradual, one stone at a time, the body and mind become accustomed. When the last stone is abandoned, death will come. I am glad you feel that way.' She paused, her eyes on mine. 'Forgive my testing.'

My hands and heart warmed under her touch, and my relief was boundless. 'I will consider the question of your forgiveness, Nyth.'

She smiled. 'I shall consider the course of your future lessons. Come to me tomorrow. I trust you are in no rush.'

I shook my head. 'I have all the time in the world.'

CHAPTER 48

Varia

Ydrin looked up as I entered. He smiled. 'Would you mind finishing here, Ona?'

'Not at all.' She did not glance at me.

I understood her reluctance to leave her patient. Although I wished to meet her, Garanth would prefer to introduce me to Ona personally.

'This way.' Ydrin led me upstairs into a small common room. 'I'll send for a meal.'

'I took the liberty of ordering something on my way to find you. Meals have been somewhat lacking recently.'

He laid his hands gently on my shoulders and studied my face. 'I see sleep has been lacking too. You need to take better care of yourself.'

'I will, when I have time to do so. Lately it's been one crisis after another.' I chose a table near the stove. 'Have you seen my reports?'

Ydrin nodded, took the tray from the server, closed the door and sat opposite me. 'Eat first. Then we'll talk.'

'I must return to Tormene tonight.'

'The empire can manage while you sleep for a few hours.' His eyes narrowed. 'What's happened that isn't in the reports?' He touched my hand. 'Never mind. That can wait.'

I might have argued, but I had already tasted the stew, which reminded me how hungry I was.

Ydrin demolished his meal, pushed his plate away and rested his hands on the table.

My appetite sated, I gave him the background to my reports.

'You did well.'

'Not with Jas, I'm afraid. The elders won't be pleased with my inference.'

'I'll speak to them. Their supervision of raithen has been lax in recent years. Action such as you've taken is long overdue. Have you heard how Gereyn is progressing?'

'I haven't enquired. Nyth disagrees with me on the advantages of speed.' I sipped my ale. 'I will call on Garanth, but then I must leave. God knows what's happening in Tormene in my absence. Next time I trust we'll have longer together.'

'I'll make sure of that, if I have to come to Tormene to achieve it. Varia, tread cautiously with Ona. She regards you as a rival.'

'Surely not!' I spread my hands. 'I understand. I'll be careful.'

'You may as well know now. She is pregnant. It's a boy.'

* * *

Garanth drew me close for a kiss of welcome. 'You took your time, Kadron.'

'War takes priority over old friends, to my regret. Ona, I'm delighted to meet you at last. Blessings on your marriage.'

Ona ignored my outstretched hand, bobbed a curtsey and said woodenly, 'Thank you, my Lady.'

I took a half pace forward, gathered her into a tight embrace and kissed her cheeks. 'Don't you dare keep me at arm's length! Garanth is as close to me as a brother. I suggest you accustom yourself to being part of my family.'

Ona blushed and glanced at her husband. 'I beg your pardon, my Lady.'

Garanth slid his arm around Ona's shoulders. 'I told you Kadron wouldn't act the empress with you.'

Ona's rosy colour faded as she looked directly at me for the first time. 'I'm sorry.'

'Don't be. I've been looking forward to learning why Garanth chose you.'

'Will you join us for supper? Ona bakes a fair plum pudding.' He glanced at his wife, and she smiled.

'I ate with Ydrin earlier, but I'll be glad to taste your pudding, Ona. If Garanth reckons it fair, I know it will be delicious.'

Ona relaxed as she discovered that conversation with me was less daunting than she had feared. Aglow with her pregnancy, and my praise for her pudding, she looked sideways at Garanth. 'Lady Varia, I know Garanth won't be happy until he's back in his old place at your side. Will you take him back?'

'You know I'll be glad to have you, Garanth. Will you come to Tormene, you and Ona?'

'You have enough, and advisors and senior officers by the score.'

I shook my head. 'My advisors have never seen action, and my most experienced officer is Ludran, if he still lives. I've received no report from him.'

'Last seen somewhere in the Ridges allegedly plotting to overthrow the empire and attracting all manner of banditry to his side? He'd have neither time nor inclination for reports. You need someone to watch your back.' His eyes met Ona's, and she squeezed his hand. 'You've convinced me. I'll come.'

I had not heard that rumour, but soldiers were worse than women for spreading speculation. Tomorrow I would make enquiries. 'Make it soon. I'm counting on you.'

* * *

It was unwise to shift when tired, but I could not justify even a night's delay. I arrived at Tormene during the second watch of the night and bypassed the battlement guards, two of whom were out of position. Fatigue overrode my instinctive reaction to report their dereliction to the duty officer. Tomorrow would do. I took the back stairs to my chambers, meeting neither servants nor guards. After weeks of travel, when my sleep had been snatched and mostly uncomfortable, a cold bed and inadequately aired sheets would serve me well enough.

Instead, fires blazed in the hearths, warming pans aired the bedding and a flask of wine stood on the table.

'Welcome home, Lady Varia.'

I spun, drawing my sword, the tip at Porel's throat before I recognised him and lowered my blade. 'You hold your life cheap, Porel.' Did he always keep my bedchamber ready for my return?

'Needs must in the circumstances.'

His odd reply and his strained expression cut through the fog of my weariness. I drew a chair to the table and shook my head when he lifted the wine flask. 'I shall need my wits. Sit down and tell me the worst.'

Porel perched on the edge of his chair and sighed. 'There has been trouble in the city – food shortages and looting. Lord Ludran has imposed martial law and curfew.'

'Ludran! You tell your tale backwards! When did he arrive, and since when has he led the army? No, don't tell me. In my absence, he would claim seniority.' Why had I assume him deserted or dead?

'He came three weeks ago, my Lady, two days after you left for the eastern border. Less than half his troopers were the same men he left with. I did not recognise the remainder. No one challenged his orders.'

I compressed my lips. 'No one could. Damn him! I gave him loyal men. What has he done with them, and where did he find his replacements?' Even if I had taken Garanth's rumour seriously, I was already too late. Clearly, I had underestimated Ludran. He had been watching for my departure from Tormene to make his move.

'A prize was dangled before him and then snatched away, my Lady. He seems determined to have that prize one way or another.'

'Wise words, Porel. I must work at keeping that prize from him.' As if I didn't have enough to contend with. 'How did he gain control of the palace and what is his position now?' I recalled the battlement guards out of their assigned positions. If I had investigated that, I should have walked into a trap, and still might.

'He rode in as if his return was expected, my Lady. Once inside, his men overwhelmed the guard, and took over the barracks. He had the officers locked in the cells, and their men confined to their quarters. One of Ludran's new recruits is second-in-command, a man named Makah. I've heard no word of Captain Jud or Training Master Dom. If either survived, he'll be in the cells.'

'I trust both live. Well! Whoever controls the palace holds Tormene. Have Ludran's restrictions improved matters in the city?'

'Quite the opposite, my Lady. There were riots yesterday. Thirteen men are reported dead.'

'Men only?' In my experience, women and children suffered first when things went amiss. Damn Ludran to the deepest hell! I made an effort to control myself. 'Are farmers still bringing produce into the city?'

He shook his head. 'The flow stopped after a few days, and Lord Ludran refuses to open the city storehouses.'

'He'll choose his moment for that. Are any trade ships in the harbour?'

'Two only, my Lady, I have not been able to establish their cargo. Lord Ludran holds the ships' captains in close confinement.'

I blamed myself for presenting him with such an opportunity when I relocated troops to the borders. Although I had little choice at the time, I should have kept a closer watch on Ludran. Instead, I had made his takeover easy. 'Where are the nearest loyal troops?' I should have known the answer, but it escaped me.

'Rumour has it Captains Frenn and Barys are camped outside the walls. Lord Ludran refused them entry, accusing them of unspecified crimes.'

'I must speak with them. You get some rest. Thank you, Porel.'

'Be careful, my Lady.'

'I will. Tell no one you have seen me.' Although I needed allies, Porel was no soldier. Whatever the odds against me, I would not ask him to walk into danger for me.

I shielded myself, checked the passage was empty and ran soft-footed down the nearest servants' stair to the kitchen passage, slipped through the outer door, stepped to one side and listened. A distant murmur of voices and nearer approaching footsteps. With no time to linger, I shifted to the dark and silent storage yard. My searching fingers found the trapdoor half concealed under a tarpaulin. I folded that back and lifted the trap. A hint of conversation, almost beyond hearing range. Friend or foe? I stepped on to the ladder, descended two rungs, tugged the tarpaulin across as far as possible and eased the trap down. Sliding my sword from its sheath, I hesitated. If the men below had heard me, they would be ready at the foot of the ladder, but they would not expect a raithan.

Shield firm, I shifted, landed two paces beyond where any ambusher would wait and discovered no ambush had existed. Darkness filled the vast practice hall, although subdued light leaked from the half open door of a side chamber. Another short shift enabled me to see a handful of men gathered round the table, talking in low voices, Jud and Dom among them. I thanked God and threw the door fully open. 'What's this? Rebellion?'

Jud sprang up.

Dom grinned. 'It certainly is, Commander.'

'Count me in. Watch the ladder, and the tower door. I'm not expecting company, but Ludran knows both entrances.'

Two men slipped past me, swords drawn. 'Got it, ma'am.'

I scanned the remaining faces: troopers, except for a sergeant I recognised but could not name. I had sent him off with Ludran. 'What have you to say for yourself, Sergeant?'

He met my eyes. 'Sergeant Wulf, Commander. It's a long story. Briefly, we were outnumbered and outmanoeuvred. I surrendered to save my men. By the time I realised their plan it was too late to start a useless fight.'

'Wulf and Midge risked their lives to warn us,' Jud said. 'Dom and I would be dead but for them.'

Dom nodded. 'We've barely a dozen men between us. It's not enough to release our troops.'

'Porel tells me Barys and Frenn are outside the walls. Let's have them in, Dom.'

Jud's brow creased. 'How?'

Dom understood. 'The postern on the sea cliff. I'll go, but we can't get two full troops in that way. Maybe a couple dozen men, enough to take the sentries and open the gates.'

Jud's face lit up. 'My men will stand by to move on the armoury. Then we free and arm the prisoners and overpower the enemy.'

'I trust you to do just that. I'll help deal with the battlement guards. When you find Ludran, I want him taken for questioning.'

Wulf interrupted me. 'Ludran's not in charge, Commander. He takes his orders from a man who calls himself the Chief. Makah's the Chief's right-hand man, a nasty piece of work, but not as bad as his chief.'

'How many men?'

'He had over a hundred, Commander, but brought only fifty inside the palace walls. The others, including some loyal to Ludran, are standing by somewhere near. I wasn't made privy to their plans.'

I nodded. Details could wait.

'Raithen assistance might be useful.'

'This isn't their business, Captain Jud. Let's show our people they can rely on the imperial army.' Once invited to participate, how could I keep raithen out of imperial affairs?

'Yes, Commander.'

Lurking in the shadow of the Great Tower, I waited for the sentry to turn and march towards me. It felt like a childhood prank: Varryn and I creeping up on an oblivious sentry, planning to touch him and run away. Not this time. He would not survive my touch. The sentry passed me in a creak of leather and a waft of sweat and ale. I stabbed. He grunted, fell forward, and I withdrew.

The next man was lighter on his feet and quicker. I knocked his lunge aside, thrust up under his jaw and sprang clear as he slumped.

My shield vanished. Disbelieving, I raised my blade and something slammed into my wrist with a loud crack. My sword fell from numb fingers, and a shove sent me toppling towards the parapet. Darkness overcame me before I struck the wall.

CHAPTER 49

Gereyn

I woke gasping for breath. My right forearm ached, but a power-enhanced scan revealed nothing wrong. Was it Varia's pain? Whether or not, I must speak with Nyth. I tumbled into my clothes, boots and armour, and seized my sword belt, buckling it as I ran. Light spread from Lady Kirra's half-open door. For an instant I hesitated, but haste was needed, and Lady Kirra might have the same influence Nyth did. I burst through the door, and the grey-haired man swung round, sword in hand. I'd never seen him wear a sword before. Neither the man nor his sword mattered, though. Nyth was there, her hand on Leoric's, his face tear-stained.

'Tell Gereyn what has happened,' Nyth said.

Leoric sobbed. 'They've taken Lady Varia prisoner and chained her to a wall. It's dark, and she's hurt.'

'Aryth?' Rage flooded my veins.

'No. Her captors are men. They hold her somewhere in Tormene. Go on, Leoric.'

'The man who gives the orders is dressed like a soldier, but he doesn't belong to the army.'

'Ludran must be behind this,' the grey-haired man said. 'I should have foreseen it.'

'The brown-haired man's evil.' Leoric sniffed. 'He just wants to hurt people, but the other one's worse. The man who isn't there. He's taken all Lady Varia's stones.'

Lady Kirra gasped, and the grey-haired man said sharply, 'What do you mean, "The man who isn't there"?'

'I don't understand it, sir, but that's what I see. He . . . It's as if he's invisible, but he isn't.'

Lady Kirra sobbed, and the grey-haired man drew her to his side.

Nyth shook her head. 'Don't despair. Death takes time to conquer a stoneless raithan.' She frowned. 'What man can handle five stones? A man who isn't there? Do you know this man, Kirra?'

She dried her eyes. 'I fear so. My brother, Urian. He failed the test for power. Although he could handle five stones without harm, he could not use them. When my father discovered that Urian had the ability to block the use of power, he came here for advice, but Urian fled before Ydrin returned with raithen.'

I stared at her. Block the use of power? God help us!

'I don't like the sound of that,' Nyth said. 'Leoric is right, this man is dangerous. We must act swiftly. Virreld, you must warn the raithen in Tormene. You will need help. Gereyn–'

Virreld! I didn't recognise the emperor. How could I have been so blind? 'I'll come with you, sir.'

Virreld met my gaze. 'Indeed, I think you must. Against a man who can overcome Varia, handle five stones and prevent us using power, we need your power and your fighting skills. This time, you and I must work together.'

* * *

The emperor controlled the shift. At the raithen school we were redirected to the palace. Virreld shifted us into the shadows of the outer courtyard. 'That's Jud's sergeant,' he breathed and stepped into torchlight.

'Sir!' Relief flooded the sergeant's face. 'They're in the briefing room, sir.'

Virreld seized my arm and shifted.

All eyes turned as Virreld entered, and the captains leaped to their feet. Ydrin and Garanth! Jud stared at me. Ydrin had eyes only for Virreld.

Garanth held my gaze. 'Your arrival is timely.'

'As is yours,' Virreld said. 'Be seated. I see Ludran's lost control of the palace.'

'Yes, sir,' Jud said. 'The men he left here are dead or prisoners, but he's fled, with the larger part of his band of ruffians.'

'How?'

Jud threw a tangle of rope and broken iron links on to the table. 'They had two rope slides rigged to the ruined fortress on Mene's Finger. Whoever was in charge ordered the rope cut. We lost three soldiers and Training Master Dom.'

'That's not the worst of it, Virreld.' Ydrin had aged, his face seamed with worry. 'Ludran has taken Varia prisoner. I don't understand how he managed that, but that's a question for later. We need to remove her from his clutches–'

'Ludran's not important,' Virreld said. 'He would use Varia as a hostage and keep her alive and unharmed. Urian is in charge. He has taken Varia's stones. Her peril increases while we talk.'

Ydrin swayed, and Garanth eased him onto a chair as raithen and captains reacted.

'Impossible!'

'How could anyone take her stones?'

'Who is this Urian?'

'Even a five-stone raithan couldn't overpower Lady Varia.'

Ydrin took a careful breath, a little colour returning to his face. 'She was overstretched – inadequate sleep, no proper meals, too many cares. It's happened. Let's deal with what we have. Questions can wait until Varia is safe.'

Frenn stepped forward. 'If she's held in the old fortress dungeons that will be a challenge. Unless raithen can access it.'

Virreld shook his head. 'Not through solid rock.'

'Then she is lost,' Frenn said.

'I'm willing to try,' Garanth said. 'If Gereyn can take me.'

'I will go. Alone.'

Ydrin shook his head. 'It can't be done.'

'It may be possible,' Virreld said. 'Leoric saw Varia chained to a wall. The fortress may be less of a ruin than it appears from this side of the gorge. We merely need to find the space occupied by the cells.'

'Merely!'

'Between us we can surely do that. Then raithen must attack from above while Gereyn ensures Varia's safety.'

'Some of my men are climbers, sir,' Frenn said. 'We could stage a two-pronged attack. Provide enough of a threat to occupy this Urian and distract him from his prisoner.'

'We must surprise him. If he threatens Varia, I shall withdraw rather than lose her. Let us link and search.'

Raithen thoughts filled my head, confirming Ydrin's assertion. Solid rock. Impossible. A water channel. An air vent. Nothing large enough to take a man. While most raithen searched from the old tower downwards, I scanned inwards from the stream outlet where it flowed over the cliff. Following the water channel upwards, I came to a space. 'There.'

A raithan confirmed it: a cell accessed from above by a narrow, twisting stairway.

Our plans were swiftly reviewed. Raithen under Virreld's leadership to strike at Urian's force, Frenn to lead an assault from the foot of Mene's Finger, Jud to hold the palace and Barys the city walls. Virreld would not permit me to shift until raithen were in position.

Ydrin did not want me to risk it. 'It's never been done.'

'You heard Lord Virreld,' Garanth said. 'He will withdraw if Lady Varia's captors threaten her. Gereyn can make that threat void.'

* * *

Varia

I came to full awareness. Pain pulsed through my sword arm, my head ached and ears buzzed. The ground moved beneath me. Heavy shackles encased my wrists and ankles. Their weight dragged on my surely broken wrist. I lay on an uneven stone floor, my outer clothes and armour missing. The dank air carried a tang of blood and sweat. A creeping sensation on my skin warned me someone was watching, waiting for me to regain consciousness. Perhaps the person who had taken my sword.

Blind panic swept over me. How could one of Ludran's men do that? I cast my mind back. When I had ordered Ludran to take over Barys' former post, I had removed the troopers who had served him longest and replaced them with men I could trust. According to Porel and Wulf he had disposed of those loyal troopers and filled the gaps with – what? Brigands? One of those was now standing guard over me. Not Ludran. He would consider it beneath him. One of his men could touch my sword with its five stones attuned to me. If he could touch it unscathed, anything was possible. He could use it against me. Then common sense returned. If he could use my stones against me, he would have done so already.

What could I do injured, chained and unable to touch power? One of my earliest lessons: the stones merely helped you focus. Power, if there was any, lay within you. Nyth could draw on power with only one stone, the others discarded, and Gereyn had long ago learned to heal without using focus stones. However, raithen relied on stones constantly. Every act of power was done through the stones, until raithen believed they could not manage without them.

The lady of the cursed wood had shown that belief false. She had set aside two stones to concentrate her power. Might I be able to feel my stones at a distance? If I tried and failed, would my jailer sense it?

Coward! Try or die. Disregarding the agony of my wrist, I reached out, my mind searching for the stones, and found nothing but emptiness. Baffled, I tried again.

Footsteps. A voice. 'We're under attack, Chief!'

A rumble of laughter close to me. 'Someone should watch the bitch. She'll be stirring soon. Keep your eyes on her and your paws *off* her. If you try anything, I'll geld you.'

Footsteps receded, leaving fast breathing in my ear, a calloused hand on my face and my neck.

I reached out again and felt the stones not far away. A wave of pain threatened my consciousness. I forced my mind to ignore it. Care and time would be needed to heal my wrist. Such healing would neither release me nor fend my jailer off. Worse, a botched attempt at healing could kill. My wrist would have to wait. I concentrated, working at increasing the temperature of my flesh, but that was too subtle. Whatever I did, it needed to be obvious. A full body breakout of boils might work. My jailor would think it something worse.

'Shit!' His creeping hand whipped from my overheated body.

I opened my eyes and blinked the sweat of my fever away. A dark figure, his features hidden. 'Water,' I croaked.

He backed through the door, leaving it open. Dim light entered the tiny cell.

The manacles had been designed for larger hands than mine. I twisted my broken wrist, stifling a scream as the bones ground together. Almost. A pulse of anguish defeated me. I heard splashing and turned my head. The ice-cold water he flung at me mostly missed. For a moment I thought he might hit me with the jug, but he did not. He stood staring at me, his thoughts crossing his face, wanting to hurt me, but afraid of retribution.

'I pay better than Lord Ludran.'

He guffawed. 'Ludran's two weeks dead. Free you and you'll reward me? Hah! You'd see me hanged, you lying bitch!'

'I'll hang your chief, and the man who took my sword. Where is it?'

He grinned, his teeth dark and broken. 'It's here. Just outside the door.'

'Why would he leave it?'

'Forgot it in his hurry. Want to see it?'

'If it pleases you to bring it.'

'Ain't we polite? I'd have shown you all kinds of things, if you didn't have some rich bitch's filthy disease.' He threw the jug at me and ducked out of the cell. It smashed against one of the chains, the shards cutting my skin.

Screams echoed through the open doorway. He had seized the hilt with both hands, knowing no better. I held my breath, drew on the stones and wrenched the chains from the walls.

He was back, looming over me, screaming still, his hands shaking uncontrollably, jerking my sword through the air.

Gripping both chain and power, I flung my left arm across my body. The chain looped in the air, and the manacle struck his neck. He fell like a pole-axed bull, my sword beneath him.

* * *

Gereyn

Virreld's call sounded in my mind. *Now!*

I focused on the space I had found and shifted for the centre, aware of the grip on my right arm too late. 'Duck!'

I sprawled on a body, and my uninvited companion caught his foot on something that clanked. Garanth recovered first, and propped the cell door open, letting in a little more light. 'Is she dead?'

For a moment, I was not sure. My heart faltered, but resumed its steady beat as I felt hers. 'She's alive.'

Garanth kicked the body at his feet. 'This one's dead. Can you retrieve her sword?'

I laid my sword beside Varia. Her hilt slid into my shielded hand. I drew it from underneath the corpse and sheathed it. 'Apparently so.' I took up my blade.

'Get her out of here. I'll take the stairs.'

'I'm not going to leave you here.'

'You can't carry us both.'

Varia was lighter than Garanth, but with the added weight of her shackles . . . 'I can try.'

'No. Take her. I have no ambition to drop out of the sky onto the rocks below.' Garanth lifted Varia, chains and all and passed her to me. 'Go.'

'God keep you.'

Garanth grinned. 'He has so far. God speed you, Gereyn.'

CHAPTER 50

Varia

I opened my eyes. Pale sunlight flooded my room, shadowing the face bent over me.

'Don't try to move just yet, Lady Varia. Let me check your arm first.'

'Sylve! I thought you had decided to stay in Althein.' When the decision was made to evacuate all students, some ilen had chosen to remain, Sylve among them.

'I was needed here.' She lifted my hand gently. 'Your wrist is healing nicely. You should avoid using your sword for a day or two, but you'll be fine.'

I struggled to return her smile. 'I might have to do that. I seem to have lost my sword.'

'No, you haven't! It's right here, beside you.' She smoothed the bedcover and frowned. 'That's odd. Who would have taken it?'

'I imagine it needed cleaning.' The last thing I saw before I lost consciousness was the bloody tip of my sword blade, the only part visible.

'Master Ydrin took care of that before he brought the sword here, Lady Varia. I'll make enquiries once I've given orders for your breakfast.'

'Thank you, Sylve.'

She slipped out before I thought to question her further. Typically of ilen, she would want me recovered before I started worrying about what had happened. As though ignorance might be comforting.

Porel brought my breakfast tray himself. Daylight did him no favours. He had lost weight, and looked as if his cares had increased. 'What would I do without you, Porel?'

'You would manage, Lady Varia. You don't make a fuss, and you put up with things you shouldn't. The kitchen is busy this morning, and I thought it quicker to serve you myself. I'll find a woman to help you bathe after you've eaten. Don't let anyone bully you into dealing with other matters until you're comfortable.'

My smile came more naturally this time. Porel had come to Tormene with my mother, when she married my father. He had attended me for as long as I could remember. 'I won't. Thank you.'

As he set the tray on the bedside table a waft of cinnamon reached me. I stared at a plate of eggs smothered in a pale yellow sauce. He must be distracted; he knows I prefer plain dishes. I had picked up the fork before I had a flash of recall. Sunlit dust in the air reminded me of Marrton, Ossner's guest chamber and Dern's pale face as he said, 'I trust Lord Ossner is not familiar with uncommon poisons.'

I dropped the fork, picked up the knife and raised my eyes to meet Porel's.

'You slept for the best part of a day, Lady Varia. You should eat.'

'After you.'

He took my discarded fork, scooped a large mouthful of eggs and sauce into his mouth and swallowed. 'It's very tasty.'

'I'm sure it is.' Maybe I had misjudged him. Or he had taken precautions as I had done at Marrton. I reached out for the bell-rope and tugged, ignoring the twinge in my wrist.

'You have many enemies, Lady Varia.'

'I did not think to number you among them, Porel.'

'I have always served your family.' He said it without expression, as if he had learned the words by rote. Then the glint in his eyes changed. He lunged towards me, long-bladed dagger in hand, and missed as I rolled out of bed.

I snatched up the cold warming pan in my good hand and swung round to meet his next thrust. Hearing footsteps in the passage, I knew better than to turn, but Porel had never been trained to fight. His gaze drifted behind me. I smashed the warming pan against his dagger, breaking his grip and likely his hand. Stepping back, I risked a swift glance behind. Two soldiers, their swords drawn, stared at Porel.

He staggered away from me, panting, clutching his hand. As I watched he grimaced, his mouth stretching his formerly plump cheeks taut. His body stiffened and he toppled. Only his eyes moved. I held his gaze while he lay shuddering. It took him several minutes to die.

I turned to the soldiers. 'Who's in charge here?'

'You mean apart from you, Lady?'

'Do I look as if I'm in charge of anything at the moment?'

He averted his gaze from my nightgown, his face flushed. 'Yes, Lady, I mean no, Lady.'

'Who ordered you to keep watch here?'

'Captain Barys, ma'am.'

'Wait outside.' I threw on shirt, breeches and tunic, pulled on boots, mail and a plated jacket, and buckled on a sword belt holding my spare sword and dagger. 'You, take me to Captain Barys. You, stand guard here. No one enters this room without the captain's authority.'

[1]*   *   *

Barys was arguing with Frenn. In other circumstances, I might have sympathised, but now their quarrel was the last thing I needed. 'Why did you send two men to guard me?'

Frenn turned away, but Barys met my gaze. 'Captain Jud said something about guarding you. I thought he'd given the orders, but Sylve said there were no guards this morning, so I sent two men. Where–'

'Your timing was excellent, Captain. Porel tried to poison me. When that failed, he drew a dagger on me. You'll find his corpse in my room. Tell me everything.'

---

[1]

His eyes widened, but he did not hesitate. He snapped his fingers. 'Sergeant, I want two guards on this door. Inform Lady Kirra and Master Ydrin that Lady Varia is conferring with her captains and invite them to join us. Have food and drink brought, and for the love of God ensure everything is tasted first.'

'My sword is missing, Captain. I'd like it found.'

'Organise a search, Sergeant, starting in Porel's quarters. Arrange for Lady Varia's chambers to be cleared and cleaned. I want a man standing by to carry messages. At the double, Sergeant.'

'Yes, sir!'

Frenn drew a chair forward for me and seated himself opposite, ignoring Barys' glare.

'Are your differences anything I should know about?' Better to clear the air sooner, rather than later.

'No, Commander.' Barys' response was a little too swift.

Frenn shook his head.

No one spoke. I already knew the news would be dire. Sylve's summons to Tormene, Barys' reluctance to tell me anything and Porel's treachery added up to something approaching disaster. I stared at the imperial symbol on the wall facing me as if it still had meaning. When food came, it was ashes in my mouth.

My mother entered first, my grandfather close behind her. I stood, and they embraced me, holding me close, my mother's tears drenching my cheek. When she released me, I took her hand, led her to a chair and sat beside her. Ydrin took the seat next to Frenn.

Barys sat at the head of the table. 'Captain Jud's guarding the outer walls and maintaining order in the city. The storehouses have been opened, food distributed to shops and market stalls and announcements made for everyone to go about their daily business, subject to a dusk-to-dawn curfew. There's been no trouble in the streets today. I would have said the palace is secure, but your news of Porel gives that the lie, Commander.'

'What of Porel?' Lady Kirra's tone was sharp.

'He tried to kill me. God knows why.'

'Virreld trusted him,' my mother said. A tear trickled down her cheek.

'So did I.' I squeezed her hand lightly and nodded to Barys to continue.

'I'll skip the details, Commander. Dom led us in. Jud had taken the armoury. Between us we overcame some of Ludran's men, but a score or more escaped to the ruined fortress on Mene's Finger. We were too late to prevent them capturing you.'

Mene's Tower, the old fortress across the wild river had been long-abandoned. I had assumed it a crumbling ruin.

'We were making plans for an assault when raithen arrived from the school here. Lord Virreld and Gereyn came from Althein, and Master Ydrin and Garanth from Mondun.'

Why isn't my father here? Where are Gereyn and Garanth?

'Lord Virreld led raithen to assault the fortress, while Gereyn took Garanth to rescue you, Commander.'

'That wasn't planned,' Ydrin said. 'Gereyn refused to take him, but Garanth seized his arm as he shifted. Gereyn brought you here. He was about to return for Garanth when the fortress exploded. Lord Virreld and raithen were safe behind their shields, but Garanth was buried and–'

Garanth! May you rest in peace.

'I lost fourteen men,' Frenn said bitterly.

'We'd already lost Dom, with three of his men.'

'Two raithen died,' Ydrin said.

How? That question must wait; another took priority. 'Where is my father?' I feared I knew, but hope has no limits.

'He died soon after we returned to the palace. It was sudden. Perhaps his heart, or–'

'Or by Porel's hand.' I bowed my head, unwilling to accept the loss of my father.

'We might have questioned Porel, Varia.'

I looked up. Lady Kirra's tears had dried and her face was stern. My gentle mother desired justice for my father, as much as I did. 'I did not kill him. He also died suddenly after he tasted the meal he brought me. I–'

The sergeant knocked and entered without waiting for a response. 'This was found in Porel's bedchamber, sir.'

Barys stretched out his hand, and I leaped up to snatch the box. Opened, it contained three quit seeds and a dusting of red powder. 'Ydrin, will you advise the sergeant and his men on hand-washing?'

After he and the sergeant had left us, I closed the lid, placed the box on the table and dusted my hands. Quit seeds were supposed to be safe to handle until cut or chewed, but the powder residue indicated that Porel had split at least one. 'The last time I opened this box it contained five quit seeds. I guess Porel used one for my father and one for me.'

'You did not eat his poisoned meal,' my mother said. 'What caused you to suspect him?'

'I don't believe I did. Not of this.' I gestured at the innocent-seeming box. 'I was uneasy. He was not quite himself, overly solicitous, and he had forgotten my aversion to sauces. It seemed wise to ask him to taste it for me. Where is Gereyn?'

'Digging in the ruins for Garanth,' Frenn said, his voice flat.

'No one could have survived that blast,' Barys said.

'What caused the explosion?'

Both captains spoke at once. I lifted a hand. 'Frenn?'

'It was a trap, Lady. I believe most of Ludran's men had fled before they lit the fuse.'

'We found Ludran's sword in the rubble,' Barys said. 'He must have died there.'

His meaning was clear, but I disagreed. Suicide would never have entered Ludran's mind. 'My captor told me Ludran has been dead for more than a fortnight. Perhaps he was a victim too. Somehow he fell into the hands of a man who is capable of something we believed impossible. A man who could break my shield and handle my sword unscathed. I don't know–'

'Where did Ludran meet such a man?' My mother's voice was hoarse, her pallor disturbing.

Barys answered her. 'When he took over my post, watching the roads though the Ridges. As to what happened . . . Sergeant Wulf knows more than anyone, but he's busy directing the search for survivors.'

'I should not have given Ludran that posting.'

'Hindsight is a poor judge of difficult decisions, Varia.' Ydrin had brought a steaming basin and a towel. 'Scrub your hands well. You are not immune to the evil of quit poison.'

CHAPTER 51

Gereyn

I shifted to the base of Mene's Finger and checked my shield. Frenn was climbing a side column, and the man ahead of him had already gained the top, when the old fortress exploded. The blast toppled the tower, hurling men and stones towards the raging torrent that separated the Finger from the imperial palace. Frenn ducked and clung to the rock face as flying fragments bounced off the column, mostly missing him. I shifted, seized him and shifted again.

Covered in dust, Frenn coughed, and spat blood. 'Where are my men?'

I shook my head, staunched his bleeding and tried to persuade him to leave the search for dead and wounded to others. I shared his distress, having no hope that Garanth might have survived. The stairway to the cell where Varia had been chained was now choked with rubble. I scanned the tumbled boulders for signs of life but found none. As I turned something drew my attention to the summit of Mene's Finger.

One of Frenn's men ran up. 'A dozen men missing, sir. Sergeant Wulf is organising the search.'

I shifted into the shadow of Mene's Finger, where a sergeant was talking to a grizzled and scarred trooper.

'Sergeant Wulf. What can we do for you, raithan?'

'I need to investigate something up there, Sergeant. Will you lend me a couple of men to watch my back?'

'It's overlooked from the Torr. You'd be exposed to bowmen.'

The trooper whistled. 'It would be a hell of a shot from the Torr, almost straight into the sun. Anyways, they've likely fled.'

'It's still a big risk.'

'One I must take, but I'd prefer to have a bowman or two watching. Just in case.'

Wulf nodded. 'See to it, Midge. Take four men, and try not to make it obvious you're on watch.'

'Me, obvious? You must be confusing me with someone else.' He grinned. 'What's your name, raithan? So we know who to tell when someone kills you.'

'Gereyn.'

'Got a personal score to settle, Gereyn?'

'I have.'

'So have we. Hope they show their hand.' Midge casually adjusted the position of the bow slung over his shoulder. 'Here, you three, come with me, and you!' The five soon separated, calling to each other about missing comrades.

I dropped my shield and re-cast it, focusing without touching my sword. After all the practice under Nyth's eye, it came instinctively. Maybe Urian's blocking ability only worked against focus stones.

I shifted to the broken dust-clouded top of the Finger. Part of the eastern wall remained and would obstruct the view of anyone on the face of the Torr. I swung round, but saw no one on or near the base of the palace walls. Nevertheless, my sense of being overlooked persisted. I scanned my surroundings and sensed nothing. The only movement came from Wulf's men clambering around the Finger.

A gust of wind stirred the dust at my feet. Instinctively I averted my eyes, and saw the shattered body, face down in a rubble strewn depression. Invisible from any other position. The hairs on the back of my neck stood up. I shifted to hover above the unstable stones and looked down. A sword impaled the broken corpse, as if deliberately positioned for its owner to find. I landed, tugged Varia's sword free, laid it on a cracked flagstone, and gently turned the broken body. With fingers that trembled, I brushed Garanth's hair from his face and stood.

An arrow clattered on the rocks. I spun round, ducking instinctively. Did that pierce my shield, or did my move spoil his aim? The bowman must be close to the base of the palace wall, but I could not see him. I held my shield firm, considered the possibilities, gathered power and splashed fire across the opposite cliff. Dammit! Fire had struck the wall, except for one patch. Leoric's confused words came back to me. 'He's invisible, but he isn't.' If the first, I was in trouble. If the second, maybe not.

Urian, Lady Kirra's brother, had the ability to stop raithen using power. That's why I couldn't see him. I'd been searching with power. A shift to the foot of the Finger. Another into deepest shade. I dropped all power and ran my eyes over the cliff. There! He had used the same trick I had, hiding in a cleft. I needed to draw Midge's attention to the right spot before Urian killed again.

The troopers had spread out. Had they seen him? I recast my shield, gathered water from the river and flung it at the marksman, not expecting the trick to work. All Urian needed to do was ignore it. Water drenched the rock all around him, but the cleft was dry and that was enough.

One of Midge's men shouted, 'Something odd in the cleft. Aim for the dry spot, loose!'

Arrows flew.

I shifted to the battlements above the cleft, intending to call more archers, but even as I turned, one trooper fell. I dropped my shield, released all power and leaped from the wall. Plunging downwards, I had all the time in the world to prepare my stroke. Pain pierced my thigh, but I ignored it. My blade cleaved the bowman's head as I drew power to cushion my landing – too late. My ankle shattered. Fool! I should have shifted!

After I achieved what Lenathe called a 'battlefield repair' on my leg and ankle, I turned to face Midge. Wulf was running towards us.

'You got the bastard!'

'Pity it took so long.' Wulf glanced at my blood-soaked leg. 'You need to get that seen to.'

Midge spat on Urian's bloody face. 'Damn it! I wanted to claim his head.'

I understood his reaction 'You still can, Midge. Slice his head off as a trophy and sling the rest in the river. I wish we'd got that filth Makah too.'

I sheathed my bloody sword – Cap would have my guts for that – and shifted back to Garanth as Frenn led more soldiers from the palace. About time. Maybe they would be able to round up the last of Urian's men. I placed Varia's sheathed sword on Garanth's chest, lifted him and shifted back to the palace.

The audience hall echoed silence. Virreld lay before his throne, his face serene. I laid Garanth beside the late emperor. Words were inadequate, but something must be said. 'You fought all your life for those you loved, Garanth. Rest in peace now.'

My eyes rested on Virreld. 'You asked me to forgive you, and I did. But I failed to ask you to forgive me. I misjudged you, and it's too late to set that right. I'm sorry for that.' I withdrew to a dark corner and sat on the floor, absently working a full healing on my ankle and thigh while my thoughts dwelt on Garanth and Virreld.

CHAPTER 52

Varia

I could not yet spare the time to visit my father's bier; the dead must not take priority over the living. I bathed swiftly and dressed with care, as befits the imperial heir's first appearance in public as uncrowned empress. My escort awaited me at the outer courtyard, and my standard-bearer took his place behind me. Our progress through unusually quiet streets attracted no little attention: shutters were flung open, children cheered and stout housewives beamed. I smiled at the children and raised a hand in acknowledgement of my people's welcome.

At the city storehouses I consulted with the store masters, who reassured me. Although the city had lacked trade ships since Ludran had closed the port, farmers were coming to market again. The masters reported no significant shortages. I thanked them, praised their management under the recent difficult circumstances and rode on to the port with my escort. Fishing boats were returning to harbour.

Two trade ships still rode at anchor. The harbour master shook his head, 'It doesn't make sense for them to stay, my Lady. Not now their captains are back on board.'

'Perhaps they still hope to make a profit on their cargo. Fly the imperial standard and invite them in.'

I watched the exchange of signals between the two ships, my escort lined up behind me, and the imperial standard flying proudly overhead. After a short delay, two boats moored at the quay and the two captains approached. 'Welcome to Tormene, sirs. Will you accompany me to the harbour master's office for refreshments and discussion?' They bowed. Their faces had given nothing away, but I had read their signals and did not doubt they would accept the best deal they could negotiate.

Despite the short notice, the harbour master produced a fine selection of wine and refreshments. I took little part in the conversation until our guests had refilled their cups and plates. 'On behalf of the empire and the city I apologise for your treatment during our small domestic disagreement. Now that matters have been satisfactorily resolved, I trust you will feel able to resume trade with the empire as before.'

The darker-skinned captain smiled broadly, his teeth as grey as the shark's tooth hanging from his neck. 'There is the question of compensation.'

'A matter to be negotiated, Captain. Your priority, I imagine, is to sell your goods, purchase what we have to offer and return to your home port.'

The taller captain's gaze shifted from me to the harbour master. 'I understand Tormene has suffered a shortage of many things during the recent difficulties.'

The harbour master shook his head. 'On the contrary, our warehouses are full. You are free to buy whatever takes your fancy, Captain. The usual port charges will be waived.'

'As part of your compensation, to enable you to forget any discomfort during the unfortunate delay, we might pay the balance... Would a man's weight in gold enable you to forgive us?'

'What man?'

'With no intent to offend, may I suggest that we use the heavier of you two as the measure?' I paused, while they studied each other. 'If either of you has silks or sapphires to trade, I should like to see the finest. For something exceptional, I might be persuaded to pay up to twice the usual price. I'm sure the harbour master will be delighted to entertain you while you discuss the possibilities. If you will forgive me, I have other duties.'

After a great deal of bowing, I left the captains in the harbour master's capable hands. Expensive or not, I considered the deal worth the cost. Word would spread that whatever had been amiss was minor, and that trade with the empire was again profitable. Some foreigners might initially take the new empress for a gullible fool. They would soon learn otherwise.

I ordered my escort to wait outside the temple. If I was unsafe within God's house, then indeed my time had come. A lay brother bade me welcome and led me to the high priest's office. He opened a door, murmured, 'Lady Varia,' and stood back to allow me entrance. I had anticipated a suite of rooms such as one might find in the palace. Instead I walked into a small cell, furnished only with a tiny table, two upright chairs, a shelf of scriptures and a prayer desk. The door swung shut behind me.

The high priest, who wore a robe similar to that of the lay brother, rose to greet me. 'My child, you are welcome. May the good Lord comfort you in your sorrows.'

I kissed his ring and sat. The chair was more comfortable than it looked.

The high priest's eyes twinkled. 'I'm not one for regalia and other finery, though I shall wear the robes of my office for your coronation. In the circumstances, you will wish that to take place as soon as possible.'

'I am already acting as empress. There must be a period of official mourning for my father. Would two weeks be too soon for the coronation?'

'I believe three weeks might be required to ensure the appropriate degree of ceremony. Your people will be glad of a reason to rejoice. I must say, I'm surprised you felt it necessary to come in person. You must have many calls on your time.'

'I am indeed short of time to do all that is demanded of me, but I am even shorter of men to delegate to. My chamberlain and my advisors are dead, as are many of my soldiers.'

'I had no idea matters were so bad.'

'It is not public knowledge.'

'Will you permit me to offer you one of my most able servants to assist you until you can appoint your own?'

'I thank you, my Lord, but the dividing line between state and religion is best not obscured.'

He laughed. 'Forgive me. I quite agree, and have no intention of crossing that line. The man I had in mind is . . . I hesitate to say irreligious. Perhaps he is best described as one who for whom religion is of low priority. He is however loyal, able and an excellent historian and tactician.'

'You would miss him then.'

'When you discover that his single-mindedness irritates you more than his abilities, by all means return him to me. In the meantime, I shall heave a sigh of relief for my respite.'

I smiled. 'On the understanding that this arrangement is purely temporary, I accept your offer, my Lord. I am grateful.'

* * *

My first act on returning to the palace was to strip off my rich and heavy formal attire. Wearing a simple robe over the necessary mail, I called on my mother, hoping to cheer her a little with the minor successes of my day. The guards directed me to a room in the east wing, where my mother and grandfather stood over a bier, its occupant scarred and battered, face disfigured and head cloven. Such had been the force of the blow, I thought it an axe stroke.

Ydrin turned. 'Here lies a man who could handle stones of power without harm, but not use them. He could render any raithan powerless and hide himself from power-enhanced view, but could not bear to live among those who wielded power forever beyond his reach.'

'He was raithan?' That would explain the sadness in my grandfather's voice and my mother's tears.

'He was unable to pass the tests. He was my son.'

Blood pounded in my ears. 'Oh, Grandfather.'

'His loss is an old grief. I had not thought to see him again.'

I embraced my mother, and she clung to me. 'Gereyn killed him. A sword blow, since he could not use power against Urian.'

Impressive. One more reason to track down the elusive Gereyn and set matters straight. I thrust the thought aside. 'I understand your grief but cannot regret his death. He would have killed me.'

'I suspect he manipulated Porel into killing Virreld and attacking you. We know he set the trap in the old fortress, which killed so many good men. I am sorry to have to confirm Garanth's death.'

I had feared such news. Nevertheless, it was hard to bear.

Ydrin wiped his eyes. 'Have you happier tidings, Varia?'

I told them the tale of my day, and Ydrin smiled. I took my mother's hand and kissed it. 'I have a vigil to keep.'

'Eat first,' Lady Kirra said. 'You look fragile.'

'You are used to the look of padded armour. What is underneath is unchanged.'

Ydrin took my face in his hands and looked deep into my eyes. 'Eat. You will need all your strength in the days to come.'

'I know.'

CHAPTER 53

Gereyn

Varia's call came as I sat beside my campfire. I focused and sensed the evil of aryth near Mondun. At this distance I could not be sure, but guessed halaryth accompanied karyth. I dropped an airtight cover over the fire and the glowing embers died. Untied the horse and smacked its rump to send it off towards Tormene. After one final glance around I shrugged into my pack, drew my sword and shielded myself. Answering Varia's call, I shifted across the miles to its source in a matter of moments, holding my breath against the bitter chill and careful to check my shield before landing.

Aryth drifted far above Mondun's silent, empty streets, though the air immediately above the roofs was clean. Here and there streets lamps burned above closed doors, but not a glimmer of light shone through rows of heavily shuttered windows. All my senses alert, I made my way quietly along the street towards my summoner. Directly ahead an archway led into the cobbled main square, apparently deserted, but anything might lurk in the dark shadows. I hesitated, shifted a short distance, stumbled on landing and told myself to concentrate.

'Sir.'

I whirled. A lighted doorway revealed a soldier, naked blade in hand. The edge of a bandage showed at his wrist beneath his mail. I stepped inside, but did not release my shield until the door was softly closed and barred behind me.

'This way, sir.'

A short passage let to a hall crammed with raithen and soldiers, everyone's attention fixed on the blazing fire in the hearth. No, not the fire, the chimney.

Varia turned to face me. 'Do you feel them, Gereyn?'

'There are many.' They were gathering overhead.

'Fewer than there were. We have accounted for several halaryth over the past two nights. Tonight at least one nikaryth is up there.'

'More than one.' The name hardly mattered. I felt spikes of great evil, hiding behind a herd of slaves, as lightning builds to strike from amid dark clouds, impatiently waiting to accomplish their desires – destruction and death. Their constant movement frustrated my attempts to count them.

'If we wait, they will seek to break our defences when *they* choose. I prefer to take them by surprise. We must work together.'

'Yes, Lady.' I kept my voice steady with an effort. Though I feared to fall into the claws of halaryth, what now hovered over us was far worse. Nikaryth were the masters of the hunt, karyth their hounds, halaryth the huntsmen urging the pack on to kill the quarry – men. Against such might, I must maintain my shield at maximum strength for as long as needed, which might be while the night lasted, and that would drain my strength. Varia had faced this before and understood how to nurse her resources, but I had never faced nikaryth in force. Fighting one had exhausted me, but then I had been wounded. And this time my shield was stronger.

'Are you ready?'

She would not have called me to Mondun if she did not trust me to protect her. I nodded and set a barrier to prevent her emotions distracting me. Now I was as ready as possible.

'You and I will come down on them from above. Other raithen will attempt to surround them.' She touched my hand.

My shield melded seamlessly with hers forming the strongest defence yet. Like those fights with Dern at my back. I remembered to breathe.

Someone opened an outside door.

'Now!'

We shifted into darkness high above the town. Doors burst open, soldiers spilled out into the square, and halaryth swooped down. More raithen appeared. Maybe there were enough of us to do this.

I plunged my sword into the nearest halaryth's chest. Blood poured from the wound; it twisted away from me, as if to escape, but the damage was mortal. I wrenched my blade from its body, and it dropped out of sight.

A halaryth backed away, tempting me to pursue, but I sensed a trap.

Varia confirmed it. 'Stay close.'

I swept my gaze around the night sky and felt a resurgence of evil. 'Here they come.'

My sword arm trembled with the effort to maintain my shield against the malice directed at me. Nevertheless, when a halaryth advanced I found the strength to lunge, directing a surge of power through my blade. It fell in flames. Varia beheaded another. Halaryth scattered, sped away, vanished.

'Up.'

I shifted withVaria and looked down. The great nikaryth were merely dark shapes hovering on motionless wings, keeping their distance from raithen.

'There.'

We shifted to face nikaryth and raithen followed. Horned, beaked, snakelike, armoured or furred, no two nikaryth were alike. The creatures of nightmares drove karyth towards me, but Varia's strength guarded me. I was not afraid. Karyth died on my sword and Varia's, shrieking their harsh death cries and clawing vainly at my shield. Halaryth returned, fewer than before. Nikaryth drove them to attack, as they had driven karyth. When cringing halaryth came within my reach, I slew them as easily as karyth. For a time that was my overriding purpose: to guard Varia and to kill.

The night wore on until exhaustion threatened me. Its early signs could be easily dismissed, but I knew better than that. The first muscle tremors gave warning, and I tried to relax my shoulders. My aches and shakes would steadily increase, wearing away my strength. At first it would be physical misery, my muscles not working as they should, but then my mind would be affected. I would begin to make stupid decisions that might mean death, not just for me, but also for Varia, for raithen, for the soldiers still fighting in the square and for the people of Mondun. Dammit! I won't be the first to give up.

Nikaryth surrounded us, mocked my efforts to defend myself and laughed at my failing power. They might flee at dawn, but I did not know that for certain. There was so much I did not know; my ignorance might kill us all.

The nearest nikaryth, in the semblance of a giant bat, bared its great teeth and made an obscene gesture. Fury filled me, threatening to override my instinctive caution, but I dared not release even a small part of the power holding my shield in place. That was what it wanted. It came closer, almost within my reach. I allowed my sword arm to drop slightly. The still grinning nikaryth struck. Filled with loathing, I slashed with power, and the nikaryth died.

In that instant, my shield slipped. As I struggled to reinforce it, a halaryth reached out to grasp my blade, and my hold on power wavered. In panic, I tightened my grip on the hilt and sent a surge of power through my sword. The halaryth's claws sprang apart, and it fell back. Two more halaryth rushed towards me.

Varia was hurt. I could not exert full power while shielding her, but it would take all my remaining strength to fend off both halaryth. I could not even be certain of destroying them. If I was fast enough, I might be able to gain sufficient respite to reinforce the shield around Varia.

I contracted my shield and directed a strike of power at the two halaryth. It rebounded off an impenetrable barrier. My shield gave way and sudden agony pierced my side. In despair, I fought to recast my shield and maintain my failing grip on my sword. I needed to rejoin Varia, but could no longer sense her. Dark flames overwhelmed me. Surrounded by shadow, I no longer knew where I was, or where the enemy was. I attempted a blast of power, my sword fell from my hand, and darkness overcame me.

CHAPTER 54

Gereyn

Pain dragged me into consciousness, the metallic taste of blood in my mouth. I could not open my eyes. My fingers groped for my sword.

'Lie still. You are safe.'

A gentle touch brought light to my eyes, I blinked. After a moment, I recognised Lenathe. 'Drink this.'

She lifted my head. I swallowed the bitter drink and sank into sleep as she lowered me to the pillow.

When I next woke the pangs of my wounds had gone, but the anguish of my failure remained. I reached for my sword before I remembered. It was gone. Varia was lost. I attempted to sit upright. My head swam, and bees buzzed in my ears. I swayed, hands gripped me, and forced me back on the bed.

'Rest, fool. There's nothing you can do,' Burll growled.

'She is dead.'

'No.' Burll's jaw tightened. 'Lady Varia was alive when they took her.'

God save her! I swallowed. 'Give me a sword.'

'There is no sword for you.'

'Give me a sword,' I repeated, frantic at Burll's stupidity, the delay. I tried to sit up again.

Burll slammed me back against the pillow. 'Listen and understand.' He thrust his blade forward, hilt first. 'Three stones are set here. That suffices for me. Did I hand you this, the power remaining in the stones would burn you to the bone. Each stone knows its wielder, and no other handling is possible. The sword you used belonged to Varryn. You held it unscathed only because the stones had forgotten his touch. Did any raithan pass you a sword or any ilan give you stones, did you hold nine stones, you could not use them. Even the late emperor's sword, barely used recently, would kill you. There are no free stones, none that have forgotten their owner. Do you understand now?' He released me.

I met his fierce gaze. Nyth had said the same. There must be a way! I made an attempt to draw power from my one remaining stone. Weakness defeated me, and I sagged back on the pillow.

'You are fortunate. Without the stone you wear you would have died when you lost your sword. If you want to live, you must rest.'

I closed my eyes, drifting into a dream in which a dark-haired girl with Iylla's face begged me to save her. I turned my back on her, closed my ears to her screams, and woke soaked with sweat and tears. When I slept again, I dreamed of Dern bleeding, dying, pleading for help. Uncaring, I walked away from him. At my next waking, I willed my eyes to remain open.

Lenathe brought food and fed me. She bathed my face and hands. 'Do you need anything?

'My clothes.' I needed her help to dress, being as helpless as a newborn pup. My legs barely supported me, but I insisted on wearing mail under my plated jacket. At last I was fully clothed, my empty sword belt buckled in place.

She helped me downstairs.

I heard voices outside, but recognised none. 'Where's Burll?'

Lenathe shook her head. 'He was only lent to us. Now he is back with the tribes, until he is needed again.'

'I need to talk to raithen.'

'I will take you. Maybe they can persuade you to see sense.'

Leaning on her, I crossed the street, struggled up the entrance steps and stumbled over the raised threshold. She guided me past a score of pallets, their bandaged occupants unconscious or restlessly asleep, and through a door into a small courtyard. Two women sat on a stone bench. The younger woman stood and walked away, displaying no interest in another raithan. Lenathe followed her.

The woman on the bench looked up. 'Sit down before you fall over.' Her face was stern, but her eyes softened as she met mine. 'Don't blame yourself, Gereyn. Lady Varia made mistakes too. We all have our limits.'

Her voice was familiar. 'Do I know you?' I sat next to her.

She smiled. 'Once I recommended we kill you. I am wiser now. My name is Maris.'

'What can we do? Burll says there are no spare stones.'

'No one tells me such things, but it's likely true.'

'Do we sit here and wait for them to kill us? I must have a sword.' In my present state I could achieve nothing without more stones.

Maris lowered her voice. 'Did Burll tell you there is no free sword for you to use? He is mistaken.'

My heart missed a beat. Was there hope, after all?

'You will have been told to be cautious, but now we are desperate. If you can wield five stones, you may be able to add more, especially if the owner has not held them for long, provided you do not hold more than nine all told. God help you if you try that! One sword *may* meet your need, but there is no certainty. Its owner has barely handled it for several years. With that sword and the stone you wear,' her eyes flicked to the chain hanging from my neck, 'you only need three more. If you are willing to take the risk.'

I understood. Burll had assumed I would not be able to use Virreld's sword – he might be right. A chill gripped me. I met Maris' bleak gaze. 'The late emperor's sword,' I whispered. 'Where is it?'

Her eyes brightened. 'It lies on his tomb waiting for someone with the courage to seize it. If he had joined with Lady Varia and Lord Varryn when Lord Invar was taken, together they might have saved him, but the emperor would not do it. He did not believe fifteen stones would suffice.' She grimaced. 'Perhaps he was right.' She tightened her grip on her sword hilt. 'Now we have nothing to lose. No raithan has more than three stones. Without you and Lady Varia we cannot stand against nikaryth. I fear they know it. Your choice is to wait for death to find you, or try to save her. You prefer to make the attempt, even if it means falling alive into the claws of nikaryth and halaryth. Don't you?'

'Yes.' I did not hear the word, but Maris understood me.

She nodded. 'Then we must decide how to obtain the sword. Speed is essential. Every hour that passes diminishes hope.'

In the silence that followed, I could feel my heart beating. 'I can't shift to Tormene. Could you shift me there?'

Her face had paled, even her lips. 'I must try, or–'

'No!' The cry from the street brought us both to our feet. Maris ran, and I followed as fast as I could, using the wall for support. She pushed through soldiers and raithen, and I slipped through the gap she made. Lenathe crouched over a man slumped on the cobbles. Faril, his face grey, his eyes squeezed tightly shut and his blackened hand, a mere claw, clamped around a sword hilt.

'God's love!' someone exclaimed.

I knelt beside Lenathe. Reaching into Faril, I felt her healing power. If Faril were freed from Virreld's sword, she might be able to provide some measure of relief for him. Whether she could save his hand was not my concern. I reached for the sword. My fingers barely touching the hilt, I drew on power to free Faril swiftly and gently.

Faril half opened his pain-dulled eyes. 'Save her!'

I closed my fingers on the sword-hilt. The five stones did not burn me. Strength flowed into me, driving out all trace of weariness. I stood unwavering. 'I will.'

As I turned away Maris caught my free arm. Unable to accept any further delay, I raised my sword, but then I saw the stone on her open palm. I lowered my blade, took the stone – it did not burn – and set it in place. 'Thank you, Maris.' Two more raithen stepped forward; each gave me one stone.

'No more.' Maris' eyes met mine, and she smiled. 'My blessing.' She cried, 'Go with God!'

I turned my gaze upwards, drew power through the nine stones, more power than I had dreamed possible, set my shield and shifted away from Mondun.

* * *

Varia was incapable of calling me. Her despair drew me, but now I had hope. Faril, Maris and two raithen, whose names I did not know, had given me the means to save Varia. Failure and folly forgotten, power throbbed in my veins and raced through my sinews. I flung myself across the intervening heavens and into hell. My arrival, in a blaze of power-wrought light, illuminated a scene that caused my heart to skip a beat and drove out all doubts, all terror, such feelings consumed by my furious rage.

Bare rock dropped into dizzy depths and soared to sky-touching heights. Open vents disgorged acrid smoke and steam. Flames leaped from molten cauldrons and scorched their surroundings. I stood on cinders and bones, but barely noticed.

Varia dangled by her wrists, the chains a fraction too short for her to support her weight on the ledge below her feet. Stakes driven through her mail into her flesh pinned her body on each side. More chains linked the stakes to iron posts. A single stone hung from her neck. Her sword lay on the unreachable ledge.

In the mirror image of her position, hung a slumped figure barely recognisable as human. His body skeletal, his skin partly flayed, his wounds leaking blood and pus. One stone on a leather band tied round his forehead kept him alive. His burning blue eyes, on the brink of madness, fixed on Varia.

I closed my eyes against the sight and opened them immediately. If Varia could bear to look, so could I. This barely alive ruin of a man could only be her younger brother Invar, taken alive, chained and tortured for aryth amusement, and now tormented by his sister's suffering. His face, its skin stretched tight over his sunken cheeks, revealed nothing. Only his eyes, and Varia's unswerving gaze, proved he lived.

CHAPTER 55

Gereyn

A halaryth twisted one of the spikes that held Varia. It threw back its head, making a sound halfway between a laugh and a howl. I shifted, slashed its throat and swung back to behead its fellow, too busy shortening Invar's chains to notice me. Without pausing I sliced on down through Invar's stakes and chains and sent a ball of flame to consume the pitiful wing of karyth that appeared above me. If they were short of hounds, the masters must do their own killing. I cut Varia free and extended my impenetrable shield to cover her and Invar. We would live or die as one. The extended shield securely in place, I delved into Varia and Invar to provide a fraction of relief and strength. They lay as dead. A rush of halaryth and nikaryth swooped down to surround us.

My shield held. I shifted to take two halaryth by surprise, blasted them and shifted back to ensure my shield covered Varia and Invar. Nikaryth hung back and summoned black clouds of karyth. I flung lightning bolts at the hounds, destroying many outright and leaving survivors blinded, blundering into and clawing at each other. Reckless halaryth came close enough to attack me, I slew them, and deflected nikaryth's dark fire. Alone against many, I needed to shift constantly and swiftly, but dared not increase my distance from Varia and her brother. I had come to save her, and could not leave them. Flight was no answer. This was a chance to reduce – or destroy – the aryth threat. They had not expected my enhanced power. If I fled with Varia and Invar, they would be free to breed replacement karyth. Next time they would be ready for me.

An attack on nikaryth was best done sooner, before the repeated attacks wore me down. Eventually, I would succumb to fatigue, my shield would fail, and Varia and Invar would die. If they were not already dead.

I thrust that thought from my mind. Remembering my failure at Mondun, I strengthened my shield and focused my gaze on the closest halaryth. They watched me, the expressions on their faces ranging from hate to disdain. I selected one at random and sent a bolt of power through its chest. As the remainder scattered, I shifted to take myself away from their renewed attacks. With small shifts, I came at them from above, below and behind, constantly in motion, ducking and weaving, shifting away and back, to kill and wound.

Gasping for breath in the foul air, but unwilling to use power to filter it, I looked round. Halaryth and karyth had vanished. Nikaryth surrounded me, had cut me off from Varia and Invar. They had not linked together, but several were working independently to dismantle my shield. I feinted towards the two nikaryth immediately opposite me. As they struck, I shifted to land between Varia and Invar. Varia stood, sword in hand, unchained. Blood trickled from her wounds. She swayed, her free hand on one of the posts. Invar's sword lay near him, but he did not move. If he still lived, he would not have the strength to stand, let alone wield a sword. It did not matter. Added to mine, Varia's power would be enough. God grant it!

I called her, and she responded. Power flooded into me. My grip on my shield steadied as a wave of screaming nikaryth dived down. Varia stood unsupported, her blade flaring, and I fought with her: raithan and freak working together. Blazing brightly, leaking fire, I flung bolts of power, lunged, slashed and thrust. Nikaryth fell.

Weakened by injury and anguish, and surely diverting part of her shield to cover Invar, exhaustion would cripple Varia first. Even with nine stones, I would not last long without her support. Together we must destroy as many nikaryth as possible. If we failed here, Aryth would rule the world. I exchanged a swift glance with Varia. Her grim expression confirmed my suspicions. Her brow creased with pain, she pressed her free hand against her side. Yet her blade did not waver. She nodded. Together, we struck again.

A scream. It did not come from my throat or from Varia's. A nikaryth fell almost at my feet, and other nikaryth fell back in dismay.

'Join with me.' A hoarse voice, close to me.

Invar had gained his feet and grasped his sword. Now there was hope! I linked him to us and gathered power, knowing I must release it before it engulfed him. My sword warmed and glowed red. All things became possible.

Invar's voice sounded in my mind. *They have joined. You must target the one in control.*

I stared at him. *Which one?* Even as I asked the question, I felt power flow from one of the nikaryth, its body and wings as black as night, great horns rising from its head and glistening fangs hanging from its gaping maw. I shifted a short distance – the attack missed me.

Not that one. The jester!

A movement at the side caught my attention. I shifted upwards and, from my new position, identified the jester. Its body and limbs were longer than other nikaryth, as if it had been stretched. In an almost human face, it opened its mouth impossibly wide and laughed manically.

I channelled the power surging through my veins. The strike burst from three blades as one and reduced the jester to bloody fragments. The circle of nikaryth faltered. As I swept the head from the power-filled horned nikaryth, a backlash of power broke over nikaryth. Their bodies shattered, melted and dissolved into trickles of dirty liquid. Foul droplets dried into ash and dispersed into grey smoke as the heat of our three-fold power consumed them.

* * *

I fought to maintain my grip, to control my power, to establish what threat remained. Before my searching eyes could penetrate the smoke of my enemies' destruction, Invar failed. As he fell, my shield weakened. With an effort that hurt, I held the fragile shield in place over myself and Varia and fought to release excess power and extend the shield to cover Invar once more. Too late. The backlash of power caught him, a groan escaped his lips, his sword slipped from his hand and he lay still.

I turned slowly. Darkness, denser than before, pressed in on me. The last shreds of nikaryth contaminated the air I breathed. In this new form, they meant to poison me and complete their victory. That was madness! With an effort, I focused.

Total destruction surrounded me. I sensed no life among the twisted, shattered bodies of karyth and halaryth. Thank God! I released my shield slowly, and used the remnants of my fading power to draw both Invar and Varia to me. I held them close, striving to fix my mind on my destination, a place of safety. It kept slipping away. No longer capable of sensible thought, I gritted my teeth, determined to hold on to power and shifted.

CHAPTER 56

Gereyn

I awoke cold and stiff. Smoke lingered in my nostrils and throat. Despair came close to dragging me back into oblivion. I fought it. Coughing smoke from my lungs, I separated the scent of hot lamp oil from wood smoke. Panic receded. I lay between soft linen sheets under the weight of woollen blankets. The crystal clad stone hung on its chain around my neck. My sword lay nearby. I opened my eyes to a bare stone walled room I did not recognise. It was not Althein, my intended destination. Where was I? My sword rested on the bed beside me, four stones imbedded in the hilt. I blinked away tears. Thank God someone had the wit to remove the surplus stones.

A woman bent over me. I could not recall her name. She turned away to speak to someone else. 'He is awake.' She withdrew, and another woman came forward into the lamplight.

'Lady Kirra,' I managed to say before distress closed my throat.

She sat on a chair beside the bed and laid her hand on mine. 'All is well, Gereyn. You are safe at Tormene, and Varia is alive and well, thanks to you.'

I could not bear her gratitude. 'I lost Invar.'

She smiled at me, and that was hardest of all to bear. 'He is at peace. More importantly, you have freed us from the fear of aryth.'

'Invar made that possible. Without him, I would have failed. Varia would have died.'

'My dear, it was not Invar who lent you his strength, but Varryn.'

Horrorstruck, I stared at her. He died at The Tower of the Winds. Unless... the sorceress lied! She gave Varryn to her fellow nikaryth, knowing that doomed him.

'Varia and her brothers were lost without hope, until you freed them. You are not to blame. We grieve for them, yet it is a comfort to us that Invar will lie in hallowed ground in Althein.' She took my hand in hers. 'There is no shadow on our rejoicing that Varia lives.'

Unable to form a coherent denial, unwilling to disturb her calm acceptance of her losses, I was silent. I knew my guilt. It was all of a piece. I had failed Invar, and unknowingly Varryn, as I had failed Selthel... as I had consistently failed from the beginning. If Lady Kirra found ease in forgiving me, I would not take that from her. I understood grief and the need for comfort. She sat quietly beside me, and after a time I closed my eyes and slept.

When I next woke, Ydrin sat beside me. 'I see you're much better.'

Am I? 'What of Faril?'

The smile faded from Ydrin's face. 'He lost his hand. I doubt he will ever be free from pain. Lenathe works healing on him constantly, but he refuses to let his injury hinder him. He insists on teaching his students as before.'

I shuddered inwardly at the recollection of Faril's hand grasping the sword hilt. That might have been my fate. I did not understand why it had not been. 'Were the extra stones returned to Burll, Maris and . . .' I did not know their names.

'They will be returned to their original owners when your hold on them has faded. In the meantime they are in Nyth's care. Will that do?'

I could not smile. 'It will do very well.' I lay back on the pillow and closed my eyes.

As soon as I was fit to move unaided, I asked about Garanth's grave.

'As his widow wanted, there is nothing to mark his grave,' Ydrin said.

'Widow?' Did he find happiness again after all?

Ydrin explained.

'I'd like to meet her. I'm sorry, I interrupted you.'

'Rightly. Garanth would have expected nothing else. There is a memorial to him next to Virreld's tomb. I will show you.'

'I'd like to see that.'

* * *

The tombs were as cold as the palace passages had been the night I had first come to Tormene. Since then I had learned that careful use of power made adjustment to cold or heat possible. Lamps alongside Virreld's tomb brightened his stone features. Garanth's memorial stood under a skylight, his stance a familiar one, naked sword in hand and poised to attack.

'I will leave you here,' Ydrin murmured. 'Can you find your way back?'

'I think so.'

I stood alone before Garanth's statue. I had hoped to know him better. And share the promised ale.

A footstep. I slipped into the shadows. Varia knelt to pray before her father's tomb. I wish I had known Virreld better too. I waited patiently until she rose. 'Lady Varia.'

She whirled, her sword half out of its sheath before she recognised me. 'Gereyn. I am glad you are well.'

I wanted nothing more than to leave, but her words demanded a response. 'Likewise, my Lady.' I turned to go.

'There is a matter you and I must discuss.'

I cocked my head. 'Yes, Lady Varia?'

Her eyes narrowed.

'It does not need to be now. You are mourning your father and Garanth.' I moved my weight from one foot to another, resisting the temptation to shift away from her, which would only increase her anger.

'Your dealings with Captain Jud. If you remember, I began this conversation some time ago. You were not able to make a coherent reply then. I trust this time your thoughts are in order.'

She had struck me and told me what I had done was unforgivable. 'I have begged Captain Jud's pardon.'

'Do you consider that sufficient compensation for your treatment of him?'

'No . . . I was angry.'

'What had Captain Jud done to offend you?'

Nothing. 'He was unlucky. It was the emperor's summons that I found unacceptable. Why did he summon me?'

'The emperor did not summon you.'

I stared at her. 'There was a letter. It bore the imperial seal and was brought by an imperial messenger.'

'Wait here.' Her voice was sharp.

I might have left, and was tempted to do so, but where could I go that was beyond her reach? Besides flight would have been a coward's act, and I was not afraid. She was gone a long time. I used her absence to pay my respects at Virreld's tomb, glad we had made peace with each other. I half expected Varia to bring Captain Jud with her. He had reason to hate me, but he had accepted my apology.

Her soft-footed approach took me by surprise. She was alone. 'This letter is what Captain Jud was charged to deliver to you. You should see what you are rejecting.' She tossed the pieces at me.

I did not attempt to catch them, so I had to bend to pick them up. Then I held them under the nearest lamp, sensing her eyes on me. The gift of reading came from her, and the recognition of her handwriting with its loops and curls. 'This is signed "Varia I". I don't understand.'

'My father appointed me to rule in his absence. After you freed me from my fire, he travelled to Althein, to make his peace with my mother. I have been empress in name and law since then, only lacking the imperial crown. That will be remedied in a matter of days.'

I lowered myself to the tiled floor in the full imperial salute.

Varia's eyes flashed. 'Enough foolery! Read the damn letter!'

Empress indeed, used to instant obedience. Though her use of 'damn' was more like Kadron. I stood. The handwriting blurred before my eyes and came back into focus. I held the torn pieces nearer the lamp and reluctantly began to read:

From Varia, acting Imperial Highness of the western lands and all lands owing allegiance thereto,

To Gereyn, Falk's son, formerly of the eastern lands; healer-defender; foster son of healer-defender Selthel, and later of Duke Arnull of Hawdale; defender of Mondun; by whose hand the nikaryth Divasa was thwarted and ultimately slain.

I, Varia, Empress in Waiting, being without mate or issue, whether recognised by the laws of the Empire or otherwise,

Hereby offer to the said Gereyn Falk's son my hand, my heart, and my body, and joint rule of the Empire.

Signed: Varia I

I made out the opening phrases in bewilderment and read on, in increasing astonishment, to the very end. Then returned to the beginning to read it again. Impossible. She would not offer such a gift to me. Yet she had. Not once but twice, in the face of such rejection that . . . I looked up into her smiling face. 'You mock me.'

'How do I mock you?'

'I am a bastard, my mother a prostitute, her husband a pig farmer. But you know all this, and more. You knew it before you wrote the letter.' I lowered my head, reluctant to meet her eyes.

Varia stepped forward. 'No mockery was intended. Whatever your faults, that would be a poor return for all you have done for me and mine. As I believe you have heard, my father's father raised pigs, and so did Kei until my father ordered him to join the army. It is not something to be ashamed of. However, the man Falk, who forced your mother into prostitution, who sold you and your sister, was not your father, was he? That is why he hated you and your sister, because you were not his.'

'Does it matter?' It was a very long time ago.

'You owed him nothing, except perhaps payment for his treatment of you, your mother and sister, but you chose otherwise. It was not your fault you could not find your sister. After Selthel's death, you began your wanderings again and met Divasa. Look at me.'

I raised my head and saw understanding in her eyes. 'I wanted to die, but I was afraid of death in her presence. She appeared in the likeness of a woman, but I knew she was something else. I defended myself, without knowing what I was doing, only that I would not endure her touch.

'Then I did not have to endure it. There were flames, but I didn't understand what I had done, or that time was passing, leaving me untouched. I awoke knowing pain and tried to heal myself.

'Someone spoke kindly to me, anointed my hurts, gave me water and food. When I was able to endure the journey,

Duke Arnull took me to his house. Later he wanted to make me his son. It was hard to refuse him. I did so because I was ashamed of what I was, and what I am.'

'At that time you were a lonely frightened child. Now you are a man, and more than that. Healer-defender is what you are and always will be. That is most definitely not something to be ashamed of. Your deeds will be remembered long after your death.

'As you said, I know everything about you. Transference works both ways.' In a softer voice, in the slow drawl of my childhood, she said, 'Gereyn.'

She had softened the G as only my mother and Selthel had done, saying my name as 'Yereyn.' My father – my mother's husband – had never used my full name, his shouts had always been 'Yer!' She knew that too.

My gaze dropped to the letter. I still did not quite believe it. 'This is the message that Captain Jud brought?'

'It is.'

'Then I am doubly a fool.'

Varia shook her head. 'You were wise to be wary of my father. He was wrath with you, ashamed that you succeeded where he failed. Nonetheless, he knew better than to challenge you or to force you to challenge him.'

'I would not have harmed him.'

'I know, but he would have destroyed you, had he believed it could be done. It was the impulse of a moment, soon conquered, but we thought it wisest to keep you from his sight. Once he left for Althein, you were safe. However, he left orders to remove you from Tormene, and I was not then in a position to countermand those orders.'

'I am neither educated, nor trained to rule.'

'Will you refuse me for that? Such lack can be remedied. What you will be is in your own hands. Do not throw it away, I beg you.'

My legs threatened to give way. I strengthened them. 'Why me?'

'I was intrigued from the start. You know what they say about mountain girls and northern girls. I am both. Every time I have asked for your help you have come to my rescue. Why is this different?'

'There are no more aryth to kill. You don't need me at your side to rule the empire.'

Varia's smile was rueful. 'My father's interest in the empire began to fail when my mother left him. He needed her. I trust you are right about the aryth threat, but I fear you are not. If my fears are realised will you come to my aid?'

'I will.'

'Your journey would be shorter if you were already at my side.' She took my hand in hers. 'Tell me you do not love me.'

'I can't.'

Her smile was radiant. 'Then tell me you do.'

All that I was not, she was. Yet my power was greater than hers. She had acknowledged it. Recognised my deliberate choice to offer my life for hers in order to free her from her own fire. Now I understood. In that moment when she had come to herself, she had seen my peril and offered her life for mine. The transference that had taken place then had changed both of us and had made this outcome possible, if I could . . . if I would accept her offer.

If not . . . In that refusal, there would be emptiness: nothing of hope, nothing of desire, nothing of love. I had been there once in the flames, in loneliness and pain, as she had. I would not allow myself to take that place again, nor would I condemn her to that future.

In the drawl of my childhood, I said, 'How could I not love thee, knowing thee as I do?' Selthel's laughter echoed in my mind, and my beloved teacher's voice said, to me alone. 'I rejoice for thee, Gereyn.' I was glad to hear it, but it was Varia who stood before me, not Selthel. My teacher rested in peace as he had wanted. My hand closed on Varia's, and I kissed her lips.

Varia eased her blade from its sheath.

I drew my sword, conscious as rarely before of the four stones in its hilt and the fifth hanging at my neck. Cautiously, remembering Ydrin's warnings, and Nyth's, I linked with Varia, feeling her wariness, and knowing the strength of her shield, almost as strong as mine. For the first time, I saw the colour of my own power. Faint at first, but increasingly bright, warm amber light glowed around me. As its area expanded the colour mellowed to honey gold, and its radiance covered me. The outer edge of my power touched Varia, and she responded with a soft blue glow. The colours deepened, merged and changed, separating into bright whirls. Their variations ranged from amber, through gold to brilliant silver, from palest dawn to deepest blue – the colour of Varia's eyes.

'What are you doing?' Lady Kirra asked.

Varia turned towards the door where her mother stood. Our combined power moved with her, so that it covered Lady Kirra too. 'There is nothing to fear,' Varia said softly. 'Not now.'

Lesley lives in North Yorkshire. Alongside a career in Taxation and Accountancy Lesley had always written for fun. But early retirement allowed her to devote her time to writing fantasy which was her real passion. Her first novel was long listed in a Mslexia Novel Competition and later publication of a short story by Mslexia gave her encouragement to continue. The result is Changeling.

Printed in Great Britain
by Amazon